Felons of our Land

(The dead don't cry, do they?)

by
LOUIE BYRNE

FIRST EDITION
Published 1997

Felons of our Land
(The dead don't cry, do they?)

by
LOUIE BYRNE

FIRST EDITION
Published 1997

ISBN No. 0 9524278 2 6

British Library Cataloguing in Publication Data.
A catalogue record for this book is available from the British Library

Published by Premier Books, Luton
Cradock Road, Luton, Beds. LU4 0JF
Tel: 01582 572727 Fax: 01582 585868

Set in Century Schoolbook & Century 725 Black

Printed by Biddles Limited
Woodbridge Park Estate,
Woodbridge Road,
Guildford
Surrey GU1 1DA

Printed in the United Kingdom

FORWARD

Ré an Ocras Mhóir of 1845-1850 was the greatest calamity
ever to befall the Irish nation. It was a disaster that could
have been avoided for there was ample food in the country.
Despite the desperate plight of the people, England
continued to keep the docks busy as cereals,, livestock and
agricultural produce was shipped out of the hunger ridden
country.
I mention here just one pitiful drama that was played out in
Dingle in County Cork....

In a cottage near to Dingle there lived eight people. When
foraging for food they wandered too far. Unable to make the
return journey they lay down hoping that a passing cart
might oblige and take them home. By late evening they were
despondent. The strongest of the daughters without any
assistance carried her father on her back to the cottage. She
returned time and time again to bring her other sisters back.
Free from the shamed faces, for they were without clothing,
to die with dignity in the sanctuary of their cabin. Finally
worn out and dying she made a final effort to reach her
cottage with the last of her charge. Unable to complete the
journey she lay down beside a hedgerow hoping that someone
would do for her what she had done for her family. Alas, it
was not to be, she would be denied the dignity of dying in her
own home. Exhausted she covered her nakedness and that of
her charge as best she could and surrendered her mortal
body to the rats and vermin and set her spirit free.
There are many recorded stories of heroism and self denial
told. There are also many stories of selfishness and
despotism.
The workhouses unable to cope with the demand for space
packed five persons or more to each bed. This in turn
accelerated the pestilence within the building. As Monsignor
Maguire related later...
"I remember one day when no less that 80 dying persons
were brought to the workhouse in a line of carts. I

administered absolution as rapidly as I could before these poor creatures died."

Relief schemes were set up in 1845 building Famine Roads. The wages were as follows......

> 10 pence for a ten hour day for a man
> 4 pence for a woman breaking stones by hand
> 3 pence for a boy or girl.

One half pound of Indian meal was allowed for all children between nine and fourteen years of age. However this was soon stopped as being too expensive and replaced with the SOUP KITCHEN. They too were abandoned in 1847 leaving the desperate people of the south and west to their fate.

It is ironic that when the British government granted the sum of £100,000 for famine relief in Ireland, they granted £200,000 to Battersea Pleasure Gardens in LONDON.

Letter written by Nicholas Cummins, a respected magistrate
to The Duke of Wellington in the winter of 1846.....

My Lord Duke,

Without apology or preface I presume to trespass on Your
Grace as to state to you and, by the use of your illustrious
name, to present to the British public the following statement
of what I myself have seen within the last three days;
Having, for many years been intimately connected with the
western portion of the County of Cork, and possessing some
small property there, I thought it right personally to
investigate the truth of several lamentable accounts which
have reached me, of the appalling state of misery to which
that part of the country was reduced.
I accordingly went on the 15th inst; to Skibbereen, and to
give the instance of one town land which I visited, as an
example of the entire costal district, I shall simply state what
I there saw.
It is situated on the eastern side of Castlehaven harbour and
is named South Reen, in the parish of Moyross. being aware
that I should witness scenes of frightful hunger, I provided
myself with as much bread as five men could carry, and on
reaching the spot I was surprised to find the wretched hamlet
apparently deserted. I entered some of the hovels to ascertain
the cause and the scenes which presented themselves were
such as no tongue or no pen can convey the slightest idea of.
In the first, six famished and ghastly skeletons, to all
appearances dead were huddled in a corner of some filthy
straw, their sole covering what seemed a ragged horse cloth,
their wretched legs hanging about them, naked above the
knees.
I approached with horror, and found by a low moaning that
they were alive; They were in fever- four children, a woman
and what had been a man.
It is impossible to go through the details, suffice to say that in
a few moments I was surrounded by at least 200 of such
phantoms, such frightful spectres as no words can describe.
By far the greater numbers were delirious, either from

famine or from fever. their demoniac yells are still ringing in my ears, and their horrible images are fixed upon my brain. My heart sickens at the recital, but I must go on-.

In another case decency forbids what follows, but it must be told — my clothes were nearly torn off in my endeavour to escape from the throng of pestilence around, when my neckcloth was seized from behind which compelled me to turn. I found myself grasped by a woman with an infant just born, in her arms and the remains of a filthy sack across her loins- the sole covering of herself and her babe. The same morning the police opened a house on the adjoining lands, which were observed shut for many days, and two frozen corpses were found lying on the mud floor, half devoured by rats.

A mother, herself in fever, was seen the same day to drag out the corpse of her child, a girl about twelve, perfectly naked and leave her half covered with stones. In another house, within 500 yards of the calvary station at Skibbereen, the dispensary doctor found seven wretches lying unable to move, under the same cloak- one had been dead many hours, but the others were unable to move themselves or the corpse.

To what purpose should I multiply such cases? If these be not sufficient, neither would they hear who have the power to send relief and do not, even though one came from the dead.

Let them however, believe and tremble that they shall one day hear the judge of all the earth pronounce their tremendous doom, and ye gave me no drink; naked and ye clothed me not. But I forget to whom this is addressed. My Lord, you are an old and justly honoured man. It is yet in your power to add another honour to your age; to fix another star and that of the brightest to your galaxy and glory. You have access to our young and gracious Queen-lay these things before her. She is a woman and will not allow decency to be outraged. She has at her command the means of at least mitigating the sufferings of the wretched survivors of this tragedy. They will soon be few, indeed, in the district I speak of if help be longer withheld.

Once more, my Lord Duke, in the name of the starving thousands, I implore you, break the frigid and flimsy chain of official etiquette and save the land of your birth- The kindred of that gallant Irish blood which you have so often seen lavished to support the honour of the British name. Let there be inscribed on your tomb, SERVATA HIBERNIA.

I have the honour to be, my Lord Duke,
Your Grace's Obedient humble servant,

N.M Cummins, magistrate.
SKIBBEREEN DECEMBER 1846.

"I said to a man who stood
At the gate of the year
Give me a light
That I may tread safely
Into the unknown"

DEDICATED TO MY WIFE

BRIDGET

THE FAMINE YEARS

Weary men, what reap ye? 'Golden corn for the strangers'.
What sow ye? 'Human corpses that await for the avenger'
Wanting forms, all hunger stricken, what see you in the offing?
'Stately ships to bear our food away amid the stranger's scoffing'.
There's a proud array of soldiers- what do they do round your door?
'They guard our master's granaries from the thin hands of the poor'.
Pale mothers, wherefore weeping?- Would to God that we were
dead;
Our children swoon before us, and we cannot give them bread.

Little children, tears are strange upon your infant faces,
God meant you but to smile within your mother's soft embraces.
'Oh! we know not what is smiling, and we know not what is dying;
But we're hungry, very hungry, and we cannot stop our crying;
And some of us grow cold and white- we know not what it means;
But, as they lie beside us, we tremble in our dreams.'
There's a gaunt crowd on the highway - are ye come to pray to man,
With hollow eyes that cannot weep, and for words your face is wan?

'No; the blood is dead within our veins; we care not now for life;
Let us die hid in the ditches, far from children and from wife;
We cannot stay to listen to their raving, famished cries-
Bread! Bread! Bread!- and none to still their agonies.
We left an infant playing with her dead mother's hand:
We left a maiden maddened by the fever's scorching brand:
Better maiden, thou wert strangled in thy own dark twisted tresses!
Better infant, who wert smothered in thy mother's own caresses.

We were fainting in our misery, but God will hear our groans;
Yea, if fellow men desert us, Will he harken from his throne!
Accursed are we in our own land, yet toil, we still and toil;
But the stranger reaps our harvest- The alien owns our soil.
O Christ! how have we sinned, that on our native plains
We perish houseless, naked, starved, with branded brow, like Cain's?
Dying, dying wearily, with a torture sure and slow-
Dying as a dog would die, by the wayside as we go.

One by one they're falling round us, their pale faces to the sky;
We've no strength left to dig them graves- there let them lie.
The wild bird, when he is stricken, is mourned by the others,
But we, we die in Christian land we die amid our brothers-
In the land which God has given like a wild beast in his cave,
Without a tear, a prayer, a shroud, a coffin, or a grave.
Ha! but think ye the contortions on each dead face ye see,
Shall not be read on judgement day by the eyes of Deity?

'We are wretches, famished, scorned, human tools to build your pride,
But God will yet take vengeance for the souls for whom Christ died.
Now is your hour of pleasure, bask ye in the world's caress;
But our whitening bones against ye will arise as witnesses,
From the cabins and the ditches, in their charred, uncoffin'd masses,
For the angels of the trumpet will know them as he passes.
A Ghastly, spectral army, before great God we'll stand
And arraign ye as our murderers, O spoilers of our land !

THE FAMINE YEARS
BY LADY OSCAR WILDE (1820-1896).

Extract from a letter written by an overseer on the relief scheme to a friend on seeing scores of emaciated workers die on the famine road works . . .

'I hope never to see such a winter and spring again. I can truly say, in looking back upon it, even now. That it appears to me, not as a succession of weeks and days, but one long continuous day, with occasions of nightmare sleep. Rest one could never have, night nor day. When one felt that every minute lost a score of men might die.'

Extract from a letter sent by a midshipman who came ashore at Schull not far from Skibbereen . . .

'We proceeded to east Schull (Near Skibbereen) on quitting Shirkin. Inland we passed 500 people half naked and starving. They were waiting for soup to be distributed amongst them.
They were pointed out to us, and I stood looking with pity and wonder at so miserable a scene, my conductor, a gentleman residing in East Schull, and a medical man, said to me;
"Not a single one of those you now see will be alive in three weeks time: It is impossible.
The death rate here averages 40-50 daily. twenty bodies we buried this morning, and they were fortunate at being buried at all.
The people build themselves up in their cabins, so that they may die together as a family with their children and not be seen by passers- by.
Fever, dysentery and starvation stare you in the face everywhere- Children as young as nine years old look like decrepit old men and women, their faces wrinkled, their bodies bent and distorted with pain. their eyes looking like those of a corpse.

Babes are found lifeless, lying on their mother's bosoms. I tell you one thing that struck me as peculiarly horrible;
A dead woman was found lying in the road with a dead infant lying on her breast, the child having bitten the nipple of the mothers breast right through trying to derive nourishment from the wretched corpse.
Dogs feed on half buried dead, and rats are commonly known to tear people to pieces, who, though still alive, are too weak to cry out. I went into the one and only shop in the place to try and get some bread to give away. I was obliged to leave immediately, for I could not stand the stench. On looking again I discovered the reason-one body lay stretched on a door and I saw the outline of a form, although covered with a heap of rags, I perceived was also dead. Instead of following us, beggars throw themselves on their knees before us, holding up their dead infants to our sight.

Skibbereen 1846.

FELONS
OF
OUR
LAND

HOME AND FAMILY

The Flynn family lived in the townland of Skibbereen in the County Cork for as far back as anyone in the village could remember. Most cottages in Munster could boast a Flynn somewhere within the family.

My father held a lease on a smallholding which consisted of a cottage, a haggard and about half an Irish acre of land.

It was leased from the estate of Brigadier William John Cornwall Stone. In return for this privilege, Father was required to till and sow some three acres of his Lordship's land annually. This crop he would surrender to the estate in part payment of rent. He would also have to give three days of the week working on the estate.

My mother, for her contribution, would be required to give her services as a seamstress, when and if required, which I might add was more often than not.

They were bonded serfs in their own land with no rights. It was considered a privilege to have a fine stone cottage and one half acre of land on which to support their family.

Father accepted this situation as did his father before him.

It was far better than the living conditions that others had to endure in their one room mud cabins covered in rushes.

Mother never really accepted this situation. She was a true Fenian with the proud blood of her race running through her veins.

Our piece of land was not enough to sustain a growing family and the inevitable would have to happen.

I or my brother Brendan would have to flee the nest when we came of age.

Father was still a young man and an asset to the estate. It would be many years before I would be considered for a tenancy and only then if someone had died or been evicted. Not a lot of prospects to look forward to.

There were four persons in our family; Father and Mother, my brother Brendan and I.

We reared a pig each year and killed it in the autumn when fodder became scarce. Most of the carcass we sold in the village. The offal and head we pickled in a barrel for our own use.

As far back as I can remember it was my duty to carry out the task of feeding the pig and cleaning out the haggard.

1

There was many the nasty nip I got from a crabbit pig, I can tell you.

My brother Brendan was far from well and unable to leave his bed. Therefore this menial task and many more were placed on my young shoulders.

We also reared a few hens and ducks to supplement our diet.

Father was a proud man and a dreamer, rest his soul.

He often boasted that were it not for the prohibitive cost of a church pew, the family could occupy their own private seat in the front row of the chapel. Now that would be a chastisement to many and envy to more, he said.

"Just think of it, our family name on a brass plate before the high altar," he would often say and he with that far away look in his eyes.

Mother, well she resented anyone having the audacity to be able to lay claim to the front seats of the church, just because they could afford them.

"It's an affront to Almighty God, so it is. It should not be tolerated. The Bishop should take measures to stamp out such a privilege. The very cheek of them sitting there lording it over the best seats."

Yet the irony of it was that it was the bishop who was selling the seats.

"And why, tell me, shouldn't they? He who pays the piper calls the tune." Father would defend the right to buy a seat in the church.

"A right indeed is it? Blasphemous so it is. Just who do these 'CRAW' thumpers (Chest Beaters) think they are anyway. Are we not all supposed to be equal in the sight of God. Remember, a shroud has no pockets."

Mother would philosophise and point a wagging finger at father.

We were used to this good natured bantering and anyway it always petered out peacefully.

Mother's maiden name was Bridget Clancy. Father's parents heard of her when they went to the matchmaker looking for a bride for him.

Matchmaking is a way of life in rural Ireland and a respectable method of marriage. The father casts his eye around for a suitable girl for his son who will inherit his smallholding when he passes on. In Kerry and Limerick it was the custom to give the elderly couple a field and a room in the cottage after the nuptials. There was a lot of jealously between the sons after the father made his choice. In some cases, regrettably, it resulted in murder.

The father of the boy approaches the matchmaker to sound out what assets the girl in question has to offer.

Can she cook and sow and milk? Will she suit his son and be willing to marry before Chalk Sunday?

Her family in turn will enquire as to the character of the man wanting to marry their daughter. Is he of a sober disposition and good on the land.

If they are willing to 'Draw it Down' the matchmaker will make arrangements for the fathers to meet in the local and, after a few drinks to soften the tongue, so to speak, the girl's father will ask what dowry is expected of them. They will ask as to how many beasts are on the farm and its size. What kind of a cottage will they have, etc.. It matters not that they all know each other and what each other has on offer, the ritual must take place. Customs must be honoured.

"My son will take her off your hands for £350 and not a penny less."

"No, I'll not be insulting the company but my client is willing to throw off £50, so he is. Then there's the luck penny."

The matchmaker continues bargaining without consulting the parents. An old hand at it and who would question his/her judgement.

The good natured bantering continues until the figure is finally agreed at around £275, plus the matchmakers fee.

The drinking continues and all have a grand old time.

Then comes the walking of the land.

Before the girl's parents arrive to inspect what is on offer the house is whitewashed, drinks purchased and a fine meal laid on the table. If all goes well there will be eating, drinking and the 'CRAIC' until the early hours .

Next day comes the niceties when both parties go to the solicitor and get the talking down on paper. With the writings completed the farm is handed over and then the marriage can go forward.

'That's the way we do things here in Munster. It is a respected and ancient tradition, so it is.'

Mother's family lived in the village of Ballyheigh in the neighbouring county of Kerry. My mother was a seamstress of some considerable talents. Her prowess with the needle was known as far afield as Cork and Limerick City. She would be called upon by the nuns of the cities to embroider the elaborate robes of a newly ordained priest.

It was said, complimentary of course, that it was none other than Bridget Clancy who taught the spiders to spin their gossamer webs. She dismissed all these compliments, to her. It was a gift from God and not of her doing.

"There are many far more nimble with the needle than me," she would say . Whatever else mother was a modest woman.

She was a very religious person and took a pride in teaching us our Christian duties.

"Always pay attention to your Catechism, children. Remember that there are Seven Deadly Sins. These are an affront to Almighty God and are to be avoided if you want to enter the Kingdom of Heaven."

This would be her opportunity to call us to her and instruct us in the true faith.

"Remember the Seven Deadly Sins that I told you about. They are Pride, Covetousness, Gluttony, Lust, Envy, Anger and Sloth. Carry their rejection within your hearts always if you want to see God."

She never made any effort to explain their meaning and so they remained a mystery to us. Whenever we questioned their meaning the answer was invariably the same.

"There's yet time to grow up and learn all these things."

I often wondered if she knew the meaning of them herself.

"You would think they would be capable of replacing a few buttons at least." She would look over her glasses at father as she pushed the needle and thread through the cloth with the help of her thimble.

Seldom did he reply. He was an avid reader and spent his leisure time deep within his Sugan chair. There he would sit puffing on his cré dúidín oblivious to all around him with his eyes glued to the page.

If there ever was a dreamer then my father was one.

Father was no time-served tradesman. He was a general handyman, very good with his hands if one takes my meaning.

Whatever the task set before him was a challenge to be mastered.

"Sure if someone had the God given ability to make it, then I see no reason why it cannot be repaired." This was his philosophy.

"Will you not be making it worse than it is, have some sense and send for Tom Flynn," many the housewife was heard to chide her husband as he struggled in vain to repair a broken object.

It is well documented that it was none other than he who repaired the large carved front doors of the Big House.

The doors were made from the finest English oak. The timber to make them had come from a forest across the sea in England.

Did not the Brigadier boast that it was from this same

4

forest that King Henry the Eighth had the timbers felled for his finest men-o-war. That is what he boasted and who was there to challenge him.

His family coat of arms had been emblazoned on the two great panels by some of the finest craftsmen in London.

The great doors arrived at the Manor in grand style. The dray was drawn by two magnificent Shire Horses. Two first class joiners from England accompanied the doors. They sat upright on the front seat with their arms contemptuously folded.

That was a proud day for the Brigadier, so Father told us. "It's a long way to fetch two handymen just to hang a few doors," Father remarked sarcastically at the time.

No Irish oak, it was claimed, could hold a candle to the quality of English oak. The day the doors were hung was a day of celebration within the great house. From that day on, it became incumbent on the butler to ensure that the boot boy kept them waxed and polished with best beeswax.

I tell you, the fine doors were tried by a few years out in the Irish weather. The Atlantic storms soon tested their mettle and put paid to them.

Father was summoned to the Big House and asked for his assessment as to how the doors might be repaired.

What a sorry sight they were. They could not be opened and were as crooked as Biddy Lanagan's sow's tail, and that was saying something.

Father studied the great doors and the dressed stone surroundings. One of the two rampant lions guarding the entrance had been knocked lopsided by the swelling doors.

"Fine wood and a fine setting, I'll agree." Father ran his hand over the grain of the wood and dug his chisel into the lead filling holding the door frame firmly in the stone.

"Never mind the compliments, man, can you repair the doors?"

His Lordship had little patience with Father. Perhaps he never understood the Irish ways.

Little did he realise that Father was not being complimentary but using Irish sarcasm in a witty way..

"Well now! It's like this your Lordship, I can and I cannot. Now if that is not good enough then I suggest that you look elsewhere." Father stood back a pace and studied the doors.

"Oh get on with it man, I have no time for your chatter."

He returned to the house through the conservatory, this being the only way into the front of the house now that the great doors were jammed shut.

With the help of the hired hands from the Manor farm, Father removed the two great doors and transported them to the large workshop on the home farm. He made a temporary door to replace them and hung it in place.

"It's not as elegant as the others but at least he can now get in and out of his mansion."

He laughed as he eased the door to and fro on its temporary hinges.

Returning to the farm he carefully removed the wooden dowels holding the great panels in place and dismantled the doors.

Some days later his Lordship was passing through the great barn when he came across two large iron troughs filled with water and two huge millstones sitting on top. Curiosity turned to horror and anger when he saw his great doors disembowelled beneath the water.

We were told that there was míle murder in his eyes when he saw the carnage.

Immediately he despatched his estate manager to our home. Father was to report at once to his Lordship and explain his conduct.

Father was not one to hurry on the beck and call of anyone and told the agent that he would come as soon as it was convenient.

I remember it well, the casual way he sauntered to the door and removed his caubeen from the peg.

"I'll be home later, Bridget. Keep the sup of tae warm." With that he left the house in no great a hurry.

He arrived at the great barn some time later only to find his Lordship pacing up and down the cobbled yard beating his riding crop against his boot.

"So you finally condescended to honour us with your presence Tom Flynn." His lordship stood before father like a suzerain.

"Is there a problem, sir?" Father queried, ignoring the challenging stance.

"Will you look at my doors, what do you think you are doing?" he demanded as he rushed across to the troughs.

"I was of the opinion, your Lordship, that you would understand the necessity of soaking the timber."

Father calmly explained that what he had done was necessary.

The doors had to be dismantled and the wood soaked to straighten it without splitting it, there was nothing for him to worry about. The doors would be reassembled better than any fine English tradesman could do it.

Father's Fenian upbringing always came to the fore when he had one over on the gentry.

Needless to say, his Lordship took some persuading before he was willing to accept that Father knew what he was doing. Nevertheless he had little alternative but to welcome his explanation.

Father did assemble the doors, and gave them a good soaking in Linseed oil. He reset the cut stone and straightened the crooked lion. When all was ready he rehung the doors. He was proud as punch as he moved the doors to and fro on their hinges. When closed not a breath of wind passed through them. They stand to this day as a memorial to a fine craftsman.

I can still see him now, looking proudly at the fine doors.

"There's many the stack of barley that will fall before they jam again," he would tell us.

A fine man, a fine man indeed was my father, God be good to him and all deceased members of my family.

My younger brother Brendan was named after the great voyager Saint Brendan. He died from the 'Ocras' during the Great Hunger.

He suffered from a weak chest or so mother would have us believe. We knew it was consumption, better known as T.B. Family pride would never allow the word to be used.

I would have to flee the nest when the time came. I often heard Father tell Mother that Brendan would have to be cared for always. God in his mercy relieved them of that burden and gave Brendan peace.

Skibbereen was a small straggling village. A village where care for the community was paramount. A stranger would be watched and discreetly questioned as to his reason for calling. Were they related to someone or were they looking for someone.

It is not a large village, there is but the one road through it. There are two churches as in most villages, one Catholic and one Protestant.

At the far reaches was the blacksmith's forge owned by one Seámus Hennessy. Seámus was the only person in the village who had not been born there. He had come some years previously from Newcastle West in the neighbouring County of Limerick to serve his apprenticeship and stayed on after the old blacksmith died.

Skibbereen was not a village of note until the 'Great Hunger' of 1845-1850 . . .

THE BIG HOUSE

Like all the gentry, his Lordship's family had their mansion built to personify all the essential characteristics of wealth. This was indeed a substantial house on a grand scale.

It was built to impress upon the observer the grandeur and wealth of the occupiers, and in the vain hope that a member of Royalty would at some time grace its portals.

Father maintained that it was like a hive awaiting the Queen Bee, who never arrived.

Many surrounding villages had been obliterated to create and enlarge the estate. Not one brass farthing had been paid in compensation for the loss of their homes and smallholdings to the indigenous population. They were given the ultimatum of becoming servants or getting off the land. Should they agree to stay then they would be given the lease on a half acre of their own land on which to support themselves and build a cottage. In return they would have to plough and sow three acres of land for the Brigadier. They would also have to pay rates and taxes on the holding.

Like an ever growing octopus out of control, the estate was enlarged until it encompassed all the lands within the Parish. The mansion was built high on the top of the hill known locally as 'Finn McCools Hill', the top of which had been decapitated to accommodate the mansion.

The river Llen that had flown through the village since time began was diverted to the front of the mansion and dammed in order to create a huge lake.

Father told me that the lake was lined with clay that had been brought all the way from the brick fields of Limerick to make it watertight. The clay came in large drays drawn by heavy Shire Horses.

The boys from the surrounding countryside were ordered to strip naked and plaster the sides with the clay. They worked a ten hour day on the lake throughout the spring and summer months trampling and spreading the clay. Many died from cold and malnutrition during its creation.

The family were noted for their military prowess and could trace their leadership in battle back to the reign of William and Mary of Orange.

The present Lord of the Manor was a brigadier in command of his own regiment of dragoons. They were staunch Anglo Saxon and considered Irish Catholics beneath their contempt.

The Brigadier stood six feet tall and walked with the gait beholding his rank. He was always immaculately dressed and groomed. Not a hair was ever out of place.

Father maintained that he must have been born in the saddle for he was seldom seen off the back of his chestnut mare.

He was a strict disciplinarian, yet generous and understanding within limits.

His wife, Lady Elizabeth was Mistress of the Manor and let it be known to all. She took personal charge of all the servants, male and female, within the household. She ruled the manor with a rod of iron and would not hesitate in taking a rod to chastise any servant for the least misdemeanour.

She was forever in conflict with the Head Gardener and considered the walled garden her personal domain. It was she and not the Head Gardener who dictated what grew within its confines. Yet should the kitchens find they were short of any produce then it was he who shouldered the responsibility.

Her rose garden was the envy of the countryside. She claimed that she could grow roses where others could not grow grass. Not, mind you, that she ever dirtied her hands on the task. She dictated as to where the roses were to be grown and it was the duty of the gardener's to see that her wishes were carried out to the letter. Woe betide any gardener who failed to meet her standards.

There were two children in the family. Master William James Cornwall-Stone, the son and heir, and Harriott Elizabeth Cornwall-Stone, the daughter. They spent most of their childhood under the watchful eyes of their German governess. They looked so sad compared with the boisterous children of the village. With all their wealth they never seemed to be happy. They were being groomed for better things and were afforded little time for childish pleasures.

When in the garden they would spend their time sitting on the balustrade learning French or German.

They reminded me of a song that mother used to sing . . .

> "I'm only a bird in a gilded cage,
> A beautiful sight to see.
> You may think I'm happy and free from care
> I'm not! though I seem to be,
> For my beauty was sold, for an old man's gold
> I'm a bird in a gilded cage."

It was to the manor that I was sent at twelve years of age. I was considered old enough to be apprenticed out to the estate. It is from here that the story of Seámus Flynn really begins.......

A CALLING TO THE BIG HOUSE

"Seámus Flynn! Seámus! Is that you?"
It was old Seámus Hennessy, the farrier from Newcastle
West in the neighbouring county of Limerick standing by
his workshop. He was waiting as usual for one of the local
boys to make his appearance.
"It is indeed, and what can I do for you this day?" Seámus
replied.
"Will you take these along to the Big House, like a good
boy. It's the special cages for the broody pheasants". Old
Seámus had made the cages with his own hands. He was
no Gobán when it came to making willow baskets, cages,
cribs, ciscéans and anything made from willow. He was
also the village blacksmith.
"I've put them on the cart for you."
In anticipation of some garsún passing, the baskets were
already roped securely to the cart.
Old 'Long Ears' his faithful donkey was already
harnessed to the cart and patiently standing outside the
workshop.
Seámus took his place on the tuige suideacán and, taking
the reins in his hands, encouraged the donkey to move
forward.
"See that you put them into the hands of Gerry Donneely
and nobody else, and when you are at it be careful of old
Long Ears." He stroked the donkeys ears affectionately.
"He's safe with me Mr Hennessy. Come along Long Ears,
let's go." This would be a great opportunity to see the
grand house for the first time.
"He's getting a bit long in the tooth like myself, so do be
careful," old Seámus warned.
With a jerk of the reins, the donkey responded to the
command.
Long Ears dug his hoofs into the gravel and the cart
slowly left the village at a steady pace. Long Ears would
have it no other way.
Looking back along the road he saw old Seámus waving
his Shillelagh in salutation. The old donkey looked
around and wiggled his ears. Seámus guessed that he was
waving 'Goodbye' to the donkey and not to him.
He had never set eyes on his Lordship nor for that matter
on any of his family. This would be a wonderful
opportunity for him to get at least a glimpse of them.

It was by choice that his lordship had isolated himself and his family from the village. Following the 'yellow' plague of 1835, (Cholera), his Lordship decided that passing through the village was putting his health and that of his entire family in jeopardy.

Consequently he had a private road constructed through the old spinney down by Drocsaógal Carrig. As the road bypassed the village he could now avoid any contact with the village and its occupants.

He was neither shy nor ashamed to send his agents into the village to collect his tithes and taxes when due.

Seámus, a garsún of eleven years of age at the time, wondered as to how his Lordship was still on God's earth. The very mention of his name brought profane 'Pishogues' from every man in the surrounding countryside. Not, mind you, that they ever uttered a word within hearing distance of his agents.

It must have been the charitable prayers of the womenfolk that protected him from a fate worse than death. He thought that if the women stopped praying for his Lordship's well-being then as sure as God made apples, something would surely happen to him. His mother was of the opinion that the Blessed Lord would punish him in his own good time.

"The hand of the Lord will touch him, sooner than later, you mark my words," she would proclaim. Not, mind you, but that she was the most charitable of women and would never wish harm on anybody.

The more the villagers prayed for his demise, the more prosperous he became. The hand of the Lord had indeed touched him and it was most bountiful.

As he reached the incline leading to the home farm Long Ears was showing signs of fatigue. Leaping from his seat Seámus took the reins in his hands and encouraged the donkey up the hillock.

As they came nearer to the gates he spoke to the donkey.

"Come on Long Ears, we are about there." He encouraged the donkey to make the effort.

On reaching the entrance he halted the donkey and looked up in awe at the enormous iron gates. Their impressive size and height frightened him. Never had he seen such gates as these.

Atop each gate was the family crest of his Lordship. These consisted of two rampant unicorns holding a golden chain between them. Resting in the centre of the chain was a golden crown.

This was the estate of his Lordship and he was letting all and sundry know it. The intimidating size of the wrought iron gates and the challenging unicorns spelt it out loud and clear. 'No Trespassing'.

Taking the handle of the long call chain in his hand he pulled it down. The bell set some distance from the gate clanged loudly.

He waited for some moments, there was no response. He again took hold of the handle, this time in both hands and pulled it several times. Clang! Clang! Clang! The bell tolled its message, 'There's a caller at the gate!'

Seámus continued pulling the handle, the bell continued sending out its message.

Finally the door of the gatehouse opened and a frail old lady hobbled from the shelter of the porch. Shading her eyes from the sun's glare she waved her hands in annoyance.

"Will you stop ringing that bell, we're not deaf, if you must know."

She continued to hobble into the garden.

"Do you have business here, son?" she called on seeing him, yet making no effort to come to the gate.

"I've got the cages for the birds from Old Seámus Hennessy," he informed her.

"Can you wait awhile, I'll need to go and fetch Pat to open the gate." Without waiting for his reply she hobbled back into the house and closed the door behind her.

He returned to the cart and sat on the straw seat. After a long wait there was still no sign of the gates being opened. Jumping off the cart he led the donkey to a taoscán of lush green grass growing beside the brook that ran along the roadside.

The old donkey soon got the message and wasted little time in reaching the spot. As he pulled at the clump of grass and began to chew it, he looked behind at Seámus and waggled his ears in gratitude.

"Come here boy, what do you think you are doing there?"

It was, he presumed, Pat, who was standing beside the half open gate and he adjusting his bríste fadas. He must have been abed and the calling disturbed his slumber.

"Coming sir!" Seámus took hold of the reins. The donkey grabbed the last mouthful before being led towards the open gate.

"Take yourself up the back drive and give the basket to Mr Donneely and to no one else. Do you understand now. You'll find him in the compound, I have no doubt," he warned and instructed, all in the same sentence.

"Get along there". Seámus flicked the reins across the back of the donkey.

Long Ears once again dug his feet into the gravel as the

cart moved slowly up the slight incline. Reaching another iron gate, not so ornate as the others, he guided the donkey into the cobbled courtyard. Stopping outside a long stone barn he saw a man pulling hay from a rick.

"Would you be Mr Donneely? " he asked as he removed his caubeén out of respect.

"No son! You'll find him over there in the ice house." He pointed across the yard. All Seámus could see in the distance was a blank stone wall. There was no house of any description that he could distinguish.

Not wishing to upset the man nor to bring his wrath down on himself, nor perhaps a clout across the ear for his troubles, he took the reins in his hands and crossed the yard towards where the labourer had pointed.

At the far end of the cobbled yard he saw an open door set into the ground. A salting barrel lay in front as a hazard warning, a haze of fog rose silently from within its confines.

Dismounting from the cart he cautiously approached and looked inside. A flight of stone steps led down into the bowels of the earth. He took a step back in fear and trepidation. Holding the rim of the salting barrel he again looked down into the hole. A haze of fog hung around the entrance which was icy cold.

'This must be what Hell is like, only it's made of fire,' he thought, as he nervously peeped inside.

Through the haze he saw a man bent over a bench. He was not too sure though, for the man was covered from head to toe in a thick coatamore and was wearing heavy gloves.

As his eyes became accustomed to the darkness he saw that he was setting out poultry on a long slate shelf. On the opposite side on a corresponding shelf were the carcasses of two stags complete with horns.

All were encased in broken ice and snow. As it was early Autumn he wondered where they got the ice and snow from.

Better still, how did they keep it from melting.

"Are you Mr Donneely, sir?" he called keeping a tight hold on the barrel.

"I am that." The man looked up before he carefully placed the last of the birds on the slab.

Having ensured that all was in order he ascended the steps and closed the stout oak doors before he secured them with a large bolt and lock.

"Now what brings you here looking for me?" He placed a friendly hand on the shoulder of Seámus.

"I've got the cages for you from Old Seámus, the gaba.

They are sitting on the cart, sir."

"Good on you son. I've been waiting for them." Together they approached the cart. Seámus reached out to help in removing the cages.

"Leave them son, I'll look to them."

Mr Donneely was indeed a strong man as he picked up both baskets one in each hand and took them inside the long barn.

Inside two young girls were plucking game birds. Seámus asked one of the girls for some of the big coloured feathers but she giggled and looked shyly away.

Mr Donneely selected several of the biggest and best feathers and gave them to him.

"You can stick one or perhaps two in your caubeén if you wish, and be the envy of all the other boys."

Seámus blushed as the girls put their hands over their mouths and began to giggle.

"Now girls, get on with your task," Mr Donneely chided.

As they left the barn to retrieve the cart Mr Donneely took two apples from the pocket of his coatamore.

"These are for you, son."

He smiled as he held out the apples to Seámus.

"Oh thank you sir, thanks a lot." He reached out and took the apples. One he put in his pocket, the other he rubbed and rubbed on the sleeve of his geansaí until it glowed. He wanted to keep them forever and ever but, like Eve, temptation was too near to resist.

He resumed his position on the straw seat of the cart and left the farm. On the way down the long drive he kept looking at the apple. Then, with his resistance gone, he bit into the succulent fruit and relished its sweet flavour.

Long Ears kept looking back at him and licking his lips. Seámus soon got the message and taking one last look at the generous core he jumped off the cart and gave it to the donkey. He suspected that, like himself, this was the first real apple that he had ever tasted.

Old Seámus was sitting outside his workshop with his legs crossed making a pannier when they returned.

"Not been pushing him son, have you?"

Putting the pannier to one side he rose and began to examine the donkey. Satisfied as to his well being he put his arms around the old donkeys neck and stroked his nose. Seámus could see that these two were long associated companions.

"Oh no sir! I let him have his own way most of the time. I even gave him one of my apples."

He saw no reason for telling Seámus that he only let him have the core.

15

"God bless you son, you'd best be off home now. This is for you."

He gave him the almost obligatory "Cross of St Bridget" which he had woven from the reeds.

This was the usual payment in kind. Most, if not all the mothers in the village had a barn filled with them.

A FATHERS ANGUISH

Reaching his own threshold he could hear his mother singing. Why, he thought, does she sing such melancholy songs. Still who could blame her, there was not much to sing about in Ireland these days, what with the Great Hunger and the transportation to Van Deemens land.

"Is that you Tom," she called on hearing the footsteps.

"No, it's only me, Ma!"

Seámus entered the scullery and handed her the cross.

"I see you have been running errands for old Seámus Hennessy again. Where to this time?" She looked down at the cross.

"I had to take some ciséans up to the big house for him. You should see the place, it's huge."

He began to tell her all about the mansion.

"Here, my hands are full, take it to the barn and leave it with the others." She was showing little interest in his most recent adventure.

"How is Brendan today?" Seámus asked on his return.

"Not much improvement, I fear. Don't waken him son."

"I brought him a fine apple from the big house, so I did, look!"

Seámus took the apple from his pocket and rubbing it on his sleeve held it up for her to see.

"I'm afraid he needs more than apples, but he will appreciate it all the same." She sighed.

"What's in the pot mother? It smells real good."

"It's a coinín stew, your father found a dead coinín on the roadside. A gift from God, I have no doubt ," she added.

"Is there some for Brendan. He could keep the apple for afterwards."

"Of course, and there's some for him and for you too, look!" She scooped the ladle through the pot and carried a variety of vegetables and a piece of the rabbit to the surface.

"Now go and see if Brendan is awake. He will be glad of the apple."

Opening the door Seámus peeped into the dark silent room and gently called to his brother. There was no response but the rasping breathing coming from the bed. Slowly he retreated from the room and closed the door.

Brendan had been ill for some time and there was little that they could do for him. What he needed was lots of fresh milk and good wholesome food. There was little prospect of that without the money to pay for it.

17

His father did not receive much in the way of payment from the big house. What he got he spent mostly on what food and clothing he could afford for his family.

Seámus, anxious to give his brother the apple, returned to the bedroom.

"Are you awake yet, Brendan?" he gently called as he looked down at the wasting form of his younger brother.

"I may have my eyes closed but I knew it was you."

Brendan, opening his eyes, looked up at his brother with a mischievous smile.

"Look what I brought you. I got two from a man at the great house." Seámus gave the apple a final polish and presented it to him.

"You went to the big house, did you. What is it like?"

Reaching out he took the big red apple and began to polish it on the bed clothes.

"You should see it, it is huge and filled with more food than they can store in the house. They keep it under the ground in big rooms filled with fog."

"Like Hell is it?"

Brendan's eyes opened wide.

"Is what like hell? Don't eat the apple just yet. Ma has made a stew," Seámus told him.

"Do you know, I thought I smelt something good cooking." Brendan sniffed the air.

"Pa found a fine coinín on the road and brought it home, that's what you smell."

Seámus sat on the side of the bed and began telling him all about his day at the mansion. As he looked down at his brother he noticed that he had again fallen asleep. The precious apple lay on the bedspread. Picking it up he laid it on the window ledge and left the room.

"He's gone asleep again, Ma. He doesn't look too good."

"Don't you ever let me hear you say those words again Seámus Flynn, never, do you hear! God is good and Brendan is getting better!" His mother stamped her foot and began to wipe her hands in her apron. He knew this meant she was annoyed.

"Sorry Ma, I thought that......"

"Something smells real good and I'm famished." The figure of his father filled the door frame.

"It's the coinín. I managed to make a stew from that and a lot of vegetables. I hope it is alright Tom."

"Sure there's nothing to worry about. Wouldn't it have been a sin to leave it for the madra rua. What is the matter with you, why are you crying?"

"Seámus remarked on how Brendan looked and I chastised him with my tongue, so I did. I know that I

18

shouldn't have. He loves his brother so he does, he is so good to him. It's the Ocras." She ran from the kitchen and entering the back kitchen began to beat the wall with her fists.

"You're not upset, are you son. It would take more than that to upset our Seámus, so it would. Now where is that stew?"

Tom found it best to let his wife alone when she was upset. What could he do to alleviate the situation?

"'Tis sorry I am for my behaviour, sit yourselves down." Bridget came from the back kitchen, wiping her eyes in her apron as she apologised.

That evening they sat as usual by the fireside talking of this and that. Both were trying desperately to keep off the subject of Brendan's illness.

Bridget was knitting a geansaí from a load of old wool she had recycled. She kept glancing at Tom who was sitting in his sugan chair reading. She knitted faster and faster and finally flung the whole lot to one side.

"Say something! Will you say something for God's sake Tom Flynn, say something." She held her head in her hands and began to weep. There was a silence from Tom, a silence that said more than words.

"I'm asking you Tom, I'm begging you! In God's Holy Name, what is to become of us at all, at all. Today we had rabbit stew but Brendan couldn't eat it. What of tomorrow, what of our son?"

"I wish to God that I had an answer for you grá geal mo croide, I really do. The Ocras is everywhere. Don't you know how I feel, listening night after night to the hungry cries of my wife and children. Don't I know that our youngest son is at deaths' door? I wish that God in Heaven would take us away from this cursed land."

"I know Tom, I know it is not your fault. It cannot go on year after year. God has punished us enough. You'll see. The potato will crop next year."

"Next year is it, does it matter Bridget. Next week or next year? I know that it will be too late for our Brendan."

"Perhaps it is best that we said the rosary and went to bed. There is little to stay up for and the candle is burning low." Calming the tense situation Bridget rose from her stool.

"Call Seámus and leave the door open for Brendan to answer." Tom went and took the family rosary beads from the back of the chair and knelt on the flagged floor.

"Molad le Dia," (Blessed be God), Tom started, without waiting for the other members of the family to join him.

"Molad le na Ainm Naomta." (Blessed be his holy name),

19

Bridget replied as she entered the kitchen carrying her mothers old rosary."Molad le híosa Criost ata 'na fiór- Dia agus 'na fiór duine" (Blessed be Jesus Christ, true God and true man).

They could hear their two sons answering from the confines of the back bedroom.

"And God bless Brendan and make him well again," Seámus prayed at the conclusion of the family prayers.

His mother again looked towards her husband and began to weep.

"Good night, I'm off to my bed and so should you be."

She wiped the tears from her eyes and left the room.

Tom remained kneeling by his chair and once again took his beads from the back of the chair.

"Merciful infant Jesus of your divine love for the family I implore you to give us some help and relief." He prayed as the light from the candle flickered in the breeze coming from under the door. A slight zephyr moved the curtain to and fro. From the small back room came the grating restless breathing from their son as he fought bravely to stay alive.

Supernatural shadows appeared and disappeared within the stone walls of the kitchen as he prayed.

On the conclusion of his prayers Tom blew out what remained of the candle and sat by the fire. He watched the shadows' dancing on the wall and could not help but feel for the agony that his wife was suffering. If only he could get his son into the fever hospital, he thought.

It was nearing dawn when he woke from a restless sleep. Rising, he quietly made to climb the raking ladder to the bedroom in the rafters. He looked in at his two children cuddled in their bed. The patchwork quilt that his grandmother had made in years gone by lay in a crumpled heap on the floor. Retracing his steps he picked it up and laid it over the sleeping children.

"Jesus of your infinite mercy, if you cannot spare me then please spare my children," he again prayed as he looked at the picture of the Sacred heart hanging over the bed.

He listened to the rasping and shallow consumptive breathing coming from Brendan. He knew that there was no hope of a cure. Still, in some far recess of his mind and in his unquenchable faith in his God he hoped for a miracle. At least his son was still alive and there was a glimmer of hope. For that he thanked his God.

He removed his clothes and lay down beside his wife.

"You're late Tom, what have you been doing?" she asked sleepily.

"Nothing, nothing at all, just dreaming. Go back to sleep."

THE BATA SCOIR

Early next morning Seámus rose from his bed and collected the four sods of turf for the school fire. His father had bundled them in a straw rope the night before. Each pupil had to contribute four sods of turf to the National School daily.

With his slate under his arm he set out along the old boreen. His only meal was a drink of water from the well below the house.

"Does it ever stop raining in Ireland?" he thought to himself as he tried to protect the precious turf under his threadbare geansaí. The master would not be too pleased to be presented with a bundle of wet turf. On the road he was joined by other boys and girls all in their bare feet. Each carried the obligatory four sods of turf and their slates.

By the time he reached the school he was wet from head to toe. Luckily some of the other boys, for this was an all boys class room, had got there before him and had a good fire ready. He tried to instil some warmth into his numbed bones. As the numbers of pupils increased so did the competition for space at the fire. Soon he found himself ousted by the bigger boys.

"Give us a look too, that is my sod in the fire," he pleaded as he found himself deprived of the comforting heat.

"Druidim De," (Push off), challenged one of the older boys. All looked shocked on hearing the boy speak Irish.

Seámus found himself being pushed farther and farther back as a general melee took place for a space at the fire.

A bell rang in the schoolyard. The pupils vacated the warmth of the fire and hurriedly entered the yard. This was divided in two by a dry stone wall. Girls lined up in one half and the boys in the other. Both teachers, male and female stood by the doors of their respective classrooms and ushered the pupils forward .

With the pupils inside the classroom the teacher entered and closed the door behind him. Mindful of his authority they rose to their feet as one.

The day began as usual with prayers for her majesty Queen Victoria, Queen of Ireland. This was followed by the roll call.

With the roll call completed the teacher went to the blackboard and began to write down the long tables. He was interrupted by a gentle knocking at the door. The door was opened to a ragged boy standing in the doorway. "Sorry I'm late master, I slipped when crossing the stream," he apologised, as he stood shivering in the doorway.

Smoke began to fill the room as the draught caught the fire.

The boys seeing the state of their comrade found it amusing and began to laugh.

"And just what is there to laugh at?"

The teacher looked around at his pupils who soon stopped their merriment.

"Close that door and come here at once." The master had the cupboard open. The boys knew what this meant.

"Over here boy". He pointed with the long saileac slat to a spot before him.

"Fell in the stream is it. Lies! Lies! Lies!" He banged the cane hard on the desk.

"You slept in is more the truth. Hold out your hand."

Six of the best landed on each numbed hand of the miserable pupil standing shivering before him.

"Go and sit down and tomorrow be on time or else."

With this warning and a final lash across the buttocks he dismissed the pupil.

The lessons slowly progressed throughout the morning with little respite from the monotony of the routine.

"Cuir cugám an cailc, má sé do toil é." (Pass me the chalk please) Seámus called to Michael Quigley who was a close friend of his.

"James Flynn come out here at once, and bring your tally stick with you," the teacher ordered on hearing him speaking Irish.

Seámus rose from his hard seat and picking up his 'Beata Scóir' came to the front of the class. He knew what to expect for the teacher had the saileac slat in his hand.

"James Flynn, this is the second time today that I heard you speaking the Irish. This is a barbarian language and is not to be spoken. You know what happens to boys who persist in speaking that language, don't you?"

"I'm sorry sir, but I forgot. It won't happen again, honest."

He knew before he ever appealed that there would be no clemency.

"Forgetting won't do, will it."

Reaching out his hand he took the Beata Scóir from Seámus.

Seámus watched as the teacher put a notch in it and returned it to him.

"Now hold out your hand."

Obediently he held out his hand palm upwards. For his

disobedience he received three slaps with the saileac slat on each hand.

He had broken a cardinal rule by speaking Irish in the classroom. Speaking or writing Irish was strictly forbidden.

The school was dismissed at four o'clock but not Seámus and three others. They would have to stay behind and receive their punishment according to how many notches they had accumulated on their Beata Scóir.

"James Flynn, on three separate occasions you deliberately spoke Irish today. Yesterday you ignored my instructions four times. You are the ringleader of this conspiracy and are determined to disobey me. You will have to learn your lesson the hard way. Bend over boy."

Seámus was severely beaten with the saileac slat.

He found it hard indeed not to break into the Irish tongue. Irish, being the native language, was spoken in most houses in the Southwest of Ireland.

It was dark evening before he set foot on the threshold of his father's cottage.

"How did you fare at school today Seámus?" His mother asked as he entered the cottage.

"Alright, but a waste of time. I'll be glad when the summer

comes and I can leave and earn some money. How is Brendan?" he added as an afterthought.

He entered the bedroom and called softly to his younger brother.

"Brendan! Are you awake, Brendan?" He slowly approached the bedside.

"Boo!" Brendan pulled the blanket from his face and looked up at his brother.

"I was awake all the time and saw you sneaking about, so I did." He half laughed, then he took a fit of coughing.

"Guess what I found to day in the boreen." Seámus held his hands behind his back.

"What? Something good I hope!" Brendan asked as he struggled for breath.

"Look! I found him sitting on top of Mary O'Leary's wall." Seámus held out a huge frog towards his brother.

"That's the fattest one that I ever saw. What will you do with him?" Sitting half up in the bed he smiled at the frog.

"He's for you, we will put him in a basin on your window sill."

"What would Mother say and how could we feed him?" Brendan asked between coughs.

"He will catch all the flies and I will bring him home the odd worm or two. You can give him a name." The frog began to croak loudly.

"I'm going to call him Cromwell so I am. He was slimy and grumpy too." Both children laughed at their audacity.

"Mother is making some stirabout, it should be ready soon," Seámus told his brother.

"Stirabout, it tastes awful. Where does it come from?" Brendan grimaced at the thought.

"I heard father tell that it comes from America."

"Well! Tell him to tell the Americans to keep it."

"There is little else to eat now that the praties have gone," Seámus informed his brother.

"There will be plenty of praties soon again. I heard Ma and Pa telling each other."

"When did you hear all this then and you in bed?"

"I heard them talking when they were digging in the quarter acre."

"I hope that they are right. Everyone else is talking about the hunger."

"Bfuil Ocras ort?" (Are you hungry)

"Ta Ocras orm anois." (I am hungry now)

"There is no need to go hungry. I heard Pa telling Ma that they send cattle and wheat from the big house to Bantry bay. From there it is put on ships and taken to England. My stomach is as empty as mother's cupboard." Seámus rubbed his stomach and laughed as it rumbled.

"Why do they take it to England. They must have plenty of their own"

"Our corn you mean? It is taken to feed the workers in the great factories where they make clothes and steel. He told Ma".

"I hate the Sasacnacs. Do you think that they will ever leave Ireland?"

"It is told in the Sean Scéals that one day the great army of the Tuatan-de-Dannan will rise from the dolmens and together with the Red Branch Knights will free old Ireland. It is also the prophesy that when the Shamrock and Palm are worn on the same day then Ireland will be free."

"Won't that be a grand day to see, Seámus. Do you think that I will be well by then," Brendan pleaded with his brother.

"You'll be long better by that time. God is good you know. Tell you what, we will go down to Queenstown on that day and wave them 'Slán Abaile' so we will, you'll see."

"Won't that be a day to be seen in old Skibbereen. You and me carrying the Green flag with the Maid of Eireann sitting prettily in the centre." Brendan was more chirpy now.

"A grand day indeed, a grand day Brendan, as you say."
Seámus looked out from the window and listened intently
for the sound of the waves breaking in Baltimore bay.
Yet the only sound that he heard was the mournful cry of
the gulls and the Banshee crying in the wind. He felt that
there was a foreboding over the cursed land.

"Never mind the hunger, what do you think Ma will say
about our frog when she sees it?" Brendan interrupted his
daydreaming.

"He'll be alright. Ma will understand that he belongs to
you."

"Why are you standing there like that. Why don't you sit
down?" Brendan looked at his brother standing with a
stoop, making no attempt to sit down on the bed.

"Standing like what? I always stand like that."

"No you don't, you were given a good mollafustering on
the bottom with the saileac slat by the teacher. You were
so you were, was it sore?" Brendan looked with sympathy
at his brother.

"I was not, and anyway it is none of your business, so
there."

"Well! You were either beaten with the saileac slat or you
scuttered your trousers." Brendan began to laugh which
in turn brought on another bout of coughing. He reached
under his pillow and took out the linen cloth and held it
over his mouth.

"Now see what happens when you curse. God doesn't like
it when you curse. Father says that every time you curse
you put another nail in God's poor hands on the cross."
Seámus took the handkerchief from his brother and wiped
his mouth for him. He noticed that there was blood on the
cloth.

"Did you cut yourself?" Seámus looked for a wound.

"No! But I lost another tooth today." Brendan opened his
mouth and displayed the gap between his teeth.

"How could you lose a tooth, who would you be fighting
with anyway?" Seámus asked.

"I did really, they come loose and I shake them out, see."
He reached under his pillow and produced three teeth.

"Your stirabout is on the table Seámus." He heard his
mother approaching the bedroom. In her hand she held a
bowl of watery yellow gruel.

"Look at Brendan, he lost another tooth today, so he did,"
Seámus remarked as he left the room.

"Oh Jesus, Mary and Joseph come to our aid." His
mother's hand shook, spilling some of the stirabout on the
floor.

"Did you see what Seámus brought me, Ma?" Brendan

25

interrupted her as he produced the frog from under the blankets.

"You cannot keep a frog in the bed," she remarked as the frog let out a croak of annoyance.

"Don't be silly Ma! I know that. Seámus is going to put him in a basin on the window sill for me. Can I keep him, please?"

"Oh very well, but I don't know what your father will have to say. Give me the frog for now and eat up your stirabout."

Brendan was about to object to the evil looking food when he thought better of it. She might change her mind about the frog if he complained. Reluctantly he ate the contents of the bowl.

That evening as Bridget sat by the fire knitting, the latch lifted and her husband entered.

"Go mbeannuigid Dia annso" (God bless all here). Tom removed his cap and placed it on the peg behind the door.

"Go mbá h-amlaid Duit", (The same to you) replied Bridget as she continued with her knitting.

"I saved you some stirabout, Tom. Will you have it now?"

"No! Keep it for yourself and the boys. I had something to eat at the big house. Here, I was given this".

He laid a small parcel of food on the table.

"Something nice, I hope, Brendan is not able to hold down the stirabout." Bridget put her knitting to one side and, rising from her chair, pulled the pot from over the fire.

Tom sat down in the sugan chair and placing his hands on his chin stared intently into the fire.

"What is it Tom? Is there something that you are not telling me?" Bridget returned to her knitting and sat down.

"It's the Big House. They are evicting a lot of their tenants from their cottages.

What with the failure of the potato crop last year, many of the tenants are behind with their rents. Did you know that the Terry alts and the Peep O'Day Boys are active over in the Limerick area. They are killing sheep and cattle on the big estates in order to prevent the landlords exporting them. We have been instructed under pain of eviction and deportation to report any activity in the area."

"Good God! Does this mean that you will be dismissed also. What would we do?"

"No, I'm safe enough for now. It's the tenants who are being dismissed and evicted. However they have no further need for my services. You know what this means, don't you?"

Tom stared into the flames not venturing to look at his wife.

"Do you think the potatoes will crop this year, Tom?" Bridget ignored this latest calamitous news and changed the subject.

"It's too early yet to tell. I was lucky to get a few stone of Crechán Prátie (small potato) seed. We can but pray and hope." No mention of the dreaded blight would be made. Mentioning the cursed word they believed would only awaken it.

"Seámus brought a frog home today for Brendan. It is in a basin on the window ledge." As she spoke she noticed that her Tom was growing old with worry before his years.

"A Cnádán! Well that is something different so it is. Are you going to let him keep it?"

"That's not all, he has lost more teeth today". Bridget worked harder at the needles.

"Should something happen to him it will break the heart of our Seámus so it will."

"We must be prepared for the worst Tom. When I pick him up I notice that he gets lighter by the day. My Brendan is going to die and there is nothing that we can do about it. Is there a God in heaven at all to listen to a mother's prayers?"

"The spring will soon be upon us and then he will mend. God is merciful and good, you will see. Don't be fretting too much for him now, Bridget my croide." Tom blessed himself.

"Amen, amen to that." Bridget calmed herself and looked across at her husband's face as it reflected in the light of the turf fire.

She could see the deep furrows on his brow and the sunken eyes in his head. His gaunt and haggard look frightened her. He was only thirty five years of age this summer gone and he looked like a man of sixty. What nightmares were at this moment haunting him. Would he too become another victim of the great Ocras.

"Oh God, forgive me for such dreadful thoughts," she silently chastised herself.

"This land, this cursed land, when will the Ocras leave it. Could Hell with all its torments be any worse?" The nightmare visions of a mother and wife haunted her.

"What am I knitting this geansaí for, he will not live to wear it, so he won't. Oh God in heaven, will you not listen to a mother's prayer?" Leaving her knitting to one side she left the room closing the door behind her. Tom let out a sigh and rising to his feet looked across at the closed door.

What torment his wife was suffering he well understood. Yet what comfort could he offer? If only they could speak to each other and bring into the open the mental torture that they were both suffering.

Rising he crossed the kitchen floor and opening the door went out into the night.

A PEEP INTO HISTORY

Following the signing of the ignominious treaty of Limerick and the 'Flight of the Wild Geese' in 1691 came the 'PLANTERS'. These were Protestant and Presbyterian settlers who were granted the fertile lands of Ireland. An act for the abrogating of the Oath of Supremacy of 1691 and other oaths put paid once and for all to any semblance of England honouring the treaty.

The indigenous population of Ireland had been forced by cruel laws (i.e.Corn laws etc.;) to depend on the 'planters' for a piece of their own land on which to build a cabin and feed themselves a starvation diet. In return they would surrender a portion of their crop to the 'PLANTER' (Landlord).

Imports of foreign wheat and corn were forbidden under the corn laws. This to keep the price of corn grown by the farmers of Britain high. This put the price of flour beyond the reach of the poor Irish. What cereals they grew went to pay their rates and taxes. Bread, cakes and scones became unknown in the cottages of Ireland. It is doubtful if any Irish housewife outside the great houses had any knowledge of baking bread or the rudiments of cooking basic food.

The Irish were now forced to depend on the potato and to be content with a bowl of boiled potatoes and a mug of buttermilk, (when available), or water. This was the state to which the people had been reduced. They were forced to live off, (because they knew no better), the 'LUMPERS', 'HORSE POTATOES' or for a better name 'STONERS'.

These were the rough and coarse potatoes that gave a heavy yield and could sustain man and beast for nine months of the year. The growing of this one variety of potato, year in year out in the same plot of land was a contributing factor to the potato blight. The fungus Phylophthora Infestans which attacks the potato can lie dormant in the ground awaiting the next setting of the new potato crop. Rotation of all root crops is essential to preserve the health of the land. With the small acreage of land allocated to the Irish it was impossible to rotate the crop.

A pig or perhaps a handful of fowl would be reared within the confines of their mud cabin together with the family and be fattened on the same potato diet as the family. These would then be traded in payment of their taxes and rents or for clothing for the family. The three months between the consumption of the old crop and the coming of the new became known as 'THE CORN MONTHS'. During this period they traded their labour or sold their pig and chickens for a bag or two of meal on which they survived awaiting the new crop. It was their basic instinct to survive that sustained them before, during and after the Great Hunger.

When clothing was needed for their families or when their rents were due then they paid with their labour. Money seldom, if ever, changed hands. The Irish were reduced to the lowest scale of human or animal existence. It is recorded that the slaves of the New World were treated far better than the Irish were in their own land.

The rapidly increasing Irish population were now dependant on the one crop, the potato. This was a disaster waiting to happen, for every year there were failures in this unstable crop.

Yet what were the people to do? They could not own their own land and were dependant on the landlords and their agents for a half acre of land or less on which to grow their needs and pay their rent and taxes. There was an excessive demand for a piece of land on which to build a cottage and raise a family. Rents were artificially high in relation to the value of the produce reaped from the poor soil. Tenants took little care of the land because it would never be theirs. The landlord or his agent could ,at the 'Doff of a hat', evict them.

Here then was a nation reduced to the lowest state of humanity by its occupiers. There was no incentive for them to get off their knees and improve their standard of living, on the contrary, should they rise above their status they were soon put back in their place. This was proven by the many minor skirmishes against the might of the English crown. It was a case of 'Us and them, the Irish'.

There were the so called Irish towns where squalor, famine and depredation existed. Then there were the English towns of fine houses, wealth and prosperity. To this day an example of the social contrast of the period can be seen in the grand squares in the cities of Dublin, Cork, Limerick, Derry and Belfast. There one can see the grand houses of the English town in contrast to the smaller cottages of the Irish town.

Yet the British government of the day were unashamedly to announce through the media of the press that the Irish were an ungrateful nation......

'They were neither shy nor ashamed to take of our charity. They have hardly been decent whilst they have their bellies filled with our corn and their pockets filled with our money'.

'IRISH PROPERTY MUST SUPPORT IRISH POVERTY".....

This was the view of the English 'Whigs' (TORIES) who had no love for the absentee landlord. There were no Irish landowners as by an act of English Parliament the Irish were not allowed to own property.
'The state of Ireland is to the last degree deplorable and enough to induce despair. Such general disorganisation and demoralisation. Here we have a people with rare exceptions besotted with obstinacy and indolence, reckless and savage, all from the high to the low intent on doing as little and getting as much as they can, unwilling to arouse themselves, looking to England for succour and snarling at the succour that they receive. Their masses brutal, deceitful and idle, the whole state of things contradictory and paradoxical.
While menaced with the continuance of FAMINE next year, they will not cultivate the ground and it lies untilled and unsown. There is no doubt that the people were never so well off on the whole as they have been this year of the FAMINE.
Nobody will pay rent and the savings banks are overflowing.

With the money they get from our relief funds they buy arms instead of food and then shoot the officers who are sent to regulate the distribution of that relief.
Whilst they crowd to the overseer and demand employment, the landlords cannot produce hands, and sturdy beggars calling themselves destitute are apprehended daily with their pockets bulging with money.

Such were the sentiments echoed time and time again from the hallowed halls of Westminster.
What a paradox of self justification this was from a government who cared little for the welfare of the Irish.
The abuse of what relief there was available was widespread.
Following the outbreak of the 'Great Hunger' there was no seed available for the following season. In 1847 a consignment of seed was made available to the people at a price which was beyond their reach. In the West of Ireland it was given free to the landlords for distribution

to their tenants. In too many cases, as in the Barony of Erris, of which Belmullet was one of the principle towns, the people refused in the first instant to accept the seed.

"Why should we grow the crop for when it is ripe the landlord will claim it," they cried.

This was strongly denied but was to be proven when it came to the harvest. Landowners came and took the crop in payment of rent due.

In other cases the landowners themselves were receiving food and aid from the state as their tenants starved and died inside their hovels.

In other cases, through mismanagement and squabbling between landowners and government officials, the seed arrived far too late for sowing.

As the drain on resources continued and the hunger bit deeper, a new law was hastily drafted.

This law became known as 'THE GREGORY CLAUSE'.

WILLIAM GREGORY. A member of Parliament (DUBLIN) Stipulated in the POOR LAW AMENDMENT ACT of 1847, that anyone holding more than one quarter acre of land, no matter how rocky or poor, would not be deemed to be destitute. No member of that family would be eligible for any relief nor would they be accepted into the poor houses.

'Only widows with legitimate children under the age of nine years would receive relief for a period of eight weeks or two calendar months.

That they had to be resident in the immediate townland for a period of three years and registered on the electoral registrar for that same period.

That they must have slept within that townland for a period of three years and produce proof of same.

That they should be destitute, disabled, widows with two children or more under the age of nine years or fever patients before they would become eligible for outdoor relief'.

On the West coast of Ireland where the fishermen had pawned their nets and boats or had them confiscated by the landlords and bailiffs in lieu of rent, a new scheme was proposed.

The sum of £5,000 was made available by the government in the spring of 1847 to make loans to the landed proprietors. This was to enable them to distribute funds to their tenants to buy seeds and redeem their nets and boats from their landlords.

SIR JAMES BURGOYNE was in charge of the administration of the funds available.

He made the following observation to SIR CHARLES E

TREVELYAN who was then the chief secretary to Ireland.

'I have made many inquiries for the purpose of repayment, but have always made it a point that there should be a decided prospect of any advantage being repaid, and it is here that the matter hangs. The officers all report that they doubt being able to get the money back. It is necessary to be firm on this point, that I have not made any use of a penny of the sum and have recommended to the SOCIETY OF FRIENDS that they reserve their funds also until a better mode of expending them is found.'

The Society of Friends, (Quakers), ignored this advice and assisted the poor fishermen where possible to redeem their nets and boats.
The Admiralty too, also ignoring this advice, delivered a large amount of surplus seamen's' clothing to the Society for distribution among the poor fisher folk in the West.

EMPLOYMENT AT THE BIG HOUSE

Spring came to the little village of Skibbereen and brought with it all the hopes and aspirations of the people. Gone was the despondency of 1845.

It had been an act of God, that the country should be chastised in this way, they claimed. Who were they to question God's Holy will?

Did not the wise priest tell them that it was the will of God and that it was not in their domain to question him. It would be blasphemous to think otherwise.

The Flynn family planted their quarter acre in potatoes and set aside a small plot to the rear of the cottage for the growing of the root crop and cabbages.

Now that the weather had taken a turn for the better Brendan's' window was left open a little at the top. He had insisted that his mother should place a piece of lace curtain over the gap to prevent 'Cromwell' from escaping.

His health had not improved but he was still with them and for that they thanked their God.

As the hunger continued to affect the village, typhus began to take its toll and people began to die. Hoping to contain the disease the school was closed.

Seámus, glad to be away from the school and the cruel teacher, went seeking employment.

With little income from the despondent tenants there was no longer any demand for adult labour. Landlords resorted to child labour. It was to meet this demand that Seámus found himself knocking on the great door of the mansion of Brigadier William Cornwall-Stone.

On the appointed day Seámus Flynn presented himself at the big house. He looked at the huge carved doors before he took the bell chain in his hands and pulled. The door was opened by the butler.

"Who are you and what do you mean by calling at the front of the house?" He looked Seámus up and down.

"I'm Seámus Flynn, sir, I was told to report here this morning." Seámus removed his caubeen.

"You should not have come here. Go across to the back drive and report to the head gardener in the home farm. Should you meet her ladyship you will remove your caubeen and address her as 'Madam'. Do not speak unless you are spoken to, do you understand?"

"Yes sir." Seámus replaced his caubeen and raced around to the back of the mansion and on up the drive to the

34

home farm. Once there he was directed to the large potting shed and told to wait inside. He waited for some time but nobody came to see him. Leaving the potting shed he began to wander around the walled garden.

"Come here, boy, what are you doing there? A man with the legs of his trousers tied halfways up with string called him forward.

"I'm waiting for her ladyship sir." Seámus again removed his caubeen.

"You are waiting for who? Are my old ears deceiving me now? Did you say her Ladyship?" The man came over and stood looking down at him.

"Yes indeed sir, I am. I was told to come and wait here for her," Seámus confirmed.

"Told by whom and who are you anyway?"

"The butler told me. I'm the new boy from the village. My father is Thomas Flynn."

"Well now bless my soul. Your the son of Tom the handyman are you not. Did you not come here before with some ciscéans?"

"Yes, sir."

"Waiting for her ladyship indeed." He placed his hands on his hips and laughed good naturedly.

"Come with me boy." He escorted Seámus back into the potting shed.

"This is where you belong, young man. Her ladyship will not be gracing you with her presence, of that have little doubt."

Soon he was to learn just what his duties were. He was required to wash all the empty clay pots. Then he had to sort and stack them on their sides in order of size. Any cracked or damaged pots were to be smashed into pieces and placed on a pile in the corner. These pieces he was told would be used as drainage in the good pots. It was to be a laborious, boring and messy task with little respite. Yet he persevered for he hoped that one day he would be promoted to the glasshouses, should he prove himself satisfactory.

As he diligently scoured a pot one fine spring day he looked across the garden through the murky window and saw the gardeners preparing the ground for sowing. 'Will my day ever come?' he thought to himself.

That afternoon as fate would have it he was instructed to report to the office. Seámus wondered why he was being sent for. He entered the office and stood before the large desk occupied by the head gardener.

"Seámus, do you know what this is?"

Rising from his desk the man picked up a wooden mallet

with a long handle.

"Yes sir, it's a pot sounder."

"A pot sounder. Well, it's as good a name as any. Tomorrow you will report to the glasshouses."

"The glasshouses sir. Oh thank you sir, thank you." Seámus raced from the office and returned to the potting shed. In his excitement he scrubbed harder and harder at the pots.

That evening he related to his parents in glowing detail that he was now in charge of all the greenhouses on the estate. This was a gross exaggeration and well his parents knew it.

He was to be disappointed next morning when he was presented with the mallet. His duties were to walk along the long rows of pots with the mallet in one hand and a watering can in the other. Should the pots sound hollow he was to water them. If not he was to leave them alone.

He was annoyed to find that his ambitions were once again thwarted. He would do no more than water the pots and keep the benches in order.

One afternoon as he carried out his boring task he observed her ladyship approaching. As instructed he moved to the rear of the greenhouse and waited with his caubeen in his hand.

Her ladyship was accompanied by none other than the head gardener.

"Who is that boy there?" she asked on seeing Seámus who was trying to make himself as inconspicuous as possible.

"He is our new apprentice, the son of Tom Flynn the handyman. He is showing a lot of promise Mam, if I may say so."

"Bring him here so I can see him."

Seámus nervously stepped from the shadows and bowed before her Ladyship as instructed.

"Well now Gerry, he is not very robust, is he?" She looked Seámus up and down as she addressed the head gardener.

"I fully agree Mam. Yet what the Good Lord in his wisdom has denied him in strength he has more than compensated for with good sense. He is one smart garsún so he is". These were compliments indeed for which Seámus was grateful.

"Well spoken Gerry, I'll keep him very much in mind". They left the greenhouse without one word to Seámus.

As he was now proving himself to be a trustworthy apprentice he was entrusted with more demanding tasks. Promotion followed quickly and he was given his own set of tools. This was what he had worked and waited for.

He was now entrusted to take cuttings from the various plants, and root them in the cucumber house. His delight knew no bounds when he tentatively removed his first rooted cuttings and planted them. He watched over them and nursed them until he saw the buds burst open and the first leaves appear. This to him was the greatest achievement of his young life. He had now grown plants that were likely to find their way into the gardens of the manor. Although the hours were long and he was still required to scrub the floor of the houses he was content. The day was approaching when he would become a qualified gardener.

On his fourteenth birthday he was instructed to report once again to the office. He knocked and entered. The head gardener and his understudy were deliberating over a large plan of the flower beds set out before them.

"Seámus, you have done very well so far. You are a very lucky boy indeed." As he spoke he picked up his pen and began to alter parts of the plan. Seámus glanced at it and noticed that it was a plan of the twin gardens laid out to the front of the mansion. The head gardener returned to the plan and pointed out several beds to his assistant and began to scratch his head with the pen. Finally he put the pen to one side and addressed Seámus.

"Son, you are to report to the rose garden immediately. It would appear that her ladyship was most impressed with my testimonials of you. Don't go and disappoint me now, do you hear?"

"Thank you sir. May I go now?" Seámus shuffled from one foot to the other as he awaited his dismissal.

He was not too keen on the promotion. He had been told by other apprentices that her ladyship was not adverse to boxing the ears of any apprentice who displeased her. She would not tolerate it should she find one rose out of place. Should she find the dreaded black spot on any of her precious roses, then woe betide the person in charge. He would be dismissed from the estate without as much as a farthing of any wages due. It was more in fear and trepidation that he reported to the rose gardens than love of them.

Seámus was not long into his work on the roses when he came in direct conflict with Her Ladyship. One morning as he laboriously hoed between the roses he inadvertently broke one of the stems. At that moment Her Ladyship was coming down the drive and saw what he had done. Running up to him she took the hoe and beat him across the back with it. From then on he was no longer her favourite. The more he tried to satisfy her the more she demanded. The stems were too long or too short. The buds were not open enough or else they opened too soon. There always seemed to be one problem or another. He concluded that she must be a very unhappy person and sought comfort in her roses. Why should she spend so much of her time in the rose garden when she had such a beautiful family and home. He tried to meet her every demand and tolerated all the sarcastic comments she made.

When the weather permitted it, the German governess would come into the garden with Master William and his sister Harriott. Seámus would greet them and encourage them to take a little interest in the roses, so dear to their mother.

Should the governess be absent they would come and sit on the balustrade and listen to him tell tales of old Ireland. As they were all about the same age they found plenty to talk about.

The children wanted to know all about the village and the people who lived there. Did they attend school and what kind of houses did they live in. Their knowledge of the village was confined to what the governess had told them.

The Irish, according to the governess, were a savage race. They would kill any stranger entering their village, just for the sake of killing. The English had been sent to Ireland by Pope Adrian to civilise the people. This bigotry had been long implanted in their young minds. Seámus reminded them that although they were born in the big house they were nevertheless Irish too. This information came as a great surprise to the children.

He found it necessary to plead with them to keep their conversations in the strictest confidence. Should it emerge that he was divulging information that they were forbidden to hear then he would find himself out of a job. His parents would be evicted from their smallholding and be left on the highway. With this fear hanging over him he decided that from now on he would avoid any contact with the children whatsoever. They would learn from their own experience of the injustices perpetrated on his people.

GHOST VOICES

My man lay dead for days
My paps withered and dry,
I smothered it in my skirts
When it gave its first cry.

They pulled the thatch down over us
Was it a girl or a boy?
Nettles grew out of its eyes
A stalk out of its mouth.

Scouring the beach for sea weed,
My brother and me,
When he fell down dead,
I hacked gobbets of flesh
From his soft parts, buttock and shank
And washed them in the waves.

Then I covered him with stones
And muttered a few prayers.
That night I slept without pain.
In the morning
My belly was growling again.

We ate bark from the trees,
Nettles and weeds,
We drank blood from the veins of cattle
And stuffed our mouths with leaves.
We ate the soft parts of each other.

Deep in ditches, under bushes and trees,
In abandoned beaches
Without marks or crosses,
We lie everywhere.

And sometimes, when the wind stops
Whispering through the grasses,
And birds for once lapse into silence
Might you hear us.
Listen! Do you hear us?
Hear us, hear us.

                                   Anon.

SEÁMUS FINDS TROUBLE

It was late evening of an autumn day when Seámus
finished his duties on the estate. Taking the road through
the home farm he entered the woods intending to leave by
the back gate which led directly into the village. Passing
along the primrose path he noticed that some bracken
had been plucked. Curiosity getting the better of him he
followed the trail which led him deeper into the woods.
Someone had been trespassing in the woods that
afternoon. At the end of the trail he discovered a snare
with a dead hare strangled in the wire loop.
Suspecting that the poachers were watching him, he
decided that it would be best to remove the hare and hand
it in at the gatehouse for collection by the game wardens.
Removing the dead animal he lay it to one side. Winding
up the snare he put it in his pocket. The hare he slung
over his shoulder and left the shelter of the woods. Taking
a short cut through the meadow he came to the long drive
leading to the gatehouse. He had gone no more than fifty
yards before he was accosted by two of the gamekeepers.
"Just where do you think you are off to with that hare?"
One of them held a lamp close to his face.
"Glad I met you, I found this hare in a snare in the woods.
I was about to leave them in the gate house for you but
you seem to have saved me the trouble." Seámus handed
the hare to one of the keepers and removed the snare from
his pocket.
"So you found him in the woods, did you, and you were
going to leave him with old Tom for us?" He sneered as he
looked towards his companion.
"Come on now, stop your joking. You don't think that I
snared him, do you?"
"You said it not us. Old Tom locks up and retires early, we
all know that."
"How did you intend to get out of the estate, Fly," his
companion sarcastically remarked.
"Look here, you must know me. I'm Tom Flynn's son,
Seámus. I work for Her Ladyship." He began to get
worried by the accusations being made against him.
"Well now, we'll take the snare and hare to his lordship
and let you get off home." One of the gamekeepers took a
key from his pocket and opened the gate.
"What did you say your name was? Oh yes! Seámus Flynn
and you work for Her Ladyship."

He heard the gate slam shut and the key turn in the lock.

"You're very quiet tonight Seámus, something the matter?" His father looked up from his book.

"I got caught carrying a hare." He told his father what had happened. As he was about to leave the kitchen there was a knocking on the door.

Looking towards the half door he was surprised to see the gamekeepers standing in its shade.

"What do you want now? I thought I left you at the manor"

"We wish to have words with your father."

"What can I do for you men?" his father asked .

"It's about your son, Mr Flynn."

They explained as to how they had found Seámus with the hare under suspicious circumstances. They reported the matter to his lordship. Seámus was to stay at home in the custody of his father pending the outcome.

"Did my son not explain to you both how he came to be in possession of the hare?"

"Yes he did, after he was caught," one of them sneered.

"What kind of neighbours are you anyway, treating a boy in this way. He told you what happened. I'll bid you both goodnight"

"If that's your attitude then there is nothing more for us to say. No doubt you'll be hearing more of this."

"Good night to you both." His father closed the door.

"I wouldn't worry too much about it son. It's all a misunderstanding. I'll have a word myself with his Lordship." His father, nonchalantly dismissing the allegations, returned to reading his book.

Seámus was summoned to the head gardeners' office the next day and asked to again explain how he came to be in possession of the hare.

Once again he related how he found the snared hare and pleaded his complete innocence.

"I see, Seámus. From my point of view it should at least be a lesson to you, out you go." He left the office none the wiser as to his fate.

The following day he was once again called to the manor and to the office of the head gamekeeper. In the office he was confronted by the Lord of the manor, the Head gamekeeper and a member of the local constabulary. They sat behind a long table in the most intimidating manner. Again he was called upon to repeat his version of events. He could see by the way they looked at him that they did not believe one word that he told them.

"You admit that you did have a snare in your pocket and a hare over your shoulder when you were apprehended," the constable remarked.

"I know I did sir. As I told the gamekeepers I was taking them to old Tom at the gatehouse."

"So you keep telling us. Yet it is common knowledge that old Tom locks the gates early and retires to bed. Why did you pick on this way to return home? You never went that way before." Again the constable questioned him.

"How did you intend to leave the grounds? Tom would not rise from his bed for anyone after he retires"

Questions without answers were put to him over and over again.

"This is a matter for the magistrates to deal with. The lad is dismissed for now." The brigadier rose from his seat and without as much as a glance at Seámus left the building.

Seámus was escorted from the estate like a criminal and told to return home and await the hearing. He began to worry that something terrible was about to happen to him. He found little comfort as he tossed and turned in restless sleep.

His father, the proverbial optimist, kept encouraging him, telling him that it was all a terrible mistake. The court would realise that he was innocent, nothing to worry about.

The weeks went by and still there was no word from the court. His father was now beginning to worry for his son.

The tension within the family was growing daily.

"Tomorrow I'm going to go to the manor and explain to his Lordship the agony and upset this is causing to my family. He is a reasonable man and I'm sure he will understand," his father promised.

They knew by the look on his face when he returned next day that there was no good news.

"I went and saw His Lordship as I said I would. He politely listened to me for some time in silence. Then he began to pace the floor. Backwards and forwards he walked with his hands clasped behind his back. Then he stopped in front of the open fire and looked at me."

"Mr Flynn, were it in my power I would let the boy go with a caution. However it is out of my hands. The law must take its course. I will put in a good word for the boy. Sorry I cannot do more."

"But sir, all you have to do is to drop the charges. Please for my wife's' sake. For God's sake, I beg of you." Tom pleaded in vain.

"Is that all he had to say? Sorry! After all we done for them. All this upset for a miserable hare that in all probability never came from the estate. His mother looked

across at her son and ran from the room crying .
"Try and not upset yourself Bridget. All we can do now is pray and hope."
This news came as a shock to Seámus. He was now resigned to his fate. He could expect no more justice from the court than had thousands before him. His mother prayed day and night for his deliverance. She firmly believed that divine intervention and her firm belief in his innocence would exonerate him.

On the Friday afternoon a constable came to the cottage door and handed the official summons to Tom Flynn. He would be required to present his son before the court in Cork to answer the charges of Theft and Trespass.

The family rose early on the following Monday morning and made preparations for the long journey to the courthouse. Mother refused to go. She would stay at home and continue praying for her sons' deliverance.

On their arrival at the courthouse Seámus was separated from his father and taken into custody by two jailers.

His father joined the relatives of other prisoners and adjourned to the public gallery.

"All rise". The usher banged the floor with a long staff he carried in his hand.

A bell sounded as the presiding judge entered the courtroom. Tom looked around the hostile court crammed with gentlemen and lawyers in long intimidating wigs.

The judge in his robes and sash looked more like an executioner than an administrator of Justice.

"Bring up the prisoners," the usher called, his voice echoing around the sparse courtroom.

The gathering gasped when they saw the prisoners come up the steps from the jail below the court. Their hands and feet were manacled together. A long draw chain ran through the manacles and was secured by a large lock. Two jailers guarded the prisoners.

Seámus was first to be called to answer the charge brought against him.

"How does the prisoner Flynn plead?" the clerk called.

Seámus looked across at his father, then at the judge.

"Swear the plea at once." The judge shuffled in his seat and looked sternly at Seámus.

"I found the hare, honestly I did sir," he pleaded.

"Just answer yes or no, keep your pleading for later," the judge warned him. Then as an afterthought he added.

"The court must take this as a 'Not guilty' plea. Proceed."

Each prisoners' name was called in turn and the same question was put to them.

Those who pleaded guilty were sentenced and removed

from the court.

With all the charges read to the prisoners the court settled down to listen to their pleas'.

The case against Seámus was the first to be heard.

The bailiffs were called to give their version of events. They confirmed what Seámus had told them.

He was again questioned as to how he came to be in possession of the hare. He repeated to the court as to how he had found the hare and of his intention to leave it at the cottage.

"Had I left the hare in the woods then a fox would have got it."

Then came the damning examination of evidence by the Crown Prosecution.

"You told the court that you found the hare, is this not so?"

"Yes sir, so I did. I swear I..."

"Just answer 'Yes' or 'No'." His explanation was interrupted.

"You told the court that you went into the woods and accidentally found the hare covered in bracken. More likely that you knew where the snare was all the time and that you were poaching. Is this not the truth?"

"I swear, I swear that I found the hare snared. It was not mine. I never owned a snare." Seámus clutched the iron railing of the dock.

"You were told to answer 'Yes' or 'No'. You do understand plain English?" the judge reprimanded him.

"You set the snare in the morning and sneaked back under the cover of darkness to collect your ill gotten gains, is this not the real truth? You abused the trust placed in you by your master and took advantage of his generosity."

The evidence was building up against him. He bowed his head and remained silent.

The judge tiring of the whole case and seeing that there were other cases pending decided that he had heard enough. He called for an end to the proceedings and wound up the case.

"I have given the felon ample opportunity to put his defence before this court. From the beginning of the case he has proven himself to be a well rehearsed liar. Like all Irishmen he could not tell the truth from lies if he tried. I doubt if this is the first time that he has abused his masters' generosity. He was given a position of trust by his master, the Right Honourable Sir William Cornwall-Stone, Brigadier and benefactor to this parish. A well respected and generous landlord. What gratitude does this wretch show? He sneaks into his woods, like the thief

44

he is and steals. What else he has stolen in the past we can only guess."

"May it please the court." The Brigadier rose to his feet.

"At your service Sir William." The Judge smiled and invited him to address the court

"Having listened to this case and taking into account the loyalty of his father Thomas Flynn and the age of the boy, I would ask the court to show leniency on this occasion and dismiss him into the custody of his father." With these words the Brigadier resumed his seat.

The court was quiet for a few moments as the judge consulted with his learned clerk.

Clearing his throat he looked at Seámus shivering in the iron clad dock.

"Seámus Flynn, I have taken into account the generous and magnanimous plea by Sir William on your behalf. A gesture I hope you will appreciate; otherwise!

You are hereby placed into the custody of your father on the understanding that should you commit a further felony then you will be brought back to this court and you will be deported to 'Van Deemens' land for a period of three years hard labour. Do you understand what I am saying?"

"Yes Sir, indeed I do and I thank you."

"Very well then. Release the prisoner."

Seámus had to wait until all the other cases were heard before he was taken to the cells beneath the court house to have his chains removed.

His father on seeing the Brigadier leaving the courthouse ran forward and fell on his knees before him.

"Thank you, thank you sir. May God and all his angels watch over you". He cried as he held the brass handle of the coach.

"Let this be a lesson to your son and further let it be understood that he is no longer an employee of mine. Should he be found trespassing on my estate then I will have no hesitation of returning him to his gaolers. Drive on."

He heard a cheering coming from the entrance to the courthouse. He saw his son approaching rubbing his wrists.

"Seámus, thank God. Thank God you are back with us."

STRANGERS IN THE VILLAGE

The Brigadier was not unsympathetic when he heard how Tom Flynn and his family were suffering following the dismissal of Seámus. He would not however give any further employment to Tom on his estate, nor would he evict the family from their cottage.

The alleged breach of trust by Seámus was a matter of principle. Were he to overlook this serious matter then others might take advantage of his generosity.

With no income and little food from the relief committee Tom and his family were now in dire straits.

That afternoon at a meeting of the board of governors of the workhouse, of which he was chairman, the Brigadier recommended that Tom be given a vacancy that had arisen.

"Bridget! Did I not tell you that God would answer our prayers."

"What is it Tom? Good news at last, I hope."

"Good news indeed. I have been offered a position in the workhouse. Thanks to the Brigadier"

"In the workhouse is it indeed." Bridgets' head dropped.

"We must not shy away from it. There will be a sovereign or two in it and food for all of us."

"Tom Flynn, do you not know what you are letting yourself in for?"

"What ails you Bridget? Sure I thought that you would be pleased."

"Pleased is it indeed. Do you call it an opportunity removing the dead from that place. You know it is riddled with plague. What man with an ounce of sense would want to even consider working in that hell hole?"

"We don't know for sure what I'll be asked to do yet ,do we? Show a little charity in God's Holy Name."

"You go and do what you want, Tom Flynn, but mark my words, it could be the death of you. Then what would become of us?"

"I'll go and see what the work entails. If it is as bad as you say then I can leave."

"Of course Tom, you do just that. I'm sorry to appear so ungrateful, but matters are getting beyond me."

"The soup kitchen will be opening soon, have you scalded the can?" Tom looked out of the window as people began to gather in the square.

"Soup is that what they call it? Is this what the Flynn

family are reduced to. It runs through Brendan and Seámus like water through a stream." Bridget collected the can from the scullery and banged it down on the table. "With the biscuits it will help to keep the Ocras from the door," Tom more or less apologised as he picked up the tin can and left the house.

Bridget followed her husband to the door and looked with derision at the assembled starving people.

"Is this what we have become? Half starving and depending on an army biscuit and a cup of watery soup. Get off your knees and be proud that we are Irish. Better be a dead Fenian than a grovelling beggar."

The assembled people, many on all fours and half naked, some fully naked, took little notice of her bantering. They were too enthralled, watching and waiting for the soup kitchen. Proud rhetoric mattered little to a downtrodden, starving people.

"I have a wife and six children waiting for a little help."

An attenuated corpse of what was once a man held up a three legged iron pot and apologised.

"You're not expecting to get that filled are you mister"?

A man with a woman beside him spoke. Strapped to his back was a boy whose appearance was more like that of a shrivelled dwarf than a child. What age was he, what ages were his parents? It was impossible to tell, for their faces were drawn and haggard. The boys stomach protruded to such a degree that he bounced like a rubber ball every time his father moved. He expectorated a green slime from his ever open mouth as he gasped for breath.

"In God's Holy Name cannot you put that boy down some place," a man called as he held his hand to his nostrils. The boy was in a filthy state and suffering from dysentery.

Yet the man made no effort to leave his place in the shuffling queue.

When the kitchen finally opened the obsequious mass shuffled, crawled and moved towards it.

A bell rang out and the multitude came to life. Those without cans were herded to a long table beside which stood a large cauldron containing soup. To this was attached a ladle on a chain. Beside them were containers filled with surplus army biscuits. Each person was allowed one ladle of soup and two biscuits. When they had partaken of the soup they were ushered out the back door. Those with cans were lined up at a separate table and asked to produce their vouchers. As each voucher listed the names of those entitled to soup so they received that amount of soup filled ladles and biscuits.

Tom was lucky this day for he received his rations of four ladles of soup and eight biscuits before the soup and biscuits finally ran out.

Those who were unlucky would have to take their chances again the next day and hope for success. Included in these was the man with the three legged pot. He too would have to await another day.

Tom returned to the cottage and laid the can and the biscuits on the table.

"I'll warm it over the fire. Sit yourself down, Tom".

Bridget took the can and poured the contents into a pot. Hanging it on the crane she pushed it over the coals.

"There is a little yellow meal left that I have been saving. Do you think that I should add it to the pot Tom?" she asked as she stirred the watery soup. Before he could answer a pleading voice called from the laneway.

"In God's Holy Name, can you see your way to give us a little food, or if not then a share of the warmth at your fire."

A woman with the support of a blackthorn stick appeared in the open doorway. In a ragged bundle tied around her neck was a naked infant. She was soon followed by two emaciated children.

These attenuated ghosts made no effort to enter the cottage. They stood in the doorway and apart from a piece of dripping wet blanket that covered their skeleton shoulders they were naked. Their stomachs were swollen almost to twice their normal size but their legs were no larger than the handle of a slán. A soft down was growing on their faces yet their heads were sparse of hair. Their eyes were large and watery. They neither blinked nor did they speak. Had this family come from the grave itself? Tom tried to look away but their haunting gaze would not give him peace.

"There was no soup left for me and my children. My husband is lying dead in our cottage. We have walked five long Irish miles this day only to find that there is no soup left". She tipped the rusting tin can that she carried upside down in front of Tom as proof.

"Who are you talking to Tom?" Bridget removed the spoon from the pot and stood up.

"Jesus, Mary and Joseph protect us all, where did you come from?" Blessing herself she looked at the woman and her two children silhouetted in the doorway. She could not believe what her eyes were beholding.

Táimid caillte leis an Ocras, mar táimid ar an mbótar ó maidin. (We are starving with the hunger and have been on the road since morning) Again she tipped the empty can upside down.

"We have no spare food, I only wish to God we had." Bridget stood motionless as the contents of the ladle spilled on to the hot coals.

"Could I beg a little heat from your fire then. The road to Creagh is long and weary. We will be of little trouble to your good selves. God rewards the generous giver."

"Did you say Creagh, out by Inisbeg is it not. Good God woman, whatever brought you to Skibbereen?"

"The very place missus. It's a long story and I have no doubt but you have your own troubles. If you don't be minding it is better let it rest."

Like a chastised dog the woman began to creep slowly into the cottage, her hands held before her. Her emaciated children hiding in the folds of her ragged skirt crept beside her.

"Come nearer the fire and sit yourself down. Come on, you too." Bridget invited them into the cottage. The two children reluctantly approached the open grate. Forming a semi-circle they sat on the stone floor as near to the fire as was possible. Removing the infant from the wet cloth she half dried him and placed him in front of the fire. Taking the liberty she placed the cloth on the crook to dry. Tom rose to his feet and went into the scullery.

"Bridget, could you help me here please?" he called.

Entering the scullery he motioned to her to ease the door to.

"Could we not spare a bite, no matter how small. How could we eat with them looking at us. Sure the soup would stick in my craw."

"You're a fine upstanding man, Tom, and a credit. Did you think that I would share out what we have and let them go without?"

Tom returned to the table and sat down. Bridget took the rest of the meal and added it into the soup. Reaching up, she added water from the iron kettle to it. This was the only way to ration out what was on offer.

"How are matters over your way?" Tom asked by way of conversation.

"I can tell you mister that it would not be worth listening to. But as you want to know then I see no harm in telling. The day before yesterday I left our cottage on the shore of Baltimore Bay. Inside I left the body of my Sean. I heard that there was food for the asking here in Skibbereen. You see how wrong one can be."

"What will you do now?" Tom asked.

"We will make a 'Scalpeen' along the boreen and wait until tomorrow. God is good, we may be in luck. Do you

49

know if the soup kitchen will be opening then?"

"I expect so, but there is no telling. There's a dry cottage down the boreen empty. You and your children could bed down there for the night. I'm sure that I could get a bale of fresh straw and there is plenty of turf for the asking," Tom suggested.

"That's more than charitable of you and God will surely reward you."

The conversation continued as Bridget waited for the meal to cook. Having finally inspected the contents of the pot she invited then to partake of the family meal.

"Come on now, sit yourselves down, it is not a lot that we have to offer, but you're welcome to share."

"Do you mean us Mam ? May Jesus and the Holy family reward you." The woman was on her feet and looking intently at the dishes being filled with the watery soup.

"I do indeed, you'll need to excuse me for a minute or two." Bridget picked up a bowl of the soup and left the kitchen.

"Is there a sick person in the house then?"

"There is indeed. It's our youngest, Brendan. Been ill now for a long time. Sure he is in God's hand's, so he is."

"God be good to the cratur and to all of you. We'll be praying for him, of that have no doubt, and you too for your charity this day." The woman sprinkled a little salt on her dish of soup and called on her children to join her.

"Who's in the kitchen Ma?" Brendan asked as his mother entered the room.

"A woman and her children looking for a little Christian charity."

"Are they boys or girls. Do I know them?"

"A boy and a girl about your age. I doubt if you know them for they come from Creagh. Now drink your soup before it gets cold."

"Ma, do you think that they would come and talk to me?"

"Why not, you are a proper little chatterbox. Now drink up and we'll see."

"Sorry about that, it's our son, Brendan. He is not all that well and wants to know if the children would like to talk to him," his mother apologised on entering the kitchen.

"Sure that's no trouble at all. Go in and talk to your friend now," she told her children.

"Let them finish their soup first. there is plenty of time."

It did not take long to drink what soup there was on offer. Having finished the soup the two children stood beside the table and glanced at their mother with their big watery vacant eyes.

"They are ready to call on your son, Missus," the woman told Bridget.

50

"Perhaps it would be better if they borrowed a couple of coats for now." Bridget looked sorrowfully at the two naked children.

Brendan looked up from his bed at the two children silhouetted in the doorway.

"Hallo! I'm Brendan and this is Cromwell." The children looked across at the frog sitting on the edge of the basin.

"I'm Mary and he is Pat, I'm the oldest." Mary pointed to herself and then to her brother.

"She is only a year older, you know," Pat replied.

"We never saw a tame frog before. Why do you call him Cromwell? "

"Cromwell was a grumpy English general and I don't like the English". Brendan changed the tone of his voice.

"You love your frog, don't you. Can I stroke him?" Mary looked at the frog and hesitated before approaching him.

"If you want a good frog I'll ask my brother Seámus to get you one. Would your father let you have one?"

"Our father is dead and we have no place to keep a frog." Mary stroked the frog.

"Yes we have. If he can keep one in a basin so can we. Where is Seámus?" Pat was determined that he too should have a frog.

"I don't know, but when he comes back I'll ask him to look out for a frog for you." Brendan lay back on his pillow and began to cough.

"Are you sick then, what is the matter with you?" they questioned.

"That's enough for now children." Bridget called the children from the room.

"He gets tired easily," she apologised .

"I understand Mam. I suppose we should be on our way. Where did you say the cottage was, Mister?"

"I'll come with you. Questions will be asked if you are seen entering the cottage without permission."

"I thought that you said it was abandoned and empty."

"It's empty alright, for the people left for Liverpool some time ago. They are seeking passage to America."

"Here, I hope you won't be offended." Bridget held out two well worn geansaís to the widow.

"There now, say thank you to the good woman." The widow dressed the children in the geansaís and stood back to admire them.

Leaving the house they made their way down the street.

"Here it is then." Tom went and opened the door of a sturdy cottage.

"It is a fine cottage, a fine cottage indeed. God speed all who lived here to the new land." The woman looked

around the cottage and called on her children to join her.
Tom left the cottage hoping to obtain a bundle of fresh
straw from the blacksmith.

"Is it yourself. What brings you here so early?" Seámus,
the blacksmith greeted Tom.

"I have little doubt that you saw me open the cottage of
Joe Kelly."

"I did of course, sure I'm not blind yet. Who might they
be?"

"Should anyone ask, Seámus, tell them that I took the
liberty. They are from Creagh, a widow with an infant
and two older children, God help us. They are waiting for
the soup kitchen to open tomorrow. They missed out on
the soup today but are hopeful to be successful tomorrow.
God help us and them, what else could one do?"

"There will be no questions asked in Skibbereen, you done
a charitable act, so you did Tom Flynn and God will
reward you."

"They won't be staying, but I wonder, could you oblige me
with a bundle of straw for them to make a shakedown
with."

"Did they really come all the way from Creagh hoping for
a bowl of soup?"

"They did Seámus, and I have little doubt but we will see
many more before the Ocras is past."

"Owe me, is it an insult that you are putting on me. I
would no more ask a penny under the circumstances than
I would shoe the soles of old Diabal himself. I might ask
Mary to do the calling," he added as an afterthought.

"Calling to where may one ask?"

"You may ask away Tom Flynn. To the cottage if you don't
be minding."

"I suppose I deserve the chastising for interfering in the
legitimate affairs of others. Slán leat agus go bfagaid Dia
an sláinte agat.(Good bye and may God spare you the
health.)"

Tom returned to the cottage and laid the bundle of straw
on the floor.

"I see you got the fire going then. It is known about you
and the children being here, so don't fret. Tomorrow if you
wish I'll return with you to Creagh and bury your
husband, God rest his soul. You know that your infant is
back in my cottage."

"You'd do that for us and we strangers. You are a good
man so you are, Tom Flynn."

"Will you hold your whist, it's no more than you would do
for us, were the circumstances reversed."

"I'll tell you....."

"Are you the widow woman from Creagh"? At the door stood a tall woman with a shawl wrapped tightly around her.

"I am that and who is for the asking?"

"It is yourself is it not. Seámus said that you might be calling." Tom greeted the woman standing at the door.

"This is the blacksmiths' wife, Mary. It was from him that I got the straw." Tom introduced the two women.

"I brought a little something; not a lot I fear, but it all helps." Mary opened her shawl and took out a parcel and laid it on the table.

"May the infant Jesus bless you for your charity." The widow opened the parcel to disclose two herring and a turnip.

Dean tusa an rud céadna ar mo son-sa. Abair paidir ar mo son anois." (You'd do the same for me, say a prayer for me) Mary smiled.

"I'd offer you a suideacán but.." The widow looked around the empty cottage.

"I saw you coming down the road and had little doubt as to where you were heading." Into the cottage came another neighbour.

"You did that Nora, I suppose you were talking to my Seámus".

"You won't be offended I'm sure but... Ah well, here".

Nora held out a bottle filled with fresh milk.

"That is indeed generous of you. Go mbeirimid beó ar am seo arís. (may you be alive this time twelve months)"

Tom left the women gossiping and returned to his cottage. That evening the woman called at the cottage and collected her infant son.

Next morning he saw the widow and her children waiting patiently for the soup kitchen to arrive.

"She won't be the one to miss out this day."

"Who won't?" Bridget joined her husband at the half door. The widow waved to them.

Tom picket up his can and joined her in the queue.

"If you call in sometime this afternoon I'll accompany you back to Creagh and bury your husband," Tom promised.

Seámus came to the cottage door of Tom Flynn sitting on the straw seat of his donkey and cart.

"Have they arrived yet?" He asked as he jumped off the straw seat.

"Have who arrive? You mean the widow and her children?"

"And who else would I be talking about?"

"They're here if you must know."

Bridget pointed to the widow and her two children making their way to the cottage.

"Can they say farewell to Brendan before we get on our way. They got on so well together."

"Why of course they can. He will be glad to meet them again".

Brendan promised faithfully to remind his brother that Pat wanted a frog just like his.

"I'll be beholding to the people of Skibbereen so I will". The widow thanked them and with her children took her place on the cart.

"Stop! Stop the cart". The widow tugged at Seámus's arm.

"What ails you, is there something wrong?" He brought the donkey to an abrupt halt.

"There is indeed, will you look. I forgot to give them back to your good wife. Whatever will she think of me"? The widow pointed to her two children wearing the old geansaís of Seámus and Brendan.

"Is that all, sure my Bridget wanted you to have them, they're not the best but they'll do a turn." Tom told her.

In order to ease the burden on the donkey Tom and Seámus took it in turns to walk behind the cart throughout the journey.

Seámus stopped the cart outside the cottage and stood aside as the widow opened the door.

"He's inside, so he is." The woman, blessing herself, returned, and, stepping to one side, invited Tom and Seámus to enter the cottage. She made no effort to enter herself. Inside they saw the body of a man lying face down on the floor.

"Where should we bury him Tom?" Seámus looked down at the corpse..

"I'll ask if she has a family plot near by," Tom replied.

Leaving the cottage Tom went outside. Calling the widow to one side he asked where the family plot might be.

"We have no family grave, the graveyard is out on the headland. Would you be able to take him there?"

She pointed to a little graveyard some distance away.

"Sure we can. Take the children away from here for now would you." Tom ushered her and her children away from the cottage.

In the haggard Tom found a shovel and a slán, and calling on Seámus to help they placed the body on the cart.

"I hope she won't mind but we will have to do the decent thing." Seámus pulled the door off the haggard and placed it over the body.

The sad cortege wended its way slowly up the incline to the graveyard.

Having dug the grave they placed the corpse in the open grave and covered him with the door before closing the grave.

When all was completed Seámus called to the widow and her children.

"It is all over now, Mam, would you like to come forward?" Tom was standing over the grave with his rosary beads in his hands.

In ainm an atar agus an Mic agus an spióraid Naoim. (In the name of the father and of the son and of the holy ghost) Tom blessed himself.

"Amen," replied the widow and her children.

"Go mbeannuigtear duit, a muire atá lán dé grastaib. Tá tiegearna leat is beannuigte tu tar na mnaib agus is beannuigte torád do bruinn, íosa.

A naom Muire a matair Dé guid orm na peactacacaib anois agus ar uair ar mbas." Tom recited the 'Hail Mary' in his native tongue.

"Amen," replied the widow and her children.

"Gab mo leitsgeal, tá brón orm" (Please excuse me, I am sorry)

Tom apologised and retreated from the graveside, leaving the widow and her children to their private sorrow.

He knew that her thoughts were more concerned with the welfare of her children than with the death of her husband. There was little that she could do for the dead. Her thoughts were more concerned with finding food and shelter for her three hungry children.

These were the hungry years and he knew that there would be many more deaths from the Ocras before the year passed.

The men returned to the cart leaving the widow to her private sorrow.

A HOPEFUL DREAM

She stood bare headed at the foot of her late husbands grave. The winds, the cruel cold howling winds of the Atlantic bit deep into her ragged shawl. Kneeling on his fresh grave she ignored the Ocras and the biting cold. She spoke to her husband for the last time in her native tongue.

"Sean a Mic, Ní bíonn ar aon rud act seal agus le congnam Dé beid déiread leis an Ocras seo sar e bfad agus beid siotcain agus saóire atainn. A cuid de'n tdsaogal brón go dti mise. Go mbeannuigid Dia duit agus go saóraid Dia sean Eire ".

(Sean my love, nothing lasts but for a time. With God's help the hunger will end and we will have peace and freedom. You left me nothing but your share of this world's sorrows. May God have mercy on you and may he free old Ireland.)

The woman, calling her children to her, wrapped them in the folds of her ragged skirt and dragged her emaciated body away from the graveside. It was doubtful if she would ever see the grave of her husband or Creagh again.

Slowly, followed by her two children, she made her way inland.

Glancing over a stout stone wall she saw the well filled barns of the local gentry. She was sad and angry, she released her pent up resentment by beating the barren stones with her blackthorn stick.

"God in Heaven, if only the table of my cottage had at least a pot of boiled potatoes my Sean would be alive this day. Instead all we can show for our labour are the white skeletons of our Fenian dead." She placed her hands around her children as she prayed. She hugged her infant to her breast. Her brow was furrowed and wrinkled although she was still a young woman of twenty two years. Would they too succumb to the great Ocras as had her husband. Her thoughts and prayers were with him as she comforted her innocent children.

Would her God again desert her and leave her a barren widow without kit or kin to bury her. Worse still would she become bleached bones by the wayside leaving her children to die agonising deaths? She knew the grim pangs of hunger as did her children. She knew of her constant companion, 'The Grim Reaper', forever waiting and watching.

Where now were the songs of the birds, the scent of the primrose and the blue of an Irish sky? Her mind was in turmoil. She stopped and called her children.

"We must rest here, children, for the road is long and I am too weary to continue." She took shelter beneath the covering of a Holy well situated beside the road.

Having rested she rose to her feet and again called to her children to join her. She saw the reek rising from the chimney of a distant cottage. Tightening her shawl around her children she hurried down the road. Perhaps there would be an Irish Céad míle fáilte waiting her, she thought.

She approached the door and knocked, then stood back and waited. Again she approached the door and laid her palm against its old Irish oak wood.

"This door is warm children, beyond it lies an Irish heart," she predicted as she encouraged her children to have hope.

The door was opened by an elderly man with a twinkling smile.

"Tar isteac agus fáilte roat. Níl go leír arán agam. Tá an tein deas. Caitfid go Bfuil tuirse ort, suid síos agus leig do sgít. The man held the door open wide.

(Come in and welcome. I have little food but I can offer a warm fire. You must be tired, sit down and rest yourself.)

The woman saw the warm glow from the fire and smelt the tempting aroma from a pot sitting over the coals.

Slowly and with the watchful gait of a stoat she entered the cottage. In the folds of her skirt she hid her children for protection, as would a swan her cygnets in her down. She felt that she was intruding, committing prevarication by being there. Why she felt like this she did not know. Her stomach was crying out for nourishment, her heart was broken, her children starving. Her prayers remained unanswered, her God had forsaken her. She was deeply depressed and unable to relax.

"Come near to the fire, there is a little broth in the pot to share". She awakened to the magnanimous words of their benefactor.

"Why! Why are you being so charitable to us"? She cried with uncontrollable gratitude as she clung to her children. "These are all that I have left in this cruel land. Today I buried my Sean, tomorrow perhaps a wayside grave without a coffin. What is to become of us?"

As she spoke a little head of matted curls peeped out from the folds of her skirt only to vanish again within its confines.

"Come sit yourself down, you'll feel better with a little

broth inside you." The elderly man guided her to a seat by the table ignoring her rambling questions.

Like a gaggle of shackled geese the woman and her children let themselves be herded towards the table.

Taking five assorted dishes from the dresser the man laid them on the table. Then removing the pot from the fire he filled the bowls before returning it to the crane.

"Take no notice of me, you eat up." Picking up one of the bowls he left the room and entered a small back bedroom. In the absence of the man, the woman and her children took their places at the table and partook of the welcoming meal. She fed her infant son, removing his wet swaddling cloth, dried him and made him comfortable before placing him near to the warmth.

"You may rest here by the fire. I have to attend to my sick wife. I'll leave you now in God's care". Bidding them 'Goodnight' he returned to the bedroom and closed the door.

It was early morning when the children awakened their mother. Rising she picked up her shawl from the line over the fireplace. She had placed it there the previous night to dry.

When all was ready she picked up her child and wrapping him in her shawl she prepared to leave the house.

"Are you away then?" Looking back she saw the old man silhouetted in the doorway of the bedroom.

"I was not aware that you were out and about. I'm not one for prying or disturbing people. I'll be thanking you again and wishing God's blessing on you for your charity," she apologised.

"Wait, wait will you, I'll not delay you too long." Leaving the kitchen he entered the scullery. On his return he held a tin can in one hand and a quarter scone in the other.

"This is for you and your children. Will you please remember us in your prayers." He held both hands out to the woman.

She looked into the can, it was half filled with the white blood of life. Here was a saint of a man sent to her by God Himself to give life to her and her children. A God that she had blasphemed against the previous day. For this she was truly sorry.

"God will reward you and your good wife. You have the humble prayers of a grateful widow and her orphans." Taking the can she reached up and lifting the latch opened the door.

"Bennact De lib go leir agus to n-eirigid do bótar leat." (God's blessing on you all and may your journey thrive with you). The old man waved to them as they left the cottage.

The children ran down the old boreen waving their thanks to the old man.

Having said her thanks once again the widow took to the road. She looked up at the new dawn with renewed hope for the future. A mist obliterated the heather on the hillside. Disinterested she continued on down the long sorrowful unending road. She was grateful that her God had given her one more day of hope, but what of tomorrow?" she thought.

She smiled as she saw the mist being burnt from the hillside and a warm sun rise above the horizon. She watched a wayward frog sitting nonchalantly on her bare foot. She smiled as she remembered Brendan Flynn and said a silent prayer for his recovery. As she moved the frog took a leap to the safety of the far hedgerow.

She felt the magnetism of her love for her children. She saw them running up the boreen to rejoin her.

Her heart beat faster, she reached out and in a spontaneous and involuntary act of love held her protective arms out to them. They were God's little flowers and no cruel landlord would or could destroy them. Opening her shawl she looked down at the smiling face of her child.

"When you're talking to the angels remember your brother and sister to them," she spoke to her child.

Tightening her shawl around her infant she walked slowly down the road to conserve her energy. She now knew that she was appointed by God to be their guardian angel.

After some miles she called on her children to rest by the wayside, she wanted to gather her thoughts.

Holding the can out she encouraged them to partake of the white blood of life. Then breaking the scone she handed them a piece each. She thought of how Christ had shared the bread and chalice with his disciples so very long ago. She remembered how he had been nailed to a cross shortly afterwards and let die an agonising death. She too was suffering crucifixion, both mentally and physically. She thought too of her country and her starving people. Again tears streamed down her face. She was sad, vexed and depressed. Her burden was great and her rewards small.

"What right had the British Crown to steal the bread from the mouths of her children. Food that had been grown by their parents on Irish soil?" Again her mind was wandering, the safety of her children was paramount.

Was not her Sean lying in the clay of Creagh. He tried to

59

hide from her the gnawing Ocras pains for the sake of her and her children. To the end he denied himself the little share of their sustenance in the hope that they at least might survive the Ocras. She would continue that pilgrimage for her children's sake.

"I'm glad that you are gone, Sean, gone from the Ocras and the sorrow of this cursed land. You'll grieve no more, mo cusla, but why! Why did you leave me your sorrow?"

She looked down at the last of the bread and milk and speculated as to where the next meal would come from.

Would she live to see the summer, would she live to see her children grow to adulthood?

Again she looked into the faces of her children and was grateful that she did not see the dreaded sign of impending disaster. She hugged them to her on that bleak hillside in the county Cork and dried her tears.

They were her 'Children of Lir', her swans, the Tuatan-de-Dannan. Her children of Lir would survive the Ocras, of this she was certain.

Rising she walked down the old boreen with her shoulders back and her head held high.

She was a daughter of Eireann, a Fenian. A proud and brave race. This was her land, a land in which a new dawn would awaken. She may have to suffer the pangs of hunger a little longer, but the new dawn was coming of that she was now sure.

The nation would dry its tears and the land would no longer be cursed. This she firmly believed as once again she set out to find shelter and food for herself and her three swans.

This then was the situation that the widow and her three children found themselves in somewhere on a bleak mountain road on the Cork/Kerry border that spring day of 1847.

THE STATE OF THE LIMERICK WORKHOUSE RECORDED BY S.G. OSBOURNE, CHURCH OF ENGLAND CLERGYMAN 1850.

The first union house we visited was that at Limerick. Last year when I went over it, I found it clean and in good order; I now find it in every way the reverse. In the parent and auxiliary houses there is no less a number than 8,000 paupers.

Every department, except the fever hospital, showed evident symptoms of gross neglect. I have no words with which I can give any real idea of the sad condition of the inmates of two large yards of the parent house, in which were a large number of female children; many of them were clothed in the merest of dirty rags, and of all these they wore but a scanty allowance; they were in the dirt collected on their person for many weeks; there was not about them the slightest evidence of any of the least care being taken of them; as they filed before me two by two, they were a spectacle to fill any humane heart with indignation: Sore feet, sore hands, sore heads; opthalmia evident in the great proportion of them; some of them were suffering from it in it's very worst stage; they were evidently being eaten up with vermin — many were mere skeletons: I know well what the appearance of a really famine stricken child is; there were, it is true, some here who had brought their death-like appearance into the workhouse with them; but the majority were as the type in which one word NEGLECT was printed in no mistakable characters — the neglect of the latter state, not the consequence of the former state.

BLACK 47

The year 1847 came carrying with it all the misery of the previous year.

Rain and sleet fell in a constant deluge, there was little respite for the starving people. What little Indian corn there was in stock was reserved for the local workhouse. The nearest depot with any corn, they were told, was in Limerick docks. A messenger was sent to the city requesting that some supplies be sent to Skibbereen as soon as possible to alleviate the distressful situation there.

The messenger returned empty handed, there was no good news. Limerick did not have any corn to spare. Her workhouse was in a worse state than theirs. He gave a miserable account of the situation in the county.......

The workhouse had been built to house 450 inmates in the main building and 200 lunatics in a separate complex to the rear. With the starving from Clare/ Limerick and Tipperary demanding entry the figure had risen dramatically. There were now 8,000 inmates far in excess of its capacity. There were as many more encamped outside the doors hoping to gain entry, the situation was desperate.

To add to their misery a deadly flu was raging throughout the county. Bodies of the dead were piling up outside the little graveyard at Killeely on the Clare/Limerick border. There was no one available to dig the graves and no coffins in which to place the corpses. Even the sliding coffins were worn out.

He reported on the obscenity of cereals, livestock and agricultural produce leaving Limerick docks under armed guard bound for England. To add insult to injury the ships taking away the food were anchored in Arthur's Quay across the water from the workhouse.

Much as they would have liked to help there was nothing that they could do for them. This was little comfort to the starving village of Skibbereen.

Tom awoke from a restless nights sleep. He heard the rain and wind rattling the window panes. He rose fatigued from his bed and drawing the curtain looked out at a dark, miserable, wet, windy cold dawn. He knelt beside the bed to pray. He heard his wife carrying out her chores in the kitchen.

He tried desperately to pray but could not find the words.

How could he pray to a God that was inflicting such punishment on them. They had done nothing wrong, why then was he so vindictive to them?

He heard the continual wheezing from his son Brendan, as he fought bravely to stay alive for another day.

He knew that this was blasphemous thinking and as such any prayers he may say were as chaff in the wind. Unable to pray he rose from his knees, his mind in turmoil.

As he entered the kitchen he saw his wife leaning over the fire stirring the pot.

In the reflection from the fire he saw on her face all the sorrow and anguish of a desperate mother.

He sat down on a chair and stared into the fire.

"Seámus has not come home yet, Brendan is restless with worry. He hardly slept last night. May God guide his feet home." She continued stirring the pot.

"He'll be home soon, do not fret. We must have faith in the Almighty", he consoled her.

"He must have found a shakedown for the night," he added as an afterthought.

Rising he took the candle and entered the small bedroom shared by their sons.

"How is my Brendan today, not forgetting Cromwell?" He held the candle near to his sons' face.

"I'm alright Da, where is Seámus?"

"He's stayed with a neighbour and will be home later. Your mother will bring you a warm bowl of stirabout. I'm off to work." Tightening the blanket around his son he left the room.

"Brendan seems to be getting better, thank God," he remarked as he removed his caubeen from the peg behind the door.

"Surely you are not going to that place without a morsel to eat," his wife asked on seeing him with his cap in his hand.

"I suppose there will a meal included and there are the boys to think of."

"If you don't look to yourself then what will become of us. Here sit yourself down and eat this." Looking at the tempting bowl of Indian corn and feeling the craving hunger he reluctantly returned to the table.

Tom met Joe Mc Bride on the road out of the village on that wet morning.

"Where are you off to at this hour?" Joe stood and waited for him.

"Me, I'm going to the workhouse, the Brigadier found me employment there."

"I hope you know what you are letting yourself in for,

Tom. It takes a strong constitution to stomach that place."

"You don't say, is it really as bad as people make out? Do you know when I told Bridget, she advised me not to take the position."

"She spoke the truth, I only stay there because of my children. Without the few shillings we would starve."

"We had best be getting on, I would not wish to be late on my first day." Tom stepped out ignoring Joe's warning.

Both men tightened their coatamores around them and made their way to the workhouse which was situated outside the village.

Tom reported to the warden and was sent to work with his friend Joe.

They passed several emaciated families all purposefully seeking sanctuary within the grim walls of the workhouse.

"Will you look at them Tom, in God's Holy Name, look. How many will get through the damned gates and how many will die outside?" Tom pulled his coatamore closer to his body as the rain increased in intensity and ignored the remark.

"It looks as though we are to work together Joe." Tom entered the stock room where the tackle and carts were stored.

"Good, give me a hand with this then." Joe took the shaft of a flat cart and waited for Tom to grasp the other. Together they pulled the reluctant cart out into the compound.

"You were right Joe, this is a terrible place." Tom looked towards the wall of the compound. Sitting and lying along its full length were disconsolate human beings.

"Are they all dead, Joe?" he whispered as if he did not wish to disturb them.

"We don't know yet Tom, but this is the purpose for the cart." Joe stopped the cart and parked its' shafts on the ground.

"We must wait until they are called in for their stirabout." Joe sat on the cart and invited Tom to join him.

A bell rang from outside one of the buildings. It sounded like the death knell.

Slowly, like Zombies, the skeletons rose to their feet and made their way into a building to their left.

Joe nudged Tom and called on him to join him.

Not all of the inmates got to their feet. Some were still sitting or lying along the wall.

"I'll take the far end and you start here, Tom. Help those unable to walk to their feet and take them inside. Any that are dead leave them."

"I don't think that I can stomach this Joe." Tom looked away from the wall.

"Come on Tom, I'll show you." Both men went and began their distasteful task.

There were five corpses left on the ground when they finished the roll call.

"We'll need the cart." It was apparent that Joe knew what to do.

Joe walked across the courtyard and waited for Tom who was reluctantly walking towards him.

Collecting the dead they placed them one on top of the other on the cart and pulled it towards the gate. The keeper opened the gate and without any ceremony let them through.

Outside the gates they collected another two corpses and placed them on top of the others.

With Tom on the left shaft and Joe on the right they dragged the cart down the road. Tom guessed where they were going but left it to Joe to guide the cart.

A woman in bare feet and dressed in a rag of a shawl took her place in the cortege behind the cart. Like the Grim Reaper she followed slowly step for step. Her keening was disturbing Tom.

"Are you going to bury my Shanéen without a prayer or a coffin?" she croaked.

As Tom was about to address her, Joe looked at him and shook his head. He knew what the message was...'Silence is Golden'

It was not too long before he saw the gate of the local graveyard. They did not enter but steered the cart to the rear. Stopping they let the shafts rest on the ground. As they did one of the corpses fell to the ground.

A mist lay over the old graveyard and as it condensed it trickled down the moss covered Celtic crosses.

"God in Heaven, I never knew this place to look so ghastly before." Tom tightened his coatamore about him. He looked at the mist gathering around him and felt that it was trying to overwhelm him. Joe was busy laying out a corpse in the row.

"Come on Tom, don't let it get to you," he tried to encourage his friend.

The woman stood motionless some distance away looking at the cart and its' grim contents.

On the ground in a neat row lay several other corpses. None of which had been buried.

"Don't we have to bury them?"

"Just lay the others beside them, they will all be buried soon."

As they removed one of the bodies the woman came forward and held on to Toms' arm.

"You are not going to bury my Shanéen without a coffin, are you?"

"Come on Tom, ignore her, she comes to all the burials."

With their grim task completed they picked up the cart and returned to the road.

"Please don't bury my little Shanéen without a coffin." They saw the old woman on her knees weeping and calling over the row of corpses. The mist began to swallow her up as they moved away.

"Has she been doing this long?" Tom asked, staring towards the woman.

"For the last month I'm told. One of the wretched corpses is that of her son who died in the workhouse. She waits for the cart to leave and follows it."

"Where does she live?"

"In the workhouse, of course. How she is still alive beats me. I wish to God she would stop, it gives me the creeps," Joe remarked.

"I don't know if I can handle this work, Joe."

"I cannot blame you Tom, still someone has to do it. We'll bide awhile down by the brook to ease the tension."

Lighting their piopcas they sat by the brook in angry silence.

Tom removed his pipe and looked across the meandering water towards the estate of one of the landed gentry.

"Did you ever think, Joe, our people die horrible deaths, yet these are the people responsible for their murders."

"I was over in Macroom not too long ago and was shown seven large families living under the bridge. I correct myself, for many of them were already dead. These were laid along the riverside as naked as the day that they were born".

"Did anyone do anything about them?"

"Do! What could they do and they raging with the brain fever. I believe that they all died within days of each other."

"I wonder how my Brendan is?" Tom rose to his feet and meandered some distance along the bank.

HELL'S KITCHEN

My heart is scalded from night 'till morning,
With the black saucepan that makes the dip.
The grain of flour, and the sup of water,
The Devil scald you, wouldn't you make it thick.

Although still in his early teens Seámus, on seeing that
living conditions had deteriorated within his own
household, decided that he would seek employment on
one of the few relief schemes operating around the county.
He was told that a famine road was being constructed.
Where exactly this was being built his informant was not
sure. They were told that it was between the village of
Skibbereen and Killenleagh.
Early next morning he rose from his bed and, drawing the
curtains, looked out at the drizzling rain.
'Does it ever stop raining in Ireland?' he thought to
himself.
Dressing quickly and quietly he shivered in the cold of the
room.
"Where are you going to? God but it is cold." In the dim
light he saw the drawn face of his brother barely visible
above the blankets.
"Go back to sleep, I'm going to find work." Seámus
returned to the bed and tightened the coverings around
his brother.
"You are coming back, I could not live without you."
Brendan began to cough.
"Go back to sleep, I'll be home by nightfall. Why, I might
find a present for you," he added as an afterthought.
Opening the main door he took the Holy Water and
blessed himself. He could still hear his brother fighting
for breath as he closed the door behind him.
Collecting his slán from the haggard he wended his way
down the old boreen and on to the road to Killenleagh.
The rain was still falling and he hugged his coatamore
closer to his body.
At the crossroads he took the left fork and crossed the old
stone bridge over the River Hen. In the grey morning light
he noticed that the road before him was deserted. He
wondered if there was any work taking place.
Reaching an old milk churn shelter set deep into the
hedgerow he came upon a fellow traveller taking

advantage of its sparse comfort. The man was dressed in an old coatamore and on his head was perched a battered top hat. He looked as weather beaten as his tattered attire. The top hat was not in keeping with his status.

He was adjusting rags of bandages that were tied around his bared feet. Each time he bent down a cascade of water poured from the rim of the hat as if from a water spout.

"Good morning to yourself, tell me, is this the road to the relief work?" Seámus addressed the man.

"The right road to where, may one ask?" The man continued to adjust the bandages.

"I hear there is a new road being constructed hereabouts." Seámus removed his slán from his shoulder and looked down at the badly swollen feet of the stranger.

"Would you have a bite of grub on your person." He continued adjusting the bandages.

"Sorry! I'm hoping that there might be a soup kitchen where the work is taking place". Seámus, leaning on his slán, continued to stare at the man's feet.

"I know that there has been a free one moving around here, it is run by the Quakers. You would have to be quick and bring a tin can." The man finished adjusting the bandages and stretching out his legs admired his work.

"Have you no boots?" Seámus watched as he rose to his feet.

"Boots is it! I sold them yesterday to buy a bag of gruel. I have six children and a wife to support. They are back in the hovel waiting my return." Picking his feet from the mud into which they sank he slung his slán across both shoulders and straddled it with his arms. Ignoring Seámus he walked briskly down the road.

Seámus fell in beside him and together they walked on in silence.

Reaching a bend in the road they were confronted by a gathering of people jostling for position in a long straggling queue.

"Quick as you can boy, there is a soup kitchen about to open." The man began to run, as he did the bandages began to unravel. Ignoring them he ran faster into the little village. Seámus ran beside him, keeping abreast of him.

They could see the steam rising from a large soup boiler. As they came nearer they could smell the welcoming aroma of the stew. Their progress was blocked by a gathering of starving people some on all fours and half naked. They were sitting obediently in the road unaware of the falling rain. They looked like famished beasts of the field. They obediently sat with their rusting tin mugs held in their numbed hands. There were men, women and children. Many were stretched out on the roadway unable to rise.

Seámus joined the long queue and wondered if he would get any soup at all. There were so many people and all he could see was one large boiler. As he shuffled along the line the man in front of him collapsed. His tin can rolled and rattled across the road.

"Please help me, in God's Holy Name help me." Holding his hand aloft he pleaded.

Seámus looked down at the apparition that was once a human being and their eyes met. What could he do; picking up the wretch he carried him along the line until they were both standing before the boiler.

The server emptied a ladle of soup into the can of the man and told him to move on to where there was a van containing small portions of bread.

"I have six starving children back in the cottage and an ailing woman. Could you see your way to let me have an extra portion," he pleaded.

"Sorry, the ration is one ladle and a portion of bread only." The man was ushered forward.

Having collected their portion of bread Seámus carried the man to the shelter of a hedge and sat down beside him.

The man sat with his hands clasped around the warm can looking dejected.

"You had best drink your soup when its hot," Seámus told him.

"How can I drink it when my family are starving. This is for them." He held up the piece of bread and the tin can.

"You had best eat it for if you don't then you will not be fit to get home, then what?" Seámus warned.

Looking into the can, the temptation was too great for the starving wretch. With shaking hands and trembling lips he began to drink.

"I'll go and see if they can do anything for you."

Seámus rose to his feet and went across to the wagon.

A gentleman was standing beside it looking into the gathering.

"Could you spare me a moment or two please," Seámus addressed him.

"Of course what seems to be the problem." Seámus was taken aback by the polite way that the man addressed him.

"There is a man sitting over there who has travelled more than five miles hoping for a little food. He has six children at home and a sick wife, all are starving."

"There are too many starving in this townland. Find out where he lives and I will see if we can help." He looked across at the wretch who had now collapsed into a pile of rags and was lying in the hedge.

Seámus ran across the road and helped the man into a sitting position.

"Tell me where do you live and what is your name?" Seámus tried to revive him by rubbing some life into his numbed hands.

"My name is Edward Dwyer of Killenleagh, I live in Killenleagh," he repeated before again collapsing into the hedge. Leaving him, Seámus returned to the quaker.

"He tells me that he comes from the village of Killenleagh." "Killenleagh! Surely not. Do you know how far away that is? We came by there this morning and will be passing by it on our way back to Coolamane".

"I heard of the place but I've never been there. Can you help him?" Seámus pleaded.

"Bring him here, we will get him home somehow."

"Do you think that I might go with you, I'm going to Coolamane," Seámus requested.

"Course you can and welcome, there is no room on the cart though."

Carrying the starving man to the cart they placed him on a bundle of loose straw and set out on the road to Killenleagh.

Seámus walked behind the cart in a sombre mood. Forgotten was the search for work on the famine road. Down the mountain road they travelled with the wind driving the rain into their faces. Seámus was now feeling tired and held on to the shaft of the cart for support.

"That must be Killenleagh." The gentleman pointed to a scattering of thatch cottages.

On hearing the name of his village Edward lifted himself from the straw and looked down at the row of cottages.

"This is where I live, thanks for your help." Picking up his can he was more than surprised to find that it had been filled with soup.

"Is this for my family". He held the rusting can in both hands.

"Yes it is for you and yours Edward, and so is this."

The gentleman took a generous portion of cake from under the seat and, wrapping it in a linen cloth, handed it to him.

"God and his Blessed Mother take care of you and yours." He held his benefactors' hands in his and humbly kissed them.

"There is no need to thank me Edward, I only wish that

we could do more. Go home to your family and may God's light go with you."

They watched as Edward scrambled over a stone wall at the side of the road and journeyed down a well worn path to his village and home.

They watched as he staggered down the sloping field. Turning he waved to them before disappearing into a spinney. They continued on down the mountain road towards the village of Killenleagh.

"I expect Edward is home long ago." Seámus remarked as he tried to protect himself from the driving rain.

"We may stop and have a morsel to eat." The gentleman stepped down from the cart.

"I am told on good authority that there is a new road being built here about. Would you happen to know where?" Seámus asked.

"We have been doing relief work between Skibbereen and Bantry this past two weeks and there is no work whatsoever taking place that we know of. Perhaps you should try nearer to Dunmanway".

"Dunmanway is too far from my home in Skibbereen. I guess I'll have to seek work elsewhere. Thanks anyway."

"Will you look, the sun has broken through at last." The gentleman smiled on seeing the clouds part and the sun appear.

As they entered the village they were stopped by armed soldiers.

"You cannot go any further for the present," the Corporal in charge told them.

"It's an eviction, I'm sure of it," the quaker remarked.

"Another poor family to clutter up the roads, no doubt."

Tying the horse to a gorse bush they vaulted a stone wall and made their way to where the battering ram had been erected.

Surrounding one of the scattered cottages was a detachment of Redcoats (English soldiers) and sitting astride a saddle on a white steed was a gentleman. They were now more than ever convinced that an eviction was taking place.

A battering ram had been set in position within striking distance of the front door by the 'Crow Bar' gang. Villagers were pleading unsuccessfully with the soldiers and the landlord to show mercy to the family.

They were indifferent to any pleading as they prepared to gain entry into the cottage.

"Edward Dwyer, I call on you in the name of her majesty Queen Victoria to surrender this cottage," the officer in charge ordered.

"It's the man we brought home". Seámus looked towards the cottage in disbelief.

There was silence from within as once again he demanded surrender of the cottage.

"For the final time I call on you to surrender this cottage , Edward Dwyer." The officer approached the door and rapped three times on it with the handle of his sword. This would be the final demand before the forced entry was executed.

"Please leave us in peace, what do you want of us? We have no money and no food," Edward pleaded from the confines of the cottage.

The officer took a sideways glance at the landlord and waited.

With a nod of his head the landlord doffed his hat and retreated from his position near to the door.

"All right men proceed and break it down." The officer instructed the crowbar gang.

Slowly, the ram was set in motion as they gauged the striking distance to the centre of the door.

"One, two, three," shouted the square shouldered leader who was standing at the rear of the ram holding a stout rope attached to it through a steel hook. He counted out the beat as he twisted the rope around his fist.

On the count the ram was swung to and fro.

'One-two-one- two, slowly the reach of the ram increased. On the count of three he used all his strength to add weight to the ram by running forward and pulling on the rope at the same time. The ram hit the door squarely in the centre. 'Bang- Crash'. The ram hit the door dead centre and shook the old door with all its' pent up energy. These men were highly skilled in the art of demolition.

"Come on lads, put your backs into it." The leader encouraged them to greater effort.

'Bang! Crash! Bang! Crash! The ram continued a pendulum motion as it remorselessly struck the centre of the door time and time again.

Stones began to fall away from the door surround. On seeing this they were encouraged and increased the tempo.

With a crash the door complete with the jamb collapsed into the cottage.

As the crow bar gang and the Redcoats ran forward to gain entry the whole front of the house collapsed in a pile of dust, burying them in the rubble.

There was a moment's pause before others rushed forward and dragged their comrades free from the collapsing cottage.

Seámus and his new friend watched in horror. Another tragedy was unfolding as Edward Dwyer was catapulted through the gaping hole that was once his home. He was soon followed by his wife and children. They watched as Edward collected his children and held them close to his person. His wife lay on the ground muttering to herself, her arms clasped in pleading prayer. Seámus ran forward and, picking her up, took her to the safety of the little wall leading to the haggard.

They saw the contents of the cottage being hurled into the laneway. The rusting tin can that not so long ago held their salvation rolled down the lane and landed at the feet of Seámus. When the cottage was denuded of its contents a spleen (torch) was lit and thrown into the thatch. Soon the cottage became a blazing inferno.

The leader of the 'Crowbar' gang wiped the Judas sweat from his forehead and approached the landlord.

"We'll have our payment now if you don't be minding, sir," unconcerned as to the drama unfolding around him.

The landlord threw a small bag of coins on the ground and looked contemptuously at the arrogant bully.

Suddenly a tormented shout interrupted this exchange.

"You! You and your cursed English spleen, could you not see that we are destitute. Go on burn it, for it brought us nothing but bad luck. Remember that it is to my children and their children that you and your kind will have to answer to. There is an almighty God in heaven and you will have to answer to him on judgement day. I call a curse on you and all of you." Looking from one to the other he finally rested his gaze on the landlord.

A Redcoat ran forward and, raising his rifle, landed a vicious blow on the side of his face that sent him staggering to the ground.

He rose to his knees as blood flowed freely from the mortal blow inflicted. His ears burst and began to bleed. He was unable to hear the pleadings of his wife and family, yet he knew what they were saying.

Picking a bunch of shamrocks that were growing near by he held them up for all to see.

"Sin seamróigin caoin milis, díl milis na h-Eireann. (This is the dear little, sweet little shamrock of Ireland) You can no more stop it growing than you can stop us claiming what is rightfully ours." These were the last words uttered by Edward Dwyer.

As the cottage collapsed in on itself the landlord and soldiers left the scene. The body of Edward was left on the side of the road where he had fallen. The shamrock still grasped firmly in his dead hand.

His widow and children were guided away into the care of generous neighbours.

Seámus stood for some considerable time watching the cottage burn. He turned to address the quaker only to find that he had departed.

Placing his slán across his shoulders he walked dejectedly back down the road and on to Skibbereen.

Another fruitless search for work was concluded.

Asenath Nicholson, An American Evangelist on visiting Louisburgh, Co. Mayo 1848, gives the following account . . .

The little town of Louisburgh, two miles from 'Old Head' had suffered extremely. An active priest and Protestant curate were doing their utmost to mitigate the suffering, which was like throwing dust to the wind; lost! lost forever- the work of death goes on, and what is repaired today is broken down tomorrow. Many have fallen under their labours; and the prior curate and his wife were pointed out to me in the churchyard, who had fallen since the famine, in the excess of their labour; and the present curate and his praiseworthy wife, unless they have supernatural strength, cannot long keep up the dreadful struggle. The road into the Killery mountains was rough, and we constantly were meeting pale, meagre looking men, who were on their way from the mountain to break stones, and pile them mountain high, for the paltry compensation of a pound of meal a day;

These men had to put all their seeds into the ground, and if they gave up their cabins, they must leave the crop for the landlord to reap, while they must be in the poorhouse or open air. This appeared to be the last bitter drug in Ireland's cup of woe!

WHY? A poor man was asked, whom we met dragging sea weed to put upon the potato field, "Do you do this, when you expect to go to the poor house, and leave your crop to another?"

"I will put it on, hoping that God Almighty will send me the work to get a bit back" was his philosophical reply.

We met flocks of wretched children going to school for the 'Bit of bread' some crying with hunger and some begging to get in without the penny which was required for their tuition. The poor emaciated creatures went weeping away, one saying he had been 'Looking for the penny all day yesterday and could not get it'. The doctor who accompanied us returned to report to the Priest the cruelty of the relieving officer and the teacher, but this neither frightened nor softened these hard hearts. These people are shut in by mountain and the sea on one side, and the road only passable on foot on the other, having no bridge, and the path lost entirely in some places among the stones...

Though we met multitudes in the last stages of suffering, yet not one through that day asked for charity, and in one case common hospitality showed itself, by offering us milk when we asked for water. This day I saw enough to make my heart sick-sick-sick.

ON THE ROAD TO BALLYDEHOB

Next morning Seámus rose early, he would seek work on the promised road going West to Schull.

Silently he left the room, leaving his brother sleeping. On entering the kitchen he saw his mother leaning over the fire stirring the big black pot.

"Whatever are you doing at this early hour?" he whispered.

"I heard you rising and knew that you will leave without a morsel to eat."

He continued stirring the pot.

"I was told that there might be work on the famine road West of Skibbereen".

"Here, you had best get this down you before you go." His mother placed the bowl of hot gruel on the table. Then she placed a slice of scone beside it.

Seámus finished the gruel and crossed the floor. With his hand on the latch he turned and faced his mother.

"Wish me luck Ma, tell Brendan not to worry if I'm late home." Taking the holy water he blessed himself.

Opening the half door he picked up his slán and turned West towards the village of Schull. His mother came to the door and waved him goodbye. She watched as he was swallowed up in the early morning mist.

At the crossroads he turned, paused, and looked in the direction of his home. He wondered if he would ever see his mother and father again. What would happen to his brother if he failed to return? Why he had this premonition he did not know. Raising his slán in salutation he waved it into the mist. He knew that his mother would hold vigil at the door for some time yet.

The early morning mist burnt itself out on a distant hill and as yet there was no sign of the elusive work.

Seeing the reek of smoke rising from a behind a distant hill he forced his tired body into one last effort.

"God bless the house and all who dwell here." Seámus left his slán outside the cottage door and made his way to the welcoming fire.

"Bennact Dé, a Cara" (God's blessing on you, my friend) A young woman came from the back room and greeted him.

"I must have travelled three parts of Cork this last week seeking work without success." Seámus leaned over the fire trying to instil some warmth into his perished body.

"Work is it, don't tell me about it. My husband Brian was

thinking of going over to Macroom. Rumour has it that there is a road being built there. My name is Mary, Mary Sweeney".

"I'm Seámus Flynn from Skibbereen. I was on the Macroom Road no later than yesterday and I can assure him that there is no work there.

He's not gone there to day, has he?" Seámus added.

"No, he went up towards the fairy hill." The woman pointed to a small hill covered in blue and white heather not too far away.

"Do you know if there is a soup kitchen in the district?"

"Soup kitchen is it, are you hungry then? Sure here is the man himself."

"Fáilte Roat". (Welcome to you) A gangly red headed man entered the cottage and took his place beside the fire.

"This is Seámus from over in Skibbereen, he tells me that you would be wasting your time going to Macroom". The woman gently pushed her husband to one side and removing the lid from the pot began to stir the contents.

"There is little if any hope of a soup kitchen in these parts. You are welcome to share our pot, is that not so Mary?"

"You can use the old ciscéan for a stool, so you can." The woman tossed the last few sods of turf from the basket and turned it upside down beside the fire.

"There now, sit yourself down, the stew will not be that long in cooking".

"That's more than Christian of you, so it is. Thanks."

The woman ladled generous portions of the stew into three bowls and invited them to partake of the meal.

Seámus, ravenous from the hunger, soon consumed the meal. What there was left he soon mopped up with the slice of scone he had been given.

"That was lovely, so it was Mam. You'll never know just how grateful I am. Excuse me".

Leaving the table he took the ciscéan and once again settled down beside the fire.

"That was the first and finest rabbit stew that I have eaten in a long time".

"Sure I'm glad that you enjoyed it, what about you Brian?"

"A grand stew, you're a fine cook Mary". Brian joined Seámus beside the fire as Mary began to clear the table.

"I had a sad encounter with a hare over in Skibbereen, so I had". Seámus told the story of how he was apprehended with the hare on the estate of Brigadier William Cornwall Stone.

On finishing his story Brian looked across at Mary and spontaneously they burst out laughing.

"What's so funny about that?" Seámus, indignant at their lack of manners rose to his feet and was about to leave the cottage.

"Sit down man, don't be so sensitive. It is not you that we are laughing at, you must excuse us." Brian persuaded him to return to his seat.

"What is the joke then, that is not at my expense, I hope ?"

"Not at all Seámus, go on Brian, you may as well tell him".

"Tell me what?" Seámus looked puzzled.

"It's like this Seámus. I went poaching in his Lordships' woods last night. It was dark night when I carefully set my snare. I returned before the dawn broke and in the snare I found what I thought was the biggest and fattest hare this side of Cork. I put it into my bag and collecting my snare I left the woods as quick as my legs would carry me. I had to make my get away before the light broke. When I got back here to the cottage I opened the bag and tipped out what I thought was a hare on to the table. What do you think I had snared?"

"Go on, don't tell me that you snared a badger?"

"A badger indeed. I had caught the finest and fattest tom cat I ever set eyes on. He was as black as the hobs of hell itself and as heavy as a lamb. I weighed him up and down in my hand and looked towards Mary; she got my meaning."

"A cat, well I never heard of anyone catching a cat in a snare. whatever did you do with it?"

"That's why we were laughing. You see the stew that you just ate was made from the cat".

"You're not serious; you mean we ate a stew made from a cat. Well I never".

"We did that, sure what is the difference. They ate them during the siege of Limerick and a hate of harm did they do them. Would it not be a crying shame to waste such a fine carcass?" Brian defended his action.

"Hunger is the best sauce they say and what with me with child, we need all the nourishment we can get." Mary held her hand to her stomach.

Seámus looked at his benefactors. The very thought of eating a cat nauseated him. Then he began to laugh hysterically.

The others again caught up in the euphoria of the situation joined in the laughter.

"Whatever do you find so funny Seámus, there is little difference between a cat and a rabbit," remarked Mary again holding her stomach.

"I was thinking of the time that I was charged with stealing the hare. What would they charge me with if it had been a cat.
"Catnapping I suppose"?
All too soon Seámus had to leave their jovial company and take the rocky road to Ballydehob.

SEÁMUS ENCOUNTERS THE
ZOMBIES FROM BALLYDEHOB

Seámus wandered along the old butter road in a sombre mood towards the village of Ballydehob.

Wet, cold and exhausted he came upon a Kerrymans table tucked neatly in the hedgerow. It beckoned him to come and rest his weary frame. Although still in his teens there was only so much that a human could endure. He sat shivering on the old seat for some time before he once again reluctantly rose and took to the road.

Through sheer exhaustion and frustration he began to cry.

"What is to become of me, in God's name what am I to do?" he cried aloud.

Once again as if in answer to his prayers he came upon a cottage. Lifting the latch he cautiously entered.

"Bennact De lib to leir". (God's blessing on you all) He nervously challenged.

There was no response, the cottage had long since been abandoned.

He noticed that a butter churn lay on its side between the kitchen and the scullery. He looked at the obligatory horse shoe nailed to the bottom of the churn. This would have been put there by the cooper who made the churn to deter the fairies from stealing the butter.

"It was not the fairies who were stealing your butter, it was the cruel and cold-hearted landlords. It was they and an indifferent government from England who so cruelly stole your butter and your freedom," he shouted at the churn in his frustration. A rat appeared from the inside of the churn and looked with curiosity at the intruder before sauntering back to his abode.

Exhausted from his lonely fruitless search of work Seámus sought sanctuary in the confines of the deserted cottage for the night. Collecting dry kindling and turf he lit a fire in the grate.

Outside in the haggard he found a bundle of dry clean straw and made himself a shakedown for the night.

Sitting beside the fire he took advantage of its heat and removing his cré dúidín from his coatamore he lit it. Taking the crane arm in his hand he swung it to and fro, to and fro. In time with the creaking and groaning of the old rusty crane he began to hum the songs of his native land. As his eyes grew heavy he tapped his pipe on the

81

crane and stopped his humming. Stretching out on the straw he soon succumbed to sleep.

Early next morning he was awakened by the caterwauling of a family of crows. It was their rookery that he had trespassed into the night before.

"Oh stop your noise, will you. I'll soon be on my way," he shouted into the dilapidated roof.

Taking his tin mug from his bundle he went to the stream and filled it. Seeing a generous bed of watercress growing by the water's edge he plucked a generous amount and returned to the cottage. He rekindled his fire and securing the tin mug on the crane drew it over the flames.

Taking the small portion of scone that the good neighbours had given him he made a sandwich with the cress.

Returning to the fire he retrieved his mug from the ashes. The water sizzled and bubbled as the mug swung freely on its wire carrier.

Sitting down on his makeshift bed he indulged himself in his meagre meal.

Finally with a prayer of thanks he packed his belongings and left the cottage to the crows and to the curious rat.

The morning sun was rising in the East and gave a warm comfort to his back as he continued his search for work.

By early morning he found himself on the crest of a hill and below him the village of Ballydehob.

With renewed energy and a spring in his step he again began to sing. As he jauntily swaggered towards the village his bundle tied to his slán swung in time with his movements.

On coming in sight of the cottages a misty rain began to fall. This did not deter his spirits and tightening his coatamore around him he hastened his steps.

To his left he saw two cottages within a distance of some yards before him. Both had recently been put to the spleen and he knew that the crowbar gang had been at the devils' work. In the small fields he noticed the lazy beds where once the proud stalks of the cursed potato grew. Only now they were a pale silvery grey, a sure sign that the blight had come over the land. The beds that had been created so neatly by the previous occupants were now but testimonials to their existence.

Moving further along the road he entered the village proper. On each side of the road lay abandoned hovels denuded of their roofs. The grim destroyer had taken his revenge on the little village of Ballydehob. Here was devastation, dilapidation and revenge that was both obscene and obnoxious in its entirety..

His pace slowed to a crawl as he looked with incredulity at the carnage manifesting itself before his eyes. Were these the tombstones to a vanished people. Were the little unattended fields with their long mounds of lazy ridges their graves. Where were these proud Gaels of Cork, had they been swallowed up or carried away by some demons from the other world, the world of the undead? Seámus was letting his mind race with fantasy.

With a deep sigh he stopped, all was silent. So silent that he could hear his own heart beating.

"God in Heaven be my guide," he prayed as he looked with foreboding down the deserted muddy street.

As if in answer to his prayer several creatures appeared from behind the gable wall of a hovel that had been denuded of its roof, door and windows. They could not be described as human beings, these half naked spectres, standing in front of the casement of the hovel. He was of the opinion that they were the living dead and that the hovel was their tomb.

There were four such creatures in all, two children, a man and a woman. These were he presumed, a family and the occupants of the hovel. The man on seeing Seámus turned and tried to enter the hovel, only to stagger like a drunkard on his match like legs. He looked wasted and on his back was the rotting upper half of a coatamore. His frame of a skeleton was covered in folded layers of parchment flesh. Where there should be life filled eyes there were but two deep dark recesses.

This semblance of what was once a man reached up a hand that favoured the dead twig of a tree to support himself on what had been the jamb of the door. Slowly he entered the hovel and vanished from view. The woman, whose naked breasts hung empty and sallow like two deflated bladders stood with her arms around her children. He could not see their feet for they had sunken deep into the mud. It looked as if they were slowly being consumed by the slimy mass.

"Ashes to ashes," he thought as he looked in astonishment at the three spectres standing before his eyes.

"Uisge! Arán! má sé do dtuil é, in ainm Dé". (Water, food, please in God's name) The spectre croaked pointing to the two children.

As if drawn by some unknown force the male spectre once again manifested himself from within the tomb and again glanced towards him. Seeing Seámus he made to approach the rickety gate of the garden.

Seámus took a step back in fear and trepidation. How in God's Holy Name could he greet such abominations, these

83

sick wild beasts with their incoherent cries for help and this pitiful wretch who was once a man. What was he waiting for? He was so far gone that he could not articulate. It would be a charity indeed to put, not alone him, but the whole family out of their misery.

He was brought back to reality when the wretch tried to steady himself. It was to no avail as he fell forward with a splash and landed face down in the muddied water, where he remained still.

The wretch, covered in his own excrement, was being eaten alive by lice.

"Are you alright, can you stand?" Seámus called from the safety of the gate, willing the man to regain his feet. He felt shamed and sorry that he could not bring himself to go to the man's assistance.

The woman, ignoring the plight of her partner and the scene of horror playing out its last act before her, continued to plead.

When Seámus did not respond she turned and guided her children back into the hovel. He watched as she continued on into the hovel without as much as a downward glance at the wretch, who he presumed was her husband, suffocating in the muddy water.

He stood for a while longer looking at the empty doorway before he reluctantly left the scene. Moving on down the road he stopped and glanced back. He was hoping that the wretch had regained his feet. There was no movement from the spectre lying beneath the rotting coatamore.

The dejected village was, as far as he could see, a place of the dead. Not a pane of glass was left unbroken, not a roof remained intact. The landlords and their lackeys had succeeded in annihilating the village. That was with the exception of the family of shrunken apparitions that he had previously encountered.

He was pleased to find himself once again in open countryside.

Tired and weary he lay down under the shelter of a large chestnut tree and soon succumbed to sleep.

In his dreams he saw the people of Cork in line after line pass by him. They held their heads high and smiled. These were not the attenuated corpses that he had left behind in Ballydehob. No! these were fit, healthy and proud . They walked with a determination in their step and they sang with the steadfastness of a proud people.

Behind them came screaming spectres with worms falling from their eyes and mouths.

He awoke shivering from the nightmare, a cold sweat covering his body.

THE DEATH OF BRENDAN

Seámus arrived home tired, hungry and weary both in mind and body to his cottage home.

It was two weeks to the day since the widow and her children returned to their cottage by the sea.

"God in Heaven, how time flies," he thought on seeing his brother sitting beside the fire.

Brendan was showing signs of improvement. Although they faced hunger and possible death daily they were still a family. For this they duly thanked their God.

Brendan could now leave his bed and sit beside the fire for a couple of hours each day.

Seámus entered the kitchen and placed his slán against the wall.

"Bless me, if you are not a silver lining to a cloudy sky," he remarked on seeing his brother sitting by the fire wrapped in a blanket.

"Doesn't he look the healthy boy, you must be surprised at seeing him sitting there?" His mother entered the kitchen smiling. Seámus saw from her smiling face that a great sorrow had been lifted from her heart.

"I'm nearly better and I'll soon be able to leave the house. Did you bring me anything nice?" Brendan greeted his brother.

"Of course I brought something nice."

"Show me then." Brendan took on a fit of coughing.

"You're looking at it! Me! Are you alright?" Seámus looked worried.

"He's alright aren't you son, don't get him over excited though."

"I'm fine Ma, honest."

"Have you still got 'Cromwell' or did you let him escape."

"Of course not, he is still in his basin."

"Tell you what, tomorrow I'll take you into the village. That is if mother agrees."

"How do you intend to get me there then?"

"I'll carry you on my back if necessary, that is, if you want to come."

"You'll never leave me , will you Seámus. I'll always wait for you to come home."

"Of course I'll not leave you. Why are you asking such silly questions?"

"You won't be taking me any place, will you, Seámus?"

"Of course I will, I'll stay home tomorrow and borrow the

cart from Seámus Hennessy and take you for a drive up to the Big House. How about that?"

"Do you think you should Seámus, is it not too soon? Let him get his strength back first," his mother cautioned.

"Oh please, Ma, let me go. I'll be ever so good."

"Alright then, but you must not leave the cart, promise?"

"It's back to bed for you young man." Seámus, picking up his brother in his arms, left the kitchen.

"Now tell me how you got on, did you get any work?" Brendan now propped up in his bed pressed for answers. Seámus related his adventures on the road to Ballydehob. All too soon he noticed that his brother had once again fallen asleep.

Next day, true to his word he got the loan of the cart.

"All ready for the off." His father carried Brendan to the cart and, placing him in a bed of clean straw, tucked a blanket around him.

"Seámus whatever you do, make sure you don't overtire him". His mother came to the door with the obligatory bottle of Holy water in her hands.

"Guid orrainn, a naom Matair Dé. (Pray for us, O Holy Mother of God) She sprinkled the Holy water on her sons and the donkey and cart.

"Ionnus go b'fiú Sinn cun geallamna Críost d'fagail".(That we may be made worthy of the promises of Christ), Seámus replied and blessed himself.

"Now away you go and don't stay away too long." Their parents watched as the cart trundled down the boreen. Brendan weakly raised his hand in salutation.

On their return Seámus saw his mother standing in the boreen looking up and down the road.

"Thank God you are back. I was worried that something had happened."

"Are they back then". His father came from the cottage wiping his hands in a cloth.

"Ma! We went as far as the estate of the Brigadier and looked in at the mansion. It's huge, you should see it." Brendan getting excited began to tell all about his adventures.

"Come on, let's get you into the house first." His father picked him up from the well of the cart and brought him into the cottage.

"It was great Da, tomorrow I'm going to see more." Brendan continued his rhetoric until a bout of coughing stopped him.

"Come on now, it's bed for you, tomorrow is another day." His father waited for his bout of coughing to finish before picking him up and taking him to the back bedroom.

"Now, I've got something special for you." His mother entered the room with a steaming mug.

"Not stirabout Ma." Brendan looked with abhorrence at the mug.

"Stirabout indeed, what I have here is a mug of best broth. Can you manage or do you want me to feed you."

"I'm not a baby Ma, can I go with Seámus again tomorrow, please Ma"?

"Here drink up your broth, then we'll see."

"What do you think of our Brendan then. Was there any problems with him?" his mother, pleased with herself, asked.

"No trouble at all, he was as good as gold. I won't be able to take him tomorrow though".

"Are you off looking for work then?" his father asked.

"If the weather holds I might try my luck again. If not then I might take Brendan down to the forge for a little break".....

The family prepared to say the evening rosary. The door to Brendan's room had been left ajar. This to allow him to hear the prayers and to answer.

"In ainm an Atar agus an Mic agus an Spióraid Naoim." (in the name of the Father and of the Son and of the Holy Ghost) Pat taking his rosary beads from the back of the chair began the prayers.

"Amen" answered the family.

"D'foillsig Aingeal an Tigearna do Muire" (The angel of the lord declared unto Mary)

"Agus do gab si o'n Spióraid naom" (And she conceived by the Holy Ghost)

The Angelus concluded and the Divine praise began.....

"Molad le Dia" (Blessed be God) Pat led his family into the prayers.

"Molad lé na Ainm Naomta" (Blessed be his holy name)

The monotony of the prayers that had for generations past been recounted in the cottage continued.

As Tom led the prayers he hesitated after each one and listened as Brendan weakly replied.

Halfway through the prayers there was no reply from Brendan

Again his father repeated the prayers, there was still no response.

There was an eerie silence now within the cottage. Tom looked across at his wife.

"Brendan, are you alright?" his father called quietly not wishing to disturb the silence.

"Perhaps he has fallen asleep". His mother interrupting the prayers rose to her feet and entered the room.

87

Brendan lay on his side his right hand extended beyond the bed. His rosary beads swung slowly in his bent fingers.

"Are you alright, son?" she gently called, lifting his hand and placing it under the covers.

Looking down at his emaciated face she knew that he was no more.

"Oh Brendan, Ocóne! Ocóne! Mo Gra geal mo cróide (Joy of my heart) why did you leave us?" Cradling the dead body of her son close to her breast she rocked backwards and forwards lamenting.

Seámus on hearing his mother crying looked across at his father. As one they rose and entered the little bedroom.

By the light from the flickering candle they saw his mother settling Brendan back into the bed.

"Is he alright Bridget, in the name of God what is the matter?"

"Here they are Tom, Seámus was right". She held her hand out displaying two teeth to her husband.

"Is he gone from us Bridget?" Reaching out he took his wife's hand in his and felt the pressure of the two teeth in his palm.

"He is gone Tom, gone from you and me. My Brendan is gone from the Ocras and the pain forever"

"He's not dead Ma, He is sleeping, so he is." Seámus went to the side of the bed and stroked the face of his younger brother.

"He was waiting for you to come home Seámus. He wanted to say goodbye to you so he did."

"Wake up, wake up Brendan, I'll take you wherever you want to go. Only please wake up." Seámus held his brothers' hand and called through his tears.

"My Brendan will not awaken ever again, He is gone to the angels, so he has. Gone to where the Ocras and the pain can no longer torment him". His mother came to the bedside and joined Seámus.

"Leave him be Seámus, he is now in the arms of Jesus." Gently his father placed his arm around his shoulder.

"We must say the prayers." His mother took the candle and held it close to her sons' eyes. She instinctively closed the dead eyes of her youngest son and knelt beside his bed.

His father knelt beside his wife, she took the right hand of his dead son and held it in hers. He took his left hand and began the act of contrition......

O mo Dia! tá doilgeas croide orm fá fearg a cur ort; agus tá fuat fírinneac agam do mo peacaidib os cionn gac uile nid, de brig go Bfuil siad mí-taitneamac in do látair-se. A

Dia, a tuilleas mo grád to h-iomlán I dtaob do maiteasa do- coimsigte agus tá run diongbálta agam. le congnam do naom-grásta gan fearg a cur ort aris to brát.

(Oh my God! I am heartily sorry for having offended Thee, and I detest my sins above every other evil because they displease Thee my God, Who for thy infinite goodness are so deserving of all my love and I firmly resolve by thy holy grace never more to offend thee and to amend my life).

"Amen, Amen, mo cúsla, mo brón." His mother kissed the dead hand of her son over and over again until her husband restrained her.

He blessed his son and left the room. He heard his wife speaking to her dead son as if he were still alive.

"Mo leanb boct, (My poor child) I knit this just for you and now it is to become your shroud. We cared for you, mo cusla, We loved you with all our hearts. Why! Why did you leave us. We loved you so." He listened awhile before treading softly away from the door.

"You'll need to sleep in the kitchen this night Seámus." Removing the 'Connail na Marb (candle of the dead') she took it to the little bedroom.

"Mo Mavourneen, mo mavourneen boct!, here is the light to guide you from this cruel world. Your heart was brave and you suffered in silence. You are now with the angels, free from this cruel and cursed land. Smile on us mo cúsla and pray to the infant Jesus for those left behind." Kneeling beside the bed she placed her hands in those of her youngest son and prayed.

(A lighted candle known as 'The Candle of the Dead' was always left in the room with the corpse. The belief was that as a person came into this world by the light of life, they would not be able to leave it without a light. The door would not be closed for the spirit of the dead child would remain with his mortal body and when ready to leave would need the light to guide him to the spirit world.)

Rising to her feet she returned to the kitchen and procured a pinch of salt.

"Sleep Mo cúsla, sleep in peace". Sprinkling the salt across the doorway to protect his spirit from evil she left him to make his own arrangements for his journey from this world.

These were old Celtic customs to honour the dead and were respected.

It was early dawn before they finally retired. Exhausted from the trauma his father was soon sleeping a restless sleep. Time and time again he was awakened by his wife tip toeing from the room. He saw her shadow silhouetted in the flickering light from the 'Connail Mor' as she continued speaking gently to her dead son.

"You're gone from us now mo naoidean. Remember us always and our love for you. Remember too your brother Seámus, he loved you so much. He is all we have left now and he needs your prayers in order to survive the 'OCRAS'.

Persistently she returned to the children's room with some remembered message for him to take to the next world.

It was early morning light when Tom was again awakened. His wife had left the room for the umpteenth time. He was not surprised to find her hunched over the corpse of her son, asleep.

Gently closing the door he left her with her child. It would be the last time that they would spend together on God's earth.

After a meagre meal she prepared her youngest son for burial. She laid him out on the bed in a clean white shift and in his hands she entwined his rosary beads. Then, removing the Connail Mór from the linen drawer, she kissed and lit it before placing it in the window. The neighbours would now know that there was a death within the cottage and call to offer their condolences and pray for the soul of the departed.

There were few callers to the wake of Brendan Flynn in Skibbereen that cruel spring. The people were not indifferent to the calling to the wake. They were tired, exhausted and demoralised. Death occurred from the great 'Ocras' in most of the cottages daily. There would be no keeners to lament over the body of Brendan. His parents would have to perform the task alone.

Looking through the window she saw her Tom walk discreetly past the window. In his hands he held several planks of timber. He did not look at her but passed on and entered the haggard.

Rising to her feet she crossed the threshold and called through the door.

"There is a little stirabout left in the pot, you should eat something." Her sad eyes were red raw from a night of crying.

"I've got business to attend to Bridget if that is all the same to you." He closed the door gently.

She listened as the wood was cut and she felt every blow of the hammer in her heart as her husband continued his sorrowful task alone.

After a time there was silence, it was a strange echoing silence. She thought that the world had suddenly stood still.

90

Her silence was disturbed as she heard the blackbirds challenge for nesting spaces. She heard 'Cromwell' croaking, it was Spring. A time when new life was born. There was no new life in Skibbereen that year. There would be no nest for her fledging. He was free, free from the cruel landlord, the Ocras and the cursed land.

She knew that the task was completed. She listened intently to the creaking of the haggard door. She did not wish to look, she knew what it meant; but look she did as before her stood Tom with the hammer in his hand.

"It is ready Bridget, I'll be bringing it in soon." Closing the door behind him he entered the cottage and stood looking down at the body of his youngest son.

"Seámus come and say goodbye to your brother Brendan." Ignoring her husband she called Seámus forward.

Blessing himself her husband left the room and returned shortly with the crude coffin.

"Will it be alright Bridget?" Standing in the doorway he held the small rectangular coffin in both arms. Tears welled up in his weary eyes and slowly trickled down his face.

"Oh Bridget, it's sorry I am but........."

"It is grand Tom, so it is. I know that Brendan would be proud of you."

At least her son would be buried in a coffin and not thrown into a pit without respect or pity.

Tom placed the coffin on a chair and spread fresh straw inside. Removing the body of his son from the bed he placed him gently inside.

His mother came to the side of the coffin and looked down at her child. He looked to be sleeping comfortable. She did not cry, there were no more tears left. She touched his tousled curls and stroked his dead face gently. For a fleeting moment she was happy. He was free of the Ocras and the cruel land. The Banshee, she knew would not cry for her son. She too was exhausted from crying for the sons and daughters of Eireann.

Brendan was her youngest and God in his mercy had plucked him from the pain and distress and taken him to paradise.

"Slán leat, átar mo croide, bennact Dé leat." (Goodbye forever, joy of my heart, may God bless you)

In unison and without any prompting they knelt around the crude open coffin and recited a decade of the rosary.

Tom rose to his feet and, picking up the lid of the coffin, stood to one side awaiting his wife to finish her prayers.

"Will you give the blessing before......" He looked questingly towards his wife.

Bridget, without any further prompting, rose, and, taking the bottle of holy water from the mantle she blessed her son for the last time. Then she blessed the other members of the family.

"Wait! Please wait". Seámus left the cottage. When he returned he held in his hand a bunch of primroses and cowslips. These he placed over the clasped hands of his brother.

That evening they knelt in prayer around the coffin and waited. They knew that the spirit of Brendan their youngest was about to flee the nest. They heard the keening and they heard the knocking.

"The Banshee did not forget to do the calling on my baby," his mother proudly proclaimed as she listened to the low murmuring outside the door.

Brendan Flynn was leaving the house and Skibbereen for the last time.

On hearing the knocking she faced the door and was about to run to the half door when her husband stopped her.

"Let him go Bridget, did we not hear the knocking and the calling. His spirit is now free."

"He did not forget to do the honours. He remembered us as he left, did he not, Tom?"

"He did that, Bridget. He is now in a better place away from the Ocras and the pain".

Yet she could not let him go without saying her last goodbye.

"Mo cúsla, mo buacaillini deas, slán leat a Mic." (My love, my dear child, Good bye) She held her hands open and glanced at the half door. There was no response for her son was now a free spirit.

Seámus joined his mother at the front door and stood outside waiting.

Tom nailed the lid on the coffin and gently lifting it in his hands joined his wife and son in the boreen.

The sad cortege made their way to the family plot in the little graveyard.

The people of the village came to their doors and, standing in respectful silence, blessed themselves as the family passed. What sympathy could they offer. All too soon another sad cortege would follow the coffin of Brendan Flynn .

They did not follow the funeral as heritage demanded. The old traditions were dead; what people remained were exhausted and demoralised. There were too many worn steps to the little graveyard and too much disturbed earth. The Grim Reaper did follow the coffin though, gloating in yet another victory.

The village of Skibbereen was being raped and plundered of its people by the Grim Reaper as the arrogant landlords looked on indifferently. The great Hunger was bleeding the village to annihilation.

Later that evening Seámus took Cromwell to the family burial plot and released him.

The frog sat on the grave and looked for a moment bewildered.

Then with a croak and a giant leap it made its escape into the marshes.

A CRADLE SONG

O, Men from the fields
Come gently within.
Tread softly, softly,
O! Men coming in.

Mavourneen is going
From me and from you,
Where Mary will fold him
With mantle of blue.

From the reek of the smoke
And the cold of the floor,
And the peering of things
Across the half door.

O! men from the fields;
Softly, softly come throu';
Mary put round him
Her mantle of blue.

Padric Colum

THE HORROR OF THE WORKHOUSE

Seámus returned from yet another fruitless search for work and saw his mother in the quarter acre field. She seemed to be weeding the potato crop that had been planted that spring in the lazy ridges.

"Leave that mother, I'll see to them" he called as he opened the five barred gate and entered the small plot.

"Seámus look, the potatoes! Tell me it cannot be happening again. It cannot be I tell you!" his mother repeated as she made a vain attempt to support the stalks of the potatoes which were collapsing quicker than she could place earth around them.

"It's the Potato Cholera, there is nothing that we can do." Seámus looked dejected at the ridges which were slowly being denuded of potato stalks.

"Seámus will you not stand there bladdering! Go and get your father!" She continued trying to support the crumbling stalks.

"Mother, for God's sake get off your knees. There is nothing that you nor I can do."

"They'll be alright Seámus, it is not the cursed blight. Last night there was a ground frost." She continued trying to support the stalks without success.

"It is summer mother and there was no frost last night. Stop deceiving yourself, the potato crop is finished."

"Finished! Is that all you have to say. Where in God's Holy Name are we to find food?"

"I don't know, I really don't know." Placing his hand gently around his mothers' shoulder he guided her towards the cottage.

"Where will it all end?" Seámus sat down on the stool and removed his well worn boots.

"Today I walked as far as Dunmanway. There I got a bowl of soup and a crust of bread. There is no relief work in the county. I'll not be taking the road tomorrow". He examined a hole in the sole of his boot as he spoke.

"I'm sorry son, whatever will your father say when I tell him that the curse has struck?"

"What can he say or do for that matter. Perhaps we should pack up and try for our passage to America".

"America it seems is the dream of every Irishman."

"So you're back from the workhouse then," Bridget remarked on seeing her husband come through the half door. Ignoring his wife and son he went and sat in the

95

sugan chair and began to shake uncontrollably.

"Tom, I'm talking to you, are you alright? Seámus thinks the blight has struck again. Flying in the face of Almighty God he is. Tell me Tom, tell me in God's Holy Name tell me that it is not true." Bridget went to his side and began to shake him.

"I know! God, don't I know it! In the name of God will you shut up about the blight. Are you deaf woman or worse; cannot you hear the whole village crying like the Banshee. They are crying in the village, crying to a God that mocks their every prayer. A God that left our Brendan suffer for years. Finally he snuffed him out like a candle as he prayed. If it is not one thing then it's another. Even in my own house I am tormented." Wringing his hands he continued to look into the fire.

"Sorry Tom. Did something happen today?"

"Today, tomorrow, what does it matter. I cannot stand anymore I tell you. The curse of Christ is on this blighted land."

"Tom, please I beg of you do not blaspheme so. I am sorry but..... Oh Jesus, Jesus! Jesus where are you?".... Bridget returned to the fireplace and sat traumatised looking into the fire.

"What I saw this day will live with me until my dying day". Rising he began to pace the floor. Like a soul tormented he kept up a steady pace, wringing his hands and muttering unintelligibly.

"Saw! What did you see to make you so frightened. Has it something to do with the workhouse?"

"Yes, it was the cursed workhouse if you must know."

Spittle began to form on the sides of his mouth, this he wiped away with the sleeve of his coat.

"You had best tell us. Now sit yourself down and try to tell us rationally what happened". Gently she guided him back to the chair.

Taking a deep breath he regained his composure and looked from his wife to his son.

"I was instructed to go to the dormitory where the children are. Joe Mc Bride came with me to collect two children. You know Joe and his wife Peggy?"

"Sure, I know Joe and his family as well as I know anyone, but what happened?"

"I went to the door first and opened it, I expected to hear children laughing, crying or playing about. I was more than surprised to find most of them huddled in a corner like penned sheep. Not one of them was speaking nor were any of them crying. This I can tell you frightened me, why I do not know. Here before my very eyes I saw a room filled with children, yet it was as silent as the grave. If only one of them, just one of them at least would cry.

Before me stood a boy and a girl holding hands. They were, from what I could determine, between five and seven years of age.

"That young, Tom, how cruel, are you sure?" Bridget interrupted.

"Does it matter what age they were, Good God woman, I told you they were children." He paused and again rose to his feet.

"Sorry love, but I cannot forget it." He apologised and returned to his chair.

"I presumed by the way that they were holding hands that they were brother and sister. Their bodies were swollen to about three times their normal size. Their arms were longer than that of most children and were as thin as rushes. They too were as naked as on the day that they were born. A downy hair grew from their bodies and faces but the hair on their heads had receded. Tears constantly wept from their eyes which were as big as saucers. I knew instinctively that they were pleading for something, but what could I do. I thought that they would say something to me but they just stood there and looked and looked. Not once did they blink, I looking into their eyes. I was transfixed and mesmerised for some moments. Yes Bridget, I read it in their eyes, they were blaming me, I was their guardian and I had failed them."

'I am not to blame'. I told them, but they ignored me.

Then stealing my gaze away from them I went deeper into the large room.

As I crossed the floor the children made way for me. I was shocked when I reached the far wall of the room. Before me lay the bodies of two boys. It appeared to me that they must have been supporting each other before they died. Their stomachs had collapsed into their backs and I could count each and every bone. Oh Bridget! the sight of their poor bodies, it was as if they had been covered in parchment.

As I moved nearer to the bodies some of the other children, and there were about twenty in the room, stood aside. It again came to my attention that not a single child spoke, laughed nor cried. They looked like little, shrivelled up and very old men and women. Their backs were curved and their stick-like hands extended to nearly touching the ground. The skin covering their skeletons' frames literally hung in folds. Their eyes seemed to be as black as those of the shark and had sunken deep into their skulls. They kept looking at me and I felt guilty.

I felt like screaming at them 'What are you looking at me for it is not my doing'. Yet I could not bring myself to chide them. They were so innocent looking and appeared to be saying 'Why us?'.

Some were leaning against the bare walls for support as their stick-like legs could no longer support them. How long they had been standing there I could not tell, but I never saw them move. It was as if they feared that in trying to move they would fall over. They just stared and stared, not at me, not at the room, but they stared."

"Tom! Stop crucifying yourself, it is not your fault". Bridget went to his side and cradled his head in her arms.

"Oh for Christ's sake woman. There you see, you too tell me that it is not my fault. Don't I know that? Well, don't I? Stop making unnecessary excuses for me. God in heaven, will you listen to me! It is not the fault of Tom Flynn! I must tell you, I must tell someone or I'll go mad so I will".

Reaching out he angrily ran his hands through his hair. He looked at his wife and son as unashamedly the tears streamed down his face. Then he began to walk round and round the room wringing his hands. Here was a man whose soul was tormented by what he had witnessed that day.

"'Why don't some of you say something! Go on, cry! Laugh! For God's sake do something,' I screamed at them. My voice seemed to echo all around the room as if within a tomb. They ignored me and just kept staring, at what I'll never know. But they never uttered a word, Bridget, so they didn't. Not one single word, mind you".

His voice tailed off and he looked deep into the face of his wife.

"I thought of our son Brendan, and I thanked God for taking him from this cursed land, so I did. Say what you will, call me what you want but I thanked God for taking our youngest son and I make no apology for it. My youngest son, Brendan, lying in the clay of Skibbereen, the only piece of his native soil that he will ever inherit and I am glad. What do you think of me now Bridget Clancy? Go on say it, why don't you?"

He returned to his seat and looked again at his wife expecting to be chastised for his unchristian remark. Bridget ignored it and stood holding the edge of the table.

"Joe McBride who was assisting me, warned me to be prepared for the worst when we lifted the dead children. I was soon to find out just what he meant but I never expected it to be so upsetting. Jesus have mercy on us all Bridget. As we lifted one little body, his arm which was bent under him swung towards the floor. The flesh what there was of it came away in a long strip".

He held out his arms as if he were carrying a child.

"On some of the beds there were three and on others four children, some were sitting up and not moving, others were just lying there awaiting death. They all had that vacant stare and their skin looked like the stretched transparent stomach of a goat. Joe warned me not to pick up any of the children nor should I touch them. They did not cry, they did not speak," he again repeated himself.

"Why don't they speak,? Why don't they cry, Joe?"

I pleaded for an answer. Looking across at the row of beds and avoiding my questioning glance he told me.

"The reason is this, Tom. Their jaw bones are so fragile from starvation that they are clamped to the roofs of their mouths. There is no cure and soon all the children in the room will die. Touching them in any way would only accelerate their impending deaths."

Did they know that they were about to die and succumbed to death, or were they hoping that I would put them out of their misery. Would I be their executioner? I don't know, I wish to Christ that I did."

He paused and wiped the spittle that was again forming on his mouth with his cravat.

"Many are bald headed, yet there is an unnatural growth on their faces like a downy hair. Can you imagine it Bridget, hair growing on the faces and bodies of children? In many I saw that it covered their chests as well. It was all so unnatural, so it was. I wish to God Almighty that I had never taken on the work. They will die, so they will, without the comfort of kit nor kin. Their little bodies will be buried without a shroud or coffin in mass graves. Can you imagine our baby son looking like that, well can you? I thank you God, I really do, for taking him away from this cursed land."

"I told you Tom Flynn so I did, and there is no denying it, you should not have taken that work. Cannot you let our Brendan rest in peace."

"Will you shut up woman and listen. Would it make a hate of difference if Tom Flynn or someone else saw what I saw, would it?"

He banged his fists on the sides of the chair in his frustration.

"That place, that cursed place has a jinx on it. It should be burnt to the ground, so it should. Do you know that they totally segregate men, women and children. Families are divided up and when one dies the other is not told. They die alone calling for their loved ones, that is those who can

99

cry out."

He was more composed now that he had told most of his story.

"Many are without beds in the overcrowded dormitories and fight with each other for a filthy bed from which a corpse has been removed.

The men are taken to a large shed at the rear of the workhouse. In it are mounds and mounds of rotting animal bones. They are each given a hammer and told to reduce the bones to powder. It is used on the lands belonging to the gentry.

The women are sent to attend to the sick and dying or to wash the clothes taken from the corpses. They repair them for other inmates bereft of clothes. Breakfast such as it is consists of a watery porridge. This is served at 6 a.m. and a days work follows until eight in the evening when dinner is collected. This is most days a watery soup with two surplus army biscuits.

These are biscuits left over from the wars with France and are as hard as stones. The same biscuits that are given out at the soup kitchens. At nine all must retire to their cold, overcrowded dormitories. Any noise from the inmates after this, and the paupers, for that is what they call them, are evicted out into the countryside. I don't think that I could face another day working in that house of death, forgive me Bridget. I'll not go back there ever, I would rather starve in our own home".

"You'll not go back there Tom, of that have little fear. Seámus and I were talking only this afternoon, were we not Seámus?"

"Talking about what may I ask?"

"America, I hear tell that there is work and food for all there."

"America! The American wake is it. Now where would we get the money to go to America?"

"Tom Flynn, there are thousands in a worse position than us and they are going to America"

"Free passage, is that what you are thinking about? Have you no sense woman, free passage indeed. Unless our landlord is willing to meet the cost of our passage we will die in Skibbereen. Ships bring timber from Canada and North America to Ireland. Others bring coal from England. Now these ships need ballast for the return journeys. Loading the ships with rocks and stones is time consuming and expensive. It is cheaper to load them with cheap Irish migrants who have a pittance to subscribe to their passage."

"Are you sure, Tom. Who would do such a thing?"

"Do you know, Bridget, that sometimes you are so naive that you should have been a nun. I was over in Limerick some time ago in a village called Castleconnell. There is a field near by called the 'Famine Field.' In this field is dumped the ballast for the ships. Some call it the 'American Field'. There is little use for it now that they have human ballast.

We must talk of this another time, Bridget. Be very cautious when you talk of emigrating. Only today Tony Quigley was found dead on the road to Kinsale. He was a good worker and saved hard intending to go to America and earn enough to bring his wife and two daughters over. He was on his way to Queenstown hoping to bargain a passage for himself and his family. He must have got caught in a storm and with little clothing to keep him warm and with no food in his belly to talk of, he died from exposure."

"Tom, sure that poor man,rest his soul, was in no fit state to take to the road. Whatever possessed him to go all that way alone. What will become of his daughters and widow?"

"I take it that you have not heard then?"

"Heard what, did something happen?"

"The constabulary went to the cottage to inform the family of the death of their father, so they did. They were shocked to see the state that the family were living in. The two daughters were lying more or less in the ashes and they scantily covered in a threadbare blanket trying to keep warm. The widow greeted them sitting at the table which had not seen food for two whole days. She is in bad health and there is fear that she will never recover. With Tony now gone what hope is there for them?"

"What hope indeed father, and what hope is there for us, may I ask. Did you not see the deserted cottages in the village? If the Ocras is not decimating the villagers then it is the famine ship," said Seámus.

"Free passage indeed! There is no such thing as free passage. I've heard enough! Enough do you hear! I'm taking myself off for a breath of fresh air, so I am".

Leaving the cottage Tom vaulted the stone wall and crossed Primrose meadow.

THE GLEANERS IN THE MANURE HEAP

He had not gone far when he came across several villagers gleaning stinking turnip and cabbage tops from a pile of manure.

"What do you think you are doing, you cannot eat this muck," Tom reprimanded them.

Ignoring him, they continued gathering up the decaying tops from the rotting manure heap stacked outside the walled garden of Lord Carbery.

His lordship had little if any interest in the welfare of his captive tenants. As long as he received his income in the region of £50,000 in rent and taxes from them per annum they were free to enjoy the hospitality of the piece of land that he rented to them. Failure to meet their rents would result in a visit from the crowbar gang. These were fellow Irishmen who for a meal and a Saxon shilling were willing to do the dirty work for the landlords.

His conscience did not bother him when he saw the miserable, wretched Irish queuing up for a bowl of watery soup and a hard biscuit. Yet there were many landlords in the region who were no better and no worse than His Lordship.

Sir William Brecher who owned most of the town of Skibereen was another landlord who cared not for the plight of his tenants. His annual income of approximately £10,000 helped to keep him in luxury as his pauper tenants starved. There would be no remittance of rents until the harvest improved.

'Give in to the Irish and where would it all end? They, (The Irish) were an ungrateful lot, if it is not famine then it's a plague. They always seem to have problems, don't they. Why cannot they sort them out themselves instead of putting their problems on the shoulders of the English? As we feed them and cloth them they show no gratitude'.

As Charles Wood the then chancellor of the exchequer said at the time.......

'They have hardly been decent whilst they have their bellies filled with our corn and their pockets with our money'

He addressed his speech to the honourable Members of Parliament in London with his tongue in his cheek.

These were hard hearted business people whose

sympathies lay with their bank balance and not with their starving Irish tenants.

There were at least another dozen known avaricious landlords in the West county of Cork who acted like medieval barons. However much contempt we may feel for the conduct of these landlords, what excuse can one offer for the Reverenced Stephen Townsend. He was one of the local Protestant clergy, a man of the cloth, as they say. He too was a landlord siphoning off £8,000 from his wretched starving tenants each year. One wonders did he justify his unchristian conduct by referring to his tenants as 'Papist Irish Peasants'.

Whatever the reason for the conduct of the landlords it was the Irish destitute tenants who were suffering and dying.

There was food in plenty available in the country for those who could afford to buy it. Of this fact there was no disputing. This option was not however available to the starving evicted wretches. Where were they to find the money to buy food? Nor was it open to the diseased tenants who had sealed themselves up in their cottages to avoid the shame of their neighbours seeing their emaciated bodied raked with plague and stinking of dysentery.

Tom knew of all these happenings but they mattered little to him. His concern was for the survival of his wife and son. He had lost one son to the Ocras and hoped to God that he would not lose the other.

If only God in his divine mercy would listen to his prayers. Did not his Christ die nailed to a cross unable or unwilling to save himself. He dismissed these blasphemous thoughts from his mind and falling to his knees began to pray.

Curiosity got the better of some of those scavenging in the manure heap. On seeing Tom fall to his knees some looked across at him, only to returned disinterested to their task.

A wretch of a woman half covered in a rotting shawl in which she cradled an infant rose from the midden. In her hand she held the decaying top of a turnip. This she placed in her mouth and began to chew. She regurgitated the mash she created into her palm and fed it to her infant.

On faltering bare feet she left the manure heap and approached the spot where Tom was kneeling in prayer. Using Toms' shoulder as a crutch she knelt down beside him and began to pray aloud.

Soon others joined them and formed themselves into a

circle. Tom removed his rosary from his pocket and led them into the prayers. What were these people praying for. Was it for their own intentions? Was it for the wretches who were about to die? Their prayers and their pleadings were as secret as the confessional.

Tom too sent a special message from his heart to his God. He pleaded to escape from this cursed and wretched land. It was here that the fit, the starving, the plague ridden, the dispossessed, the widows and the children all bereft of their last vestige of pride prayed in their shame. A rag tag army on the march with only one goal in life, to procure enough food to keep them alive for one more day. Instinct compelled them to keep going for just one more day. In too many cases their emaciated bodies, no longer able to sustain them, gave up the fight.

They competed with the rats and other scavengers for the chance of survival. They gorged themselves on the rotting garbage from the great houses. The rats gorged themselves on the bodies of the victims of 'The Great Hunger'.

The only ones well fed were the dogs, cats, rats, vermin and landed gentry.

The occupants of the Castles, Manors and Great Houses that overlooked the villages from Bantry bay, Schull, Ballydehob, Skibbereen, Clonakilty and all the intervening villages between were indifferent to their plight.

It mattered little to them that the inhabitants of the villages slowly and systematically perished from disease, hunger, plague and sheer exhaustion. This then was the state of Southwest Cork. Those who took on the long road to Cork City found not hope but rejection. The gates of the city were closed to them. State and church had no time for these disease ridden parasites. They were looked on with fear and derision by the dignitaries of the city.

"Return to your villages, there is nothing here for you," they were told.

Those who were willing to leave the outskirts of the city were given a mug of soup and two hard biscuits or a hunk of bread to sustain them on their way.

"Where do we go to, we are dispossessed and our village destroyed," they pleaded.

"Go where you will, but there is no place here for you".

Those who lingered were encouraged to leave with the threat of a beating.

With the prayers concluded they left the hillside and returned to their hovels, their booleys, the hedgerows and the highways.

A CHARADE

As the wet summer of 1846 gave way to the autumn, matters were taking a turn for the worse. England found that it was now too late to buy any corn with which to feed the starving Irish.

The English Government came to the bizarre decision that all to the West of Ireland would probably need some help. Those living in the East would survive on what supplies were available.

To this end the food depots of Limerick and Cork would be opened when it was proven that all the produce of the land had been consumed. When there were no longer supplies available to purchase from the corn merchants only then would help be given. A line was drawn up on the map of Ireland, and all to the West of that line would receive some help. The rest would have to survive on their own resources.

There would be strict rationing of supplies.

This one act was to cause resentment throughout the country.

On hearing of the plan many moved into the West hoping to obtain a share of what relief there was. They were soon informed that only those who had been domicile in the West for three years would qualify for relief. They would have to return to their own homes East of the line and hope for survival.

The people found it hard to understand just what the English meant when they refused to release any food until all the harvest had been exhausted. There were no potatoes in Ireland as the crop had totally collapsed in July of that year. What cereals there were had to be surrendered to the landlord in payment of rent. Those with work found that their pay for a weeks' work was not enough to pay the exuberant prices being asked for a meal sufficient to feed a family for one day. They were being asked to decide as to which members of the family should live and who should die. This policy was draconian and cruel.

Time and time again urgent messages were despatched to Westminster warning that if no food was released from the depots then there would be starvation on a colossal scale.

Lord Trevelyn and Sir Randolph Routh ignored all these warnings. They made it abundantly clear that the depots were to remain secured and guarded and would not be opened until they authorised it. To enforce this directive more troops were despatched to Ireland from mainland Britain.

The weather which had been wet and cold all Summer was now showing further deterioration. The roads into the villages were becoming impassable and the only open roads were the bridleways. Local magistrates warned time and time again that time was running out. Unless immediate steps were taken to replenish the depots with corn then there was no hope of any of the villages surviving the winter.

Once again Lord Trevelyn made it clear that no fresh supplies would be available from the Americas until December or January of 1847 at the earliest.

The people were led to understand that the central depots in Cork and Limerick were filled to capacity. As these depots were central to County Cork, Kerry, Limerick, Tipperary, Clare and Galway it was assumed that in due course they would be opened and supplies would be made available.

What Lord Trevelyn and Sir Randolph Routh did not tell the magistrates was that the depots were far from overbrimming with corn.

The depots in Limerick contained less than 200 tons of unground corn. This was corn left over from the previous year. It was far short of meeting even the basic demands of County Limerick let alone the other counties.

Cork depots which were supposed to hold reserve stocks were all but empty as were the depots in County Limerick. The truth was that the government were of the opinion that the potato crop was safe. This although there was ample proof that all was not well with the crop. No corn whatsoever had been purchased in 1846. As Autumn gave way to Winter a stock list was taken of all available corn, biscuits and other foods in Ireland. The sum total amounted to less than 3,000 tons to feed the nation. An impossible task, and unless the promised corn arrived from the United States by early January then many thousands more would die.

Sir Routh assured the magistrates in the Autumn of 1846 that ample supplies had been assured from America. They would arrive in late December or early January. Yet it was already far too late. France had purchased vast quantities of the crop in advance of the harvest. The Prussian Empire had secured what supplies of Rye that would be available from the new crop. There would be little if any available for the English market. This was well known by the English government of the day. Knowing that its hesitation to secure supplies on the world market would have catastrophic results in Ireland they took panic measures far too late.

The Irish nation would be decimated. Writing to Lord Trevelyn, Sir Routh asked him....

"What am I to tell these people when they discover we lied to them?"

This cruel charade of the English Government would bear fruit in Irish dead.

A MOTHERS TEARS

Seámus rose early and, having completed his ablutions, he lifted the latch.

Placing his caubeen on his head he took the road to Macroom. He had been assured that there was relief work between Dunmanway and Macroom. He looked across at the outline of Mount Kid as the darkness of the night gave way to the dawn.

He tightened his coatamore around him as an icy wind beat into his face. He thanked God for the gentle mist that was rising off the moor. Although the weather was overcast there was no rain. On reaching the cross at Drimoleague all his assurances of a fair day were shattered. Sleet and driving rain raced across the moorland turning the road into a swollen stream. He could go no farther and would have to find shelter. It was doubtful if there would be any road works taking place in such austere weather.

Seeking shelter he saw a group of hawthorn bushes and ran towards them. They offered little protection, for the wind raced through their branches, drenching him in the process. He would be as well taking his chances in the open.

Rising wearily he trudged along the road, his bare feet sinking deeper and deeper into the cold mud. Rain ran off his caubeen and into his coatamore which was now a mud stained rain sodden hindrance. Although it offered little if any protection to his numbed body he could not discharge it. It was all that he had to protect him. With God's help he would find shelter and be able to dry out.

To his left on the sheltered side of the hill on the road to Coolkellure he saw a cottage. He would have to seek sanctuary within its walls. There was no alternative. He could not go forward nor could he return home. If he continued on then he too would surely become a victim of the 'Great Ocras'.

With grim determination he hastened to the door. Crossing the threshold he tried to raise the latch and enter but the door was bolted from within.

"Is there anyone inside, open the door in God's Holy Name," he pleaded.

After what seemed a lifetime the door was opened slowly. A gaunt man made his appearance. He made no attempt to welcome Seámus. If anything he made it clear that there was no 'Cead míle Fáilte within.

"What is your business here? We are of little trouble."
The man questioned and answered at the same time.

"Will you open the door and show a little hospitality."
Seámus shouted at the closed door..

"This is an 'Ocras' house, there is little that we can offer."
Reluctantly the man drew the bolt and opened the door.

Seámus crossed the mud floor and made his way to the
fireplace where a poor fire was smouldering.

"It's a foul day so it is. I was on my way to the relief work
on the Macroom road when I was caught in the weather."
Seámus began to make conversation as he removed his
wet coatamore. An old broom lay beside the fire and he
took the liberty of hanging his coatamore on it. With little
heat coming from the fire there was little hope of it
drying.

The cottage consisted of one room with an open loft above,
the entrance to which was by means of a raking ladder.

The one window had been obliterated with a mixture of
stones and clay.

Apart from the flickering flame from the miserable fire
the cottage was in darkness.

A shakedown of stinking malignant straw was set on the
earth floor in one corner. This seemed to be the fellows'
bed and was covered with several layers of rags. In the
centre of the floor sat a homemade table and two stools.
This was the sole furnishing of the cottage. Several rats
were scurrying around in the filthy straw.

"Do you live here alone?" Seámus asked as he glanced
around the miserable room.

"My wife and son live here too. Would you have any food
?"

"Food, now where would one get food in the County Cork?
I was hoping to come across a soup kitchen in my travels".

"Soup kitchen out here, have a little sense. The nearest
soup kitchen when it turns up will be at Macroom or
Skibbereen."

"There was one over on the Killenleagh run by the
Quakers some two weeks ago. I know for I got a mug of
soup and two biscuits from them and grateful I was."

"Killenleagh you say, Why you must have been there
about the time the eviction took place." The man looked at
Seámus suspiciously.

"I was there with the poor wretch on the very afternoon of
the eviction, God rest his soul. You could say that me and
the Quakers were in some way responsible for his death."

"Is that so, and how did that come about?" The man was
now all attention and had forgotten his hunger.

Seámus told him how it all happened.

"It was the will of God and there is nothing that you could have done about it. I see no reason to put the blame on yourself," the man replied on learning of what had happened.

Seámus was distracted by coughing and groaning coming from beneath the rotting rags.

"It's my wife and son, she is not all that well. I was replied hoping that you might have a little food to help," said the man as he noticed the look of shock on the face of Seámus.

"Your wife is sick, I am sorry. I only wish that I could be of assistance," he offered.

"It's a man of the roads Mary, he's come in out of the rain." The man went and pulled the blanket to one side. As he did two huge rats ran from the makeshift bed.

Seámus looked in at the gaunt face of a woman who was being slowly consumed by fever and hungry rats. There was little doubt but that she was dying and had been for some days.

She was so near to death that she was unable to articulate. He knew that she was pleading for some relief by the way she looked. There was nothing that he could do, she was being eaten alive by the rats.

Perhaps all she craved for was a drink of cool spring water to ease her burning fever. He listened to her incoherent cries sending their message through her large still eyes. He felt shame, for he could not bring himself to approach her.

"Are you aware that your wife is seriously ill and may not last the night. Could you not give her a drink of water at least? " Seámus kept his eyes transfixed on the vacant face of the woman.

A sweet smell permeated from the bed. Seámus knew what that smell was. Had he not buried his brother not too long ago?

"Where is your son?" Seámus asked, fearing the worst.

"He is in the bed beside my wife, why do you ask?" The man paused for a moment and then looked towards the bed.

"Jesus and Mary be good to us. No!"

Leaning over the body of his wife he picked up a horrifying spectre, or what was left of it, from the straw.

It was the body of a naked boy. The body was bloated to three times that of a normal healthy child. A watery slime oozed from his ever open eyes. His arms were longer than his entire body. He was covered in a hairy down from his head to his feet. His cold arms and feet were no larger than a rush and swung freely to and fro as his father cradled him in his arms. He was unmindful of the foul smell permeating from the corpse of his son.

Seámus knew what this meant for had not his father told him of it happening in the workhouse not too long ago.

Holding the child close in his arms, the father began to rock to and fro and calling to him. He seemed unaware that his son's corpse was being eaten by the rats.

"You're not dead Pádraig, you're not dead." He stroked the bared head and sallow face of the bloated child. His wife raised her hands from the putrefying straw and tried to reclaim the body of her son. Not one word did she speak, not a tear crossed her sad eyes.

"No Mary, never again will you cradle little Pádraig". Taking the body of their son to the table he laid him down gently.

"Do you want me to help you with the burial?" Seámus asked.

"You may leave now mister. We brought Pádraig into this cruel world and we will see him out of it. I warned you that this was an 'Ocras' house but you would not listen, would you? Will you leave us in God's Holy Name to die in the peace of our own cottage."

"You must leave this place at once, it is infested with rats," Seámus warned.

"What is wrong with you, we cannot leave here. Look! Look at our shame.I know that the rats will come for us as soon as we are unable to defend ourselves."

"Good God man, there must be something that you can do."

"Do! Do what? We have done all we could. We have made our peace with God. He will protect us from the rats as long as there is life in our mortal bodies. After we are dead it will not matter, now, will it?"

Seámus looked at the man with incredulity.

"Leave us to our fate, there is nothing to be said or done"

"But please, you must do something," Seámus pleaded.

"What do you suggest we do, commit suicide and condemn our souls to Hellfire? Please, in God's Name go; go and let us die with the last vestiges of dignity left to us on this earth. You were not invited into this 'Ocras' house. Your presence is an abomination to us. Leave us, leave us now to die without further outside interference and reminder of our shame."

Seámus retrieved his coatamore from the broom and reluctantly retreated to the door.

"God be good to you and yours."

"And to you and may you find peace on the road. Bennact De leat".

With gentle persuasion he was pushed out of the cottage of death. He heard the bolt being secured behind him. Saying a silent prayer he left the occupiers to their God. Without a backward glance he trudged his way down the boreen.

BETTER TIMES WILL COME, THEN WE WILL GET CHURCH RITES FOR THE BONES

On the road he ate shamrocks and grasses, anything edible to ease the cramp of hunger as again he braved the elements and continued on his journey to Macroom.

At the Shanacrane Cross he stopped and looked up at the lichen covered sign. Three long wooden fingers pointed in three different directions. One to his left pointed out the road to Poulnaberry Bridge. Another to his right pointed out the road to Coopen but standing high above the other two was a larger sign that beckoned him on.

It did not gently direct the traveller as the others did. It boldly declared that this was the road to Macroom and the road that one should take.

Seámus sat on a stone wall that seemed to start nowhere and go nowhere. The road to Macroom was wider than the other two but showed no welcome. A cold drizzle hid most of the road before him.

Beside him a spider sat patiently in the centre of her gossamer home. This she had woven in the centre of a blackberry bush, which had long since been denuded of its fruit. She too was waiting in anticipation of her next meal. She rose and stretched out a long leg and tested the strength of her trap. Perhaps she was bored of the long wait and decided to stretch her legs, he thought. As she did so, jewelled droplets of dew trickled down the web and formed themselves into long necklaces of transparent pearls.

Seámus watched in fascination as he awaited the next move from the spider. All too soon he felt his eyelids closing. With an empty stomach and a long road behind him he was fatigued and wearied. Should he fall asleep where he sat he knew that he may never awaken.

It was imperative that he found refuge before nightfall. Rising from his cold seat he found that his left leg had gone numb. Limping slowly down the road he rubbed it until life painfully returned.

Some distance from Shanacrane and nearing Kilmichael he encountered the company of his fellow men and women.

By the roadside sat a cart which was drawn by a donkey. The cart was loaded with a variety of apparel. Across a rack that ran from front to rear hung a variety of boots

113

and shoes. Around it gathered a multitude of what could only be described as humiliated spectres. They were standing obediently around the cart as clothing and footwear was thrown into the crowd. Each gathered up what they could catch. Without shame they stripped off their rotting rags and donned the clothing presented to them by their benefactor.

Soon the cart was emptied and taking the reins in his hands their Good Samaritan encouraged the donkey back along the road towards Kilmichael.

What a pageant of man's inhumanity to man these apparitions were. Their bodies were covered in hair as was their faces. Yet their heads were as sparse of hair as that of a corpse.

The cheeks of many were so constricted that their jaw bones were locked within their mouths.

Like zombies, they lurched down the road on their spindly legs.

They spoke little if any, as though dumb.

Seámus watched them depart. Behind them they left sepulchres of the malodorous clothing which they had discarded.

With no food to sustain them they had resorted to eating nettles, cabbage leaves, turnip tops and blackberries, even, ironically, the rotting potatoes.

At the tail end of the spectacle came two more zombies. How else could one describe them. They looked like two puppets who had escaped from their strings. They were trying desperately to support each other.

He looked with disgust and pity at the two revolting breathing abominations.

"Go back! Go back to the grave from hence you came," he mentally screamed at them. Then he prayed to his God, pleading for their welfare.

"Why am I praying for you, you are beyond any help. Why should I try to prolong your agony, you disgusting whelps." These were his mixed sentiments.

They were no more than two corpses that belonged in the graveyard, with the exception that they were breathing. They were entirely naked and their bones were denuded of flesh. In its place was a thin transparent covering of what looked like mutton cloth.

How could these corpses walk on the hard ground? Their feet were divested of skin.

They disgusted him and made him want to vomit.

The smaller of the two seemed to be encouraging the other forward. Were they brother and sister, husband and wife or were they, as he thought, refugees from the grave.

It was impossible to tell their ages. All that could be confirmed was that they were male and female.

As the female encouraged her companion forward she looked at Seámus and smiled.

"Why did this walking pestilence smile at me. Is she showing contempt for what I am thinking?"

He felt threatened by her.

Things from the grave do not smile, nor do they walk.

"Go away, let me awaken from this insufferable nightmare." His mind raced to find a rationalisation.

It was something that he had never encountered even in his worst nightmare. Here was a corpse, her mouth denuded of teeth, smiling at him like the 'Grim Reaper'.

The stricken apparitions stopped momentarily and the female tried to speak.

"Go away, leave me alone, it is not my fault. I am not the guilty party. I cannot help you".

Again his mind raced to find answers, or were they excuses?

Raising her match like hand to her throat she desperately tried again and again to speak. No words came from her parched lips. With a sigh of resignation she lifted her hand and once again encouraging her companion, they moved on.

Here were just two of the victims of the great hunger whose hearts were as stout and strong as that of a fit person. They did not complain of the cold, the hungry nor of their nakedness.

Although abandoned by their God and their fellow men they had each other's company. Would they wait a little longer. Perhaps some charitable soul would give them food 'In God's Name.' What was he thinking of, prolonging their agony? Had he no mercy, no compassion. Wait! for what should they wait?

What would happen when one or the other of the two pillars supporting these corpses collapsed as surely they must. What were their names, names indeed, what did it matter. It was all too late.

He hoped and prayed that they would disintegrate and die, here and now before his eyes. It would be charitable, where was their merciful God?

"Strike them down God, show them your mercy, or is it that you too have abandoned them. Is there not even a Drocsaógal tamhlacht available to them?" He prayed and blasphemed.

Would an animal be left to suffer such pain and misery? He inhaled the foul sweet smelling stench that corrupted the air left behind by these abominable wretches.

"Strike them down now, God. Put these pathetic revolting abominations out of their agony," he demanded as he gripped his slán tightly in his hands.

"If you don't then I will!"

. . What was he doing . . .

He gripped his slán tighter in his sweating palms and made to follow them . . . What was he thinking of?

ELIHU BURRITT PAYS A VISIT
TO SKIBBERREN IN 1847

Among the attenuated apparitions of humanity that thronged this gate of stinted charity, one poor man presented himself under circumstances that even distinguished his case from the rest.He lived several miles from the centre of the town, in one of the rural districts, where he found himself on the eve of perishing with his family of seven small children.

Life was worth the last struggle of nature, and the miserable skeleton of a father had fastened his youngest child to his back, and with four more by his side, had staggered to the door.

The hair upon his face was nearly as long as that on his head. His cheeks had fallen in, and his jaws so distended that he could scarcely articulate a word.

The children's appearance, though common to thousands of the same age in this region in the shadows of death, was indescribable. their paleness was not that of a common sickness. There was no sallow tinge in it. they did not look as if newly raised from the grave and to life before the blood had begun to fill their veins anew; but as if they had been thawed out of ice, in which they had been embedded until their blood had turned to water.

ELIHU BURRITT
SKIBBEREEN
COUNTY CORK

SPRING OF 1847 A.D.

SEÁMUS MEETS AN OLD FRIEND

Seámus was brought back to reality by the rain, the cursed rain that never seemed to stop.

Night was fast approaching and he was still many miles from Macroom. He would seek refuge in the village of Kilmichael for the night.

The rain was now falling steadily, showing little sign of easing. With his head down against the driving wind and rain he wandered aimlessly along the road. He paid little attention as to where he might be. Instinct told him that he must find a dry shakedown for the night or perish in the storm.

At the top of an incline in the road he saw smoke from behind a hillock. The welcoming sight put renewed life into him and he hastened to where the reek was rising .

He was disappointed to see before him, not a cottage, but a scalpeen. It was some four feet in height and built against an old stone wall. Several planks of wood had been placed at an angle to the wall and covered in straw, mud and stones. A hole had been left to allow the smoke to escape.

It mattered little to Seámus what it looked like. He hoped that it would be his salvation and give him shelter from the cold and wet of the night.

He walked briskly up to what he considered to be the entrance and called.

"Can a man of the road come in and share your fire?" There was silence for a moment, then a friendly voice answered.

"Tar isteac" (Come in)

Crawling on all fours he pulled the sacking aside and came face to face with a man sitting crossed legged over a warm fire.

"Thank God I found you, I would have died out there". Seámus made his way to the fire.

"I too was lucky to find this place, I can tell you. By the way my name is Gerry Donneely, make yourself at home."

"My name is Seámus Flynn." Both men shook hands warmly.

"I'd like to offer you some hospitality but this is all there is and that is not mine to give."

Gerry invited him to share the fire.

"You mean there are others staying here?" Seámus wondered as to where he might sleep.

118

"Not that I know of, the place was deserted when I came across it. I found the turf behind the wall here. I expect it belonged to whoever built it."

"If they have not returned by now, then it is doubtful if they ever will."

"Return, return to what? From the state I found it in then whoever lived here has long gone. It looked to me as if it could have been occupied by a family."

"God be good to them wherever they have gone to."

"Amen." Gerry reached up the stem of his pipe to the peak of his cap in respect.

"Tell me, what part of the county have you come from?" Gerry asked.

"Me! I come from Skibbereen. I'm making my way to Macroom searching for work."

"I'm not from that part myself. I come from Kilgarvan in the far county."

Kilgarvan, and where might that be now for the asking?"

"I can tell you that it is as near to Kenmare as is Skibbereen to Drimoleague."

"You have come a fair distance then, looking for work too I suppose."

"You could say so, I used to work in Skibbereen you know. I worked for years for Brigadier Stone. I was his head gardener. Not any more as you can see. No doubt but you know the estate well. Somehow your face seems to be familiar."

"It's a small world, so it is. I don't expect you remember me, now do you.?"

"Is there any reason why I should?" Gerry scratched his head and studied Seámus.

"Don't you remember? You were the man who gave me the two apples when I delivered the cages to the manor. Have I changed so much that you cannot remember me? I'm Seámus Flynn."

"Of course, of course, you're welcome Seámus, I should have remembered, sorry. How is your father? You have a younger brother who is not too good."

"We buried my brother Brendan this year past. The old folk took it real bad."

"Sorry to hear it Seámus. May God give him rest."

"Whatever happened to you, if I'm not intruding?"

"With little income from the estate and most of the workers dispensed with there was no further need for a head gardener. The Brigadier locked up the mansion and took himself and his family back to England. You didn't know that the manor is closed?"

"No, father was no longer welcome there after the incident

119

with the hare."

"I'm for getting my head down and I suggest you do the same."

"That makes two of us, with a good nights sleep and an early start we should come to the roadworks."

Early next morning they rose and placing their sláns on their shoulders took to the road.

They reached the roadworks at about seven o'clock that morning.

The rain had stopped and a cold mist hung along the hedgerows.

They were in luck when they came upon a soup kitchen about to open.

Both men dropped their haversacks on the road and began to laugh. Removing their tin mugs they ran and joined the ever growing queue.

"Our luck is in Seámus my boy." Gerry again laughed. They were grateful as they watched the large cauldron sending it's welcoming aroma to the sky.

There was no rush to be first in the queue. When the lid was removed they shuffled forward and gratefully accepted a ladle of soup and a hunk of dry bread.

When all were fed their benefactors called on the assembly to give thanks to God in a short prayer.

"Who are these people and what are they doing here on the road?" Gerry queried.

"They are Quakers and the most charitable people I know. They do not ask you to change your religion for a bowl of soup." Seámus enlightened him.

The men were called to one side and directed to their place of work on the road. Those without shovels were directed to the side of the road.

Seámus was distressed when he saw women and children dressed in rags, many as near naked as they could be. All were in bare feet sitting by the roadside breaking stones. It was obvious that many were too weak for the work. Blood ran freely from their numbed fingers as they continued with the task. They seemed to be oblivious to pain.

More women formed a long queue on the road. Holding their hands behind their backs each carried a large boulder. These they dropped into the foundation of the road and returned to again repeat the task. They were insensitive to the sharp stones cutting into their bare feet.

"Jesus! Will you look at that." Seámus nudged Gerry as they crossed the road.

"This is what Mother Ireland has come to. Her children are the lowest dregs of humanity." Gerry showing his

120

anger spat on the ground.

Those without shovels were sent to collect the broken stones in iron clad wheeled carts and drag them to where the road was being constructed. Many working on the road were suffering from malnutrition and plague. Yet with dogged determination they worked on as best they could. There were many hungry mouths at home waiting in desperation for their return with the eight pence in wages. This would perhaps keep some of them alive for yet another day.

Those unable to carry on retired or were carried to the hedgerow. They had reached the point of no return. At home in their hovels the children would wait in vain for their return.

Their labour on earth was finished and the only caller to the hovels would be the Grim Reaper.

England had given twenty million pounds towards the emancipation of the slaves in the West Indies without a murmur. She had reluctantly given fifty thousand pounds to save the Irish nation from annihilation and this would have to be repaid.

What a travesty of justice the whole charade was.

The work continued for the next four days without respite. They were thankful that the rains had stopped and the weather took a turn for the better.

On the fifth day they came across a man lying in the hedgerow near to the new road

They could see that he was suffering from the advanced stages of plague and malnutrition. Unable to do any more work he was trying to sell his pick and spade. This wretch had worked on the road without respite for the past four days.

"I need some money for my children, won't you buy these?" he pleaded.

By nightfall he had collapsed and was lying along the hedge still holding on to his precious tools.

Seámus and Gerry having finished their days' toil came and called to the man.

"You will need to find shelter, you could die here." They lifted him to his feet but it was obvious that he could not stand.

"What will we do with him, we just cannot abandon him." Seámus remarked as they placed him gently on the ground.

"Find out where he lives and if it is not too far then we could take him there." This solution was agreed upon.

"Tell us, where do you live?" Seámus slapped him on the face to revive him.

"Will you buy my spade, please?" The man opened his eyes and looked pleadingly at Seámus.
"Where do you live, tell us?" insisted Seámus.
"On the Teerelton Road, on the Teerelton road," he answered twice before once again collapsing.
"The Teerelton Road, where might that be?" He looked questionably at Gerry.
"I wouldn't know, I'll find out."
"Teerelton is it, take the next left you cannot miss it," Gerry was informed.
"How far might it be?"
The guide scratched his chin and gave a rough estimate.
"Well I would guess a good three to four Irish miles depending where you wanted."
"It's about three miles down the next boreen to the left. I suppose he could live this side of the village," Gerry informed Seámus.
"Wherever he lives we cannot leave him here to die." Seámus went seeking transport to carry the man .
"Will you look what I found." He returned pulling a four wheeled wooden dray.
"You'll get us deported if you steal that!" Gerry looked shocked.
"They have all gone to their homes, anyway we will have it back before morning. Sure no one will be any the wiser."
"What are we waiting for then?" They picked up the man and placed him on the cart.
"Here let us not forget these."
Seámus picked up the spade and pick and placed them on the cart beside the man.
They had gone about two miles down the Teerelton Road when they came upon a tumbled cottage. Two of the walls were still standing and a makeshift third wall had been constructed to make it habitable.
"Let us ask if anyone here knows where he lives."
Seámus let go of the shaft of the cart and approached the hovel.
"Is there anyone home?" he called as he entered the dark interior.
"What do you think, Gerry?" he whispered.
Gerry picked up a handful of straw from the floor and wrung it into a long taper. Going to the fire he lit it and holding it above his head surveyed the interior.
On a bed of foul straw in a corner lay three children. Two of the children kept their eyes firmly fixed on the two men. They scarcely blinked at all. The third child was lying on its side motionless.
In a far corner lay an adult in a sleeping position. Several

rats were roaming around the floor without fear. Seámus was about to go and call the adult when a girl with a bucket of water entered the hovel.

Over her skeleton frame she wore a large coatamore. This was her only clothing. Seámus presumed that she had got it the day before from the man with the cart.

"Is that my father outside?" Laying the bucket on the floor she left the hovel.

Both men followed her out and saw her approaching the cart.

"Your father is not too well, we brought him home," Gerry informed her.

"He is dead, why did you bring him here?" she questioned.

"No! he's sick and needs help."

Seámus went to the cart and tried to lift the man.

"The poor soul is dead, Gerry! God be good to him he must have died on the way."

"Leave him on the cart, I will take him to the graveyard."

The girl turned her back and entered the hovel. She seemed indifferent to the death of her father.

The men reeled back in horror when they saw the girl stagger into the light. On her shoulder she carried the emaciated body of a naked woman. Her long skeleton arms embracing the girl as if for the last time. Slowly she approached the cart. Both men stood back in horror and shock. They were unable to comprehend what was happening.

Laying the corpse beside that of her father she began to drag the cart down the road.

"What in God's name are you doing,girl?" Gerry stopped in front of her.

"I'm going to bury my father and mother, that is what I am doing." she told them, showing emotion for the first time.

"Leave it, you show us the way. Seámus, get the spade." Picking up the spade he placed it beside the bodies and took his position beside Gerry. The girl walked slowly in front of the cortege.

Some yards down the road they came to the little graveyard with its ever- welcoming gate.

The girl walked over several graves and came to one surrounded by a railing. At the head stood a large granite Celtic cross. On a banner cut into the stone and running from top to bottom they read "Gone but not Forgotten."

On the base it read 'The Burial Vault of the Carrington Family of Teerelton'. There were several names of past members of the family inscribed on the stone.

Four steps led down to an iron door which was locked

with a large padlock.

"This is our family vault," she told them.

"Are you sure?" Gerry asked. He was doubtful that such an elaborate mausoleum could be their property.

"Yes! This is it, we once owned most of the land between here and Coppeen."

"How can we get into the tomb?" Seámus looked over at Gerry doubting what she was saying.

From the pocket of her coatamore she produced a large key and handed it to Seámus.

Reluctantly the key turned in the lock. Both men took hold of the large ring attached to the door. As they pulled on the ring the door creaked in protest as with a final effort they forced it fully open.

Inside on slate shelves were five large coffins. There were three to the right and two to the left.

"I went to Macroom begging for a coffin for my mother some days ago. How could I bury my own mother without a coffin?" The girls voice echoed around the walls of the vault. It was as if she was apologising for not supplying coffins for her parents.

"How long has your mother been dead then?" Seámus looked across at the mummify corpse.

"I brought her to the vault some days ago but could not turn the key. That is why she has been lying in the shelter," the girl apologised.

"Will it be alright if we place them side by side on one of the empty slabs?" Gerry, anxious to see the bodies interred, interrupted the conversation..

"Do just that, when brighter times come I will get them coffins."

The girl was more concerned with giving her parents a decent burial than for her own welfare.

With the bodies interred they closed and locked the door before returning to the hovel.

They followed the girl into the dark interior and waited as she lit a piece of a candle.

The three children were still in the same position on the straw.

"Are these your brothers?" Seámus approached the filthy straw.

"This is my brother Joseph and this is my sister Mary. The youngest in the corner is Brendan."

Seámus winced when she mentioned the name.

"Don't you think you had better see to him."

"I was waiting for my father to return with some food."

"We have a little food, haven't we Gerry?"

Seámus, without waiting for Gerry's approval removed

124

what food they had from the haversack.
Having shared what they had with the orphans they left
the hovel promising to return in the near future.

THE DEAD DON'T CRY, DO THEY?

'Midnight raves in gloomy anger, hoarse and rough the ice winds blow,
And the bleak face of the darkness wears a streaming veil of snow,
But our hearth is cold and empty, and our little hut is bare,
And, O God, my gentle Eily, lies in famine fever there.
Come father, Oh come quickly with the sacrament and prayer,
My stricken angel's dying, and you have no time to spare,
God look upon my sorrow, Holy saviour dear, I pray
Recall, recall thy dread decree, or take us both away.

(Verse from 'The Evicted Peasant' Lays and legends of Thomond)

They returned the cart to their place of work and again took possession of the scalpeen. It was nearby and offered dry shelter.

The road which led to God knows where was no more than a 'Famine Road'. The only purpose it served was to offer employment to a starving people.

With thoughts on their own survival they had all but forgotten the children over in Teerelton.

Slowly the road progressed and passed Toone bridge.

Catastrophe struck without warning when a halt was called to all road building. What funds there were had been exhausted.

"What can we do. Surely you are not going to let us starve?" The workers gathered around the gigs of the engineers demanding food in return for their labour.

"Come back in the morning and we will have answers for you," they told the angry people.

This seemed to pacify the gathering and they dispersed to their homes without any further disturbances.

Next morning, as the dawn began to creep across a watery Irish sky the people began to assemble on the road.

By midmorning the road was completely blocked with milling crowds all looking for the elusive engineers.

Around noon a platoon of soldiers on horseback arrived. Behind them followed two large drays filled with sacks of corn.

The soldiers stationed their horses between the assembled people and the drays.

"The work on the road has now stopped as all available funds are exhausted," the Captain of the Guard shouted over the heads of the assembly.

126

"We will die of the hunger if we cannot work," a voice called out from the crowd.

He was soon joined by others who began milling forward.

"Keep an orderly line and I will dispense what food I have secured between all the workers," the Captain promised.

The promise of food quelled any sign of revolt.

The Captain looked along the growing line of people waiting patiently for a little grain.

"All these people could not have worked on this road," he told his second in command.

"We don't have enough grain to supply a quarter of them," he was informed by the quartermaster.

"Supply as many as you can, the troops will stand by ready to quell any disturbances," he ordered.

Slowly and orderly the queue moved forward and soon the first dray was emptied of grain. Then the second dray came forward and that too was soon emptied.

"Where is the corn for us, we worked for five days on the road and we got nothing. You gave grain to those who never done a stroke of work, why?" The people became unruly and began fighting with those who had already got a small supply of grain.

"Don't blame us, blame them. There is plenty of grain in the depots," the others shouted as they fought to defend their precious commodity.

In their anger and frustration they picked up stones from the road and began throwing them at the troops.

The soldiers were ordered to unsheath their swords. Then without any warning came the order to charge.

Men, women and children scattered as the horses bore down on them.

The people ran to the safety of the fields and ditches on either side of the road.

The Captain had no wish to add to their misery, yet he was duty bound to disperse the milling angry crowds.

He was in sympathy with their situation and had no intention of adding to their suffering if it could be avoided.

He ordered the troops to be recalled and regrouped on the road.

There was little that the people could do but sit down in the fields and hedges and vent their frustration on the earth. Some banged the ground until their fists bled. Others tore their hair out, many just sat and wept.

For the next two days they remained at the road works hoping and praying. Around the fields, covered in what shelter they could find, were assembled other potential workers. All were waiting and hoping that the agents would return and pay them their wages.

"Come and see what I found," Gerry called to Seámus.
"What is it now?"
Seámus reluctantly followed Gerry over the fence and into the field.
"Look! What do you make of that?"
At the door of a scalpeen, resting on a shelf, was a child. This was nothing new for it was the practice of the evicted to build such shelters. When they went in search of work or food they placed their children on raised platforms near to the door. This they believed would protect them from the rats. Any neighbour passing would look to the welfare of the children. At least if they failed to return then some charitable person would hopefully care for their child.
"It's a child waiting for it's mother to return, so what."
"Don't you see Seámus, there has not been work on the road for some days. This child's mother will not be returning, she must be dead."
As he approached the child Seámus called gently to it. There was no response. He looked deep into the child's eyes and noticed the vacant stare. He called on Gerry to come and look, was the child alive or dead?
"The child is alive, look at its eyes. It must be hungry and thirsty." They looked with pity at the innocent child waiting patiently for his parents who may never return.
"What do you suggest we do? We cannot look after it."
"There's a milch cow in that field over there. One of us should go and get some milk."
"Alright, I'll go, but keep a sharp look out. If the owner sees me he may shoot me." Seámus crept through the gap in the hedge and approached the beast. With his tin mug held in one hand he lay flat on the ground and extracted about a quarter of a pint of milk from the cows udder.
"I got it and it's still warm". He held the can up in triumph.
Letting the nourishing liquid flow into the child's mouth he stroked its throat encouraging it to swallow.
"That's enough for now," Gerry called as the child began to cough.
When the child stopped coughing he again encouraged it to drink. This time there was no response, the milk trickled from the mouth of the child.
Holding the child's head he began to wipe its face.
"Gerry, I think he is dead." He looked again into the child's eyes.
"We can do no more for him, he is now in the hands of his guardian angel," Gerry remarked as he closed the child's eyes.
They placed the child underneath the shelf and pulled

away the supporting timbers. The hovel collapsed, burying the child.

On the third day rumours began to filter through that there was food and work available in Bantry.

The navy, they were told, had landed ample supplies of food. There was surplus food available for all comers. This was a hopeful exaggeration of the true facts. What supplies had been sent were for an isolated community which was on the verge of annihilation.

In the vain hope of obtaining a little sustenance the road was soon thronged with half starving skeletons. There was no hope of any of them ever reaching Bantry. It would take a fit person with adequate supplies and clothing three days to make the journey. But then these were not rational people, their goal was to find enough food to sustain them and their families through another day.

By the time they reached Inchigeelagh their numbers had been decimated. None would reach the Pass of Kelmaneigh on the Bantry road.

Seámus and his companion sat outside the scalpeen making plans for their departure. What purpose could be served waiting for an agent who would never return.

"How are the orphans over at Teerelton coping?" Seámus idly asked.

"Do you know they passed right out of my mind. We could call in and find out how they are doing," Gerry replied.

"Call and see them without a morsel of food to offer them. I could not do that"

"There is plenty of food in the depot at Macroom, I'm sure that they would not miss a few handfuls of grain," Gerry laughed.

"Oh great, All we need to do is go up and ask the English soldiers guarding the place to let us have a sack or two."

"Why bother to ask them, the grain belongs to us."

"You are not thinking of rifling the depot? If we were caught we would be transported. That is if we were not shot first."

There was silence between the two men for a time.

"Oh very well then, we could go and look the place over. Don't forget, if I am caught I'll be deported for certain or worse still hanged," Seámus reminded Gerry.

Next morning found the two men in the town of Macroom. The depot was guarded by one soldier stationed at the main entrance. Going to the rear of the depot they noticed that a smaller door led to a small alleyway. A block and tackle hung above a door on the first floor. Behind the depot were open fields. If they could open the door they could get inside and steal a bag of corn each. They could be long gone across the fields before anyone noticed.

That night Gerry stood lookout at the corner of the alleyway. Seámus crept to where the block and tackle were located. Reaching up he pulled on the rope. The wheel turned and in doing so began to creak.

The noise reverberated around the countryside. Gerry looked down the alleyway on hearing the noise. Then at the sentry lounging lazily against the main door. The soldier made no movement and Gerry signalled to Seámus that all was well.

Seámus put his foot in the eye of the hook and pulled himself up to the door. He was surprised when he found that the doors were not locked. They opened freely when he touched them.

Creeping into the dark interior he dragged a sack of corn to the door and attached it to the hook and let it down slowly.

Gerry, on seeing the sack appear, took a quick look at the sentry who was still lounging against the door. Running down the alleyway he released the sack.

Seámus hauled up the rope and tied a second sack to the hook and let it down.

He slithered down the rope and was soon joined by Gerry. They removed the second sack and returned the rope to the attic door. Hoisting the sacks on their backs they crossed the open fields and left Macroom.

Soon they were on the road to Teerelton and the hovel of the Carrington family.

By early morning they were outside the entrance to the hovel. They were surprised to see that it had collapsed in on itself. Dropping the sacks they went and lifted the fallen timbers. Under the timbers lay the body of the girl. It appeared that her face had collapsed inwards. She was lying in a prone position facing the open doorway. It was as if she was waiting for someone. To all appearances the girl was dead.

Her stomach which two weeks or so ago was thin and sparse of flesh had now burst. The dress she wore had split and was hanging loosely over her back. There was no sign of any bruising and they concluded that she had died of the Ocras.

Her flesh was cold to the touch, they knew that she was long dead. Seámus lifted her hands which were as thin as rushes. They fell back lifeless on to the mud floor when released.

Against the wall in the filthy straw lay the bodies of the three younger children. Two were propped against the dry stone wall in a sitting position. The third, Brendan, lay on his side in the filthy straw. There was no need to confirm but that they were dead. Rats of all shapes and sizes were making a meal of what was left of them. This foul smelling hovel was no longer their sanctuary but their grave.

"How in God's Holy Name can we bury them?" Seámus held his hand to his nostrils and ran from the scene.

He was shocked when he saw Gerry dragging the corpse of the girl into the hovel and laying her down beside the other. As he laid her down the key to the crypt fell from her pocket.

"They won't be needing this any more, will they?" Picking up the key he placed it on the old mantle.

"What do you think you are doing, Gerry?"

Ignoring Seámus he went to the centre of the hovel and pulled away the timbers holding the roof. With a crash the whole building collapsed bringing part of the wall with it.

Pulling a handful of straw he rolled it into a torch and set it alight. Throwing it into the hovel he blessed himself and stood to one side.

What was left of the hovel was soon alight as inside the bodies of the four children were slowly cremated.

"There will be no Drocsaógal Támhlachts for these unfortunates. It is better than letting the rats consume them."

Picking up a length of timber that had escaped the fire he threw it on to the funeral pyre.

Seámus stood with his rosary in his hands and prayed as he watched the sparks reach into the sky.

"Come on, if you're ready. They don't need praying for." Gerry stood some distance away with a bag of corn on his shoulder.

Blessing himself, he returned his rosary to his pocket and, picking up the other bag of corn, joined his friend on the road to Skibbereen.

THE FIELDS OF ATHENRY

By the lonely prison wall,
I heard a young girl calling,
Michael they have taken you away,
For you stole Trevelyn's corn,
So the young might see the morning;
Now a prison ship lies waiting in the bay.

Low lie the fields of Athenry,
Where we once watched the small free birds fly.
Our love was on the wing, we had dreams and songs to sing,
It's so lonely round the fields of Athenry.

By a lonely prison wall,
I heard a young man calling,
Nothing matters, Mary when you're free,
Against the famine and the crown
I rebelled, they ran me down,
Now you must raise our child with dignity.

Low lie the fields of Athenry,
Where once we watched the small free birds fly,
Our love was on the wing, we had dreams and songs to sing,
It's so lonely round the fields of Athenry.

By a lonely harbour wall,
She watched the last star falling,
As the prison ship sailed out against the sky,
Now she'll wait and hope and pray,
For her love in Botany bay,
It's so lonely round the fields of Athenry

Low lie the fields of Athenry,
Where once we watched the small free birds fly,
Our love was on the wing, we had dreams and songs to sing,
It's so lonely round the fields of Athenry.

Trad

THE FELONS ARE APPREHENDED

They were pleased and relieved when they saw the outskirts of Skibbereen looming in the distance. Their relief was to be short lived. Outside the village they were taken by surprise by a detachment of mounted Redcoats. Escape was out of the question.
"What do we do now?" Seámus nudged Gerry as the two adversaries came face to face.
"Tell them that we got the corn in payment for working on the road," he suggested.
"What have we here?" The sergeant in charge of the platoon dismounted and approached them.
"We are on our way home to Skibbereen, we have done nothing wrong," Seámus defended himself.
"Now who said that you done have anything wrong?" The sergeant looked around at his troop and laughed.
"Alright drop the sacks and let's look inside." Two more troopers dismounted and joined their sergeant, their carbines cocked and at the ready. Placing the sacks upright on the road Seámus and Gerry undone the string and opened the sacks.
"Corn, I thought so. You are Gombeen men, so you are," the sergeant sneered.
"Out to fleece your own people. Selling them corn at a huge profit. People like you are the scum of the earth."
"You're wrong, we live in Skibbereen and were given the corn in payment for our work on the famine road," Gerry protested.
"Where was this road being built then?" another soldier asked.
"Over by Kilmichael on the Macroom road".
"That road was abandoned ten days ago. You had best come with us." They were soon manacled and tied behind one of the horses.
The corn was placed pannier style across one of the mounts.
The villagers came to their doors on hearing the troops in the street. They were shocked when they saw Seámus Flynn and Gerry Donneely being dragged behind a horse.
The news soon spread throughout the village that Seámus Flynn and Gerry Donneely had been arrested for stealing corn.
They were held in the local barracks pending further inquiries as to where the corn came from.

Seámus knew that his parents would do all in their power to visit him.

That evening, as he predicted, his parents arrived at the compound.

"Seámus, why in God's name did you do it?" his mother cried.

"We did it hoping that we could save a family of orphans, but they were dead when we got there."

Seámus explained how they had tried to save the orphans of Teerelton.

"I understand son, but why! Why you?" she sobbed.

"I know what will become of us father, it is a foregone conclusion". He was resigned to his fate.

There was little that his father could say for he knew that the English would send them to Van Deemens land or Australia.

Within a few days the news came back that the two sacks had been stolen from the depot in Macroom.

"Don't give up hope son, God is good and merciful," his father encouraged his son on hearing the damning news.

That afternoon they were taken from the barracks and transported to Cork jail to await their fate.

Tom and Bridget rose early on the following Monday morning. and prepared for the long journey to Cork city jail. Before leaving they attended early morning mass and offered it up for the release of their son and his friend.

On their arrival at the court they joined the relatives and friends of the other felons awaiting trial and sat in the gallery.

"All rise". The court usher banged on the floor with a long staff. He rang a hand bell to summons the court to order.

The presiding judge and his cortege in wigs and gowns entered through a back door and took their seats.

When all were settled in their places the judge nodded to the usher.

"Bring up the prisoners," the usher shouted, his voice booming around the court room.

The spectators gasped when they saw the prisoners enter the dock. Their hands and feet were manacled and at least a dozen Redcoats stood guard over them.

"Silence in the court," the usher demanded.

The first of the prisoners was dragged to the front of the bench to face the judge.

"How does the prisoner plead?" the clerk demanded.

The bewildered man looked at the judge and then at the gallery.

"Swear the plea at once," the clerk again demanded.

"I n...n..never done anything" stuttered the prisoner.

134

"Just answer yes or no. Keep your excuses for later. This goes for all of you prisoners," the judge added as an afterthought as he shuffled uncomfortably in his seat.
"Take that as a not guilty plea," he advised the clerk.
Seámus tried when his turn came to justify his reason for stealing the corn but without success.
"Just answer "Yes" or "No" to the questions from my learned friend," the judge warned him.
"You claim that you stole the corn to feed the poor, like Robin Hood, no doubt," the judge sneered.
"I did sir," Seámus pleaded.
"If these so called starving orphans were living in Teerelton what were you doing in Skibbereen with the corn?"
Seámus clenched the spiked iron rail of the dock. Bowing his head he remained silent.
The judge, tiring of the cases decided that he had heard enough. He called an end to the whole proceedings. He would sum up the cases on the evidence presented.
"I have given each of you ample time to put your defence before this just court. From the outset you have, all of you, proven yourselves to be well rehearsed liars and perjurers. This is not the first time that many of you have been before the court. You were given the benefit of the doubt by a merciful court then. I have no intention of going down that path. I find you all equally guilty and responsible for your actions.
You will all be transported to the penal colony at Her Majesty's prison at Bendigo on the outskirts of Melbourne in Australia. There you will each serve a period of three years hard labour. Take the felons down".
Many of the prisoners were found guilty of cattle stealing. Others were found guilty of breaking curfew under the Insurrection Act. A large number were sentenced to transportation for no greater a crime than being absent from their homes during the hours of curfew. Others were sentenced for persistently speaking the 'IRISH'. Many of the married prisoners with families pleaded for their wives and families to be allowed to accompany them. The magistrates, many of whom were landlords, were only to willing to meet this request. This was a golden opportunity to rid their estates of unwanted starving Irish.
Seámus, a youth not yet sixteen years of age looked stunned at the court and shook his head.
"You with the curly hair."
The judge pointed his finger at Seámus.
Seámus stopped in his stride and in doing so pulled the

other felons to an abrupt halt with the draw chain.

"Me, your honour?"

"Yes you! What do you mean by shaking your head and looking with contempt at me". The judge wagged his finger at Seámus and adjusted his wig.

"Nothing your honour." Seámus replied.

"Nothing! Nothing! For your contempt you will serve a further year, do you hear me. Take them out of my sight!"

His mother, too upset by the harsh verdict sat sobbing, her head sunk deep in her hands.

His father comforted her, but could offer little else. The prisoners were escorted to the cells below the court. From there they would be taken and incarcerated in Cork jail awaiting transportation to the penal colonies of Australia. Not one of the prisoners had been found innocent.

His mother came to visit him in prison and give him what support and comfort she could. She also brought some of his favourite food. On meeting they fell into each others arms sobbing, finding a little comfort in each other.

"It was not for ourselves we did it. We tried to help them and look what happened, they are dead and we are convicts," he cried.

What comfort could she offer but a mothers prayers and tears.

A week later his family came again to see him. They were shocked to hear that he was about to be transported on one of Her Majesty's prison ships to the penal colony. This would be the last time they would see him.

His mother was determined that she would fight for the release of her son. They would not transport him like a common slave, not if she could help it!

"Tom! Oh Tom, there must be something that we can do. Can you not go again and speak to the court?"

"I'll go and speak to them. They will understand that Seámus is a good boy. I'll let the clerk know that we wish to appeal." Father and mother fell into each others arms crying.

That afternoon he was granted an audience with the Chief Clerk to the court. Once again he pleaded for leniency for his son. After all he was an only child. The clerk listened in silence to Tom's plea. Much as they would like to commute the sentence it was out of their hands. All their pleas were rebuffed by platitudes. They could not intercede, Seámus would have to serve his sentence.

Despondent, Tom returned with the sad news, there would be no appeal from the sentence. They would now have to accept that there was nothing else they could do on behalf of their son.

They would now make the final journey to Cork and bid him farewell. This would be the last time that they would see their son on God's earth.

His mother made a small hamper of food to sustain them on their long journey to Queenstown.

At the first halting station Bridget opened the hamper and invited her husband to partake of the food.

"Bridget, you are not eating."

Tom passed the basket to his wife.

"Sorry Tom, I'm not the least bit hungry, but you eat up."

Putting the basket to one side she again burst into tears.

Tom, unable to eat, returned the food to the basket and closed the lid.

"Try and not worry so. I'll ask the coachman to let you have a corner seat. You should try and rest".

She was provided with a makeshift bed in the corner of the coach. Yet try as she may she found sleep denied her. Her thoughts were with her son and his predicament.

As dawn gave way to the morning sun, the mist began to rise from the surrounding countryside. The sun rose higher into the sky and the birds began to vacate their roosts.

This was the end of the line. Sea birds flew noisily around the coach begging for scraps of food. Slowly the coach rumbled on, nearer and nearer to the port.

She was awakened by the grating of iron wheels on cobbled stones. Then she heard the constant chatter of voices outside the coach.

Wearily she opened her eyes and looked around her. The coach had stopped and was empty of passengers. Looking out the window she noted too that the horses were gone. The coach was parked in a siding next to other coaches.

She saw her husband in conversation with a group of Redcoats. Looking back he saw her and waved his assurance. Leaving them he retraced his steps and returned to the coach.

"They are not here yet, I thought it best to let you sleep for a time." He held on to the brass handle of the coach. She noticed the tension in the whites of his knuckles as he gripped the handle.

"I must have dozed off Tom. Did you say that they have not yet arrived? I presume you mean our Seámus."

"There's time yet love, why don't you stay in the coach and try to get some sleep."

"Sleep, rest, how can I rest. My youngest lies buried in the clay of Skibbereen and now my only remaining son is about to be taken from me. An innocent child about to be transported to the ends of the Earth and we can do nothing".

She threw the blanket covering her feet to one side and alighted from the coach. The chill breeze coming off the sea forced her to tighten her shawl around her.

"Is that the prison ship?" She nodded towards a ship preparing to sail on the tide.

Wearily she sat on one of the bollards holding the ship's ropes. She held the rope tight as if trying to prevent the ship from taking her son away. She watched the seagulls walking and squabbling along the sea wall. Their raucous calling and squawking irritating her ears.

Tom came forward and placed his hand on her shoulder. She reached out and, taking his hand in hers, she half smiled.

Early that same morning Seámus was ordered from his hard bunk in Cork city jail. After a meagre meal of watery gruel he was marched to the courtyard and lined up with the other felons about to be transported.

"Bring out the chains, bring out the chains." The order was relayed across the compound and on into the jail itself.

Seámus found himself chained to five other prisoners. The chains were attached to their hands and coupled to their feet. A draw chain ran through the eye of each individual chain securing the prisoners together. Long drays drawn by heavy Shire horses were brought into the courtyard and the felons lined up behind them.

Unable to climb on to the drays owing to the restriction of the chains they were manually hauled on board and seated on benches secured to the floor. At each end of the dray were iron rings bolted to the floor. The draw chain was passed through the rings and locked securely.

There were twelve convicts allocated to each dray, in two rows of six facing each other.

When all the convicts were stowed on board the convoy left the jail escorted by a heavily armed military escort.

On hearing the noise of the drays, the shouting and running of feet, Bridget let go of her husband's hand and ran with the crowd. She stopped as she saw the sad cortege coming down the quay.

She heard the defiant singing of the Felons. Although her heart was heavy she was proud. They would not be transported like sullen slaves. These were Fenians and the poignant ballad that they sang enshrined the tragic facts of Irish life during that time. She saw the tears in their eyes as they sang. A lump came into her throat as she too was caught up in the tumult.

138

THE OULD FENIAN GUN

It hung above the kitchen fire,
Its barrel long and brown,
And one day, with a boy's desire
I climbed to take it down.
My father's eyes with anger flashed,
He cried; "What have you done?
I wished you'd left it where it hung-
That's my old Fenian gun.

I fondled it with love and pride;
I looked it o'er and o'er,
I placed it on my shoulder
And marched across the floor.
My father's anguish softened,
And he shared my boyish fun-
"Ah well", He said," 'Tis in your breed,
Like that ould Fenian gun".

"I remember '67 well",
He said, "When lads like me
All thought we'd strike another blow
To set ould Ireland free.
But broken were our golden hopes;
I was long months on the run;
But it did good work for Ireland then-
That brown ould Fenian gun.

"I was down there in Killmallock-
'Twas the hottest fight of all-
And you see"-he bared his arm-
"There's still the mark if a ball.
I hope the young lads growing now
Will hold the ground we won,
And not disgrace the cause in which
I held a Fenian gun".

I placed it o'er the fire once more;
I heard my father sigh;
I knew his thoughts were turning back
On days now long gone by.
And then I vowed within my heart;
"I'll be my fathers son,
And if Ireland ever wants my aid
I'll hold a Fenian gun.

That's years ago: I've grown a man
And weathered many a gale.
The long, long years was spent inside,
A gloomy English jail.
I've done my part, I'll do it still,
Until the fight is won;
When Ireland's free, we'll bless the men
Who held a Fenian gun.

Phil O'Neill

THE PRISON SHIP SAILS

Two armed Redcoats sat on the front seat, behind sat the ragged felons in their chains. On a high seat to the rear sat two more Redcoats. A platoon of mounted soldiers followed behind. They ignored the defiant singing of the Felons. They could suffer them a little longer, for soon they would be rid of them.

With her hands held open wide she called through her tears for her son. This would be her last chance to hold him in her arms

She ran from dray to dray seeking her son.

"Seámus, Mo cúsla: it's me, your mother, where are you son?" There were so many mothers, fathers, brothers, sisters, wives and sweethearts calling to their loved ones that it was impossible to distinguish one from the other. Prisoners strained at their chains hoping to see a friendly face for the last time. The convoy trailed back some distance from the quayside, then the prisoners began calling out. Somewhere in the milling crowd they hoped to see a loved one for the last time.

Seámus got caught up in the euphoria and he too began to call for his mother.

"I'm here Ma, It's me, Seámus" he cried out. He had not heard his mother calling but he knew that she would be there to comfort him.

His father followed close behind, stopping every few minutes he cupped his hands and called.

The drays were now level with the running people. Many on seeing their loved ones tried to board the drays but were savagely beaten back by mounted soldiers. This savagery did not in any way deter their determination. Like an unstoppable flood they succeeded in mounting the drays. It did not matter how often they were barbarically beaten off, they swarmed back on again. They were determined to hold on to their loved ones for as long as they possible could. Eventually the officer, seeing that he was accomplishing little but crass hardship on the families, called off his soldiers and left the families to say their final farewells.

She had not found her son on the first two drays. Anxiously she waited for the third dray to enter the compound. The gates were blocked with milling crowds and mounted soldiers were called forward to clear the entrance.

Seámus kept calling for his mother and tried to look behind him. Every time he moved the chains bit deeper. Not alone did they inflict severe wounding to him but also to the other prisoners on the dray. They had been designed to cause as much suffering as possible. His parents now stood inside the gates and waited for the final dray to come through.

"Look love, it's him. It's our Seámus." His father pointed as the third dray swept past at a steady pace.

"Seámus! Seámus. It's us!" His mother hung on to the side of the dray and tried to keep pace with the horses. Finally, with the help of her husband she was aboard and holding tightly to her son.

The dray moved on to the quayside and stopped. Prisoners were already lined up along the quay. The chains were removed from the floor of the dray and the rag tag prisoners lined up with the others.

"Seámus, my son, what have they done to you?"

His father came forward and looked with pity at his son. Seámus had been beaten, his face was badly cut and swollen. There was bruising all over his body.

He stood before them bewildered, his head bowed in submission.

As mother, father and son embraced, the chains holding him in bondage clattered and rattled. He was no longer their son, he was a convict, a felon, the property of Her Majesty's Government.

He was oblivious to the pain raking his sore body as his parents hugged him tightly.

The soldiers stood back and let the families have their last moments together. For a brief spell time stood still on the quayside at Queenstown. All around families wept, kissed and hugged each other. This would be their final farewell for they would never meet again. The length of the sentence mattered little, for never had anyone returned from the penal colonies. All too soon the soldiers called on the families to disperse and began rounding up their prisoners.

His father handed him a bag containing some clean clothing and a little bundle of food. His mother took rosary beads from around her neck. Kissing the cross she placed it around her sons neck.

"These belonged to your grandmother son, never let them out of your sight. Remember, pray always for us as we'll be praying for you."

"You'll be back home in next to no time son, be brave, they will realise their mistake. We will continue the fight to prove your innocence." His father shook hands with his son, then emotionally he hugged him to his breast.

With members of the other families, his mother and father walked by his side to the gangway. Many were still singing patriotic songs in a insolent manner. The soldiers made no effort to stop this last show of defiance against the British Crown.

At the gangway the families were pushed to one side as the prisoners were shuffled on to the deck and lined up. Seámus was in the front row and called down to his parents.

"I'll be back, don't fret. They cannot hold me in chains forever. I love you all. God save Ireland!" This cry echoed all along the quayside as the prisoners and families shouted in defiance "God save Ireland!"

His mother procured a vantage view from the top of one of the bollards and waved to her son. With the ship now ready to sail the prisoners were marched below decks. She watched as her son waved and waved until he disappeared from view.

A stevedore ordered her from the bollard. He was about to release the ropes holding the ship to the quayside.

With her sails set the little ship slowly moved out into the Atlantic swell. His mother watched as the ropes snaked across the quay and over the sea wall, only to reappear on the deck of the ship where they were rolled into coils by the deck hands. With its broad arrow on the main sail there would be no mistake, this was a prison ship.

She sat on the bollard and watched as the ship slowly dipped below the horizon and out of view. Tom came and sat beside his wife as they both looked out into the empty vastness of ocean.

She looked up into the night sky at the myriad of twinkling stars. She again prayed, and as she finished she saw a star shoot across the vast emptiness of ocean.

"Did you see that, Tom. A good omen if ever I saw one."

"Seámus is a strong boy, we will soon be united again. It's only for three years. God is good, it will soon pass." He tried to comfort his wife.

"Four years Tom, sure it may as well be four hundred. We will never see our Seámus on God's earth again." She was inconsolable in her grief as she corrected her husband.

"This is what they call British justice love. "

"May the Curse of Christ fall on England and all her unjust laws!"

Mother and father fell into each others' arms and cried uncontrollably.

The families of the prisoners moved closer to the quay as

143

if trying to reach out to their loved ones. Their crying and lamenting stopped when they heard the voices of their loved ones singing defiantly from the bowels of the prison ship. They may perish on the coffin ship, as the wild winds howled over them. They may be buried in a pauper's grave in a distant land unblessed by their mother's hand. Yet their spirits would return to claim their rights to the land that bore them.

The little ship sailed away from its native shore, the defiant singing slowly fading in its wake.

Tom and Bridget left the bollard and joined their song, then, as one, knelt on the ground and began to recite the rosary.

FELONS OF OUR LAND

Fill up once more, we'll drink a toast
To comrades far away;
No nation on this earth can boast
Of braver hearts than they.
And though they sleep in dungeons deep,
Or flee, outlawed and banned,
We love them yet, we can't forget
The felons of our land.

In boyhood's bloom and manhood's pride,
Foredoomed by alien laws
Some on the scaffold proudly died
For holy Ireland's cause.
And brother's, say, shall we to day,
Unmoved like cowards stand,
While traitors shame, greater foes defame
The Felons of our land.

Some in the convict's dreary cell
Have found a living tomb,
And some unseen, unfriendly fell
Within the dungeon's gloom.
Yet, what care we, although it be
Trod by a ruffian band-
God bless the clay where lay to day
The felons of our land.

Let cowards mock and tyrants frown,
Ah! little do we care!
A felons cap's our noblest crown
An Irish head can wear.
And every Gael in Innisfail
Who scorns the serf's vile brand,
From Lee to Boyne, would gladly join
The felons of our land.

Arthur M. Forrester

DISASTER AT SEA

Below decks in the bowels of the evil smelling ship Seámus listened in numbed silence. He heard the ropes creak as they strained and stretched. He felt the ship shudder and rock and he heard the muffled voices of the people calling. Somewhere out there were his parents, standing watching and praying as he was carried away from his native shore.

He listened for a moment as the felons once again broke into spontaneous and defiant singing. Caught up in the euphoria of the singing he dried his tears and joined in the chorus.

Again he began to cry. The heavy chains holding him in bondage to the other prisoners clanked whenever he raised his hand to wipe away a tear. Some of the older prisoners tried to offer him a little comfort. Exhausted from the trauma he rolled himself into as tight a ball as he could and succumbed to sleep.

He was awakened by the rolling of the ship and the clanking of chains. He saw the light from a whale oil lamp as it bobbed along the deck. Soldiers were coming and removing the manacles from the prisoners. Several oil lamps were being hung along the length of the deck. Wooden buckets were placed at intervals. These they were told were their latrines. There would be no washing facilities. Water was for drinking only and would be available at midday.

With their manacles removed they went seeking their companions.

Seámus and Gerry found each other and were to become companions throughout the long journey. They were soon to learn the harsh discipline of a prison ship.

As the ship sailed further into the Atlantic Ocean it was buffeted by a storm. Several of the prisoners were injured. Some died and were buried at sea, their bodies dumped overboard. There was no surgeon and no medical provisions on board.

Daily the hold was opened and the prisoners were allowed out on deck to slop out. On deck they were allowed one ladle of water each from a barrel secured to the mast with ropes.

Prisoners who disobeyed the rules were tied to the ships canon. The ships company and the prisoners were assembled on deck to watch the Captain's punishment. A block of wood was rammed into the prisoners mouth to prevent him biting his tongue. A military drummer played a tattoo on a side drum as the quartermaster called out each stroke. The Cat-O-Nine Tails left long bloodied weals on the exposed back of the prisoner. To add to his discomfort salt water was thrown over his wounds and he was then left tied to the gun for hours at a stretch. There were many who did not survive this savage punishment.

Five weeks out from Cork supplies were running low. The decision was made that rations to the prisoners would be cut. This would conserve stocks until they reached the relief ship. By now eleven of the prisoners had died and many more were in a serious condition. The captain worried that if he did not reach a supply ship soon then he would lose more of his prisoners. He was also concerned that the prisoners might become mutinous and take command of his ship. As a precaution he ordered that they be manacled individually.

Resentment was now running high. The crew were stealing part of the meagre rations destined for the prisoners.

Complaints to the Captain and his officers fell on deaf ears. He was confident that he had the prisoners securely under control. With the situation so volatile he had no wish for any conflict with the members of the crew.

He would be accountable for the prisoners and should he lose too many then he would have to answer to the governor of the colony on his arrival. The little ship struggled on past Port Nolleth. Soon they would be within sight of Cape Town. The crew would expect to be allowed ashore for a short respite.

The weather was calm and the captain consulted with his officers as to whether they should seek fresh supplies at Cape Town or press on to Prince Edward Island. There they were to rendezvous with a frigate of the line.

It was decided after an elongated meeting that they would press on. The weather was in their favour and they had ample supplies to last if all went well. It was a gamble that they felt worth taking. They would lose precious sailing time berthing at Cape Town. In order to appease his restless crew the Captain informed them that they had to meet the deadline. Their fresh supplies were waiting at Prince Edward Island. From there it would be easy sailing to Australia where the crew would be given four weeks shore leave before the return journey to England.

This promise secured the complete loyalty of the unsettled

crew, much to the relief of the Captain and his officers.

The ship sailed further down the coast and the lookout watched as the flat top of Table Mountain slowly faded away into the sunset. There would be no turning back to Cape Town now.

As the ship entered the waters of Good Hope a swell was beginning to show signs of foul weather ahead. White horses were beginning to appear in ever greater numbers in the heaving ocean.

"Batten down the hatches!"

The order rang out. Soldiers went below decks and removed the chains from the prisoners and instructed them to lash themselves to any available upright.

"It's the 'Roaring Forties', Heaven protect us," the prisoners shouted.

They had heard stories of the treacherous waters around the Southern coast of Africa. The stories they had heard were about to be experienced as the ship began to rise and plunge. Waves, some in excess of thirty feet, threatened to swallow up the little ship but still she struggled on. The canon was torn from its moorings and crashed across the deck causing damage to the superstructure. It broke through the guard rail and was catapulted through the air before plunging into the torrent. The ship rose high above the waves and seemed to be suspended in space before it was again swallowed deep beneath the boiling ocean only to be vomited back to the surface.

Many of the crew members and soldiers were washed overboard as they tried to remove dangerous cargo from the decks. The main mast collapsed and hung precariously over the starboard side of the ship threatening to capsize her. Frantic efforts were made to cut the mast free with hatchets and saws. They finally succeeded in jettisoning it over the side. Two soldiers were lost overboard in the process.

The ship was now taking water at an alarming rate. The pump crews were exhausted and unable to continue. Prisoners were pressed forward to take their places with little success. The pumps were unable to cope with the volume of water and the ship was in imminent danger of sinking.

As the ship was about to be dragged under, the order was given to abandon ship. Longboats were dragged to the leeward side and lashed fore and aft. Guide ropes were tied securely to stanchions. Using the ropes to support them, the crew and soldiers made their escape to the longboats, taking their muskets and supplies with them.

When the boats were filled to capacity the Captain,

carrying the ships papers and a sextant came on deck and took his place in the last boat and gave the order for the ropes to be cut. The prisoners were to be abandoned to their fate. They would have to take their chances with the elements and their God.

Realising they were being abandoned they tried to rush the boats. There was pandemonium on board as the soldiers were ordered to open fire. The prisoners fled as volley after volley of ball shot raked the deck. There was nothing that they could do. They watched helpless as the long boats moved further away from the endangered ship. "Murderers! Murderers!", they shouted after the rapidly departing boats.

They retreated below decks and organised themselves into groups. Some returned to man the pumps, others to jettison the cargo in order to lighten the ship.

All their efforts seemed to be in vain as the ship took in more and more water. Their God and the Ocean would now decide their fate.

The lower decks were now awash and shoulder high in water. Several of the prisoners had died from whiplash and other accidents. Their bodies were left floating in the murky water. Two prisoners had been decapitated when trapped between flotsam.

Seámus saw Gerry trying to move a heavy packing case to the port side of the ship.

"Hold on there Gerry, I'll come and give you a hand" he shouted above the storm.

Gerry did not hear him and continued to battle with the case as Seámus tried to reach him.

Suddenly the ship lurched from port to starboard.

He watched in horror as Gerry, now tangled up in ropes, was dragged across the deck before being catapulted over the side and into the bottomless ocean.

"Gerry, where are you?" Cupping his hands he shouted as he looked into the boiling foam.

There was no sign of Gerry nor of the large packing case. He knew that both had been carried to the bottom of the sea.

With Gerry gone he would have to look to his own survival.

The little ship had no intention of surrendering to the waves and bravely battled on. Time and time again it was hit on both starboard and port side by waves that submerged her. Shaking herself like a shaggy dog leaving a river she came to the surface time and time again and battled on. No mattered how often she was reluctantly dragged beneath the waves she always returned to a steady keel.

By now the prisoners were totally exhausted and tied themselves to whatever supports they could find above the waterline.

As they slept the little ship bravely battled on alone against the elements. She was steering herself by guess and by God. Slowly the ship picked up the current of the Southern Ocean and steered herself out of the storm. The waves were now receding and some prisoners claimed that it was the weight of the water inside the ship that was keeping it afloat.

Others claimed that it was in answer to their prayers and that it was their God that had protected them. Little credit was given to the brave little ship and the craftsmen who built her. The prisoners stayed below decks as the ship, although tossing like a cork, continued to fight on, helped by the Southern Ocean current.

Seámus wakened to an eerie silence, the storm had gone. There was only a slight movement of the ship as her keel slapped gently in a calm ocean.

"We're saved, saved," Seámus undid his rope and dashed from pillar to pillar awakening his fellow prisoners. God had been good to them.

Once on deck they assessed the damage. How that little ship stayed afloat was indeed a miracle. The bridge was gone and where the masts had been there were but gaping holes. Of the crew there was no sign, they were now in a vast ocean of unknown waters. Not one aboard knew how to navigate a ship.

"What do we do now?" Seámus looked around at the faces of the prisoners.

"We must bury our dead and salvage what we can in order to survive," came the answer.

With the dead disposed of they set about making the ship secure. The pumps were once again in action clearing the holds. Slowly the ship took on some semblance of organisation. They searched the ship's galley and stores for food and water without success. The crew had taken whatever supplies there were with them.

Below decks they broke open the clothing store and kitted themselves out in warm clothing. Their sparse prison garb they discarded into the sea.

There were two rockite prisoners on board and they seemed to take command of the ship and its ragtag crew. Canvas sails were set out on deck to catch whatever rain might fall.

Makeshift fishing nets were assembled and hung over the sides. A beacon was set in place at the prow of the ship.

150

Should they see a passing ship or an island then they would light it.

Slowly the ship was organised and those too ill to help were made comfortable below decks. They sweltered in the heat by day and froze by night. What fish were caught they ate them raw. They were lucky, if one could call it luck, that there was a heavy fall of rain one afternoon and they were able to save the water in casks. A constant vigil was kept on deck. They had no idea as to where they were or where they were going.

They sang the songs of old Ireland and told sean scéals to keep their spirits high. They accepted it as an act of God when one of their comrades died. They were strong in their faith that most, if not all of them, would survive the ordeal. Had not God in his mercy saved them from drowning at sea? He would not desert them now.

After eight days and nights drifting in the empty ocean many were now delirious and covered in open sores. As their numbers dwindled so did their hope. Those who were left could not expect to last much longer. Their optimism soon turned to pessimism as they watched their numbers falling.

Their faith in God was shattered, they believed that he had abandoned them. They would never be saved.

Despondent, they abandoned their previous plans for survival. Having made their peace with God they settled down to await their doom.

In the afternoon of the ninth day Seámus thought he heard voices calling to them from above decks.

"Ahoy there, ahoy!" Seámus lifted his head from his hard bunk and listened.

"Ahoy there, anyone on board?". Yes! there was someone calling to them.

Slowly he dragged his body from the bunk and crawled out into the sunshine. His eyes hurt and his mouth cracked as he tried to answer. He fell over two dead bodies and crashed to the deck. Rising he shaded his eyes and saw a ship to starboard. He fell to his knees too weak to walk and crawled along the deck. Raising his hand he waved weakly before collapsing . Others having heard the commotion were now making their way up from the holds. Grappling hooks were slung across the deck and both ships were pulled close together.

The Captain of the rescue ship ordered the crew to stand by but not to board the ship. There may be plague on board. The occupants would have to be checked over by the ship's surgeon.

Finally it was confirmed that there was no plague on

board. It was safe for the rescue party to board the ship.
"Good God, who are you and where did you come from?"
Sailors ran to help the demented and starving prisoners.
"Where is your Captain, and what of the prisoners?"
Seámus was asked as he lay on a stretcher on deck.
"Was there a mutiny?" The captain continued asking
questions.
"These men are dehydrated, there is little use in
questioning them yet, I doubt if they could answer you,"
the surgeon told him.
Slowly the prisoners were removed to the frigate and the
search of the ship began.
The captain was convinced that there had been a mutiny
on board and that the prisoners had escaped. The dead
were taken on deck and covered in the Union Flag. The
Union Flag was also hoisted on the stern of the ship. With
a final salute to the dead and the flag the boarding party
left the ship.
The frigate moved some nautical miles away from the
little ship. Then came the order for the ships crew to
assemble on deck. A general salute to the brave little ship
and to her dead was called for. A lone marine took his
place on the prow of the frigate and sounded the last post.
"Open Fire!" The Captain raised his sword and saluted as
the last notes died away. The guns of the frigate roared.
The little ship shuddered and splintered. The crew
watched as the little ship sailed on alone and defiant.
Once again the order rang out, 'Open Fire!'.
As the shells tore her asunder the little ship capitulated
and sank beneath the waves. Her bow came to the surface
in final salute before she sank to the bottom of the Indian
Ocean.
Next day Seámus, having recovered somewhat, was
brought before the Captain and his officers. He was
questioned as to what happened on board the ship. He
related that the crew and the Captain had abandoned the
ship and that all those rescued were Irish Felons.
His incredible story was not believed. Here was an Irish
felon standing before a Captain of her Britannic Majesty
and having the audacity to inform him that a fellow
officer of Her Majesty's Fleet had deserted his ship. Such
conduct was opprobrious. It was unthinkable that an
English Captain would ever desert his ship. He would
rather go down with it in honour. He would not allow his
prisoners and his ship to face certain death. Cowardice
was unknown in Her Britannic Majesty's fleet. This was
a scurrilous attack on the character of the Captain and an
affront to the Royal Navy. Seámus must be lying to order

to save himself and his fellow convicts from a mandatory death sentence.

Several other prisoners were interrogated before it became apparent that they were telling the truth.

As the Captain had heard nothing of the fate of the crew he presumed that they had drowned. This was most unlikely, as they were in several longboats. Some if not all must have landed at some remote port in South Africa and had not as yet been rescued.

Convinced by the prisoners' testimony as to what took place he was embarrassed. He had saluted the Irish Fenian dead and given them a full naval burial at sea. To his further chagrin he had dressed them in the uniform of Her Majesty's sailors. There was little that he could do until he returned to Prince Edward Island. What happened to the crew was no longer his responsibility. He would despatch his report to the Admiralty in London. He would also request that a ship be sent to rendezvous with them to collect the prisoners for transportation to Australia in accordance with the law.

He instructed his surgeon to look after the welfare of the prisoners. He would ensure that they were fit and well by the time the relief ship arrived.

The frigate returned to her station at Prince Edward Island. They were instructed to remain there and guard the prisoners until a ship could be despatched to collect them. There was a ship sailing light from Melbourne that was due within the week. It would take them to their destination.

During the following week they were well treated. By the time the ship arrived from Melbourne all the prisoners had recovered sufficiently to walk on board. The first priority was to strip them of their naval uniforms in exchange for prison clothing.

There were a lot of fond farewells exchanged between the prisoners and their jailers from the frigate.

BENDIGO PENAL COLONY

The prison ship reached Melbourne on the morning tide. The prisoners were marched from the ship and lined up on the quay. Six prisoners were detailed to each group. "Bring out the chains!" Once again they were manacled by their hands and feet. The long running chain was knitted into the rings holding their handcuffs. With the felons duly secured they were marched to the waiting drays. They knew the drill and obediently climbed onto the drays. They sat on the hard benches contemplating their fate. The drays and their compliment of soldiers moved through the city. Some onlookers called to them wishing them luck.

"I'm from the Queens county, how are matters in Ireland?"

" I'm from Tipperary, where are you from?"

It was a tonic to know that there were people from their own country walking free in the streets.

"We come from Munster!" the prisoners shouted back, and called out the names of others they knew who had been sent to the penal colony before them.

The Irish convicts were looked on by some as revolutionaries ready to overthrow the colonists at the first chance. They remembered the uprising of 1804 at Castle Hill which had to be put down with a great deal of force.

The flogging parson, Samuel Marsden (1764-1838) who took a sadistic delight in flogging the prisoners was frightened of the Irish convicts. He held them in contempt and described them as of the lowest class. They were most wild, ignorant and savage. They were criminals from the day they left the cradle, Papists, riddled in superstition, crafty, artful and full of treachery.

There was also a great deal of respect for the Irish convicts. It was appreciated that without their labour many of the great roads, railways, viaducts and buildings of Australia could not have been built.

Governor Macquarie (N.S.W) was of the opinion that good and faithful service to the colony should bring reward not alone to the colony but to the convicts. To this end he awarded them with remission off their sentences for good behaviour and diligence to their work. He brought about the 'PASS' system by which the prisoners were set free to work for a wage. This was strongly opposed by the government back in England. Australia was a penal colony and the convicts should be treated as such. All concessions to the convicts were to be revoked without delay.

They were not to be integrated into Australian society. The liberalisation of the prisoner's conditions was soon stopped and conditions were made that much harsher, if that were possible.

Many of the prisoners found guilty of lesser crimes were assigned to work for the settlers or Army personnel (Officers). They would work a ten hour day from Monday through to Friday and six hours on Saturday. In return they would receive their food and board.

Their future was indeed a game of chance. One could be assigned to a decent settler who would appreciate the valuable contribution made by the convict. Others would treat them worse than the jailers of 'The Road Gangs'. They would flog them sadistically with the 'Cat-O-Nine-Tails within an inch of their lives just for the fun of it. Not alone this, but they would keep them slaves long after they had completed their sentence. The only escape from their captors was in death. Many, seeing no respite from a life of misery, committed suicide.

Not all people were friendly. Many jeered at them and spat in their faces. According to some bigots they were murderers and thieves. They were intent on destroying the rule of the Crown in Ireland. The colonies had no place for such scum.

The dray moved out into the suburbs of the infant city and on into the open country. There were no roads and many of the prisoners were injured when the iron clad wheels dropped into large pot holes in the track.

As the unmade road dried up the prisoners were ordered off the drays. From here on they would be manhandled. They were shackled like cattle, six men to each side of the dray.

"Pull you lazy Irish bastards!" The soldiers rode up and down the line shouting.

"Come on, get your backs into it!" A lashing from a bull whip encouraged those not pulling hard enough to increase their effort.

Unused to the unmerciful heat they dragged and hauled the heavy drays. At the end of a long gruelling day they were given a mug of water and a piece of bread and told to find shelter under the drays and rest until morning.

Most of the next week was spent pulling the heavy uncompromising drays across open country. Where were they going to, they wondered?

155

Scorched by the blazing sun and tormented by vicious flies feeding on their open wounds they trudged on. Those who died were buried by the wayside. Those too ill to work were abandoned where they fell, there to await certain death.

They were relieved to see a camp in the distance. This was their destination, the prison at Bendigo. On seeing the prison they made a final effort. It did not matter that it was a stockade, it afforded sanctuary from the heat of the day.

Some distance from the shelter lay a collection of several buildings surrounded by a large white wall. This they presumed was the barracks.

On arrival, their chains were removed and once again they were given a meal of bread and water. With their meal more or less consumed they were ordered to their feet and marched towards a long open shed. Their guards showed little mercy and beat them with bullwhips. This was to be their resting place for the night.

Seámus woke from a fitful sleep to the sound of a bugle. Soldiers on horseback and on foot were rushing around like so many ants.

Prisoners free of their shackles came to the shelter carrying buckets of water. Each prisoner was given a tin mug and a spoon. These they were told were their utensils and they should take good care of them. Replacements would have to be bought dearly. They were ordered to their feet and marched on to a large square area. Seámus studied his new home and was far from impressed. Before him were the two large wooden gates surrounded by the glaring whitewashed wall that seemed to go on forever. He studied with dismay the gates and the long white wall. The heat and the glare were oppressive and hurt his eyes.

The gates were opened and the felons marched through. With the banging of the gates and the fixing of the bolts they were swallowed up inside.

He stood with the others in a quadrangle which was surrounded by several wooden buildings.

Before them the Union Flag hung limply on a flag pole. This symbol of tyranny had marked the four corners of the earth. He did not wish to look at the despised reminder of British occupation. Yet his eyes were drawn to it.

A long table was set up in the square and two officials came and sat behind it. In single file they were marched to the table where each was given a number and told to report to a lean to at the side of the square. Seámus was handed a piece of paper and marched off. He opened it and looked at it. It read '147 Flynn'.

Inside the lean to were several piles of clothing. He hesitated and looked at the assortment of rough jackets and trousers.

"Next, come on, we don't have all day." He shuffled forward to the bench and handed in his piece of paper.

"One four seven Flynn!" A clerk opened the piece of paper and shouted.

Seámus was shunted further along the line.

"Remove all your clothing!" commanded a man who was stamping the coarse clothing. He discarded his clothing as ordered and stood awaiting the next order.

"Place them on the pile over there and put these on."

He was handed a jacket and trousers with the number 147 stamped on them. They had the name of the prison and yellow arrows impregnated into the fabric. Escape would be difficult if not impossible.

The prisoners, dressed in their uniforms, were marched back to the square. There they were left standing in the oppressive heat for some considerable time. Their mouths were parched with thirst and their feet continued to bleed. Hordes of voracious flies continued to feast on their weeping wounds. Those who fainted were abruptly brought back on their feet.

"Stay on your feet, you Fenian scum!" came the short rasp from their jailers as they threatened them with long bullwhips.

Prisoners too weak to respond were lashed mercilessly. As most were showing signs of distress they were returned to the lean to. There they found sanctuary from the oppressive heat if not the flies. A wooden barrel on wheels, drawn by two prisoners, was brought into the shelter to relieve their thirst.

Those sentenced for minor crimes, such as breaking curfew, etc., were taken away to work for the Officers or local dignitaries and settlers. Those left behind were given a small loaf of rough bread and told that this was their rations for the day. Once again they were assembled and marched back on to the square.

This time a rostrum had been placed under the Union Flag. On it stood a soldier in a smart uniform, and, by his side, hung a scabbard. Someone of importance must be coming to speak to them, thought Seámus.

A dumpy man in a fancy uniform and plumed hat, flanked by two officers with naked swords, took his place centre stage.

The assembled soldiers were called to attention as once again a bugle sounded. Then all was silent, with the exception of the clanking of prisoner's chains and the snorting of the horses.

"I am her Majesty's Governor of this colony. It is my duty to see that your punishment is executed in a fair and just manner." Here he paused to take a drink from a tankard laid on the rostrum.

"The rules are made to be obeyed." He wiped his mouth with a silk handkerchief.

"Briefly, the rules are as follows...

Disobedience to any command will result in a flogging. You will be tied to the punishment wheel and flogged within an inch of your lives. Laziness, insolence, leaving your place of work or rambling off into the bush are just a few of the offences that will warrant a flogging". From what Seámus had heard so far it would appear that flogging was a daily occurrence.

"All punishments will be carried out in a fair and a just manner according to the law. In more serious cases you will be stripped naked and incarcerated in the 'cage'. This is the underground cell which you can see behind you." The prisoners looked around at an iron grill set into the square.

"You will remain within its confines for the duration of your punishment.

I have little doubt but many of you are contemplating escape. You will note that escape is possible for this is not a secure prison. There is no need for it, look around you, what do you see? A vast wilderness. A wilderness bereft of water or shelter. Where civilisation is non existent. It is feared by man and beast alike. Hostile savage tribes of Aboriginals are roaming the bush waiting to drink your blood. Behind you is the town of Melbourne. Its destination is beyond the capability of any man on foot. Beyond that lies the ocean which is patrolled by man-eating shark on the lookout for a meal. You would pray to be captured and returned after a day out there

We do not send out hunting parties to track down escapees. There is no need. They return of their own accord or else go mad and die in the bush. Obey the rules and you will make life more comfortable for yourselves and your sentence will pass quickly." With these words he vacated the rostrum.

With the departure of the Governor the prisoners were escorted back inside the building. Once inside they were allocated their cells. Two prisoners would share a cell. The cells were barely big enough to hold the bunk bed and a makeshift bench.

Seámus entered his prison cell and collapsed exhausted

on to the lower bunk sobbing.

"Look son, we have to live here together and the last thing that I want is you snivelling. You can have the top bunk as you are fitter and younger than me." An older man entered the cell and asserted his authority.

Seámus awakened to the sound of the bugler, he would get used to this. As he rose from his bunk he heard the doors being opened.

"On your feet you lazy scum!" He heard the order ring out. Several prisoners were standing outside their cells by the time he entered the corridor.

"You slept well, I'll say that for you. My name by the way is Tom Clery." His companion held out his hand as he joined Seámus in the corridor.

"I'm Seámus Flynn, what time is it?" Before Tom could answer they were ordered to collect their Billy cans and parade outside.

They noticed that a scaffold had been erected in the centre of the main square.

"Will you look at that, there is going to be a hanging for our benefit." Tom shaded his eyes and looked at the grim spectacle.

On the platform stood two soldiers and a civilian.

"I have no stomach for such barbarity, we will wait here until it is all over." Tom pulled Seámus to one side.

"Outside you two, and join the others". A rifle butt was prodded into Tom's side.

The prisoners were lined up in front of the scaffold.

After a short period of time a coach entered the compound followed by mounted soldiers.

From it stepped the gentleman in full regalia with a plumed hat on his head and a chain around his neck.

The soldiers took up positions on either side of the scaffold.

The horses shook their heads as myriads of flies tormented them. The soldiers were not so lucky, for they had to sit to attention.

Two soldiers dragging a half dying prisoner between them entered the compound and mounted the platform .

"Richard Dowd, you have been found guilty of escaping from the prison at Bendigo and in doing so you severely injured one of your jailers.

In keeping with the laws governing this colony, you are hereby sentenced to be hanged by the neck until you are pronounced dead. Have you anything to say?"

The prisoner remained slumped between the two soldiers.

There was an eerie silence in the compound.

"Then may the Lord have mercy on your soul." The

hangman took a black cowl from his pocket and placed it over the head of the prisoner.

Stepping back he looked towards the governor. He in turn removed his watch and with a nod returned it to his pocket.

The hangman released the lever and the body of Richard Dowd dropped into the recess below the platform.

"Whatever did he do to deserve that? God be good to his soul." Seámus blessed himself.

"He probably gave himself two choices, freedom or death. Either way we will never know."

Under the lean to was a kitchen of sorts with long wooden tables. They were marched inside and given a meal of porridge, a loaf of bread and a billy can of water.

"Go easy on the bread young one, that is your rations for the day," a prisoner sitting opposite warned Seámus.

With the meal completed they were marched out of the prison confines and along what was a partially constructed road.

The road seemed to be going deep into the bush. Accompanying them were two drays carrying all the accoutrements needed for road construction. They travelled several miles until it came to an abrupt end.

"You are now the road gang and you will continue with the construction of this road. Now get to work!"

Throughout the day they toiled and sweated in the relentless heat. By midday they were hungry and near to exhaustion when a halt was called.

"Well Seámus! What do you make of it?" Tom joined Seámus under the shelter of the dray.

"Not much, I doubt if I will last the day." He took a swig from his billy can.

"Oh you'll be alright. You are lucky, you are young and strong."

Tom and Seámus formed themselves into a partnership helping each other whenever possible.

The rest periods were few and all too soon they were back to the task of building the road.

They soon learnt that the road was to be a service road between Melbourne, the prison and beyond.

As the weeks became months and the road grew, precious working hours were being lost returning to the prison. A statolith camp was set up alongside the road. There would no longer be any need to return to the prison. To supplement their monotonous diet they took to capturing rodents and kangaroo. Soon they learnt how to live off the bush.

One afternoon, as they were trying to dislodge a large

boulder, the crowbar slipped. Seámus was levering the boulder and Tom was guiding it with his shovel. As the crowbar slipped the handle of the shovel broke.

Tom reported the accident and sought a new shovel. For breaking the shovel both he and Seámus were taken to the lashing wheel. These were large cart wheels set between two stakes. The purpose of these were to restrain the prisoner as the punishment was carried out. A block of wood was trust into each of their mouths, this to prevent them biting their tongues.

Seámus received ten lashes from the cat-o-nine tails. His offence was not considered as serious as Tom's.

Tom received twenty lashes and was left tied to the wheel for the rest of the day in the merciless heat.

This would teach them to be more careful in future with prison property.

When Tom had completed his punishment they were both taken before the commander.

"You two cannot be trusted with precious tools. From today you are both consigned to the oxen gang."

They knew only too well what the oxen gang meant. Twenty men yoked together with chains. A large tree trunk would be attached to the chains and the prisoners would have to drag it along the rough road levelling it as they went.

They would also be required to pull heavy ploughs. These were used to open up the ground in preparation for stone laying. This work was so exhausting that no more than six hours a day could be spent on it compared with the usual ten hours normally spent on other tasks.

Throughout all their adversities Tom and Seámus continued to work as a team. When times got rough they encouraged each other.

One night Tom noticed that Seámus was not his usual self. He was in a sombre mood and lay on his bunk in complete silence.

"Time will soon pass Seámus, you've completed the first six months," Tom encouraged.

"Don't you worry about me, Tom, you'll soon be home with your folks in County Galway. Why, I'll make the trip from Cork just to visit you."

"I never did tell you, come to think of it, why I was sent to Bendigo, did I Seámus?" Tom took a deep breath.

"No! But I have little doubt you are about to tell me."

"It was so very long ago now, yet I can still picture it as though it were yesterday. I come from the village of Athenry in the county Galway.

It's an insignificant place in many ways, but to me it was

the garden of Eden. I was sixteen years of age at the time and like all garsuns in the village I was full of devilment. I met up with a young lass by the name of Theresa Gorman from the neighbouring village of Kiltullagh. It was at the crossroads dance below the bridge where the river Radford flows. Now laugh you may, Seámus, but we were wed within the year.

Theresa had no more a dowry to offer than I had a wedding ring to offer her. Sure both families were as poor as church mice. The neighbours gathered round to help and built us the neatest Cushen Dhub that you could lay eyes on. We had a large kitchen with a bedroom off it. I was proud of that cottage and I always intended to go over to the quarry at Monivea and get enough slabs to make a good dancing floor. You see we were good at the steps, I tell you". Tom rose from his hard seat and danced a little jig to convince Seámus.

"Ah Seámus! I can see us both now on the night of the Sean Scéals and the Craic and we both dancing like Leprechauns across the floor. The fire reflecting our shadows on the whitewashed walls.

Time passed and we were soon blessed with a son. We christened him Joseph after my father, God be good to his soul.

There was never enough to eat, but then you would know all about that. There was many the night that I watched in anguish as he suckled her empty breasts looking for nourishment.

We were devoted to each other and somehow we managed to survive.

It happened one night, little Joseph would not stop crying. We knew why he was crying, there had not been a sup of milk nor a crust of bread in the cottage that day and no prospects of any.

I could no longer stand the agony of listening to his crying. I up and left the cottage and sneaked into the estate of his Lordship. I knew just what I was doing, I make no excuse for that. In one of his store houses I found sacks of corn piled up from floor to ceiling. Many had been gnawed by rats and mice and the grain was trickling slowly on to the brick floor.

Here was the corn that we had grown with our own hands, waiting to be shipped out to England." Tom again rose and held his hands open.

"You must appreciate how I felt at that moment. At home my child was dying for the want of food. I doubted if he would see the morning. When all the time there was plenty in his Lordship's barns.

I took a sack of corn and spilled half out on the floor. I tied the sack with string and was about to leave the barn. In a corner I saw a fine pile of carrots stacked high. Putting the sack down I filled my pockets with as many as they could hold. Content within myself I hoisted the sack on my back and was soon wading the river.

Although Theresa was worried, no more than myself, mind you, she was pleased to see so much food. The following morning I had the corn ground in the mill.

With a good feed of oats under my belt I took the road to Galway. There was a famine road being constructed near to Cashland and I got a days work on it.

That evening when I got my eight pence pay I bought a few groceries and took the road home.

My heart stood still when I saw the peeler's wagon standing in the laneway. In the doorway stood a constable. Thinking that something had happened to our baby I ran to the door. There I was apprehended by another constable. Soon he was joined by his comrade who had been on lookout at the back of the cottage.

Irons were attached to my feet and my hands were manacled. Theresa was holding Joseph in her arms and crying as I was manhandled into the wagon and taken away to prison in Galway.

I had been seen carrying the corn on the hillside by an informer.

The judge condemned me to transportation with three years hard labour.

Explaining my situation to the judge was a waste of time. I knew what to expect from the outset.

As I waited with the other prisoners for the prison ship, Theresa was allowed to visit me.

Some two weeks later we were informed that the prison ship had anchored in Galway bay.

It would be used to transport felons from Galway, Limerick and Clare. to the new colony of Australia.

The jailer with whom I had formed a friendship told me that he would let Theresa know when the ship was leaving.

True to his word he told her and she was at the quay waiting when we arrived.

I remember it well, for it was dark night when I heard her voice calling to me as the dray reached the quay.

'Tom, it is me, Theresa, with Joseph.' The gentle voice called out in the stillness of the night. Her voice was like a light to a stricken ship.

"Tom! I have come to bless you and say goodbye." Again I heard her call.

163

The dray stopped and we were lined up along the harbour wall.

From the gloomy shadows came several members of our families. I saw my Theresa with little Joseph wrapped in her shawl.

She removed the baby from her shawl and held him up for me to kiss and cuddle for the last time.

I reached out as best I could, considering that the chains were prohibiting my movements.

We hugged each other, so we did. I can feel her arms hugging me to this day. I felt her soft warm tears mingle with my own. Ah Seámus, it was all soon over.

We were torn from the arms of our loved ones and marched on board the prison ship.

That was the last that I ever saw of my wife and child.

I knew that she was watching and praying as the ship slipped its ropes and sailed out into Galway bay.

I know that she is still praying for my return, what do you think Seámus?" Tom looked across at Seámus but he had long since succumbed to sleep.

TOM DISCLOSES HIS PLAN

Men could not endure the hardship of the oxen gang for long, and Seámus and Tom were no exceptions. After a period of two months they were once again transferred back to the pick and shovel gang.

Tom was detailed to accompany a badly injured prisoner to the infirmary at Melbourne. The prisoner had developed a high fever and Tom was instructed to stay with him and to keep him supplied with water on the long journey.

On arrival at the infirmary he was left alone with the prisoner. Their two guards went off in pursuit of more amicable company. They warned him not to leave the confines of the infirmary, promising they would return that evening.

Tom sat on a bench beside the prisoner's bed and waited. By evening the soldiers had not returned and he was now getting impatient and hungry. What if something had happened to them, what would he do?

"What are you doing sleeping here?" He was awakened by a gentle hand shaking him. Looking up he saw the smiling face of a young nurse.

"Sorry, my name is Tom Clery and I'm waiting for my escorts to return. I was told to wait here."

"Don't look so worried, I'll not eat you," she reassured him.

"I see you are with the prisoner, is that so?" she smiled.

"Yes, I was told to wait here." Tom fidgeted on his seat.

"Did you have anything to eat today?"

"No, not yet. I'm waiting for my guards to return," he repeated

"Yes you told me all this before. Relax, come with me." Rising, he followed her down a long corridor.

The welcoming aroma of cooking food met his nostrils as they stopped outside the hospital kitchen.

"Will you see that this man has some food and a place to rest until his escort returns?" the nurse asked a member of the kitchen staff.

"He is a convict and has no right to be here." The cook snarled contemptuously.

"Never mind what he is or who he is, just give him some food and a place to rest. Do you understand me?"

Reluctantly Tom was given a meal and a shakedown in one of the corridors.

The guard did not return to the infirmary until the following evening.

On their return to the compound the Commander wanted to know why they were late in returning. They explained that they had spent the day looking for Tom in the infirmary but without success. They thought that he had absconded and spent the day searching the streets for him. It was not until the following morning that they found him hiding in the cellars of the hospital.

Tom tried to tell his side of the story but nobody was listening. The magistrate would be visiting the compound the following day. He would be given ample opportunity to tell his side of the story.

He would be summoned before the magistrate next day on a charge of attempting to escape and evading capture.

In the meantime he would be incarcerated in the cage to await his trial.

Tom was dragged exhausted at midday from the sweltering hell hole. He was given a drink of water before his chains were fitted and he was taken to the Commander's tent.

His guards repeated parrot fashion their previous statement.

Tom asked the magistrate to contact the hospital and ask the nurse if he were telling the truth or not.

The heat in the tent was overbearing and the ferocious flies did nothing to alleviate the discomfort of the magistrate.

"Is that all you have to say?" The magistrate fanned himself with a sheaf of notes.

"Tom Clery you will serve a further twelve months sentence to run concurrently with your present punishment."

"Whatever happened to you Tom?" Seámus asked as his friend returned to their makeshift shelter.

"It's a long story, a long story indeed Seámus." This was all the information he divulged and Seámus knew better than to press the point. There was a code among the felons. If they did not wish to reveal any information then you respected their wishes.

The work on the road continued. There was no respite from the heat and the insatiable flies. They attacked every open wound and in the process turned them septic. The only cure was to burn the wound or to treat it with very hot water to draw the poison.

Their diet was poor and what they were given was rancid and unfit for human consumption. They refused to eat the food and took to capturing wild life instead. By night they were plagued by mosquitoes, by day they were tormented by flies and heat. There was little respite from the daily punishment of one kind or another.

Tempers began to fray and fighting became a daily occurrence. The guards resorted to the only punishment they knew, flogging and incarceration in the hole. These punishments only exacerbated an already simmering resentment.

In order to ease the volatile situation it was agreed that half of the road gang would be returned to the prison at Bendigo. Those who had served the longest term on the road gang would be given priority.

Most of the prisoners felt that they had a right to be returned, but the final decision rested with the Commander. Those who continued to protest were punished severely. Many were tied to the wheel and left there until they could no longer protest.

Seámus and Tom kept themselves aloof from all the troubles. They knew that they would not be going back.

"Are you awake Seámus?" Tom whispered one night as they lay in the shelter of their lean to.

"'Course I'm awake, how could anyone sleep in this heat. " Seámus continued to squash the mosquitoes feasting on his flesh.

"I'm going to go walkabout. I've had all that I can endure in this hell hole." Tom began to cry. Seámus knew that he was on the verge of a nervous breakdown.

"Where would you go? You would die out there in the bush."

"I may as well be dead. I did not tell you, but you remember that day I was sent to Melbourne and was late back?"

"Sure I remember, why?"

"I had my sentence increased by twelve months on my return."

"Another year! You never told me. How did that come about?"

"The guards failed to pick me up that evening and did not come back until the next evening. I got the blame and the magistrate added another twelve months to my sentence. I know it is asking a lot of you, Seámus, but would you come with me?" Seámus did not answer.

"Two of us together have a better chance of survival and we have been pals from the beginning," Tom continued to plead.

"Do you know what you're asking of me? You want me to escape with you. Have you thought of the consequences if we were caught?"

"That's about it Seámus. You don't want to be buried here like a dog do you?" Tom was crying bitterly.

"You heard what they said about trying to escape."

"We could make for the coast above Melbourne. I heard tell that many American whaling vessels anchor there." Tom, more composed now, rose and sat on the side of the bunk with his head in his hands.

"Do you think they would take us home. What if they turned us over to the English?" Seámus was showing interest.

"The Americans would never betray us once we tell them we're Fenians. They would take us with them to America."

"Very well then Tom, I have no more to lose than you." Both men laughed as they shook hands.

Seámus found sanctuary in his sleep that night. He dreamt that he was back in old Ireland with the gentle breeze to his back.

He saw his mother sitting in the kitchen with a coatamore from the Big House on her lap and she replacing a button. As usual she was chiding the owner for being so careless.

Father sat in his sugan chair with a book in his hands, taking the occasional glance at a chicken slowly pecking her way across the floor.

He saw his brother Brendan running across the lazy ridges in pursuit of his frog 'Cromwell'.

There were fresh eggs, butter and milk on the table and the aroma of bacon and cabbage bubbling in the pot. He tried to reach it but found that whenever he tried the table moved out of reach.

He was transported to the lake at the Big House. Gentle billowing clouds bumped into each other and obliterated the sun for a moment. Then, opening their curtains, they once again allowed the sun to sparkle on the crystal water. Reeds parted as a mother duck and her ducklings sought access to deeper water. Once mother and family had passed through they closed their gentle drapes, making a musical sound in the process.

"What are you doing here?" He was startled by an intrusion into his dreaming. Looking behind him he saw two evil looking gamekeepers about to attack him.

One grabbed him by the arms and the other by the legs. He felt himself floating through the air where he was suspended for a moment. Then with a splash he was catapulted into the lake. Down, down into the depths of the lake he plummeted and began to swallow great quantities of water.

"Jesus help me!" he cried out.

"Did you say something son?" He awakened to the friendly voice of Tom. He was back in the prison camp. far away from his dreams and the shores of old Ireland.

"Thank God it was only a dream, Tom. I was back in Ireland and nearly drowned." There was no need for further elaboration, they all had their dreams.

THE ESCAPE

Methodically they planned their escape and made preparations for their survival in the bush. They would steal what they thought they would require a little at a time.

First they stole two large water bags and hid them in the bush beneath a marker. These were followed by a length of rope and other essentials.

Slowly their stock of necessities accumulated. There would be no turning back.

Finally they set the day on which they would escape. They agreed that they would make their bid the following Sunday when most were at Mass.

Saturday afternoon was free and the felons were allowed to relax and roam in the bush.

Not Seámus and Tom, they spent the day filling the water bags and going over their plan. Nothing must be left to chance.

Sunday morning was spent lazing around the camp awaiting the arrival of the priest.

There was a relaxed atmosphere within the camp. The prisoners were resting in their bunks. Most of the guards had gone to Melbourne for the weekend. Those left behind lazed around the camp. There was no need to be alert, for who would be foolish enough to attempt an escape from this God-forsaken place.

The priest did not arrive until late afternoon. This was indeed a great advantage to them.

They did not attend the Mass but waited until most of the guards had joined the worshippers.

"Now is our chance, take a shovel and go into the bush, I'll meet you there." Tom nudged Seámus who by now was half asleep.

"What do we need a shovel for? There's one already with the swag." He looked at Tom, puzzled.

"We don't want the shovel. If the guard sees you he will think that you are going to the latrine. That way you won't arouse his suspicion. Good luck."

"Good luck to yourself. We will need all the luck that we can muster."

Seámus, picking up the shovel, casually sauntered into the bush. There was no need to worry, what guards there were ignored him.

Tom soon joined him, and with a wry smile they went and

collected their swag.

Their absence would not be noticed until the following morning. By then they would be long gone.

It was doubtful if the governor would waste manpower sending out a search party.

The two men laughed as they slung their swag over their shoulders. Little did they care that they were now fugitives at the mercy of a hostile environment and savage natives.

They had burnt their bridges , there would be no turning back.

Seámus was worried about their clothing. Anyone meeting them would recognise them and shoot them or return them to the prison.

"Meet anyone out here? Are you serious? Who in God's name would be mad enough to venture into this?"

"We are here, are we not?"

They looked at each other and laughed.

"Come on, if we follow the road markers we should soon come to Melbourne," Tom advised

They followed the road for several miles until the light faded. They would eat and rest deep in the bush, and pick up the road again the following morning.

Seámus rose early and cooked a meal, leaving Tom sleeping.

"On your feet ,Fenian scum!" Seámus kicked at Tom's heels.

"What! What!" Tom was rudely awakened.

"Here, have some tucker." Seámus reached out a tin plate

"Don't ever do that again Seámus, it's not funny."

"Sorry Tom, it was just a piece of fun. I wasn't thinking straight," Seámus apologised.

With the meal consumed they once again returned to where the road markers were situated.

"There they are." Seámus pointed to the pegs marking the proposed route.

"There are people out there, look!" Tom pointed to a number of men gathered in the distance.

"I see them, they are clearing more scrub."

"We cannot follow the road, that's for sure."

Scratching his chin Tom looked around the empty wasteland.

"We will cross to Cape Howe in the Sea of Tasman. It's a bit longer but it's safe." Tom seemed to know what he was talking about.

"Will there be any American ships there?" Seámus looked into the vast wilderness with a furrowed brow.

"Whaling ships follow where the whales are. There's

171

bound to be at least one sheltering in the bay."

Tom set off at a steady pace with Seámus following close behind.

For the next three days they tracked through the bush, Tom checking periodically with the position of the sun.

Their confidence collapsed when Tom admitted that he had miscalculated and that they were now lost.

Seámus began to panic, what if they could not find their way out of the bush?

Tom, the eternal dreamer, assured him that civilisation was not far away, but where?

Their meagre supplies were soon exhausted, worse still their water supply was reduced to a few dregs in one of the bags. If they were to survive they would need to replenish their supplies and more so their water.

Panic and desperation made them abandon all semblance of rational behaviour. They began to hurry their steps through the sun drenched bush.

"If we are to get out of this Seámus, we must think."

"What do you suggest we do?" Seámus looked towards Tom for guidance.

"First we must find shelter from the sun. We will sleep by day and travel by night. If the abbo's can survive in this God-forsaken place so can we. Come on, let's find some shelter."

That day they spent resting beneath the spreading branches of an isolated tree deep within the bush.

They used their knowledge of snaring to trap snakes and other edible mammals and animals in order to survive.

Bird's eggs were a delicacy when they could be found. Not alone did they supply a valuable source of food, but life-giving liquid nourishment as well.

By the second week matters were getting really desperate and they were drinking their own urine.

As the sun scorched the parched bush they sought shelter under a sparse clump of bushes.They felt certain that death was not too far away. No words were spoken between them for they knew that it was only a matter of time. They were so dehydrated that trying to speak brought agony.

In this condition, one afternoon, Tom noticed a snake or lizard wriggling towards the safety of a large rock. As the animal burrowed beneath the rock he crawled forward. He was determined to catch it before it found sanctuary.

The creature was halfway under the rock by the time he reached it. In his desperation and without hesitating he grabbed it.

The snake or whatever it was turned and bit him on the

172

hand. Dropping it he pulled his hand back and, grabbing his wrist, sucked at the wound in desperation. He spent the afternoon sucking at the wound and tending to it. He continued to suck out whatever venom the creature had injected into the wound and spit it out. He felt nauseated and began to vomit. By evening he felt feverish but still never mentioned his encounter with the creature to Seámus.

Next morning he could not stand, he was shivering and felt really ill.

"I'll not be able to move on today Seámus, I'll need to rest. It must be something I ate."

He rubbed his stomach but still kept the secret of his encounter with the creature to himself.

"Sorry Tom, tell you what, you rest and I'll go into the bush and try my luck"

Leaving Tom resting he set off into the bush. Some hours later he returned with two musk kangaroos over his shoulder.

"They are not very big, Tom. Beggars can't be choosers."

He laughed as he held up his catch for Tom to see.

Tom hardly ate any of the meal and this worried him.

"Tom! You don't look all that good. Perhaps we should give ourselves up."

"Don't worry Seámus, by tomorrow I'll be as right as rain."

"Of course you will, try and get some sleep."

"Seámus, would you do me a big favour should anything happen to me?"

"Nothing is going to happen, but if it means getting a good night's sleep, then let's hear it."

"Do you remember me telling you about my wife Theresa and my son Joseph?"

"Sure I remember, how could I forget?"

"If I should die and you escape to Ireland, would you look them up and tell them what happened, please, Seámus?"

"Very well, I promise. Why you're being so morbid I cannot understand. Now will you let us get a little sleep, please."

Next morning there was no improvement in Tom's condition. If anything he looked far worse, but still he insisted they press on.

Breaking a branch from the tree Seámus shaped it into a crutch.

"You lean on me, Tom, and use this as a support."

Together they made their way deeper into the bush.

Two days and nights passed and they were still in the grip of the bush. Tom was now delirious and kept wandering off as Seámus slept. He was in no position to

173

help his friend.

"Leave me Seámus! You would have a better chance on your own," Tom pleaded.

"No Tom, we got into this together and together we will make it, God willing."

In the distance Seámus saw the outline of a baobab tree shimmering in the cruel heat.

"Come on Tom, one last effort," he encouraged his friend.

Tom was in a desperate state and hallucinating. There was no going back and no going forward, He would not abandon his friend to the scavengers of the bush.

There was nothing that he could do for his friend. He tried praying but the words would not materialise.

He would awaken from fitful sleep to hear Tom, hallucinating, speaking to his wife and family.

That night he stretched the canvas in the bush hoping to collect some of the dew from the night air. He was awakened by Tom pleading for a little water in God's name.

"How are you feeling, Tom?" Seámus rasped, his own mouth parched dry.

Rising wearily he went to the canvas. There was a minimal amount of dew in the centre. Carefully he soaked a cloth in the water and returned to his friend.

"Here Tom, drink this, it will help." He raised him on to his lap and held the cloth to his lips.

The dry heat from the bush raging down incessantly on their half naked bodies was intolerable.

"Seámus! Seámus are you about, you must go on. I have not long to live, I'll never see Galway bay again, ever!" Tom tried to raise himself from the barren ground.

"Listen Seámus! I know I have not much time left. Don't forget if you ever make it back to Ireland call up to Galway Town and tell my wife and son that I'll be praying for them. Let them know how I tried to return to them. If you can, my friend take..."

"Stop talking, Tom, please stop, it is draining your strength".

Tom did not reply.

Seámus rose and, retrieving the canvas, he stretched it across the tree casting a comforting shade over his friend.

"Is that better?"

He collapsed under the canvas and lay still, Tom did not reply. He had lapsed into unconsciousness.

Seámus watched the heat dance in the bush, he heard the call of the animals. Was it all a horrible nightmare? He ran his hand across his parched lips and in the process cracked them further. Parasitic flies swarmed over the open and septic wounds, eating him alive.

He wondered how his family were faring in Ireland. If only he could sit beside the brook and drink and drink from its cool crystal water. His whole body cried out for water but there was no relief.

He managed to clear a space for himself, and with a glance at Tom, lay down. He was now too weak to care for himself or Tom. Surely God in his mercy would take them both in their sleep. He began to mutter a prayer...

Slowly his eyes closed, he felt weak and all went black.

He was awakened by the calling of a shell duck. After some time he managed to open his eyes which had been glued together with mucus.

How long he had been unconscious he didn't know.

"Oh God in Heaven why did you not take me!" he cried.

He looked across at Tom who had rolled from the safety of the shelter and was now lying on his side half under the baobab tree. The sun was beating down relentlessly on his naked body.

"Tom! Tom" he called as he crawled to his friend's side. Reaching out he tried to drag him back into the shelter.

"For God's sake, Tom, wake up, you'll die out there"

He took hold of his hand to drag him into the shade. There was no need anymore. God had been good to at least one of them. He lay down under the canvas. How long he lay there he did not know.

It was evening when he awoke. In the centre of the canvas he found a precious amount of dew. This he carefully poured into his billy can and secured the lid. Sucking what remained of the dew into his mouth he removed the canvas from the tree. Tom's shrivelled body lay some distance away. With a final prayer he placed the canvas over the body and returned to the shelter of the tree. Taking his knife from his belt he carved a memorial deep into the bark of the tree...

"Here lies the body of Tom Clery,
late of Galway City.
I became richer and wiser
by knowing him.
A greater spirit is he now"
Seámus *Flynn (Cork 1848)*

There was no further need to delay. Picking up his swag he left Tom to his God and his Dreamtime. Perhaps he had returned to his native Galway to find his Theresa and his son Joseph.

175

THE WONGAPITJA ADOPT SEÁMUS

Desperate to reach civilisation he threw caution to the wind and staggered into the open. The heat burned into his wounds as he staggered and crawled through the bush. Where he was going he did not know, yet somehow with God given strength he staggered on. Human endurance could only stand so much.

Lost and alone he forced his aching limbs forward but to where?

His eyes burned, his swollen tongue was hanging out of his mouth. Flies by the million tormented him and slowly sucked what life there was left from his limbs. There was nothing he could do to stop them. He cried to his God to put an end to his misery.

He must find water and shelter or face an agonising death. His swollen tongue was choking him to death. He tried desperately to tear it from his mouth.

"My God, my Saviour why have you deserted me," he croaked as he remembered Christ's suffering on the cross.

Bright lights flashed before his burning eyes, he grasped at his throat in a final effort to bring relief to his oxygen starved lungs.

The bush reeled before him, he staggered and again tried to breath, Then all went black.

He awakened to hear strange voices calling.

Slowly opening his eyes he squinted, wondering what was happening. Several forms swayed and waved above him, his eyes ached, he closed them to relieve the pain and stress. Still the voices kept muttering.

Slowly he again opened his eyes. As they adjusted to his surroundings he saw a circle of aborigines looking down at him. He had been brought to the refuge of a large shaded tree. He was sure that they were about to murder him but he did not care. It was better to die now than suffer a lingering death in the bush. As he opened his eyes they again began to speak before sitting down in a tight circle around him. Regaining his composure he pointed to his mouth denoting his need for water.

A girl came forward and began to feed him the pounded root of the Nager bush. He felt pain and relief as the raspberry tasting juices lubricated his parched throat.

Again he relapsed into a coma.

When he recovered he found that he had been placed in a shallow clearing under the tree.

For the next three days he was fed by the girl who seemed to have been appointed his nurse.

Slowly he found new strength and before long he was able to walk about. He owed his life to these gentle people and wanted to show his gratitude.

Going to their leader he offered him his knife. Looking to the others the leader pointed to Seámus. Then they began to laugh. He again tried to give the knife to the leader. This was declined with another great bout of laughter. It was obvious that they had no need of his gift.

He found himself joining in the merriment that he had created at his own expense.

After some days he was feeling well enough to travel, but where to?

His problem was resolved when he awoke one morning to see them walking slowly into the bush.

He quickly realised that his only hope of survival was to follow them.

Instinctively he rose to his feet and without waiting to be invited or rejected he fell in behind them. He had no fear of these gentle people of the bush. Had they not rescued him from certain death? They had adopted him, and he gratefully ate what food was offered, whether live grubs or roasted kangaroos.

He was to learn that they were members of the WONGAPITJA tribe. One evening as they sat around their camp fire they related to him their story of the Dreamtime.

With gestures and the occasional word in broken English they related their story. Seámus thought back to the days when he listened to the Sean Scéals of the Tuatan-de-Dannan around the turf fire in Skibbereen.

It began when a Possum and a Bungarra married, they told him. Everyone was opposed to the marriage and tried to separate them. There was only one escape for them from the constant nagging and that was to go walkabout and find a place where nobody else lived. Having found a cave deep inland they began to paint it with the pictures of the animals , birds and insects that lived in the area. When they had filled all the walls with paintings they began to paint each other. This is why aborigines paint themselves, he was told.

As the weeks grew into months he formed a close bond with them and began to adopt their customs. Finally he consummated his bond by taking the girl who had acted as his nurse to be his woman.

Although he was content with living and sharing their nomadic life style there was still that nagging calling to return to his native land. He put to the back of his mind the fact that as an escaped felon he would be arrested and hanged should he ever return to civilisation.

He had no knowledge as to what year it was nor as to where he was. As he became acclimatised to their way of life he began to worry less about the world of the white man. He told his woman that from now on her name would be Sheila.

Sheila was soon with child and one day beside a gully she gave birth to a son.

Later that afternoon he placed his grandmother's rosary around the neck of the infant and took him back to the gully.

There he baptised him and gave him the name of Thomas after his father.

His behaviour at the gully caused much humorous bantering from the natives. He could not explain fully the reason for the ceremony. Finally he abandoned all efforts to explain his strange conduct and joined in the good natured bantering. He was not about to try and convert them to Christianity.

Sitting around the camp fire one evening he noted that there was a restlessness among the tribe.

"Tomorrow we must go walkabout to our ancestral places," he was told.

"I hope it is not too far. Sheila might not be able for the journey so soon."

"You will not be coming, Seámus. You and your family must now find your own walkabout."

"Not coming? You will come back, won't you?"

"No! There is no place for you with us ever again."

Next morning they assembled and said their last farewells to Seámus and his family.

As the embers of the fire slowly died away they rose. They rubbed their scent on him as a token of their brotherhood. Slowly they wandered back into the bush from where they came so long ago.

Seámus waved his last goodbyes to them long after their shadows faded into the distance. He owed them his life and he would never forget them.

As the fire gave out its last few sparks he too picked up his swag and wandered off into the bush. He looked back at Sheila and stopped. She knew that it was now time for them to go on their walkabout. Picking up their son she followed him.

What, he thought would become of them. Would they encounter hostile tribes or, worse still, Red Coats?

He knew that the soldiers, should they find them, would

178

either return him to the penal colony or kill him. His wife and child would be killed or banished into the bush. A bastard child born of a savage mother and a white man would never be accepted in the white community.

No woman with a child could possible survive alone in the bush. If they were captured by other aborigines would they accept a half caste child into their tribe? They were now alone and without the protection of the tribe. Survival for him and his family was now uppermost in his mind.

They were in luck when they discovered an area well stocked with wild life and a running brook. This was where they would set up camp . He would not subject Sheila to the trauma of the bush. He would build a shelter and settle down and wait until the baby grew in strength.

Having settled into his new home he began to inform Sheila of his home in Ireland and how one day they would return there on a great ship. Sheila looked bemused as he tried to explain all about Ireland and his people.

He was taking it for granted that she was as enthusiastic as he was at the prospects of returning home.

Yet in the back of his mind he knew that he was deluding himself. They could never leave the Australian bush. He was an outcast, a felon on the run, she was a savage. To make matters even worse she had conceived a half caste bastard son.

Their only hope for survival lay in the bush.

One afternoon as he sat nursing his son he heard voices shouting in the distance.

Calling on Sheila to take the infant and hide, he raced off to investigate.

Coming within range of the voices he crouched down in the bush and crawled closer.

Before him he saw the outline of several men on horseback. He knew that these were white men for the aborigines did not have access to horses.

Cautiously he crept towards them. Were they soldiers or settlers? It mattered little for one was as bad as the other.

Having confirmed that they were indeed settlers he returned to his shelter.

"There must be a sheep station near here," he told Sheila on his return.

"We will have to leave, if they find us they will kill us and our child." Sheila hugged her son to her breast to protect him.

"Tonight, under cover of darkness we must dismantle our camp and leave," he warned her.

Once again they moved deeper into the bush and it's

harsh environment. They had to put as much space as possible between them and the settlers.

By dawn they were tired and hungry and Sheila was showing signs of fatigue.

As if fate were to again play a part in his life they came to a Baobab tree and sought its shelter.

Seámus awoke to a refreshing breeze wafting over his face. The sun had set. Calling to Sheila he told her that he was going in search of food. She should stay under the shelter of the tree until his return.

Moving swiftly and silently through the bush he saw in the distance a small spinney.

'There are bound to be animals there," he thought.

As he came nearer he soon realised that he was within the boundary of a large sheep station. Before him stood a shearing shed and beside it a large trough filled with life giving water.

Cautiously he approached and hid inside of the pens, listening and waiting. An occasional mammal ran along the wall. Some stopped and looked at him curiously before moving on. Apart from this intrusion the place was eerily silent.

Throwing all caution to the wind he let out a 'Whoop' and ran towards the trough of water. With another 'Whoop' he climbed on to the wall and plunged into the cool water. He felt his dried skin stretch and his body relax as, like a sponge, it absorbed the water. He rested his arms on the side and, sitting down, relaxed, and planned his next move.

He was awakened by the bleating of sheep and the sound of horses.

Looking over the rim he saw a band of horsemen approaching. There was no time to escape and hide. He would have to stay in the trough and hope that they would not find him. Any movement on his part would shy the horses and alert the stockmen to his presence.

It soon became obvious that they had no intention of leaving. Taking their horses to the trough they dismounted and began building a fire.

The horses must have been very thirsty for they spent a long time partaking of the life giving water. He remained as rigid as a statue as several of the horses eyed him suspiciously. Some shied away only to return within seconds as thirst overcame their caution.

"Damn flies, they pester everyone and everything," grumbled one of the stockmen on seeing his horse shy.

He watched as they set their billy cans over the fire and ate their tucker.

It was dawn when they removed their saddles from the horses and placed them around the fire. Using them as pillows many settled into their pipes. Others, tired out, settled down to sleep.

He was worried for the safety of his wife. She would miss him and brood, thinking that some disaster may have overtaken him. Would she stay under the tree where he had left her, or would she venture out into the bush seeking him?

The sun began to rise above the horizon as the stockmen awakened from their sleep. Rising they picked up their saddles and returned to their horses. Tying their swages behind their saddles they mounted and prepared to leave.

"Hold on a minute". One of them dismounted and approached the trough.

Seámus watched, his heart pounding as he came towards him. As he approached Seámus took a deep breath and sank down in the water. Picking up a bucket from beside the trough he dipped it into the water and filled it. With his lungs about to burst Seámus came slowly to the surface. Taking deep gulps of air he again looked over the rim.

The horseman was standing over the fire quenching it with the water.

Then, mounting his mare, they left as one, leaving the station to the sheep and Seámus.

Numbed with cold he wearily rose from the trough and went outside. For once he was grateful for the heat of the bush.

The sheep had now left the station and were wandering into the bush seeking food.

This was his opportunity to obtain a meal for his hungry family.

Crawling towards the sheep he swiftly brought one down and killed it with his knife.

Placing it across his shoulders he trotted back to where he had left his family. They would not go hungry this evening nor for a few days.

He soon realised he was now in a better position than he had been by the brook. There was adequate water and food to be had for the taking. Life had taken a turn for the better for him and his family and he thanked God for the blessing.

"We could do with a bit of luck, and I guess we have found it here."

Seámus surveyed his new shelter.

He continued to steal the odd sheep when need arose. He was sure that with so many sheep wandering in the bush the owner would not miss one.

With such easy pickings he became careless and was nearly discovered on many occasions.

On one of his forages he was trapped in the middle of the flock of sheep. He had gone to steal a sheep and failed to check if the station was manned. He was about to strike at the sheep when he heard the sound of approaching horsemen. They were rounding up the stock and taking them back to the station. He was now in a dilemma for there was no escape. He could not hide nor could he find cover. He was in open country and any movement on his part would alert the stockmen.

Seámus entwined his hands deep into the fleece on the underbelly of one of the sheep and hung on. Slowly he allowed himself to be dragged across the plain. What would be the outcome when they reached the station did not enter his mind.

The stockmen herded the huge flock into the station and divided them into pens and closed the gates. He was now trapped. The smell and heat from the sheep was overbearing. He wanted to cough but dared not. He felt he would suffocate under the bodies of so many sheep.

Crawling on his hands and knees he made for the comparative comfort on the edge of the pen.

Once there he could raise his head without being seen. He was crushed against the rough wall of the pen time and time again by the massed bodies of the sheep. The smell was nauseating and several times he awoke to find he had fainted and was being trampled under foot.

By nightfall the stockmen once again retreated from the station.

At last he could leave the pen and refresh himself in the trough.

Killing a sheep he placed it over his shoulders and returned home.

His narrow escape did nothing to warn him of the dangers in which he was placing both himself and his family. Two weeks later he was once again back at the station foraging among the sheep.

He felled one and killed it . He was about to place it on his shoulder when out of the bush came the stockmen.

Leaving the carcass he began to crawl into the bush, then he heard a cry.

"Thieving Abbo bastards".

He looked up and saw a stockman with a rifle in his hand riding towards him.

He now needed all the skills and cunning taught him by the Abbo's. He zig zagged across the plain and reached

182

the bush. Once there he dropped to the ground and began to crawl deep into the undergrowth. When he thought he was safe he stopped and remained still.

He heard the thunder of the horse's hooves as they raced through the scrub. The stockmen whooped and cheered as they raced in hot pursuit of their quarry. He heard them lashing the scrub with their long bull whips trying to dislodge him. He dug himself deeper and deeper into the choking dust.

The dust being disturbed by the horses entered his nostrils and lungs. Vicious ants bit deep into his skin leaving large open weals on which malevolent flies were now feeding. He could feel their long proboscises probing deep inside the wounds. The pain was becoming unbearable. He would have to move or be eaten alive.

The posse continued to criss-cross the bush trying to flush him out. Tiring of their hunt they finally returned to the station. Seámus rose on all fours and glanced around him. The posse had indeed abandoned their search. He would have to return empty handed to his wife and child.

This set back did not worry him unduly, at least he was still alive. The stockmen would blame a wandering Abbo for the killing and forget about it. He would have to be more cautious in the future. The lives of his wife and child depended on him.

Next evening he was once again back on the edge of the grazing belt. This time he was more cautious and reconnoitred the area beforehand. He hid for some time in the bush and waited.

When he was sure that there were no stockmen about he swiftly downed and killed a sheep and left.

Was this to be all his life would be, he thought one day, as he sat beside the water trough, reflecting.

THE MURDER OF SHELIA
AND HER CHILD

Seámus took the watering bag down from the tree. Shaking it he realised that supplies were running low. He would have to return to the trough and replenish his supply.

He was apprehensive of returning to the compound and leaving his family. The stockmen were busy with the sheep. What if some wandered deep into the bush and found his camp in his absence.

"Sheila, we are running short of water. I am going to the compound to replenish our supplies. I want you to be extra vigilant, for the stockmen are shearing the sheep," he warned her.

"You be careful, yourself".

She held on to his arm.

"Don't worry about me, it's you that I worry about".

He again warned her of the dangers she faced.

"For now I will move the camp deeper into the scrub. Stay quiet and do not light a fire." He was already gathering up their few possessions as he spoke.

Sheila picked up Thomas and followed her husband.

Finding a concealed spot he erected a temporary camp.

"I must be off now, Sheila, remember what I told you." Picking up the watering bag he wandered off into the bush. Some distance from the camp he looked back. As he could no longer see the camp he felt reassured. They would now be safe until he returned.

Sheila took the infant in her arms and settled down to await her husband's return.

By midday he had not returned . Coming from the shelter of the camp she looked into the bush hoping to see her husband. To her horror she saw several horsemen bearing down on them.

In her panic she forgot what Seámus had told her. Picking up her infant son she ran deeper into the bush and in doing so exposed herself. Finding a quiet spot she lay the baby down and covered him. Then she crept back to the camp. Should the white men discover her then at least her son would be safe.

She was not to know that they had already seen her movements and were on their way to investigate.

Looking up she saw them some yards away. They came nearer and nearer and she knew that soon they would be upon her. There was to be no hiding place. In panic and fear she rose from her hiding place and began to run. It was a futile effort at escape, she was soon run down and captured.

"Please, please, my baby," she cried as she tried to escape from her captors.

"Well, look what we have here, a woman from the tribe that has been stealing our sheep."

One of the stockmen dismounted and was soon joined by his companions.

"What are we going to do with her?" another sneered.

"Do with her! Her tribe have been having our sheep, now we are going to have her."

The leader laughed as he unbuckled his belt.

They took it in turn to brutally rape her. They showed no remorse whatsoever when they finished.

"What do we do with her now?"

Without a word and in a final act of brutality one of the stockmen stepped forward. Grabbing her by the hair he withdrew his shearing knife. Forcing her to her knees he slit her throat as easily as he would a sheep.

The others stood transfixed as her blood slowly trickled along the parched earth. She made no sound but lay with her eyes transfixed upon the faces of her murderers.

"Watch her, mates, she is putting the curse of the bones on us," warned an elderly stockman.

With a kick of his boot her murderer sent her crashing to the ground.

They were distracted by the sound of the baby crying. One left the scene and went to investigate.

"Look here, this is a half caste". He held the infant up by the leg.

"Bring the little bastard over here."

The baby was brought to where his mother lay dying, her life blood slowly ebbing away.

Like a tethered lamb awaiting death, Sheila called out pitifully to them.

"Please! Of your mercy, please spare my child".

Blood oozed from her mouth as she tried to plead for the life of her son.

Yet she knew, as a mother, that there would be no mercy. The child was a half caste bastard and would be put to death.

She listened painfully as her child cried out for her comfort and security. Seeing and hearing his mother, the infant instinctively held out his arms seeking her protection from these cruel tyrants that were hurting him.

Mindful of her loving instinct for her child she somehow

185

raised herself from the ground. Holding out one hand she pleaded and cried for her child. She wanted to hold and comfort him for the last time.

The murderer took the child from his companion. Again drawing his knife he held the infant by his legs. With a swift trust of his knife he cut the child's throat and threw it to his mother.

Sheila reached out and pulled the body of her infant close to her dying breast.

Looking from one to the other of their executioners she sank to the ground. Tightening her arms around the corpse she sank to the ground and succumbed to death.

With no signs of remorse the murderer wiped his knife on his leathers, mounted his horse, and prepared to leave.

Some of the others looked away unable to stomach the wanton murders that they had witnessed.

"There's no need for you to look so pious. Would any of your wives want to bring up a half caste bastard?" he remarked on seeing their revulsion.

Without another word he rode off into the bush.

"Should we not at least bury them?" one of the remaining men asked.

There were no volunteers as, one by one, they mounted their horses and left the carnage.

SEEKING SANCTUARY
IN A SHEEP STATION

Seámus returned to where he had left his wife and child. He called to her again and again . He began to worry when she did not reply .

Some distance to his left he noticed a large horde of flies concentrated in one spot. They were in a frenzy as they rose in a huge cloud before descending again.

Fearing the worst he ran towards the spot and saw the unmistakable outline of boots and horseshoes. Moving closer he saw the bodies of his murdered wife and son. Their bodies were intermingled and a dark crimson pool of blood had formed around them.

He looked down at the carnage in disbelief. Who would perpetrate such a heinous act of horror. Who would take sadistic pleasure by mutilating and murdering an innocent child and his mother?

He knew that it was white men who committed the crimes. Whether stockmen or renegades, it mattered not.

There was nothing that he could do now except give them a decent burial. Returning to the camp he procured the spade and opened their grave. In it he placed the bodies of his wife and son and filled it in.

He could not put a marker on the grave. Should the perpetrators of the heinous murders return and find the marked grave they would know that there was a witness. They would hunt him down and murder him.

There was little doubt in his mind but that some of them would return out of morbid curiosity. With the bodies gone they would presume that wild animals had taken them.

With the burial completed he knelt down and said a final prayer.

Packing his swag he slung it over his shoulder and went deep into the bush.

Once again he was alone in the wilderness. He cried uncontrollably as he wandered aimlessly through the bush. There was to be no respite as the blinding sun burned into his eyes and flesh. He tried to find shelter under the sparse branches of a bush but to no avail. It was hotter sitting under the tree than it was walking.

Mercifully he saw the sun sink slowly below the horizon. He could now seek a little respite.

Next morning he awoke from a restless night's sleep, a

sleep filled with memories of his wife and child. Rising he lit a fire and with what little water he had left he filled his billy can. Taking some of the cooked mutton from his swag he made his tucker.

There was nobody now to share his meal except the flies and buzzards. He was alone with his God and the elements.

He finished his meal, quenched his fire and packing his swag went in search of the ever elusive coast.

For the next two weeks he searched and listened for the noise of the breakers on the reef. He searched the skies for the mournful cry of the albatross or the shrill call of the seagull, but all was silent. Nothing but the oppressive heat and the cruel flies. Would he find civilisation or a felon's grave deep in the wilderness?

Now in deep depression he began to hallucinate. He knew that he was going mad but could do nothing about it. The bush was slowly swallowing him up as it had so many others before him.

He swam in crystal clear lakes only to find that he was rudely awakened struggling in rough bush.

Like a rudderless ship he wandered aimlessly, calling, calling in vain. He knew that there would be no reply, instinct told him to call.

In fits of depression he visited his home in Ireland. He talked to Sheila as she nursed the infant. He became more and more irrational and despondent. He carelessly lost his swag and water bottle. There could be no other outcome now but an agonising death.

He came to and found himself slumped over a large trough filled with water. Dipping his finger in the water he began to draw long lines across it. then he began to laugh, hysterically.

"You don't want me to die for some reason, do you God. Why don't you leave me alone?"

He could not, however, resist the pull of the water. It may be a figment of his imagination but it looked real.

Climbing on to the rim of the trough he fell into the water. Rising to the surface he began to take in copious amounts which made him choke and vomit. Only then did he realise that it was not a dream, this was real water. Like nectar it entered his mouth and found its way to his parched stomach, its coolness soothing his burning body.

After some considerable time he began to take stock of his surroundings. He must be near civilisation. There had to be a ranch nearby.

How he had got there he could not comprehend. If it was not an act of God then what?

Should he search for the ranch house, there was bound to be one. Would they welcome him or surrender him to his tormentors?

Question after question raced through his mind. He had made it and was alive and that was all that mattered for the present.

Climbing out of the trough he sat inside the shade of the station. Exhaustion and hunger overcame him and he slept.

The sun was sending out long shadows when he awoke, he looked at his naked body and wondered what had happened to his clothing.

Leaving the station he went outside and saw before him a trail.

Returning to the station he searched for a billy can or some vessel in which to carry precious water. Finding a large earthenware jar he filled it. Placing it carefully in an old hessian sack he slung it over his shoulder. Once again he was on the trail.

With renewed hope and vigour he followed the trail which he anticipated would bring him within reach of his fellow human beings.

A dust storm rising in the distance obliterated his vision.

It was late evening when he saw in the distance a large ranch house. Forgetting the fragile jar he let the sack slide from his shoulder.

He heard the jug smash as it hit the rock hard ground. What did it matter? He had reached civilisation at last.

With no thought of his nakedness he ran like a lunatic, screaming and shouting towards the sanctuary of the house.

He was no longer cautious as like a lost sheep he raced to join his flock.

There was no response to his calling, perhaps he was too far away to be heard. Finally he found himself within the confines of a large shed. Inside he again called, his voice echoing around its emptiness.

Where were the owners, where were the sheep? He ran around the sheds calling hysterically. It was abandoned, there was nothing but the mocking echo of his voice.

"I'm here, it is me, Seámus Flynn, why don't you answer me?"

He ran to a large paddock surrounded by other buildings. Once again he looked into every door and stable. He crossed to one of the buildings and on opening the door found himself in a long room with bunk beds. This must be the shearer's quarters, but where were they?

Looking out of the window he saw the ranch house. There

189

was bound to be someone in the house.

He approached the front door and knocked, there was no response. He banged louder and called. He lifted the latch, the door swung open freely on its hinges.

"Anyone home?" he called nervously as he pushed the door fully open.

Cautiously he entered and kept calling, hoping to attract attention to himself. There was an uncanny silence about the place.

Entering the kitchen he saw several scones of bread and a large pitcher covered with a muslin cloth. Seeing the food made him realise how hungry he was. He removed the cloth.

Surely the owner would have no objection to him taking a little of the food?

Breaking a section off one of the scones he filled a mug from the pitcher and began to eat. Returning to the room he sat down on a chair. What had become of the occupants?

Then he saw another room leading off the parlour. Rising he approached the door and cautiously turned the handle. He found himself in a spacious bedroom in which was a large brass bed.

Convinced that the ranch was empty he took advantage of the situation and flopped down on to the bed.

The long journey had taken it's toll, and before he could finish his meal he fell into a deep sleep.

CAPTURED BY THE STOCKMEN

He was awakened by the sound of the door opening and people speaking.

Rising from the pillow he was confronted by three stockmen and a woman gathered around the bed. They were looking at him in amazement.

"I'm Seámus Flynn, I got lost in the bush." He held his hand out to them.

"Stay just where you are mister," came a curt reply as a gun was cocked and pointed at his chest.

They looked shocked at the man sitting upright in the bed. He was stark naked. His hair and body were caked in dried mud. His beard covered most of his face and grew towards his waist. Out from the matted hair stared two red raw eyes. There was disbelief on their faces as they stood transfixed before him.

The man holding the gun came towards him in a threatening manner. He stood over the bed and looked down at Seámus.

"How did you get here, there's nothing between us and Adelaide but a thousand miles of scrub."

Seámus could see that they were more frightened of him that he was of them.

"He must be one of them murdering Fenians, you know, the ones from the chain gang," another volunteered.

"Let him speak for himself. We asked you where did you come from?" The woman stepped to the fore.

"I am a whaler from a ship down the coast," he lied.

"How come you are so far inland ?"

"A group of us came ashore looking for water and fresh supplies and were attacked by abbo's. I ran inland to escape and got lost in the bush."

"From a whaler down the coast, don't make us laugh. You a whaler? An Irish con more likely. Does he look like a whaler?" The others laughed as the man holding the gun began to prod him.

"You're no whaler, just another dirty Irish convict from a road gang, aren't you?" The woman came forward and spat into his face.

"Lock him up for now and when we go to Adelaide we can take him with us. There is bound to be some reward," another suggested.

"A reward for an Irish felon? Don't make us laugh. They wouldn't thank you."

"She's right, you know. When they catch them they hang them."

Seámus remained silent as they debated his fate.

"Best to shoot him here and now."

"Do you know, I could do with a bit of help around here. You men are away most of the time."

She looked Seámus up and down and smiled.

"Take him Kate! You can have him as a present for whatever he's worth."

The men laughed and teased the woman.

"Shackle him and put him in the barn for now," she told them.

"Come on you, outside!"

Rising from the bed he stood before them unaware of his nakedness.

"Come on, move yourself!"

Seámus felt the muzzle of the gun stuck menacingly into his back as he was marched from the house.

Outside they manacled his hands and feet and placed a steel collar around his neck. To this they attached a long draw chain.

"You won't get out of this in a hurry," his captors laughed, as they pushed him into the barn and locked the chain to a post.

Seámus slid to the floor unable to comprehend what was happening to him. He was awakened with a hefty kick from the woman.

"On your feet young man". He rose to his feet and stood against the pillar. The woman stood in the jamb of the door with a cloth in her hands.

Opening the lock she removed the chain and replaced it with the halter.

"Come on, follow me and no tricks."

Holding the chain she dragged him like a shackled beast across the yard and into the house. Inside she placed some food and drink on the table and invited him to eat.

As he ate she spoke gently to him as she closely studied him.

"You do what I tell you and we'll get on fine, just fine," she cackled.

The woman was middle aged and had few teeth in her head. She seemed kind.

Seámus finished the meal and thanked her for her kindness. Rising to his feet he made to leave the kitchen.

"Where do you think you are off to, young man?" She jerked on the halter, causing him intense pain.

"I'm returning to the barn Mam. Where are the men gone to?"

"Don't fret your head about them. They have their work to do as we have ours, don't they?" She continued to study him intently. This disturbed him.

"Now, come with me and forget any plans to escape from a defenceless woman."

She rose to her feet and began to cackle.

"There's nowhere to go, and that's for sure," she laughed.

"I won't try to escape, all I want to do is to return to my ship," he lied.

"Ship indeed! Ships in the desert! I'll say this for you, you are full of fancy Irish stories. Come on move." She tugged on the halter and dragged him outside.

"Wash that muck off yourself. you look more like a black savage than a white man." She led him to a cut down barrel filled with water.

Once again he was tied to the halter within reach of the barrel.

"Step into the barrel and I'll wash you," she ordered.

"If you don't mind, I'd rather do it myself."

Stepping into the barrel he began to wash himself.

The woman stood for some time watching him, before she returned to the house.

He was glad when she had left, her presence was causing him acute embarrassment.

His relief, however, was to be short lived as he saw the woman return with a cloth in her hand.

Too weak and subdued he allowed her to wash him.

His fear was soon realised for she was obviously interested in more than just washing him. There was no doubt in his mind but that this obnoxious woman intended to seduce and abuse him.

With his ablution finished he was once again taken back to the house. Taking a scissors from a sideboard she trimmed his beard and cut his hair.

For some time she stood looking at him with penetrating eyes.

"Come in here."

She ordered him to follow her into the bedroom and made it clear that from now on this was where he would sleep.

In the bedroom she continued to massage him. To his embarrassment this eventually brought on an erection which excited her.

Mounting him she brutally used him and continued to do so until she had satisfied her lust for him.

On completion she made it clear that he would not be given any clothes and would remain shackled.

Was this then to be his fate? He would rather be hanged from the highest gibbet than suffer such humiliation.

Occasionally she sadistically beat him with a bull whip when he failed to satisfy her continuing lust for him.

He was glad when he saw the stockmen return. Ignoring him they entered the ranch house to be greeted by the woman.

"I see you still have the Irishman," one joked.

"You leave my Seámus alone, he is a good worker and we get on just fine. Don't we Pat?" the woman sarcastically remarked as she patted his nakedness, much to his embarrassment.

"'My Pat' is it? I see you keep him naked, willing and able". Another slapped his leathers and began to laugh. The others joined in humiliating him.

"You lot are jealous that he loves me, don't you, Pat my love," she mocked.

Whatever thoughts he had of seeking help from the stock men in his bid to escape were now shattered.

They took their cue from the woman and began to kick and humiliate him. Should he fail to have a meal on the table on time or saddle a horse at a moments notice he was brutally beaten.

He rehearsed over and over again a million plans for escape. These he would amend or abandon as flaws appeared in them.

Weeks became months and he was in the depths of despair. He no longer feared the bush.

Anything was better than what he was suffering.

ESCAPE

Christmas came and the old woman organised a party for her stockmen. There would be no respite for Seámus. He would have to help the woman with the cooking.

On Christmas Day the festivities started early with a heavy bout of drinking. This was followed by the Christmas Dinner which was followed by more drinking.

In the afternoon he was ordered to prepare a barbecue. Long into the night he was forced to fetch food and drink in order to satisfy their gluttony and demands for more and more drink.

Half demented from the orgy they looked for more entertainment. Collecting their bull whips they went into the stockade and began lashing the terrified captive horses. Others went into the bush and began shooting the sheep. They were completely out of control and Seámus was terrified when they caught him and tied him to a post.

They decided that they would give him a sound thrashing with their bull whips just for the fun of it. Each would give him three lashes. They were so drunk and incapable that many could not stand, let alone beat him. This was to his advantage. The whole loathsome drama culminated with the old woman giving him a final beating as he lay in agony on the ground.

Bloodied and weakened and with the shackles eating deep into his flesh he was ordered to his feet to again fetch and carry food and drink.

Whenever he collapsed he was horsewhipped to his feet.

By early morning they had drunk themselves into a stupor. One by one they fell into a deep sodden sleep.

Seámus looked at the sleepers. This presented a golden opportunity for a spontaneous escape. All the horses were at the station and the stockmen were too drunk to care or notice should he go missing.

Retreating into the kitchen he held his shackles tight to prevent them rattling. Although they were unconscious from the drink, he could not afford to take any chances. What if one of them found him trying to escape?

Opening the bedroom door he crept inside. On the bed lay the woman and one of the stockmen. Both were naked and snoring loudly.

Cautiously he approached the bed, holding tightly to his shackles. He need not have worried for they were both dead to the world and would not waken for many hours .

The key to his freedom was on a cord tied around the woman's neck. On the floor lay the leathers and belt of the stockman. Beside them lay his shearing knife.

His first thoughts were to stab the woman and the stockman in revenge for the humiliation he had suffered.

Picking up the knife he approached the bed and raised the knife. Should he cut the old woman's throat in retaliation? Then he thought of how Sheila must have suffered. He looked at them with contempt.

He realised that should he kill them he would be remorselessly hunted down and hanged.

"You're not worth it!" he spat, contemptuously

With a swift move he cut the cord holding the key from the woman's neck. Slowly he drew the cord towards him trying not to disturb the sleepers.

The key slipped from the cord and lay on the pillow. As he reached down to pick it up the woman moved and the key disappeared under her head. He was so near to freedom and yet so far. The key was now trapped between her head and the pillow.

Then he remembered an old trick he used to play as a child. Leaning over the bed he blew gently into the woman's ear. Raising her head she scratched at her ear to remove the offending irritation. He stopped blowing and moved back into the shadows. He waited until she had settled down.

Returning to the bedside he again blew into her ear. This time she turned over completely as he had anticipated she would.

There on the pillow lay his ticket to freedom. Picking up the key he returned to the kitchen and removed his manacles. He filled two panniers with food and a water bag with water.

From the paddock he selected one of the finest horses and saddled it. He took the horse to a post and tied it securely.

Returning to the house he collected all the guns, with the exception of one which he put to one side. The others he threw into the deep trough together with the ammunition.

Picking up his manacles he entered the bedroom. Lifting the man's right leg he brought it within proximity of the woman's left leg and locked them together with the manacles. Passing the chain through the iron rails of the bed, top and bottom, he closed the lock and turned the key.

From the men's store room he selected what he required and dressed himself. He looked into the mirror and smiled, perhaps for the first time in years. Picking up the gun he slung the gun belt over his shoulder, and was once again on his way to freedom.

Outside the house he opened the gate to the paddock and stampeded the horses into the bush. Opening the sluice gate he released their water supply into the ground.

Mounting his chosen horse and without looking back he vanished into the bush.

THE RIVER OF GOLD

Using all the skills taught him by the aborigines he followed the trails made by their ancestors.

These trails would lead him to water holes. This was most critical for he would need plenty of water for himself and his horse if they were to survive.

After three days he was full of the joys of life. He had found two watering holes and was optimistic as to his future. He was making excellent progress and felt sure that it would not be too long before he reached a settlement or a town. Late one evening he came to the banks of a river, here he would spend the night. This was as good a place as any to hunt for food. There were bound to be animals in the area seeking water.

Having refreshed himself and his horse he went deep into the bush and, unsaddling the horse, tied him to a tree. Returning to the river bank he lay down with his rifle at the ready and waited.

Hearing horsemen approaching he concealed himself.

"Thank God we found the river. I was giving up any hope of your scouting abilities, Tom".

One of the men dismounted and removed his bush hat. Scooping up the cool water he poured it over his head.

"Which river might this be?" another asked.

"It's the Murray, the little Murray, cobbo," another laughed as he cascaded water over himself.

So this was the river Murray. He was travelling inland instead of towards the coast.

'I should have looked at the flow of the water,' he chided himself.

Had he kept on his present course he would have crossed Swan Hill and into New South Wales. This was desert territory and as barren and bleak as that he had just escaped. He shivered at the thought. By following the river he would come to the Southern Ocean and the town of Adelaide in South Australia.

He gleaned from their appearance and conversation that they were Bushrangers. They would show little mercy to anyone crossing their paths.

They settled down on the river bank to rest. It would be many hours before they decided to leave. Some lit their pipes and sat back talking. Others placed their bush hats over their eyes and surrendered to sleep.

Seámus awoke next morning and was surprised and

delighted to see that the horsemen had gone.

Rising stiffly from his hiding place he went and collected his horse.

Having watered and inspected her he placed a long halter over her neck and allowed her to wander as she may.

He washed the grime and sweat from his body before settling down in the river's cool waters to take his bearings.

He let his mind wander back to his home in Ireland. He wondered how his family were faring and if they were praying for him. He thought of Sheila and his son buried deep in the bush.

He listened to the river dance as the water made its escape over the stones. He compared this to the Rinnce Siublac in his father's cottage so very long ago.

Dancing was a regular occurrence in his father's cottage, it having a good flagged floor. He remembered the 'Craic' and the Sean Scéals and he remembered his brother. He remembered too the day his freedom was so cruelly taken from him and he but a lad of sixteen years.

Tears welled up in his eyes.

The table he remembered was on one occasion laden with pig's heads, scones by the gross and bacon and cabbage bubbling in a big iron pot. It was so big that it was bending the crane over the coals. In the corner sat a barrel of porter and beside it another to replenish it when it was exhausted.

In the corner next to it sat Seámus Hennessy, the basket maker. In his fist he held the biggest tankard that Seámus ever laid his eyes on.

Whose wedding was that?" he thought.

He thought of how his mother chastised Seámus for tapping his pipe out on the flank of bacon hanging in the chimney.

He smiled through his tears for he knew that his mother would be praying for him. With her prayers and with God given strength he would soon be back in the old country again.

Tears once again blurred his vision and he cried unashamedly.

"Here I am, an innocent man before God, running like a cornered deer. Why am I being punished so much?"

When his emotions had passed he washed his tears away.

Walking along the river bank he picked up stones from the shallows. These he pitched into the water and tried to make them skim along the surface. He had often done this as a child back home in Ireland.

Reaching down he picked up a fresh supply of skimming

stones. As he was about to cast one he was more than surprised to see a nugget of gold in the water.

Dropping the skimming stones he picked it up and rubbed it against his shirt. He looked at it and prayed that it was real and not fool's gold.

He rubbed it once again on his shirt, and then he bit it.

"It's gold! It's gold!" he shouted as he jumped up and down in the water.

Composing himself he went down on his hands and knees and began a methodical search of the riverbed.

Nuggets of all shapes and sizes glistened in the crystal water calling on him to come and collect them.

God and his Blessed Mother had rewarded him in return for all his suffering. He was elated as he found more and more nuggets.

He laughed aloud as he continued his bountiful search.

Returning to the bush he hid his gold in his saddle bags . Taking his horse by the halter be brought her to the stream. There he tied the halter to a large rock and let her graze freely.

Opening his swag he lit a fire and cooked his tucker before resuming his search.

He spent the next week on the river searching for any evasive nugget that may have escaped his attention.

Satisfied that he had recovered all the gold he buckled his saddle bags and left the area.

He worried that he might come face to face with the Bushrangers. They would not hesitate in killing him and stealing his hard earned gold. He was determined to reach civilisation as soon as possible. By following the river he knew that he would eventually reach a town or settlement.

After a week he crossed the border into Southern Australia and continued his journey along the banks of the River Murray.

For the first time in as many weeks he finally saw signs of human habitation. Some miles down river he came upon the town of Mildura. It was not a town of any significance but to Seámus it was paradise.

Kicking his heels into the flanks of his horse he encouraged her into a gallop. Soon he was in the main and only street.

His first concern was the safety of his gold. Outside a wooden building he saw a simple notice hanging under the veranda, 'Assay Office'. Taking his pannier bags from his saddle he entered and looked anxiously about him.

Seeing a man sitting half asleep behind a desk he approached.

"Are you the official Assayer?" he asked.
"You have come to the right place, are you a prospector?"
Seámus did not reply. Opening the buckles he spilled the gold out on the desk.
"Is this real gold?" he asked anxiously.
"Don't you know?" The assayer picked up a nugget and studied it. "It's gold alright, lets have a closer look." The assayer graded the gold, weighed it and valued it.
"This is a lucky strike, you do know that there is a government duty on your find?"
Seámus could not believe it when he was told the value of his find, he was now a very rich man. The assayer handed him a receipt for his gold.
"Take this to the American Bank across the street. They will deposit it in an account for you".
Having deposited his cheque he withdrew what money he thought he would need for his immediate needs and his passage back to Ireland.
He disposed of his horse and took lodgings in the only boarding house. Tomorrow he would continue his business.
All he wanted for now was a hot bath and a good night's sleep.

A FAST CLIPPER TO IRELAND

Seámus rose early next morning and went in search of the local magistrate.

Once there he related his story as to how he was sent to Australia as a felon. Having served his sentence he was given a "Ticket of Leave". This made him a free man . Not wishing to return home a pauper he and his friend decided to try their hand as prospectors. He related how his friend died in the bush, leaving him alone and lost. Then he was attacked by savage aborigines, robbed and left for dead. Having survived this assault he wandered through the bush and was again attacked by bushrangers who left him beside a river. It was when following the river seeking civilisation that he discovered the gold.

He knew that he was taking a gamble telling the story more or less as it happened. Were he to deviate from what he told him then he may suspect the truth. He felt sorry having to say that he was attacked by savages. He felt that if he told the truth and said that the aborigines befriended him he would not be believed. Having suffered so much and made it so far he had no intention of jeopardising his fight for freedom.

He need not have worried for the magistrate was more interested in the gold coins lying on his desk than in what he was hearing. Smiling, the magistrate reached out and picked up the money.

"You are indeed a very lucky man to survive such an ordeal."

Rising to his feet he went to a cupboard and returned carrying a large bible.

He called on Seámus to swear on the Bible that what he told him was the truth and nothing but the truth. With this formality concluded he opened the desk drawer and withdrew an official document. Dipping his pen into his inkwell he confirmed in writing that Seámus Flynn was a free man. Shaking the document dry he embossed the official seal of confirmation on the parchment and handed it to Seámus. With a final handshake he carefully rolled up the document and left the office.

He was now a free man and should he be stopped then he had his ticket of leave to prove it.

His next task was to purchase a fresh horse and ample supplies for the final leg of his journey to Adelaide.

Although he was anxious to return to Ireland and home

he had no intention of taking any undue risks. He waited at the hotel until others were going on the same route. The road to Adelaide was patrolled by bushrangers waiting to attack and rob any unwary traveller. There was safety in numbers.

Three days out from Mildura as they were preparing their meal a band of bushrangers entered the camp.

"Got any food to spare for fellow travellers?" the leader demanded. Then ,without waiting, they began to open the bags of the travellers and empty them on the ground.

It was clear as to what they were and that they had no interest in food. What they were after was money, jewellery and especially gold. Gold was safe and untraceable.

As some were emptying the bags and cases, others began to search the saddlebags.

One of the victims, seeing his worldly possessions being stolen, attacked the culprit. The bushranger was too busy stuffing his pockets with the man's possessions and failed to notice the attack until it was too late.

Both men fell to the ground locked in combat. They screamed and kicked at each other as they rolled over and over on the dust covered ground. The bushranger broke loose and scrambled to his feet. Raising his boot he gave his victim a vicious kick that sent him rolling down the bank and into the river . Before his victim could regain his feet the bushranger was upon him and, raising his knife, plunged it deep into his chest.

With a cry his victim fell backwards into the water. Slowly the water changed from crystal clear to a watery red.

As some of the bushrangers found more profitable booty than others they began to squabble between themselves.

They were so intent on robbing each other that they failed to notice a platoon of mounted Redcoats coming over the hill. The victims watched in relief and amazement as the robbers continued to fight, oblivious to the approaching danger.

The officer, drawing his sword, called on his men to advance at the trot.

This was the one time that Seámus was grateful to see Redcoats.

All too late the bushrangers saw the impending danger and tried to escape. They had no time to mount their horses nor to escape. Running into the bush they tried to hide but to no avail. Soon they were rounded up and roped together.

The officer and two of his subordinates remained with the

travellers checking their credentials and returning their property.

Then they gave them an escort as far as the road to Adelaide. Seámus smiled to himself as he held a congenial conversation with one of the officers. Little did he know that he was talking to a Fenian from the road gang.

On reaching Adelaide he booked into a hotel near to the quay. His next task was to seek a passage to Ireland on the first available ship.

This was his lucky day for he was informed that a fast clipper was due to leave on the tide. The clipper was delivering mail and dispatches to Dublin and London and would be berthing at Queenstown.(Cork) He could hardly contain himself on hearing this good news. There was a passage available, but at a price. Seámus took this as a good omen, passage on these ships was at a premium. He could be home in Ireland in half the time or less that it took a conventional ship. Returning to the hotel he packed his belongings and boarded the ship.

On board he was soon to learn that all was not well in Ireland. Nothing, it seemed, had changed and this made him apprehensive .

Within six weeks the ship docked at Queenstown. Seámus set his feet on Talab-na-hEireann once again. It was from here that he had been so cruelly transported halfway across the world so very long ago.

What his return held in store for him he had yet to learn.

WILLIAM BENNETT, Quaker on a visit to ERRIS, Co. Mayo describes the state of the cabins in Belmullet in march 1847

Language utterly fails me in attempting to depict the state of the wretched inmates. I would not willingly add another to the harrowing details that have been told; but still they are the facts of actual experience; for the knowledge to which we stand accountable.

I have certainly sought out the most remote and destitute corners; but it is still within the bounds of our Christian land, under our Christian government, and entailing upon us- both as individuals and members of a human community- A Christian responsibility from which no one of us can escape. My hand trembles as I write.

The scene of human misery and degradation we witnessed will haunt my imagination, with the vividness and power of some horrid and tyrannous delusion, rather that the features of a sober reality.

We entered a cabin. Stretched in one dark corner scarcely visible from the smoke and rags that covered them, were three children huddled together, lying there because they were too weak to rise, pale and ghastly, their little limbs- on removing a portion of the filthy covering-perfectly emaciated, eyes sunk, voice gone, and evidently in the last stages of actual starvation.

Crouched over the turf embers was another form, wild and all but naked, scarcely human in appearance. It stirred not, nor noticed us-On some straw, sodden upon the ground, moaning piteously, was a shrivelled old woman, imploring us to give her something, baring her limbs partly to show how the skin hung loosely from the bones as soon as she attracted our attention. Above her on something like a ledge, was a young woman, with sunken cheeks- a mother I have no doubt-who scarcely raised her eyes in answer to our enquiries, but pressed her hand upon her forehead and looked with unutterable anguish and despair.

Many cases were widows, whose husbands had been taken off recently with the fever, and thus their only pittance, obtained from the public works, entirely cut off. In many the husband or sons lay prostrate, under that horrid disease, the result of long and continued famine and low living- in which first the limbs and then the body swell most frightfully, and finally burst.

We entered up to fifty of these tenements. the scene was one and invariable, differing little but in the number of sufferers, or of the group, occupying the several corners within... perhaps the poor children presented the most piteous and heart rendering spectacle.

Many were too weak to stand, their little limbs attenuated, except when the frightful had taken place of previous emaciation- beyond the power of volition when moved Every

infantile expression entirely departed; and in some, reason and intelligence had evidently flown. Many were remnants of families, crowed together in one cabin; orphaned little relatives taken in by the equally destitute, and even strangers, for these poor people are kind to one another to the end. In one cabin was a sister just dying, lying by her side was her little brother just dead, I have even worse than this to relate, but it is useless to multiply details, and they are , in fact unfit. they did but rarely complain. When enquired what was the matter? The answer was alike in all- Ta mé Ocras- (I am hungry) We truly learned the meaning of that sad word OCRAS.

WILLIAM BENNETT ERRIS
COUNTY MAYO

IN THE YEAR OF OUR LORD MARCH 1847.

A SAD AWAKENING

From a stables in the city he purchased a horse and was soon on his way to Skibbereen and home.

Coming over the crest of a hill he saw the straggling village. His heart beat faster as he looked down at Skibbereen.

Time, it seemed had stood still.

Riding through the village he was shocked to see that it had deteriorated so much. Most of the cottages had tumbled and there was no sign of life.

What had happened to Skibbereen and where were all it's occupants?

All around him there was decay and neglect.

Dismounting he took the reins in his hand and walked towards the workshop of old Seámus. The workshop had long since been abandoned as was evident by the profusion of yellow wallflowers growing on the gable end. Nailed to the mullion over what was left of the casement was a tattered, yet discernible Saint Bridget cross.

Memories of the times and of the errands he ran for old Seámus crossed his mind.

Mounting his horse he urged him on through the village. A steady drizzle began to fall, making him shiver in his already wet clothing.

"God in Heaven this is indeed a miserable place," he thought as he pulled his cloak closer around him.

He was roused from his daydreaming by a call from a woman in a long shabby skirt and shawl. Her skirt was caked in mud. Rain dripped from the tassels of her shawl. Her bare feet were caked in mud and she seemed oblivious to the rain and sleet.

"It's not yourself in the flesh is it, Seámus Flynn, as I live and die"

The old woman stopped in front of him.

"It's me, alright, and who might you be?"

"Don't tell me that you have forgotten Maisie O'Neill?"

"Maisie, sure, of course I remember you. How could I forget? Tell me, where are the others?"

"Ah, God help you, you have been away so you have. You won't know then, will you?"

"Know what, tell me?"

"They're all gone Seámus, so they are. All gone."

"Who is gone? What are you saying?"

"Your parents, Seámus, they died during the Great

Hunger, together with the village. Turn around and leave this accursed land. In God's Holy Name."

Like a soothsayer she clung to his saddle and gave a graphic account of the tragedy that had befallen old Skibbereen.

Without waiting for any further explanation he urged his horse to the home of his parents.

He was shocked to see that the roof had collapsed in on itself. Dismounting, he ran towards the old house.

He placed his hands on the rusting gate and pushed it open. As if protesting at being disturbed the old gate groaned and reluctantly gave way.

Apprehensively he stood before the door and, with a deep sigh, forced it open. The door had been bolted from within. He now feared the worst.

The house had changed little since he had been taken away all those years ago. Every stick of furniture was in place as if caught in a time warp.

The interior smelt of damp and decay, yet the rain had not fully penetrated the collapsed roof. Crossing to the window he tried to open the curtains, but they disintegrated and fell to the floor.

He was shocked to see the window bricked up. He knew the horror of what this meant. This he tried to dismiss from his mind and searched for some other explanation.

He had a strange premonition as he went deeper into the cottage. He felt that his parents were present and watching his every movement.

Yet the cottage was as silent as the grave and he could hear his own heart beating.

At his parent's bedroom door he paused. He had a feeling that he should not enter. There was something within the room that did not warrant intrusion.

"Please stop! Go away! Do not enter this hallowed place," an inner voice warned him.

Ignoring his feelings he gripped the latch and lifted the bolt. Once again he paused. Why was he being discouraged from entering the room.

Shrugging his shoulders he put it down to a figment of his imagination. With a final push he had the door open. He looked into the dark interior. This window too had been boarded. This was the room where he and his brother Brendan had first seen the light of day. A glimmer of light pierced the sealed window and made a round circle on the opposite wall.

The dark room smelt of decay, and a steady drip from the roof tattooed a tin plate on the floor.

He was sure that there was someone or something

watching him from the darkness.

"Who's there?" he challenged on hearing gentle movement somewhere within its confines.

There was no reply, the room was once again as silent as a tomb.

"I know you are here, come out now and all will be well," he challenged the phantom .

The steady pulse of the drip on the tin plate continued to mock him.

Returning to the kitchen he pulled dry thatch from the roof and lit it from his tinder box.

He returned to the room. The incandescent light sent dancing shadows along the wall as he moved. Elongated beings looked down at him questioning his intrusion. He delayed looking towards the bed for as long as possible. Turning to face it he looked up at the picture of the Sacred Heart hanging on the wall.

"I will bless the house in which the image of my Sacred Heart is exposed and honoured."

He read and reread the promise to the right of the sorrowful picture of Christ with his heart exposed.

A spider had built her trap over the left side of the picture. He watched her as she sat waiting for her prey.

At the base of the picture he read the names of his parents followed by his name and that of his brother Brendan.

Below was the signature of Father Clery, the parish priest who had blessed the picture for them.

He gave a wry smile as he read the inscriptions and the name of Father Clery.

He was reminded of a time, during the Stations, when Father Clery came to bless the house and all within. He was instructing Brendan in the true faith and asked,

"How would you know Jesus if you saw him, Brendan?" and Brendan had replied,

"That would be easy, Father, for Jesus wears his heart outside his shift..."

On the edge of the picture hung his mother's old Scapulars into which the spider had entwined her trap. As he reached up to remove them he dislodged the spiders web and disclosed a further promise....

"I will give peace to their families."

'Peace', he thought, 'Does this God know the agony that I am suffering?'

He approached the brass rail of the bed and, raising the torch high above his head, he looked down upon the bed. In the dim light he saw the outline of the patchwork quilt. He gripped the torch tighter and approached the bedside.

The light travelling ahead of him came to rest at the head of the bed. Squeezing the torch tighter he stood transfixed. In the bed were two skeletons lying side by side as if asleep. In their hands were entwined their rosaries. Had he found the last resting place of his parents?

Blessing himself, he stood indecisive as to what to do next. He stood for a considerable length of time looking down at what remained of his parents. Then, picking up the ends of the quilt, he covered the remains.

Although he was sure that these were his parents he hoped that he was wrong. They might have left and others taken over the cottage.

Searching the house failed to reveal the identity of the two corpses in the bed. With no clues in the kitchen he returned to the bedroom. Knocking the stones and mud from the window he continued his search. He was reluctant to search the bed .

Still with no inkling as to the identity of the corpses he returned to the kitchen and sat on a stool to gather his thoughts.

With his chin in his hands he looked into the empty grate. Then he remembered the secret hiding hole at the back of the chimney.

If there was a final message for him from his parents, then they would have put it there for him to find.

Removing the slab he reached deep inside the recess and was delighted when he found the family deed box.

Inside was a letter addressed to himself and the finder. It asked that should it be found it was to be be sent to him in the penal colony. Inside the letter was a half sovereign to cover the cost.

His father, being a methodical man, had written down full details as to how they had died.

On the night of October 31st 1848, the village was cut off from the outside world by a blizzard. There was no food and most of the villagers were dying of hunger and plague. They too had contracted the plague which was raging along the SouthWest coast of Ireland. There were no doctors and no food available. They knew that they had not long to live and could not bear the shame of the vile stench coming from their emaciated bodies. Returning to their cottage they bolted the doors and barricaded the windows. His mother set about cleaning the house and his father sat down and wrote the account of all the happenings since Seámus was taken away before placing it in the wall. When all was prepared they would place the 'Connail Mor' in a saucer and light it before retiring to their bed. They were sorry that he would not be there to receive their blessing.

It was all that they had to leave him in this world and that too was denied them.

Still, God was merciful, and would understand that their final Rosary was for him. They would make their peace with God and pray for his safe return. Then, having said their goodbyes to each other, they would settle down to die without shame.

They hoped he would soon be released from the prison colony and find them before the crowbar gang came with the landlord and set their cottage on fire with them inside. They worried that they would go to their punishment in the hereafter hungry for a final prayer from their son and they would not be laid to rest beside their youngest, Brendan. They would pray for him always and wait for him in the next world. They requested that they be laid to rest beside their son Brendan in the village graveyard.

With tears streaming down his face Seámus read on and on...

They were sorry that they had nothing to leave him but their prayers. Life had been cruel to them since he was deported. The village that he loved so much and most of his schoolmates were dead. Many had died in the workhouse and were buried in mass graves somewhere on the hillside. No cross marked their graves.

"I am now a rich man, if only I had arrived sooner," he cried. He knew that they had been dead long before he escaped from the penal colony.

The rain continued rapping on the tin plate. He looked down at the plate which was upside down on the floor. 'Was this the plate that held their last meal?' he thought His mother, being a tidy woman, would never leave a plate sitting on the floor. Picking it up he held it to him and again said a silent prayer.

Taking his mother's Rosary he kissed the old wooden cross and knelt beside the bed, as he had so often before. He prayed for the repose of the souls of his parents. He prayed too for his brother Brendan and sought his intercession with the angels.

He remembered the prayer with which his father always finished the Rosary.

He too would finish his Rosary, in his parent's cottage, as had they for all those long years ....

'Go raibh Críost agus Muire

Dar dtionlaic feadh an bhóthair;
Agus turas é in aistear,
Gura tairbheach gach orlach'.

('May Jesus and Mary
Go with us the length of the road;
May our journey not be in vain
But may every inch of it be for our good.')

Rising he looked once again at the blanket covering the remains of his parents.
He felt a peace and calm as he placed his hands affectionately on their covered heads.
With a sigh he placed the box under his arm and, closing the door, left the cottage of death.
Carefully he closed the main door, promising to return and honour their wishes

SEÁMUS RETURNS TO THE ESTATE

There were several houses belonging to the estate lying empty in the village. He would approach the administrators with a view to renting one.

On reaching the manor he was more than surprised to see that the gates were flung wide open, and the gatekeeper's cottage derelict and deserted.

The once immaculate driveway was overgrown with rhododendrons and briars. It was now passable only on horseback or on foot.

On entering the compound of the home farm he noted that this too was deserted and empty. The offices and outhouses were abandoned and open to the elements. Doors swung at crazy angles, some on one hinge. This was no longer the well-managed estate that he had been so cruelly taken from all those years ago.

Tying his horse to a post he left the compound and approached the manor.

He noticed that the wooded shutters on the windows were locked securely. The great house was also showing signs of neglect. The once immaculate flower beds were now a mass of choking weeds with the odd rose bush making a vain effort to survive.

As he approached the great doors he noted that they were now splitting and would need urgent attention. Whatever would his father say if he saw them? But father was dead and by the look of the estate it too was dead.

Seámus lifted the heavy knocker and banged on the door. The sound vibrated throughout the house.

He waited but there was no answer. Going to the side of the house he looked through the drawing room window which was not shuttered, and looked inside.

The room was furnished, and from it's tidiness seemed to be occupied.

"What are you doing there, is there something that I can do for you?" He looked up startled to see a young woman standing before him.

"Excuse me, is the manager or the brigadier available?" Seámus removed his cap as he did when he was a servant. Old traditions die hard.

"I asked you, what is your business here?" the woman asked once again, ignoring his remarks.

"I've come hoping to rent one of the cottages in the village. I believe that they still belong to the estate."

"Oh those! I'm sorry, but they are not for rent." She returned to the house and closed the door.

Seámus walked a short distance down the drive and, stopping, looked back at the house in disbelief.

As he did so he saw the great doors open and the young woman once again appear on the steps.

"Excuse me, young man. Did you say that you were looking for a cottage?"

"Well! Yes I am . Do you know where I might find one?"

"There are some gatehouses available on the estate. Perhaps one of them may suit your needs."

"Would it be possible for me to see one, I really am desperate, if you must know," said Seámus, returning to the door.

"By all means, you can take your pick. The prettiest ones are down the main drive. If you wait, I'll fetch the keys." After a short time she returned and handed the keys to him.

"They are all empty now." She seemed sad and lonely.

"Would you please return the keys." He took the keys reached out to him.

He inspected many before he decided that the best one was at the main entrance.

"I'd like to have the one at the end of the drive, that is, if it is alright by you," he told her on his return.

"If it is to your satisfaction, then sure, fine, it is yours." She smiled for the first time.

"Where might the Brigadier and his family be. I only ask because..." He hesitated. "Well, the estate looks abandoned."

"You knew the Brigadier, then. May I be so bold as to ask who you are?"

"To tell you the truth, my father and I worked on the estate many years ago. It was my father who repaired those doors." He ran his hand affectionately along the panels.

"What is your name, I cannot place the face".

"I'm Seámus Flynn, son of Tom Flynn, rest his soul." Lifting his cap out of respect he immediately replaced it.

"I was wrongfully accused of stealing a hare and deported to Australia, in chains."

"Now I remember you, you were the one who used to tell us stories about Ireland. Seámus Flynn, so that is your name. Welcome to Ireland, such as it is". She held her hand out in greeting.

"I see that you are puzzled and don't remember me. I am Lady Harriott Elizabeth. My parents and brother are long dead. I'm the last survivor." Clutching the keys tightly she turned away.

"I am sorry, indeed I am. I would never have known you."

"I'm not surprised, look at the state of me and the estate."

"Oh! I did not mean that, please, I'm sorry."

"There is no need to apologise, I understand. You don't seem to know much about what happened here. You don't know of the Great Hunger?"

"Know! Of course I know. Did not your father have me deported in the middle of it?"

"You have good reason to be bitter, then."

"I am really sorry for you, I really am. I have only recently found both my parents dead in their cottage."

"We are all sorry, that is all anyone says in Ireland. Being sorry never brought the dead back."

"I am sorry" Seámus half smiled. "There I go again. Well, now that you know who I am I guess you will not want me as a tenant. I'll bid you good day."

"Don't be so presumptive. If you want to rent the cottage then you are more than welcome. As you have seen, the estate has fallen on bad times."

"Then that is settled. As I'm here could I have your permission to look around the estate some time?"

"I have little doubt but that it will bring back sad memories, but you are more than welcome."

"What rent will you be asking for the cottage?"

"Let's say £40 per annum, does that suit you? and," she added as an afterthought, "Yes, free run of the estate."

Thanking her he took his leave and returned to the village. Once there he made arrangements to have his parents interred in the family plot beside his brother Brendan.

With the burial completed he returned to his new home . He would have the furniture from his old home brought to the gatehouse.

LADY HARRIOTT TELLS HER STORY

With little to occupy him he painted and decorated the gatehouse and was soon a familiar figure in the village. He took to riding his chestnut mare through the estate. Life for Seámus Flynn was changing for the better.

One afternoon as he was returning from a long walk through the estate he heard a clap of thunder and looking up saw the ominous dark clouds racing across the sky. He retreated as quickly as he could to the safety of the mansion. Standing under the porch he looked out at the sleet and rubbed his hands together to keep warm.

He heard the door behind him being opened.

"Won't you come in out of the rain?" An elderly servant stood with the door open welcoming him in.

"Thank you, that is most kind of you."

Seámus entered the hall and removed his coat.

"Here, let me have that." The woman reached out and took his coat.

"Come in, Mr Flynn, and warm yourself," He heard the familiar voice of Lady Harriott call from the drawing room.

Seámus entered the room and apologised for the state of his attire.

"Don't worry about it, come sit by the fire." She pointed to a chair opposite hers.

"I did not know that there were servants in the house."

"Servants! There is only Mary and I here. She is a Godsend. Most of the house is locked and deserted."

"I took the liberty Mam, if you don't be minding." Mary entered the room carrying a tray of refreshments.

"You're an angel Mary, thank you."

"Will I pour Mam?"

Mary stood before the fire. Seámus saw the lines of age on her face in the glow from the turf. She was still the servant and obedient to the last.

'How sad,' he thought. Here was a woman who had served the household from childhood, yet she had nothing to show for it.

"No Mary, I'll see to it, thanks". Mary genuflected and gently closed the door behind her as she left the room.

"You must wonder at the state of the estate. You see a big change since you were ....."

She stopped herself from bringing up old scores.

"From the look of the place , I would say that it is in bad

need of good management."

"That is the easy part. There is no income whatsoever from the estate. The Great Hunger put paid to whatever resources we possessed. There has been no help from the government and the village has been left to die."

"What of the rents from the village, surely this would have helped?"

"Income from the village? I have little doubt but that you saw the state of the village. Father returned from England hoping to rescue the estate. He spent every penny we possessed and more to try and keep the estate solvent. Then the government brought in a law that proclaimed that Irish rates should support Irish poor. That was the final nail in the coffin for father could not meet those draconian demands."

"Did he not explain all this to his tenants?"

"Explain! He called a meeting in the Village Hall and tried to divulge to them the seriousness of the situation. The villagers, without listening, put the blame on my father. Then they walked out leaving father to solve all their problems."

Shortly after that he contracted the plague and took to his bed. Then mother and my brother took ill with the same malady. The village was in quarantine and it was impossible to obtain any help from outside. Father died a few days later and two workmen from the estate helped to inter his body in the family crypt. With no income and no means of paying the workers they left us to our fate. Who could blame them?

Mary, God bless her, stayed with us and helped with the nursing of mother and my brother. Within the week they too were dead and Mary and I took their bodies and laid them in the crypt. So you see there is nobody left apart from myself and my servant, Mary."

"Surely you cannot blame starving tenants for the demise of your estate?" Seámus was not convinced by the argument.

"Of course I blame them. My father looked after them and gave them work and food."

Seámus was about to say that the land belonged to the people in the first place. Giving them a pittance of their own land did not make the land grabber a benefactor.

He thought better of it; what was the use in arguing with the converted?

A REMINDER OF OLD TIMES

Entering the village one afternoon he was accosted by a ragged wretch of a person.

"Please come and help me," he begged, holding on to the reins of the horse and forcing her to stop.

"What is the matter with you? Let go of my horse at once!" Seámus reached down and pushed the man away.

"Please, in God's Holy Name, please help me!"

Looking behind him Seámus saw the man with his hands joined. He was now kneeling in the road, pleading.

"What is it that you seek?" Seámus returned to where the man was kneeling.

"It's not me, sir! Oh please, my wife is in bad need of a doctor."

"You're mistaken, I am not a doctor."

"Would you please come to my cabin and at least offer a little comfort. Please!"

"Very well then, but I can promise nothing."

Seámus dismounted and, throwing the reins over the horse's back, followed the man down the road.

Reaching a half-finished famine road the man led him down a muddy track. Overgrown blackberry and hawthorn bushes threw obstructions across their path. Seámus, fearing that his horse might be blinded by the bushes, tied her to a post and continued on foot. The track smelt of decay and death and there was something portentous about the place.

In a hollow screened by bushes he smelled the reek of smoke.

"We are here, sir, may God bless you for your indulgence." The man ran ahead and stopped at the door of a dilapidate cottage. The roof was sagging and in a dangerous condition. The door or what was once a door was closed, there may as well have been no door at all. The bottom had rotted away and hessian sacking had been nailed to what remained.

Raising the latch the man opened the door. As he did so another piece fell off of what remained.

"I must make a new door one day," he apologised as he picked up the piece of wood and threw it to one side.

Seámus entered the foul smelling hovel. As his eyes adjusted to the dark he noticed the damp earthen floor covered in fungi. It was from this that the smell was coming.

Looking across at the pathetic smouldering excuse of a fire he noticed a three legged iron pot. It was stained with the remains of Indian corn that had been long since been eaten. What was left hung in long transparent slivers over the side.

His attention was distracted by a woman lying in the leaba suidheacán mumbling her beads.

'If there was a God in heaven then surely he would hear her prayers,' thought Seámus.

The only signs of a well filled belly was that of a huge rat. The rat kept scurrying in and out of a hole behind the fireplace.

On seeing Seámus the woman stopped praying and rose up in the bed.

"In God's Name, sir, please fetch the priest and don't let me leave the world without the sign of absolution," she pleaded.

"Fetch the priest, son, before it is too late. I do not wish to rot in hell," she again pleaded before collapsing on to the bed.

The wind howled and moaned around the cottage blowing the sacking covering the door to and fro.

Ignoring the woman's pleas he went to the ciscéan and took several sods of black turf and screwed them into the fire. Sparks and flames leaped up the chimney sending a warm glow around the room.

The rat, curious as to what was happening, came cautiously from his burrow. His whiskers bristled as he smelled the air. He began to preen himself, but on seeing the two men retreated swiftly to the safety of his burrow.

Ignoring the rat, Seámus went to the side of the fire and, taking the handle of the bellows in his hand, began to turn it. In response the fire began to send a comforting heat throughout the room.

"I'm Jimmy Murphy and this is my wife Anne."

He approached the fire and could not resist turning his back to the warming heat.

"I'm Seámus Flynn, Tom Flynn was my father." He let go of the handle and reached out his hand in greeting.

Seeing that the fire was now engulfing the three legged pot he reached across and pulled it clear of the flames. They had enough problems to deal with. A cracked pot would only exasperate the situation further.

"Where do you expect to find a doctor for your wife?" Seámus queried.

"I just don't know, she is now in God's hands."

"If you kept the house warm and gave her a hot meal, it might help."

219

"There is little problem with the fire. I have a haggard filled with dry turf. With all the problems I let the fire run down, so I did. There is no food in the house and we have not eaten this week. That is the truth, mister," he apologised.

"You mean that both you and your wife have not eaten this past week?"

"That's the truth of the matter, but then who has? What can we do?"

"Here, give me a hand to carry the bed nearer to the fire, leaving her in that damp corner could kill her."

"God Bless you son, I feel better already." The gaunt face of the woman looked up at him in gratitude.

"I'll go and see what I can find. In the meantime, put the pot on the boil, I'll not be too long away." Seámus left the hovel and returned to where his horse was tethered.

On the way to the village he met with a woman carrying two hens in a basket.

"Are the hens for sale, Mam?" Seámus looked down at the scrawny birds.

"They are indeed, sir, and fine laying birds they are."

She lifted one of the birds out by its wings and weighed her up and down in her hands. The bird cried her protest before the woman placed her back inside the basket.

"How much are you asking for them?" He looked at the miserable birds who under normal circumstances would be laughed out of the market.

"I'm asking four shillings for them and not one penny less will I take."

"Four shillings it is then, but I'll need the basket as well."

"Sure, I'll throw the basket in and we'll say nothing of the luck penny."

Approaching his stirrup she handed over the birds.

He was lucky in finding some vegetables for sale but at a cost that was beyond the means of the villagers.

He returned to the cottage happy with himself. He was sure that if the couple could get a little food then they had a chance of survival.

He helped to kill and boil one of the birds and added a generous portion of vegetables to the pot.

"This should last you for a day or two. I must make my apologies now".

As he left the cottage the night was dark and a chill wind was blowing from the East. Turning up the collar of his coatamore he returned to his gatehouse.

NOTICE TO QUIT

Pinned to the door he found a note from lady Elizabeth asking him to call at the manor on his return. Unsaddling his horse he left her loose in the meadow and went up the drive. At the door he was met by Mary.

"Come in sir, Her Ladyship is waiting for you in the drawing room."

"Is that you Seámus?" He heard the familiar voice call from within the room. Entering the room he paused and looked towards the fire. A high backed chair hid from view the occupant. He knew that it could be none other than Her Ladyship.

"Come in and make yourself at home. Mary, would you be so good as to fetch a tray."

"What is so urgent? Has something happened to make you change your mind?" Seámus took his place in a chair at the other end of the fireplace.

"There has and it is not for the better."

She fidgeted with a letter she was holding.

"It cannot be all that bad, surely." He looked deep into her young face.

"Here, read it for yourself. You will see how important it is." She reached the letter across to him.

"Good God, this is bad news indeed. Whatever will you do?"

"Do! What can I do, they intend to dispose of the estate. I can no longer afford to stay here."

Rising, she went and stood before the fire with her hands clenched. He looked across at her and knew that it would cause a lot of heart rending to see her home sold.

"I know that I took your money for the renting of the cottage for a year. I swear I never knew of this. I am really sorry but I cannot return your money."

She held the letter out towards him.

"What is there to worry about, it is not your fault that the banks have foreclosed on you. As for me, I am the least of your worries."

"You are so understanding. I'll speak to the new owners and ask if you can stay."

"From what the letter states the bank has not taken possession yet. Anyway, who would want to buy it. There are dozens of estates on the market at the present time."

"You are right, it could take years, there are a lot more for sale and in a better condition. That, however, will not stop

221

the banks seizing it." She looked lovingly around the room. "Oh I don't know, it's a bit shabby and run down but sound enough. I doubt very much if what it fetches will clear the debts on it."

"What valuation have the agents put on it?"

"I am told that the most I could expect would be £2,000. This would still leave me in debt."

"£2,000. I suppose it is as much one could expect with the present state of the country. You know, of course, that there will be few looking for estates, if any."

"I know all that. Still, I was hoping to have enough over from the sale to buy a little cottage for myself and Mary."

"Mary! The servant woman?"

Why , of course, don't you approve? I could not abandon her now. She was born on the estate and is as much part of it as I am."

"Sorry! I did not mean to intrude, where would you go to? This estate has been in your family for generations. Why, all your family are interred in the crypt on the estate."

"Don't you realise that I know all this without you reminding me. I don't want to leave here, but what choice do I have?"

"What are the debts, then, and who apart from the bank are your creditors?"

"Most of the debts are due to the crown from the famine days and they amount to about £1,000. The rest is our overdraft due the bank."

"You are in a dilemma. No matter which way the cat jumps, you just cannot win. Sorry."

Seámus was not being too diplomatic.

"Look at it this way, Seámus, if I had enough money to pay off my present debts it still would not be enough. I would still need money to refurbish the estate.

No, the estate is like an albatross around my neck. The longer I delay the sale the more I get into debt. There is interest on the overdraft to be considered". Opening her hands she looked in despair around the room.

"I'm sorry that I cannot be more helpful. I could not advise you one way or the other. I'm sorry. I'm pleased that I no longer find myself in such a precarious position."

"Aren't you the lucky one, Seámus Flynn."

"You could say that it was luck or divine intervention. If I tell you how it all came about will you treat it as confidential between us?"

"Of course Seámus," she promised, "You can rely on my discretion to keep your secret."

"It all came about after we escaped from the prison camp." Seámus related to her his adventures and his gold find.

"That was one fruitful adventure," she remarked as Seámus finished his story.

"The hour is late, so I'll bid you 'Good night'. Try and get a good night's sleep. God is good." Gently he closed the door and left.

"God is good, that has always been the Irish philosophy." She looked at the closed door and smiled.

TREACHERY

Some two months had passed without any offers on the estate.

Seámus lay on the top of the blankets with his hands behind his head. He was thinking about the estate and it's potential. He had more than enough money to purchase the estate and refurbish it. If it had handsomely supported the Brigadier and his family in the past then there was no logical reason why it could not support him and give him a profitable return.

The following afternoon he returned to the mansion and presented himself to Lady Elizabeth.

"Any developments yet?" he asked over the proffered cup of tea.

"You mean about the estate. Don't tell me that some miracle has happened?"

"No! There is no miracle. I'm willing to make an offer on the estate. There is no obligation to accept it. Perhaps you would rather it went to one of your own?"

"You, Seámus Flynn, what possible use would an Irishman put an estate to?"

"That is my concern. Would my offer be acceptable or not? I will require a straight answer here and now."

"Of course, your offer would have to be accepted by the bank and my creditors. As I told you, it is now out of my hands."

"That is settled, then. If you would come with me to the bank in Cork we can discuss the matter."

"You mean today, now?"

"No time like the present, perhaps then you could get a good night's sleep." Seámus smiled.

Having stated the purpose of their visit to the chief clerk they were invited immediately into the manager's office.

"Your Ladyship; Mr Flynn. Please sit down."

The manager waved his hand at two seats.

"Now Mr Flynn, I believe that you are considering buying the estate of the late Brigadier Stone."

"That is correct,providing we can come to an agreement."

"What are you offering then, for this valuable estate?"

"I'll not beat around the bush. My offer is this... I will clear all debts on the estate providing that they do not exceed £2,000 or £2,500 at the most. I will allow Her Ladyship and her faithful servant Mary to occupy one wing of the house. They may stay there until one or the other dies and then the survivor will have to seek alternative accommodation. In return I will take the freehold and all or any furnishings and chattels in the house and farm. What I intend is that the estate will be handed over to me in its entirety. Should this be acceptable then I am ready to sign as soon as is convenient."

"That is indeed a tempting offer, sir. I cannot give you a reply here and now. There are other considerations. I will, however, give your offer careful consideration and let you know within the week. I presume I can contact you at the Manor. Good day to you."

They rose to their feet and were about to leave the office when the manager asked Lady Elizabeth to remain behind..

"Would you wait a moment, Your Ladyship?" the manager asked.

"I'll wait for you outside." Seámus presumed that the manager wanted to question her alone as to her feelings on the matter.

"Perhaps you should consult with your legal adviser before you come to a decision," he advised on closing the door.

He avoided going to the Manor for the next week. He felt that she may think he was putting pressure on her.

It was six weeks later that a letter dropped through his letter box. Breaking the official seal he opened it and took out the contents. It was from a solicitor in Cork.

His client, Lady Harriott Elizabeth Cornwall Stone was willing to accept his offer for the freehold of the estate.

Should he be willing to proceed with the purchase it would be necessary for him to come to Cork. There were outstanding debts to be paid to the bank and to the Crown and he would need to make a goodwill deposit before completion.

Returning to the city he made arrangements with his bankers to transfer the required deposit to a bank in Cork. He also arranged for them to appoint a solicitor to act on his behalf in the transaction.

Returning to the estate he entered the enclosed courtyard. He had not been here before. The courtyard was surrounded on three sides by dressed stone buildings. At the far end an arch led into a small square in the centre of which was a square building with steps leading down to an iron door. He knew that this was the family crypt.

'What would the Brigadier think if he knew that Seámus Flynn was shortly to become Lord of the Manor?' he thought.

"Did you get my letter then." He turned and saw Her Ladyship standing in the square.

"Yes, I got it and have been to Cork to appoint a solicitor to act on my behalf."

"So the estate is more or less yours now, Seámus Flynn. What does it feel like as you hope to step into the shoes of my father?"

"Not as yet, we will have to find out what the bank has to say in the matter."

He ignored the last cutting remark.

"I presume that you will be making changes when you become Lord of the Manor". Resting her hand on the cut stone of the family mausoleum she looked down at the steps leading into the vault.

Did he notice resentment and regret in her voice as she spoke. Perhaps she did not want an Irish peasant gracing the portals of the family estate.

He looked into her eyes but could read nothing.

Next day he found himself back in Cork to honour his appointment with the bank and government officials.

He was surprised to see Lady Elizabeth and several officials present.

"Please take a seat Mr Flynn." The manager pointed to a vacant chair.

"Now sir, regarding the purchase of the estate of the late Brigadier Stone. I understand that arrangements have been made to discharge all debts to this bank and to Her Majesty's Government, is that so?"

"Should we reach an agreement then I presume so. However, I would like to delay these negotiations until my solicitor arrives."

"There will be no need for him yet. Let us proceed. We understand that as you have access to substantial funds there will be no problem. Is that not so?"

One of the officials left the room and returned in the company of a sergeant and constable of the Royal Irish Constabulary. They took positions one on each side of the door.

"There is no need for them, I have not brought any money with me." Seámus laughed nervously. He was apprehensive and suspicious.

The official returned behind the desk and nodded to the Sergeant. He came forward and stood behind the chair of Seámus.

"What is going on here, and why the constabulary?" Seámus looked over his shoulder at the Sergeant.

"Seámus Flynn, on information supplied by Lady Elizabeth and as a result of our enquiries, I am arresting

226

you in the name of the Queen as an escaped Felon and murderer. Get to your feet." The Sergeant laid his hand on his shoulder.

"What is the meaning of this? I am a free man and have a document of freedom to prove it. I never murdered anyone!"

"Seámus Flynn, put out your hands. You are under arrest."

A pair of handcuffs on a long chain were produced and screwed to his wrists.

"There is no use in lying, we have the statement of Lady Elizabeth which you made to her of your own free will. We have the details of your escape from the penal colony at Bendigo with another felon by the name of Thomas Clery. After your escape a guard was found battered to death. We have all the details so there is no use in lying to us. You will tell us where you have hidden the stolen money and the whereabouts of the second felon. Do you hear?"

"Why did you do this to me? I was trying to help you!" He turned towards Lady Elizabeth.

"Did you think that I would let my father's estate go to an Irish Papist, a liar and a murderer. You robbed my father in life and I was not about to let you dance on his grave. I saw the sneer on your face as you looked at the family crypt."

She spat her venom at him.

"I might have known. Leopards never change their spots, do they, Lady Elizabeth?"

"Enough! We have endured you long enough. Take that murdering Fenian down, sergeant!"

The constable stepped forward and, taking hold of the chain, dragged Seámus from the room.

"It may not be today, nor tomorrow but the day will come when you and your kind will be driven from the shores of Ireland. God save Ireland!" Seámus shouted as he was dragged struggling down the corridor.

At the barracks he was chained and handcuffed to other prisoners and taken in a prison van to Cork.

Once again he found himself incarcerated behind the grim walls of the city jail.

Looking around his dirty prison cell he remembered how long ago he had suffered in a similar cell. That time he was being transported to a penal colony. This time his fate lay at the end of a rope.

He was offered a deal, if he would tell them where he had his gold hidden, his hanging would be commuted to life imprisonment.

This inducement he defiantly refused.

227

This was a cruel irony. After all his years of trial and tribulations there was to be no escape for Seámus Flynn.
"It would have been far better had you hanged me in the first place!" he shouted at the stout door.
He was now despondent and alone.

THE LAMENT OF THE IRISH EMIGRANT

I'm sitting on the stile Mary, where we sat side by side,
On a bright May mornin' long ago, when first you were my bride;
The corn was springing fresh and green, the lark sang loud and high-
And the red was on your lips, Mary, And the love light in your eyes.
The place is changed little, Mary, the day is bright as then,
The lark's loud song is in my ear, and the corn is green again;
But I miss the soft clasp of your hand, and your breath warm on my cheek,
And I still keep listening for the words, you never more will speak.

'Tis but a step down yonder lane, and the little church stands near-
The church where we were wed, Mary, I see the spire from here.
But the graveyard lies between, Mary, and my steps might break your rest-
For I've laid you, darling, down to sleep, with your baby on your breast.
I'm very lonely now, Mary, for the poor make no new friends;
But oh! They love the better still, the few our Father sends!
And you were all I had, Mary, my blessing and my pride!
There's nothing left to care for now, since my poor Mary died.

Yours was the good, brave heart, Mary, that still kept hoping on,
When the trust in God had left my soul, and my arms young strength was gone:
There was comfort ever on your lips, and a kind look on your brow-
I bless you, Mary, for that same, though you cannot hear me now.
I thank you for your patient smile, when your heart was fit to break,
When the hunger pain was gnawing there, and you hid it for my sake;
I bless you for your pleasant words, when your heart was sad and sore-
Oh! I'm thankful you are gone, Mary, where the grief can't reach you more!

I'm bidding you a long farewell, my Mary-kind and true!
But I'll not forget you darling, in the land I'm going to:
They say there's bread and work for all, and the sun shines always there-
But I'll not forget ould Ireland, were it fifty times as fair!
And often in those grand old woods, I'll sit and shut my eyes,
And my heart will travel back again to where my Mary lies;
And I'll think I see the little stile, where we sat side by side,
And the springing corn, and the bright May morn when first you were my bride.

Lady Dufferin

A MEETING ON THE QUAY

Unable to settle he spent most of his time pacing backwards and forwards in his cell. Contemplating what might have been and cursing the treachery of Lady Elizabeth.

'Serves me right for disclosing my past to her. I should have known better. How could I have been so naïve?'

He kicked the leg of his bunk in his frustration.

Late one night he heard the key turn in the lock and saw two jailers enter.

"Is this it then, don't I get to see the priest to hear my last confession?" He had mentally prepared himself to meet his maker.

"We are not here to take you any place, we hear you pacing the cell every night and wondered if you fancied a game of cards?"

"A game of cards, anything to pass the time. Just a chat would suffice, thank you." Seámus felt the weight leave his shoulders.

He became friendly with his jailers and a bond began to form between them.

He related to them how he and his friend had escaped from the penal colony and how his friend died in the bush.

"Is it true that you have a fortune hidden away in Australia?"

"True as I'm here with you, but I would rather leave it where it is than let the bastards get their hands on it."

"Whatever will happen to it when you, you know...."

"You mean when I am hanged? You may as well say it as think it. If I have anything to do with it they will never stretch the neck of Seámus Flynn."

"You are not thinking of trying to escape from here. That would be impossible."

"I suppose it would be without outside help. Tell me, how would you like to be rich men?" Seámus laughed.

"What do you mean by rich?"

"You help me to escape from this hell hole and I will make you rich beyond your wildest dreams!"

"That's a tall order, so it is," one jailer said as he rubbed the stubble on his chin.

"Think it over, there's no hurry, I hope."

Seámus half laughed as he held his hand to his throat in a choking gesture.

His jailers did not return to his cell the next night and he presumed that they were frightened and had thought better of his offer. He would have to think of an alternative escape route.

Lying in his bunk that night he heard his jailers whispering outside his door. Then the key turned and both men entered his cell.

"We have given careful consideration to your escape plan. We would like to help you, Seámus, but we have families. Your money would be no use to us swinging from the end of a rope beside you. We will not tell of your plans to escape. We would like to help a fellow Irishman to escape, but you do understand?" they apologised.

"Don't you think that I know all this, my plan is this. There are many American ships berthed in Queenstown waiting to transport immigrants to the New World. What if I could secure safe passage for you and your families on one of those ships?"

"Us emigrate to America, we never thought of that!"

They looked at each other and laughed.

"If you were in a position to secure our passage to Boston and some money to get settled there, that would be a different story."

"You mean that you would help me to escape?" Seámus was excited.

"Escape, would we not all like to escape from this cursed land had we the means?"

"You need look no further Seámus Flynn. We are with you to a man, we will not betray you. However, let's not get too excited about it. There is no way that we would get through the docks at Queenstown without being seen. Remember, there are prison ships docked there awaiting their prisoners. The place is guarded night and day," warned the senior jailer.

"What about Tralee then?" Seámus suggested.

"Tralee. Your chance of finding an American ship there is remote. Anyhow you would be noticed straight away in a small port. We need a busy port where there are plenty of ships loading and unloading."

"There is Limerick and Galway up the coast, there are ships coming and going there all the time," the other jailer suggested.

"Galway! Why of course, there are many cornmills there. What do you think Seámus?"

"Galway it is then. Now in the morning this is what you must do. Make arrangements for your families to travel to Galway on the early morning coach. Don't tell your neighbours that you are leaving. We don't want to arouse any suspicion.

When you come on watch tonight you will let me escape. In the morning make all haste to Galway where I will meet you at the quayside. Do you understand all that. Try and not be late for as soon as I'm found missing there will be all hell let loose. In the meantime I'll do my utmost to book passage for us all."

Seámus was shocked that night when his cell door was opened by his jailers.

"In here you." He looked out into the dark corridor and saw a prisoner being escorted between them.

"Out you come and bring your belongings. You are being moved." Seámus once again felt betrayed. He was dumbfounded when he was ordered from his cell.

He was escorted along a long corridor to a side gate.

"This is it Seámus, it is now freedom for us all or the hangman's rope."

Opening the gate one of the jailers went out into the darkness.

"No, not yet." The other jailer held Seámus back as he attempted to follow.

"You put the fear of Christ into me back there. Tell me, why did you transfer that prisoner to my cell?" Seámus asked as they waited in the shadows for the second jailer to return.

"That was Tony's idea. When the morning watch comes on they will not be any the wiser. So long as they have a prisoner in the cell."

"The coast is clear, Come on, get away as quickly as you can. Remember, Seámus, we are trusting the lives of our families in your hands. Good luck and may God guide your feet. See you in Galway Bay!"

Making all haste he was soon outside the city and into the countryside. By dawn he had crossed the county border and was inside County Limerick. Reaching the village of Adare he boarded the coach to the city. Later that morning he entered Limerick, from where he took the early morning coach to Galway. Tired from the journey he entered a hotel and ordered a meal, a room and a bath. He slept long into the afternoon.

Refreshed he returned to the docks and to the agent of his American bank where he asked to see the manager.

"Please come inside, Mr Flynn. What can I do for you?"

"I need some money from my account for a business transaction in America. I have the receipt for my money held in your branch in Australia." Seámus produced the official document.

"That seems to be in order, have you any proof of identity?"

"Yes, of course, this is my ticket of leave from the English Court in Australia."

"Tell me sir, have you booked your passage as yet?"

"Not yet. You see I am taking a rather large party with me, relatives you know. All hoping for a better life in America"

"I know how they feel. Pity that so many have to take the coffin ships. Your relatives are lucky that they have you to pay their passage on one of our ships.

Do you see that coal ship over there? Would you believe me when I tell you that it will be loaded with human ballast on the return journey to Liverpool. It is cheaper, they tell us, to use humans as ballast rather than stones. Sad days for Ireland, don't you think?"

"Are there any American ships leaving for Boston or New York this evening?" Seámus, interrupting the agent, asked.

"There is one travelling light, I believe. It will be leaving on the tide at midnight. Should I arrange passage for you and your relatives?"

"By all means. What is the name of the ship and where is she berthed?"

"The name of the ship is the S.S. Calypso. You will find her on the quayside opposite. It is only a few hundred yards down the quay."

"Very well then, the 'Calypso' it is. Tell the Captain that we will do our best to be there on time. I will also require $500 in cash for the voyage. Can you arrange it for me?"

"I'm sorry Mr Flynn, but there has been a run on our reserves. I can let you have $250. This should not present any problems. You will have no need for money on board and I will arrange for the cost of the passage to be deducted from your assets. Should you need any more funds then I dare say you will find ample funds in Boston. Now if you would be so kind as to sign here."

"I thank you sir, for your concern and courtesy and will have no hesitation in bringing it to the attention of the manager of the bank in Boston." Seámus rose from his seat and shaking hands with the manager left the office.

Returning to the hotel he ate a late meal and spent the time relaxing in the lounge.

Later that evening he moved to the dining room and waited in trepidation. He watched in fear and suspicion every soldier and official who came and went.

As he had time on his hands he decided to take a stroll along the quay.

"Please sir, of your charity would you have a spare copper?"

Seámus turned to see a young woman dressed in a ragged shawl of Galway Grey looking at him with her hand extended.

He was about to reach into his coatamore for his purse when the woman looked around her and called to a boy swinging on the chains.

"Come here Joseph, you're being silly. You know it is dangerous to play on the quayside."

"Coming Ma." The child returned and stood obediently beside his mother.

"Excuse me, Mam, could I be so bold as to ask what your name is?"

"Why should you want to know who I am? Still it is no secret, for my name is Theresa Clery"

Seámus looked in surprise at her.

"Is your husband's name Thomas?"

"It is that. Do you know him, then?"

"A Thomas Clery served time with me in a penal colony in Australia."

"That's my Tom. How is he?"

"Come with me to the hotel and I will tell you everything."

Seámus told her of Tom's request and his love for her and their son. There was silence between them for some moments.

"Mo cusla, your Father will not be coming home after all."

Ignoring Seámus she cradled her son to her and wept.

"How are your circumstances?" Seámus interrupted.

"Circumstances, now that is a fancy word indeed. We live where we can find a shelter and we beg on the quayside."

"I promised your husband that I would look after you should anything....."

"You may as well finish it. Should he die."

"It's like this. I am leaving with some friends at midnight for the States. Now, if you wish, I will take you and the boy as well."

"To America, is that what you are saying?"

"Of course. It would be a great opportunity for you and the boy. I owe this to my friend Tom."

"God bless you, Seámus Flynn, God love you."

She began to cry uncontrollably.

"Come on then, we had best go and get you and the boy dressed for the voyage."

"We are going to America with this kind friend of your father's, so we are Joseph".

She adjusted her son's clothes as she spoke.

You sit there and wait. Now don't you move or else I might lose you. I must look for my other passengers."

Looking up at the wall clock he noticed that it was now

234

ten o'clock. What could be keeping them so long. Surely the families had arrived in Galway by now?

Would they arrive in time and what would he do should they fail to meet him? Should he go on and leave them to their fate?

Questions without answers raced through his mind.

Coaches came and went and still there was no sign of his elusive passengers.

He knew that he could not abandon them now. He would have to wait until they came, and hope for a later sailing.

He again looked at the clock. It was now ten-thirty. Time, it seemed, was racing to zero hour.

Were all his carefully laid plans to be dashed?

He returned to where Theresa and her son were patiently waiting.

"What is delaying them? They should be here now."

Banging his fists together he returned to the hotel foyer

Again he looked up at the clock, it was now ten forty-five.

He returned to his seat by the window and sat down.

"Come on! Come on! What's holding you?"

Where in God's Holy Name had they got to, surely they could find the hotel. Had they been apprehended?

If they had then it would be his fault. He thought of the children, how many there were, he did not know.

If they had been captured would they betray him?

'How could I live with myself if they were captured and hanged. Who would look after the widows and children?'

He heard the clock strike the hour of eleven. He was now despondent and despairing for their arrival.

He was now more sure than ever that something dreadful had happened to them.

Surely some of them had escaped. They would come and tell him eventually.

Rising, he placed his hands behind his back and again paced the floor.

He did not wish to look at the clock again, and why should he?

All his well laid plans were now in tatters and he was in danger of being arrested again. This time there would be no escape for him.

Forcing himself he cast his eyes at the clock. The pendulum seemed to be racing backwards and forwards at an incredible speed. He looked at the face of the clock, it was now midnight.

Leaving the hotel he crossed to the quay. The tide was in full flood and would soon begin to ebb. Several ships were making ready to sail, other were trimmed and heading for open waters.

235

"Good God, I forgot all about Tom's wife and child, what of them?"

His mind was in turmoil as he watched Coffin Ships leaving the port with their cargo of Irish human ballast. A ragtag army of starving stood on the deck waving to those they left behind. They had little idea, if any, of what lay ahead, yet it could only be for the better.

Returning to the hotel he entered the dining room and stood with his hands deep in the pockets of his coatamore.

"Is it yourself, Seámus, sure we thought that you had deserted us!" came a welcome voice.

"Thank God! It is you, are you all here?"

"This is my....."

"Never mind that for now! Will you look at the time!" Seámus interrupted the introductions.

"We are all ready, Seámus, did you get passage?"

"Yes! Yes! But we must hurry, for the ship should have sailed some time ago. Can the children run?" Seámus dragged one of the jailers out of the hotel complex.

"I don't think so, Seámus, but we will try."

"No, never mind. The ship that you want is the S.S. Calypso. It is berthed a few yards down the quayside. I'll run ahead and ask the captain to delay the sailing. But please try and hurry. Can't you see that the tide is on the turn? Follow me!" Seámus ran on ahead.

"Seámus," the jailer shouted, "Where did you say it is?"

"Go down the quay opposite," Seámus turned and shouted in reply, running backwards now.

"You cannot miss it, the name is on the stern. For God's sake come on, get going".

Seámus called on Theresa and her son to join him as he raced ahead leaving the families to make their own way to the ship.

A SAD AND FINAL FAREWELL
TO DEAR OLD SKIBBEREEN

He came to an abrupt halt when he saw the Calypso in mid stream with her storm lantern swinging to and fro.

"Good God, you could have waited a little while longer," he screamed.

"Where's the ship, Seámus?" panted Tony as he came up beside Seámus.

"That was our ship. We will have to wait and hope that there will be another tomorrow."

Seámus pointed to the ship as it moved out into deep water.

Soon the women and children gathered around Seámus, who was sitting dejected on a bollard.

"What will happen to us now? You are bound to be missed and the ports will be watched."

"Don't I know this? However I see no reason for you to suffer. After all it was not your fault".

"What do you mean? We have no intention of abandoning you now, have we?" Tony looked at the others to confirm his statement.

"What I mean is, I will give you the money for your passage. It is me that they want and it is me that they will be searching for."

"You forget something. We are now as guilty as you. If we don't get out of Ireland we will all hang."

"Well then, what should we do? We cannot sit around here."

"We should go and get a bite to eat and then discuss what to do," suggested one of the women.

"Look, what is that?" Tady pointed to a carriage drawn by two horses coming along the quay.

"Don't panic, it's not the Redcoats, they don't use fancy coaches," Seámus assured them.

"Whoa! Whoa!" The driver, who was sitting on a high sprung seat to the front, pulled on the reins.

"What are you doing here Mr Flynn? You should have been on the Calypso."

Seámus looked up to see the agent for the shipping line looking down at him.

"My relatives were delayed and by the time they got here the ship had sailed. Do you know if there are any passages available tomorrow?"

"Sorry sir, the next sailing will be in two day's time and

that is for Baltimore. I doubt if they could accommodate you and your relatives."

"That's it then, we will have to try Limerick." Seámus looked at the gathering before him.

"You're welcome to come with me to Spiddal, the Calypso will drop anchor midway between Spiddal and Inismaan. I'm sure the fisherfolk would take you to the ship if the weather permitted. Come on, climb on board, there's plenty of room," invited the agent.

"It's a chance worth taking and we thank you. Come on, what are we waiting for?" Seámus encouraged the others.

"With the extra load I'll need to stop at Bearna and change the team," the agent informed them.

"We are in your hands and whatever the cost I will pay it," Seámus assured the agent.

"There is no extra payment, it is all part of the service." With all aboard the agent cracked his whip and sent the team forward.

The horses were being changed at Bearna Seámus and his passengers went for refreshments. Inside, seated at the table, were several Redcoat's drinking.

"Good evening, and where might you be off to at this hour of the night?" the Sergeant asked Seámus.

"They are passengers for America joining their ship at Spiddal," answered the agent.

"You shouldn't have let them spend so much time shopping in Galway," laughed the Sergeant as he looked at Theresa and her son in their new clothes.

"You're right, but then, what say have we men got?" Seámus laughed.

"Safe voyage to you all, can't say I feel sorry for you. I only wish that I were going," retorted a soldier, the worse for drink.

"The horses are harnessed, let's get moving. Goodnight to you all."

The agent lifted the latch and opened the door.

In Spiddal they found a crew willing to ferry them out to the ship in two boats.

"Ahoy aboard the Calypso." The agent cupped his hands and called to the ship.

"Ahoy to you fisherfolk, what is your business?"

"We have your passengers aboard, would you put down the gantry?"

"Gantry away! Welcome on board!" came the greeting from the ship.

"We have women and children on board! Can you offer assistance?" came the request from the boats.

As the fishermen held on to the gantry, sailors from the

ship assisted the women and children on board.

Seámus stood on deck talking to the agent and the captain for some time.

"Time to leave now, Mr Quinn," the Captain addressed the agent.

"Thanks for everything Mr Quinn." Seámus took his hand in his.

"There's no need for this, I told you it is all part of the service."

The agent looked at the sovereigns in his hand.

"Just a little gift to remember us by, you best get off now, or else you will be coming with us."

"Goodbye and God speed ," the agent shouted and waved as he sat in the prow of the boat.

The captain saluted the agent. The gantry was hoisted and lashed securely to the side of the ship.

"Up anchor," came the order.

Slowly the sleek ship faced towards the open seas. With heavy hearts they watched as the ship sailed past Oiléan Arainn (Aran Islands).

Seámus knew that he would never set foot on talab na hEireann again. His heart was sore and he wished that he had been given the opportunity of making the 'TURAS'(Pilgrimage) to the 'Leac an Uaisgne' (Stone of Loneliness) deep in the wild hills of Donegal. He would never see the sun go down in Galway bay.

He was once again a unwilling exile from his native shore.

"Bennact Dé leat, talab na hEireann. Bennact Dé tú mo Atair and mo mátair agus go dti tú mo deasbrátair.(God's blessing on you the land of Ireland. God bless you father and mother and to you my dear brother, Brendan)

I'll never lie beside you when my life span is over. In spirit I'll return to DEAR OLD SKIBBERREEN."

Sin Deire.

This then is the story of Seámus Flynn late of Skibbereen in the County Cork.

A great deal of water has flowed under the bridges at Cork and a lot of barley has been stacked in dear old Skibbereen since that day.

How did Seámus and his friends fare in the new land? . . . I guess that is one for the history books.

EPILOGUE or EPITAPH?

"I have come to this indescribable scene of destruction, desolation, and death; that I might get nearer to your sympathies; that I might bring these terrible realities of human misery more vividly within your comprehension. I have witnessed scenes that no language of mine can portray. I have seen how much beings, in the image of God, can suffer on this side of the grave, and that too in a civilized land"

ELIHU BURRITT appeals to the people of the United States Of America to save Skibbereen and Ireland.

His report from Skibbereen and its vicinity February 1847.........
Rev. Mr F--- called with several gentlemen of the town , and in their company I took my first walk through this Potter's Field of destitution and death. As soon as we opened the door, a crowd of haggard creatures pressed upon us, and with agonizing prayers for bread, followed us to the soup house. One poor woman, whose entreaties became irresistibly importunate, had watched all night in the grave-yard, lest the body of her husband should be stolen from his resting place, to which he had been consigned yesterday.
She had left five children sick with the famine fever in her hovel, and she raised and exceedingly bitter cry for help. A man with swollen feet pressed closely upon us, and begged for bread most piteously. He had pawned his shoes for food, which he had already consumed.
The soup house was surrounded by a cloud of these famine spectres, half naked, and standing or sitting in the mud, beneath a cold, drizzling rain. The narrow defile to the dispensary bar was choked with young and old of both sexes, struggling forward with their rusty tin and iron vessels for soup, some of them on all fours, like famished beasts. There was a cheap bread dispensary opened in one end of the building, and the principal pressure was at the door of this.
Among the attenuated apparitions of humanity that thronged this gate of stinted charity, one poor man presented himself under circumstances that even distinguished his case from the

rest. He lived several miles from the centre of the town, in one of the rural districts, where he found himself on the eve of perishing with his family of seven small children. Life was worth the last struggle of nature, and the miserable skeleton of a father had fastened his youngest son to his back, and with four more by his side, had staggered up to the door, just as we entered the bread department of the establishment. The hair upon his face was nearly as long as that upon his head. His cheeks were fallen in, and his jaws so distended that he could scarcely articulate a word. His four children were sitting upon the ground by his feet, nestling together, and trying to hide their naked limbs under their dripping rags. How these poor things could stand upon their feet and walk, and walk five miles, as they had done, I could not conceive. Their appearance, though common to thousands of the same age in this region of the shadows of death, was indescribable. Their paleness was not that of a common sickness. There was no sallow tinge to it. They did not look as if newly raised from the grave and to life before the blood had begun to fill their veins anew; but as if they had just been thawed out of the ice, in which they had been imbedded until their blood had turned to water.

Leaving this battle field of life, I accompanied the Rev Mr F----- -, a Catholic minister, into one of the hovel lanes of the town. We found in every tenement we entered enough to sicken the stoutest heart. In one, we found a shoe-maker who was at work before a hole in the mud wall of his hut about as large as a small pane of glass. There were five in his family, and he said, when he could get work, he could earn about three shillings a week.

About the middle of this filthy lane, we came to the ruins of a hovel, which had fallen down during the night, and killed a man, who had taken shelter in it with his wife and child. He had come in from the country, and, ready to perish with cold and hunger, had entered this falling house of clay. He was warned of the danger, but answered that die he must, unless he found a shelter before morning. He had kindled a small fire with some straw and a bit of turf, and was crouching over it, when the whole roof or gable end of earth and stone came down upon him and his child, and crushed him to death over the slow fire.

The child was pulled out alive, and carried to the workhouse, but the father was still lying upon the dung heap of the fallen roof, slightly covered with a piece of canvass. On lifting this, a humiliating spectacle presented itself. What rags the poor man had upon him when buried beneath the falling roof, were mostly torn from his body in the last faint struggle for life. His neck, and shoulders, and right arm were burnt to a cinder. There he lay in the rain, like the carcass of a brute beast thrown upon a dung heap.

As we continued our walk along the filthy lane, half naked women and children would come out of their cabins, apparently in the last stages of fever, to beg for food. "FOR THE HONOUR OF GOD". As they stood upon the wet ground, one could see it almost smoke beneath their bare feet, burning with fever.

We entered the grave-yard, in the midst of which was a small watch -house. This miserable shed served as a grave where the dying could bury themselves. It was seven feet long, and six in breadth. It was already walled round the outside with an embarkment of graves, half way up to the eaves. The aperture of this horrible den of death would scarcely admit of the entrance of a common sized person.. And into this noisome sepulchre living men, women, and children went down to die; to pillow upon the rotting straw, the grave clothes vacated by preceding victims and festering with their fever. Here they lay as closely to each other as if crowded side by side on the bottom of one grave. Six persons had been found in this fetid sepulchre at one time, and with one only able to crawl to the door and ask for water. Removing a board from the entrance of this black hole of pestilence, we found it crammed with wan victims of the famine, ready and willing to perish. A quiet listless despair broods over the population, and cradles men for the grave.

SUNDAY FEBRUARY 21ST.......

Dr D----- called at two o'clock, and we proceeded together to visit a lane of hovels on the opposite side of the village. The wretchedness of this little mud city of the dead and dying was of a deeper stamp than the one I saw yesterday. Here human beings and their clayey habitations seemed to be melting down together into the earth. I can find no language nor illustration sufficiently impressive to portray the spectacle to an American reader. A cold drizzling rain was deepening the pools of black filth, into which it fell like ink drops from the clouds. Few of the young or old have not read of the scene exhibited on the field of battle after the action, when visited by the surgeon. The cries of the wounded and dying for help, have been described by many graphic pens. The agonizing entreaty for "Water! Water! Help! Help! has been conveyed to our minds with painful distinctness. I can liken the scene we witnessed in the low lane of famine and pestilence, to nothing of greater family resemblance, than that of a battle field, when the hostile armies have retired, leaving one third of their numbers bleeding on the ground. As soon as Dr D--- appeared at the head of the lane, it was filled with miserable beings, haggard, famine-stricken men, women, and children, some far gone in the consumption of the famine fever, and all imploring him "FOR THE HONOUR OF GOD" to go in and see "MY MOTHER", "MY FATHER", "MY BOY", who is very bad, your honour". And then, interspersed with these earnest entreaties, others louder still would be raised for bread. In every hovel we entered, we found the dying or the dead.

In one of these straw-roofed burrows eight persons had died in the last fortnight, and five more were lying upon the fetid, pestiferous straw, upon which their predecessors to the grave had been consumed by the wasting fever of famine. In scarcely a single one of these most inhuman habitations was there the slightest indication of food of any kind to be found, nor fuel to cook food, nor anything resembling a bed, unless it were a thin layer of filthy straw in one corner, upon which the sick person lay partly covered with some ragged garment. There being no window, nor aperture to admit the light in these wretched cabins, except the door, we found ourselves often in almost total darkness from the first moment of our entrance. But a faint glimmer of a handful of burning straw in one end would soon reveal to us the indistinct images of wan-faced children grouped together with their large plaintive, still eyes looking out at us, like the sick young beasts in their dens. Then the groans, and the choked, incoherent entreaties for help from *some man or woman wasting away from the sickness in some corner of the cabin, would apprise us the number and condition of the family. The wife, mother, or child would frequently light a wisp of straw, and hold it to the face of the sick person, discovering to us the sooty features of some emaciated creature in the last stages of fever. In one of these places we found and old woman stretched upon a pallet of straw, with her head within a foot of a handful of fire, upon which something was steaming in a small iron vessel. The doctor removed the cover, and we found it was filled with a kind of slimy seaweed, which, I believe, is used for manure in the sea-board. This was all the nourishment that the daughter could serve her sick mother. But the last cabin we visited in this painful walk presented to our eyes a lower deep of misery. It was the residence of two families, both of which had been thinned down to half their original number by the sickness. The first sight that met my eyes, on entering, was the body of a dead woman, extended on one side of the fireplace. On the other, an old man was lying on some straw, so far gone as to be unable to articulate distinctly. He might have been ninety or fifty years of age. It was difficult to determine, for this wasting consumption of want brings out the extremest indices of old age in the features of even the young.*

But there was another apparition which sickened all the flesh and blood in my nature. It has haunted me , during the past nights, like Banquo's ghost. I have lain awake for hours, struggling for some graphic and truthful similes or new elements of description, by which I might convey to the distant reader some tangible image of this object. A dropsical affection among the young and old is very common to all the sufferers by famine. I had seen men at work on the public roads with their limbs swollen to almost twice their normal size. But when the woman of this cabin lifted from the straw, from behind the dying man, a boy of about twelve years of age, and held him up before us upon his feet, the most horrifying spectacle met our eyes. The cold, watery-faced child was entirely naked in front, from his neck to his feet. His body was swollen to nearly three times its normal size, and had burst the ragged garment that covered him, and now dangled in shreds behind him. The woman of the other family, who was sitting at her end of the hovel, brought forward her little infant, a thin faced baby of two years, with clear, sharp eyes that did not wink, but stared stock still at vacancy, as if a glimpse of another existence had eclipsed its vision. Its cold, naked arms were not much larger than pipe stems, while its body was swollen to the size of a normal person. Let the reader group these apparitions of death and disease into the spectacle of ten feet square, and then multiply it into three fourths of the hovels in this region of Ireland, and he will arrive at a fair estimate of the extent or degree of its misery. Were it not for giving them pain, I should have been glad if the well-dressed children in America could have entered these hovels with us, and looked upon the young creatures wasting away unmurmuringly by slow consuming destitution. I am sure they would have been touched to the liveliest compassion at the spectacle, and have been ready to divide their wardrobe with the sufferers.

MONDAY FEBRUARY 22nd;

Dr. H.----- called to take me into the Castlehaven Parish, which comes within his circuit. This district borders upon the sea, whose rock indented shores are covered with cabins of a worse description than those in SKIBBEREEN. On our way, we passed several companies of men, women, and children at work, all enfeebled and emaciated by destitution. Women with their red, swollen feet partially swathed in old rags, some in men's coats, with their arms or skirts torn off, were sitting by the roadside, breaking stones. It was painful to see human labour and life struggling among the lowest interests of society. Men, once athletic labourers, were trying to eke out a few miserable days of existence, by toiling upon these works. Poor creatures! many of them are already famine stricken. They have reached a point from which they cannot be recovered. Dr. D.---, informs me that he can tell at a glance whether a person has reached this point. And I am assured by several experienced observers, that there are thousands of men who rise up in the morning and go forth to labour with their picks and shovel in their hands, who are irrecoverably doomed to death. No human aid can save them. the plague spot of famine is on their foreheads; the Worm of Want has eaten in two their heart strings. Still they go forth uncomplaining to their labour and toil, cold, and half naked upon the road, and divide their eight or ten pence worth of food at night among a sick family of five or eight persons. Someone is always kept at home, and prevented from earning this pittance, by fear that some one of the family will die before their return. The first habitation we entered in the Castlehaven district was literally a hole in the wall, occupied by what might be called in America, a squatter, or a man who had burrowed a place for himself and family in the acute angle of two dilapidated walls by the road-side, where he lived rent free. We entered this stinted den by an aperture about three feet high, and found two children lying asleep with their eyes open in the straw. Such, at least, was their appearance, for they scarcely winked, while we were before them. The father came in and told us his pitiful story of want, saying that not a morsel of food had they tasted for twenty four hours. He lighted a wisp of straw and showed us one or two more children lying in another nook of the cave. Their mother had died, and he was obliged to leave them alone during most of the day, in order to glean something for their subsistence. We were soon among the most wretched habitants that I had yet seen; far worse than those in SKIBBEREEN. Many were flat roofed hovels, half buried in the earth, or built up against the rocks, and covered with rotten straw, or sea-weed, or turf. In one which was scarcely seven feet square, we found five persons prostrate with the fever, and apparently near their end. A girl aged about sixteen, the very picture of despair, was the only one left who could administer any relief; and all she could do was bring water in a broken pitcher to slacken their parched lips As we proceeded up a rocky hill overlooking the sea, we encountered new sights of wretchedness. Seeing a cabin standing somewhat by itself in a hollow, and surrounded by a moat of green filth, we entered it with some difficulty, and found a single child about three years old lying on a kind of shelf, with its little face resting upon the edge of the board and looking steadfastly out at the door, as if for its mother. It never moved its eyes as we entered, but kept them fixed towards the entrance. It is doubtful whether the poor thing had a mother or father left to her; but it is more doubtful still, whether those eyes would have relaxed their vacant gaze if both of them had entered at once with anything that could tempt the palate in their hands. No words can describe this peculiar appearance of the famished children. never have I seen such bright, blue, clear eyes looking so steadfastly at nothing. i could almost fancy that the angels of GOD had been sent to unseal the vision of these little, patient, perishing creatures, to the beatitudes of another world; and they were listening to the whispers of the unseen spirits bidding them to "WAIT A LITTLE LONGER". leaving this, we entered another cabin in which we found seven, or eight attenuated young creatures, with a mother who had pawned her cloak and could not venture out to beg for bread because she was not fit to be seen in the streets. Hearing the voice of wailing from a cluster of huts higher up the hill, we proceeded to them, and entered one, and found several persons weeping over the dead body of a woman lying by the wall near the door. Stretched upon the ground here and there lay several sick persons, and the place seemed a den of pestilence. The filthy straw was rank with the festering fever. Leaving this habitation of death, we were met by a young woman in an agony of despair because no one would give her a coffin to bury her father in. She pointed to a cart at some distance, upon which his body lay, and she was about to follow it to the grave, and he was such a good father, she could not bear to lay him like a beast in the ground, and she begged a coffin "FOR THE HONOUR OF GOD". While she was wailing and weeping for this boon, I cast my eyes towards the cabin we had just left, a sight met my eyes that made me shudder with horror. The husband of the dead woman came staggering out with her body upon his shoulder, slightly covered with a piece of canvas. I will not dwell upon the details of this spectacle. Painfully and slowly he bore the remains of the late companion of his misery to the cart. We followed him a little way off and saw him deposit his burden alongside of the father of the young woman, and by her assistance. As the two started for the grave yard to bury their own dead, we pursued our walk still further on, and we entered another cabin where we encountered the climax of human misery. Surely, thought I, while regarding this new phenomenon of suffering, there can be no lower deep than this between us and the bottom of the grave. On asking after the condition of the inmates, the woman to whom we addressed the question answered by taking out of the straw three breathing skeletons, ranging form two to three feet in height and entirely naked. And these human beings were alive! If they had been dead, they could not have been such frightful spectacles, they were alive, and, MIRABILE DICTU, they could stand upon their feet and even walk, but it was awful to see them do it. Had their bones been divested of the skin that held them together, and been covered in a thin muslin, they would not have been more visible, especially when one of them clung to the door, while a sister was urging it forward, it assumed an appearance, which can seldom be paralleled this side of the grave. The effort which it made to clink to the door disclosed every joint in its frame, while the deepest lines of old age formed on its face. The enduring years of ninety years of sorrow seemed to chronicle its record of woe upon the poor child's countenance. I could bear no more; and we returned to SKIBBEREEN, after having been out all afternoon among these abodes of misery. On our way we overtook the cart with the two uncoffined bodies. The man and young woman were all that attended them to the grave. Last year the funeral of either would have called out hundreds of mourners from those hills. But now the husband drove his uncoffined wife to the grave without a tear in his eye, without a word of sorrow. About half way to SKIBBEREEN, Dr H----proposed that we should divert to another road to visit a cabin in which we should find two little girls living alone, with their dead mother, who had lain unburied for seven days. He gave an affecting history of this poor woman; and we turned from the road to visit this new scene of desolation; but as it was growing quite dark, and the distance was considerable, we concluded to resume our way back to the village. In fact we had witnessed as much as my heart could bear. In the evening several gentlemen at the house of Mr S---, among whom was Dr D-----,. He had just returned from a neighbouring parish, where he visited a cabin which had been deserted by the poor people around, although it was known that some of its inmates were still alive, though dying in the midst of the dead. he knocked at the door; and hearing no voice within, burst it open, with his foot; and was in a moment almost overpowered by the horrid stench. Seeing a man's legs protruding from the straw, he moved them slightly with his foot; when a husky voice asked for water. In another part of the cabin, on removing a piece of canvas, he discovered three dead bodies, which had lain unburied for a fortnight; and hard against one of these, and almost embraced in the arms of death, lay a young person far gone with fever. He related other cases too horrible to be published.

Elihu Burritt.

Elihu Burrit a man of great compassion sent this account to his fellow countrymen and women of the United States Of America appealing to their generous nature on behalf of the Irish nation suffering from hunger, cold, famine and disease. It brought an immediate and urgent response from the people of the United States Of America and Canada.

This accurate account from Skibbereen and the surrounding district was published in a journal by **JOSEPH STURGE** and published in Birmingham, England on the 3rd month 15th, 1847.
On its publication the people of Britain were magnanimous in their generosity.

My thanks to CORK CITY LIBRARY for their generous help in compiling this article.

GLOSSARY

AMERICAN WAKE

Emigrants leaving Ireland gathered together with their friends to say their last good byes. It was most unlikely that they would ever meet again and so it was called 'The American Wake'.

TERRY ALTS and PEEP O'DAY BOYS

> *'The Terry alts and the Peep O'Day Boys*
> *Who roused at night the sleeping county*
> *And terrified the Lords and gentry'.*

These were active secret organisations that came about during the great hunger of 1845-1850. They originated in Limerick/Clare counties. They entered the big estates and killed the cattle and sheep to prevent them being exported to Britain. They also threatened to burn the corn in the fields if the landlords tried to export it. As they were active at night thus the name PEEP O'DAY BOYS.

BATA SCOIR (The rod of reckoning)

> *'CROUCHING NEATH A SHELTERING HEDGE*
> *OR STRETCHED ON MOUNTAIN FERN*
> *THE TEACHER AND HIS PUPILS MET*
> *FELONIOUSLY TO LEARN'.*

(The Bata scoir was a tally stick and used to suppress the spoken IRISH. It was forbidden to speak or to write Irish. Pupils were forced to wear it around their necks and each time they spoke IRISH a notch was put in the stick by their teacher.

At the end of the lessons punishment was apportioned according to the number of notches on the BATA Scóir)

BOTAR DROCSAOGAL (Famine Roads)
Rough roads constructed during the Great Hunger that started nowhere and ended no where.
England had no intention of upgrading Irish roads, nor constructing railways and cuttings. To do so, they believed would encourage Irish commerce and become a challenge to their thriving industries.
many famine roads can be seen to this day in the bogs and by roads of Ireland.

BUTTER CHURNS
Irish butter churns always had an old horse shoe nailed to the bottom by the cooper. This to deter the fairies from stealing the butter

CALLINGS
At the moment of death it was believed (And still is believed in parts of Ireland) that the spirits from the other world came to escort the spirit of the dead person to the ASTRAL world. The bean Sidhe (banshee) crying woman calls to the house at the time of death to mourn and escort the spirit back to the light of the 'Spirit World'.

CHALK SUNDAY
The Sunday two weeks before Lent when all bachelors had two chalk marks emblazoned on the backs of their coats. This to remind then that there were only two weeks left to wed before the 40 days of lent.

CONNAIL NA MARB
The candle of the dead was lit on the death of a mortal and held close to their open dead eyes. This to allow the spirit to find its way out of the dead body. The eyes were then closed and all obstructions removed from the room. The door was opened wide and all stood clear to allow the spirit free passage out of the house.
In Munster the keeners (Mourners) would bang pots and pans, shout and make lots of noise. This to detract any evil spirit trying to steal the spirit as it left its earthly home. It

was most vulnerable as it passed from the shadows of the earth to the light of the ASTRAL world.

CROSS OF SAINT BRIDGET
Saint Bridget was having difficulties explaining the Crucifixion when trying to convert a gathering of pagans. Picking up some reeds near by she wove them into a cross.

ICE HOUSES
(Ice houses were storage rooms usually built deep underground in a shaded spot. Into these ice and snow would be packed in the winter months. As the room was more or less vacuum sealed the ice and snow would remain frozen throughout the summer months. This preserved and refrigerated the contents.)

CROMWELL, OLIVER (1599-1658)
Born at Huntingdon, Crushed the Irish by terrorist methods. The Irish with their Papal links was more feared by Cromwell than any other race.
'I had rather be overrun with a cavalierish interest than a Scottish interest; I had rather be overrun with a Scottish interest than an Irish interest; and I think of all, this to be the most dangerous.'
(OLIVER CROMWELL)

His first IRISH siege was of Drogheda. Before the battle he sent terms under a white flag.
"If this be refused then you will have no cause to blame me" Cromwell made it clear that failure to surrender would mean the slaughter of the entire population.
Sir Arthur Aston who was the garrison commander replied...
"He who could take Drogheda could take Hell". Replied refusing quarters. When Cromwell finally took the town he had the population butchered. Sir Arthur was beaten to death with his own wooden leg. Cromwell's men fought over it thinking that it was filled with gold. His cruel butchery of the Irish and his policy of 'TO HELL or to CONNAUGHT' made him a pariah.

GOMBEEN MEN

Racketeers who bought and stole corn and sold it at exorbitant prices to the starving Irish. When no money was available they would barter a bag of corn which was mixed with chaff for whatever chattels or tools were available.

HORSE SHOES
Horse shoes being made from iron are considered lucky and a deterrent against evil. They have seven holes in keeping with the lucky number '7'. This relates to the seventh heaven in the 'CELTIC' religion from which Astral spirits were returned to earth.
The following innovation has grown up in recent years....
From the children's story of Sinbad the seventh son who was lucky, and many other related stories to number seven came the inaccurate belief that the seventh son of a seventh son had some magical and curative powers. There is no substance in this belief whatsoever.

KNOCKINGS
The spirit of the dead makes its own preparations to leave its earthly home. When ready to depart to the ASTRAL world they stop outside the door and give three knocks on the door. This to thank the living and to tell them that they have no further use for their mortal bodies.

LAZY BEDS
Ridges approximately two feet six inches wide in which the potatoes were set (Grown). The potatoes were set in a staggered pattern. When the stalks appeared the ridges were banked up with earth from the trenches to the left and right to protect them from any early frost. The ensuing trench would form a drain protecting the potatoes in the ridge from becoming waterlogged.

LEAC AN UAISGNE
The stone of loneliness is situated in the Glen of Gratun near Letterkenny in the county Donegal. It was here that Saint Columcille made his final 'TURIS' before he sailed into exile. With a breaking heart he cried all night long for he knew that he would never see his native land again. He could find no peace. God in his infinite mercy sent an angel to take away his sorrow next morning.

In later years it became the custom for emigrants leaving for the 'New World' to make a 'TURIS' the night before they left to the 'LEAC an UAISGNE'. There they would assemble with their friends and pray to St Columcille that they, their families and friends may be spared the 'Ocras an Croide'. (Loneliness of the heart or Hunger of the heart). This pilgrimage usually followed the 'American Wake'

OCRAS HOUSE
Hungry houses or famine houses were the hovels of families who suffering from plague and dysentery blocked up their doorway and windows from the inside and died with dignity away from shame and the prying eyes of their neighbours. Many of these hovels can still be seen in remote parts of Ireland. It is wrongly believed by some that the windows were blocked to avoid the 'Window Tax'. This is not true, the tax had been abolished long before the 'Great Hunger'.

ROCKITES
Rockites also known as Whiteboys were the followers of captain Rock. A name used by the secret society on all letters, notices and proclamations. They first came to the attention of the British when they rose in rebellion in Limerick in 1821.

SCAPULARS
Two small squares of cloth containing the relics of saints, joined by a ribbon. They are usually worn around the neck as a sign of devotion.

WALKING THE LAND
On the promise of marriage and the dowry agreed.....
The girls parents went to the farm of the boy to 'Walk the Land'. The suitor stays away as does his parents. An impartial neighbour conducts the tour. If the girl's father approves of what is on offer there is a spitting on the hand. This is followed by the 'CRAIC' and the writing down before an attorney. The wedding takes place shortly afterwards.

A Stór	Darling
Amadán	Male Fool
Bábóg	Doll
Bádóir	Boatman
Bean Sidhe	Fairy Woman
Briste Fada	Long Trousers
Beart	Bundle
Béaltára	Scold
Béic	Scream
Banbh	Young pig
Bodhrán	Irish Drum
Breac	Trout
Bruscar	Rubbish
Buaircín	Spancel
Cáibín	Old Hat
Cailín	Girl
Camán	Hurley
Carrig	Rock
Caubeen	Cap
Ciscéan	Basket
Cnadán	Frog
Coinín	Rabbit
Cóir	Justice
Cogarnach	Whispering
Craig	Cliff
Craic	Merriment
Cruit	Hump
Crúisán	Little jug
Crúb	A Paw/Claw
Cre Dúidín	Clay pipe
Cuairt	Visit
Dailtín	Brat
Drocsaógal	Famine
Diabal	Devil
Fáilte	Welcome
Faoiléan	Seagull
Feamainn	Seaweed
Fúster	Fussiness
Flaithúlach	Generous
Gaba	Farrier
Gabhál	Bundle
Garsún	Boy

Geansaí	Pullover
Go Leór	Plenty
Giodam	Liveliness
Gríosach	Embers
Leachaide	Lackey
Leanbh	Child
Lorgadán	Leprechaun
Lúidar	Wallop
Mac	Son
Madra Rhúa	Fox
Mollafuster	Beating
Meas	Respect
Naoidean	Baby
Oinseac	Female fool
Ocras	Hunger
Pocán	Goat
Plámás	Flattery
Puisín	Kitten
Praties	Potatoes
Pishogues	Curses
Púca	Jack-O-Lantern
Ráimeís	Nonsense
Rí Rá	Turmoil
Rinnce Siublac	Step dancing
Saileac Slat	Willow Cane
Sean Scéals	Old Stories
Seilmide	Snail
Sasacnacs	English
Slán Abaile	Safe Home
Smidiríns	Pieces
Spleen	Torch
Slán	Spade
Striopach	Hussy
Suideacán	Seat
Suicin	Pet calf
Tamhlacht	Grave

Tuige Suideacán	Straw Seat
Turus	Pilgrimage
Tráithnin	Blade of Grass
Tré na Chéile	All Mixed Up

Many Irish words have been adopted into the English language.
Many Irish phrases are now in popular use.
i.e. Slán Abaile (safe Home) can be seen on road signs in most Irish roads as one leaves one county and enters the next. The next sign they will meet is Failte Roat (You're Welcome)
Dia is Muire Duit (God and Mary bless you)
Céad Míle Fáilte (one hundred thousand welcomes). These are just some of the greetings you will receive.
Some Irish words popular in Limerick/Clare have been used throughout the book by the author.